QUEENIE

www.randomhousechildrens.co.uk

ALSO AVAILABLE BY JACQUELINE WILSON

Published in Corgi Pups, for beginner readers:
THE DINOSAUR'S PACKED LUNCH
THE MONSTER STORY-TELLER

Published in Young Corgi, for newly confident readers:
LIZZIE ZIPMOUTH
SLEEPOVERS

Available from Doubleday / Corgi Yearling Books:

BAD GIRLS	JACKY DAYDREAM
THE BED AND BREAKFAST STAR	LILY ALONE
BEST FRIENDS	LITTLE DARLINGS
BIG DAY OUT	THE LONGEST WHALE SONG
BURIED ALIVE!	THE LOTTIE PROJECT
CANDYFLOSS	MIDNIGHT
THE CAT MUMMY	THE MUM-MINDER
CLEAN BREAK	MY SECRET DIARY
CLIFFHANGER	MY SISTER JODIE
COOKIE	SAPPHIRE BATTERSEA
THE DARE GAME	SECRETS
THE DIAMOND GIRLS	STARRING TRACY BEAKER
DOUBLE ACT	THE STORY OF TRACY BEAKER
DOUBLE ACT (PLAY EDITION)	THE SUITCASE KID
EMERALD STAR	VICKY ANGEL
GLUBBSLYME	THE WORRY WEBSITE
HETTY FEATHER	THE WORST THING ABOUT
THE ILLUSTRATED MUM	MY SISTER

Collections:
JACQUELINE WILSON'S FUNNY GIRLS
includes THE STORY OF TRACY BEAKER *and*
THE BED AND BREAKFAST STAR
JACQUELINE WILSON'S DOUBLE-DECKER
includes BAD GIRLS *and* DOUBLE ACT
JACQUELINE WILSON'S SUPERSTARS
includes THE SUITCASE KID *and* THE LOTTIE PROJECT
JACQUELINE WILSON'S BISCUIT BARREL
includes CLIFFHANGER *and* BURIED ALIVE!

Available from Doubleday / Corgi Books, for older readers:
DUSTBIN BABY
GIRLS IN LOVE
GIRLS UNDER PRESSURE
GIRLS OUT LATE
GIRLS IN TEARS
KISS
LOLA ROSE
LOVE LESSONS

Join the official Jacqueline Wilson fan club at
www.jacquelinewilson.co.uk

Jacqueline Wilson
QUEENIE

Illustrated by
Nick Sharratt

DOUBLEDAY

QUEENIE
A DOUBLEDAY BOOK 978 0 857 53111 7
TRADE PAPERBACK 978 0 857 53112 4

Published in Great Britain by Doubleday,
an imprint of Random House Children's Publishers UK
A Random House Group Company

This edition published 2013

1 3 5 7 9 10 8 6 4 2

Text copyright © Jacqueline Wilson, 2013
Illustrations copyright © Nick Sharratt, 2013

The right of Jacqueline Wilson to be identified as the
author of this work has been asserted in accordance
with the Copyright, Designs and Patents Act 1988.

The Random House Group Limited supports the Forest Stewardship Council
(FSC®), the leading international forest certification organization. Our books
carrying the FSC label are printed on FSC®-certified paper. FSC is the only forest
certification scheme endorsed by the leading environmental organizations,
including Greenpeace. Our paper procurement policy can be found at
www.randomhouse.co.uk/environment.

Set in 13/17pt New Century Schoolbook

Random House Children's Publishers UK,
61–63 Uxbridge Road, London W5 5SA

www.**randomhousechildrens**.co.uk
www.**totallyrandombooks**.co.uk
www.**randomhouse**.co.uk

Addresses for companies within The Random House Group Limited
can be found at: www.**randomhouse**.co.uk/offices.htm

THE RANDOM HOUSE GROUP Limited Reg. No. 954009

A CIP catalogue record for this book is available from the British Library.

Printed and bound in Great Britain by Clays Ltd, St Ives plc

To June Bendall
and all her colleagues
at the Florence Nightingale Museum

1

I lived with my nan. It was wonderful, just the two of us, in our cosy basement flat. We both had a bedroom. Mine was just a little box room, and I didn't have a proper bed, just a couch with a pillow and an eiderdown, but Nan turned it into a Wendy house for me, with a lovely Tinkerbell lampshade. She let me keep the light on all night because I was afraid of the dark. Sometimes I crept into bed with Nan in her room, but she never minded.

I was used to Mum coming and going. She was

sometimes away for weeks at a time. The year she had a job at Butlin's she was away from March till September, and Nan and I were ever so happy, just the two of us together. We had several Saturday trips to the seaside to see Mum, and that was fine, though we had to take carrier bags on the coach because I was usually travel sick. Nan always packed a damp flannel and a packet of Spangles to freshen my mouth, so it wasn't too worrying. Nan hardly ever told me off. I was her girl and she was my nan and we didn't really need anyone else, not even Mum.

But then Nan got poorly. We both had bad colds in the winter, and had to slather our chests in Vick and suck blackcurrant lozenges when we got to the cough stage. Nan's cough didn't get better for weeks, even though she sucked lozenges until her tongue was deep purple.

'I'll be right as rain when it gets a bit warmer. I've always hated the cold,' Nan gasped, coughing and coughing, and lighting up another Player's Navy Cut.

'Your Player's make you cough worse, Nan,' I said.

'I dare say, but they get me going,' she said.

She found it really hard to get up in the mornings. She rose really early, long before me, because she had a cleaning job. She started at the factory at five, and then came rushing home at half past seven to make our tea and toast before I went to school. Then Nan had a little nap before going to *her* school as a dinner lady. I *wished* she worked at my school. It would be wonderful to see Nan at lunch time, especially when Marilyn and Susan were being extra spiteful. But Nan worked at the secondary modern on the other side of town. I'd maybe be able to go there when I was eleven, though Nan said I was bright and hoped I'd pass my scholarship and go to the grammar and get proper qualifications.

'*I've* done all right for myself without passing any silly fancy exams. You're working yourself to death, Mum. You don't have to get up at the crack of dawn. Don't I bring enough home?' my mum said irritably.

'I don't want to sponge off my own daughter, thanks very much, Sheila,' said Nan. 'Besides, I'm saving up.'

'What are you saving for? I tell you, I'm rolling in it,' said Mum.

Nan sniffed. She didn't always approve of Mum's jobs. She was currently in the chorus of a travelling revue, wearing feathers and high heels and very little else, according to Nan.

I knew what Nan was saving for. It was our special secret. She was saving for the fare to London for when the Queen had her Coronation in June. We were going together, Nan and me, planning a proper little holiday. Nan said she'd take me to a huge great toyshop called Hamleys, and we'd eat in a proper restaurant with waitresses, called Lyons Corner

House and, best of all, we'd stand as near to Westminster Abbey as we could get and watch the Queen arrive in her gold coach. Nan had already bought me a little gilt replica of this coach with tiny white horses. I'd drive it along the carpet and across the sideboard and up and down the walls, imagining a weeny Queen being tossed about inside, squealing as if she were on a roller coaster.

'It'll be a holiday to remember, Elsie,' Nan told me. 'When you're an old lady my age, you'll tell your own grand-daughter, "My nanny took me up to London and we saw the Queen's Coronation."'

I was longing to go. Laura Totteridge was going to see the Coronation – her whole dancing class were travelling up in a coach because they were doing a special display somewhere – but no one else was planning a trip, though Marilyn said she was going to be watching on her brand-new television. Marilyn always had to be one better than anyone else.

I said I was going to see the real Coronation *and* I said we had a brand-new television too, my mum had bought it specially – but Marilyn said I was a liar. She said horrid things about Mum too. I told her to go and boil her head and she punched me right in the stomach, making me fall over. Mum told me to stand up for myself when they were mean to me at school, but it only made things worse.

I knew Nan still wasn't well. She never once complained, but she kept coughing, and she got breathless easily. I could hear her as she bumbled about our flat doing the housework, panting like a little dog.

'You sit down, Nanny. I'll do it,' I said, pulling the carpet sweeper out of her hands.

Sometimes she'd argue with me. Other times she'd simply sag onto the sofa with a cup of tea and a cigarette and let me go ahead. This was much more worrying. I couldn't get the knack of carpet sweeping at all. Every time I banged into anything, grey snakes of dust slipped out onto the carpet, so I had to creep around with a dustpan and brush, doing bunny hops.

I put the washing in to soak – Nan's huge vests and long pink knickers that hung right down past her knees, and my grey knicks and socks and my school blouse. This was meant to be white but was starting to look grey too. Nan wouldn't let me do the ironing in case I burned myself. When she didn't feel up to it either, we decided we didn't mind a few wrinkles.

Nan sometimes nodded off straight after breakfast so I had to take myself to school, but I was considered a big girl now so that was no problem. I always looked right and left and right again before I crossed any roads, and I never talked to strangers. I *did* have a little chat with Bert the milkman because he was my friend, and I always patted his horse, Jenny, and gave her a sugar lump stolen from the bowl at home.

On the way back from school I did the shopping. I kept the housekeeping money safe in a purse round my neck, along with the door key. It made a little thump on my chest whenever I ran.

I bought a tin loaf from the baker's, and Bath buns for a treat; four ounces of streaky bacon, and marge, and Robertson's strawberry jam and a bottle of orange squash from Mr Harris the grocer; potatoes and cabbage and carrots from Florrie, the green-grocer's daughter. She lined my string bag with paper so that the carrots couldn't poke through, and some-times she gave me a bashed apple or a bruised banana for nothing.

I felt as if I had gorilla arms hauling all the shopping home. My leg always started aching too, making me limp. It was hard work avoiding the pave-ment cracks when I turned into our street. I always had to do that just to make sure Nan wouldn't get any worse. I was ultra-careful, but I was clumsy in my horrible big boy's shoes, and maybe I trod on a line without realizing.

One day I came home from school and Nan was lying on the sofa, her face pale grey and her chest heaving after a bad coughing fit.

'Oh Nan!' I cried, rushing to her.

'I'm fine, I'm fine, don't you worry now,' Nan

gasped, mopping her lips with her hankie. 'I've just had a bit of a funny turn. My head started spinning. But I'm fine now, I promise.'

Nan looked anything but fine, but she was very insistent. I cuddled up beside her on the sofa, stroking her papery cheek, and after a while she rallied.

'There, chickie, I'm right as rain now,' she said, trying to sit up.

'No, you stay where you are, Nan. I'll make you a cup of tea,' I said, springing up.

I made it very carefully, warming the pot first, and letting the tea steep for a few minutes before pouring. Then I reached for the biscuit barrel. We kept the best biscuits for visitors and Sundays, making do with Woolworths mixed assortment for every day – but I wanted Nan to have a treat. She helped herself to a bourbon and a custard cream, and I had a squashed fly and a pink wafer.

'There! All better now,' said Nan. 'You're a good little nurse, Elsie. You'd better put on that nurse's apron! Oh, you used to love that nurse's kit, remember?'

Mum's friend Uncle Stanley had given me the nurse's kit on my fifth birthday. We usually didn't think much of Mum's friends, but Uncle Stanley had been lovely while he lasted. He was quite old and nearly bald, but he was very kind. He bought Mum lots of presents, and gave stuff to Nan and me too. He bought us a huge satin box of chocolates at Christmas with a picture of kittens on the front, a white one and a black one and a little ginger one.

Nan used it as a button box after all the chocolates were eaten. I loved to sit with the box on my lap while Nan sewed. I'd gently stroke each kitten. The satin was so soft and smooth it was almost as if they were real. We couldn't have pets in our flat – the landlord wouldn't even let you keep a budgie or a goldfish. I pretended instead. I played with my three kittens, Snow White and Sooty and funny little Marmalade.

Mum said I looked soft in the head, crooning to a chocolate box, but Nan understood, and sometimes joined in my games, pretending the kittens were real too.

We were both pretending now as we licked the biscuit crumbs off our lips and listened to the Light Programme on the wireless. We acted as if Nan really were right as rain again, though she was still grey-faced and shaky, and when she tried to stand she had to cling onto the edge of the sofa.

'I'm making tea tonight, Nan,' I said quickly. 'Go on, let me.'

'Well, I bought some mince – I should have got it on the stove ages ago,' said Nan.

'Oh, don't let's have mince, it's horrid. I know, I'll cook us cheesy beanos!'

Nan had got the recipe from *Woman's Home Companion,* and it was easy enough for me to make – just cheese on toast with a bacon rasher and baked beans, and a little tomato in the shape of a flower to top it off.

I made the cheesy beanos, complete with fancy tomato flowers, and served one up to Nan on a tray.

'My, you're a clever little cook, Elsie. You'll be tackling a roast with all the trimmings before we know where we are,' she said. 'Mmm, this is scrumptious. You've grilled the cheese just right and the bacon's lovely and crisp.'

She tried hard to eat it all up, but could only manage a few mouthfuls. I wasn't very hungry now either. I kept glancing anxiously at Nan. She tried to smile reassuringly each time she caught me looking, but she couldn't fool me.

'Do you think I should try to phone Mum to tell her you've been taken bad?' I asked, halfway through the long evening.

'What? Don't be such a silly sausage! And I'm not having you going out after dark. You get all sorts hanging round the Albion,' said Nan. The nearest phone box was right down the road, outside the Albion pub.

'I'm not scared of those drunk men,' I lied.

'Well, you should be! Steer clear of all of them.'

'But I'm worried about you, Nan!'

'Don't be so daft. I'm fine, I keep telling you. And there's no point trying to phone your mum. She'll be on stage right now, kicking up her legs.'

'I could phone later on, after the show.'

'You're not staying up past your bedtime. In fact, I think we should both go to bed now. It's time you were off anyway, and I could do with an early night. It'll do me the power of good.'

So we got ready for bed together. Nan started coughing badly again. She didn't bother washing or getting undressed properly – just took off her pinny and frock and corset and got into bed in her petticoat. I didn't go to my own little bed. I grabbed my elephant, Albert Trunk, and tried to creep in with Nan.

'No, lovey,' Nan said weakly. 'You'd better stick to your own bed.'

'Oh please, Nan! I want to give you a cuddle. Go on, you always let me sleep with you when I'm poorly.'

'Yes, pet, and I'd truly love you to snuggle up with me, but I don't want you catching this nasty bug,' said Nan.

'I've *had* it, Nan, don't you remember? I got better, and we have to look after you properly and make sure you get better too,' I said. 'Go on, please, let me in. I'm shivering!'

'Better not, dearie. Off you pop now.'

'Let me tuck you up, then, and give you a kiss night-night.'

'You blow me a kiss, pet, there's a good girl. I'm scared Nanny might be a bit germy,' she said, setting her alarm clock.

'You're not getting up at half past four tomorrow, Nan! You're not to go out cleaning. Have a little lie in. It'll do you good,' I said.

'Maybe I will,' Nan murmured.

We blew each other kisses and I trailed back to my own bedroom with Albert Trunk. I was a bit hurt, and wondered why Nan was making excuses. My bed felt very cold and lonely. My leg ached again and I fidgeted. Nan said it was just growing pains. I didn't know why one leg ached much more than the other. I hoped the bad leg wouldn't grow more, so I'd end up lopsided. Nan usually rubbed it for me to make it better, but I didn't like to disturb her again.

I fell asleep eventually, burying my nose in Albert Trunk for comfort. I woke up about six and went pattering into Nan's room, but she wasn't there. I wandered through the whole flat just to make sure – but she'd gone, and her corset and frock and pinny were gone too.

'Oh Nanny, you're so naughty,' I scolded. 'You shouldn't have gone to work. You're not well.'

I went into the kitchen. Nan had made herself a

cup of tea, and there were two cigarettes stubbed out in the ashtray. I threw them in the bin and laid the table for breakfast, getting the bread and the butter and the strawberry jam all ready on the table. Then I washed and put on my school blouse and my tunic and my horrible boy's shoes. I read last week's *Girl* comic for a little while, but I couldn't get into any of the stories this time. Even 'Belle of the Ballet' stayed a silly set of pictures on the page.

I got my drawing book instead and tried copying a picture of the Queen off the tea caddy. She was wearing her lacy wedding dress and looking like a fairy princess. I tried adding wings sticking out at the back, but they looked too much like umbrellas and I didn't want Nan to think I was being disrespectful. Nan loved the royal family almost as much as she loved me.

I coloured my picture carefully, shading the wings purple to give them a regal air, but they still didn't look right. I scribbled over them, crumpled the page up and threw it in the bin. I couldn't get started on another picture. I kept looking at the clock instead. Nan was a bit late home.

I told myself that she was often late. It just meant she'd stopped to have a gossip with a friend, or maybe nipped into the newsagent's for a packet of Player's and some pear drops. I tried counting to a hundred, certain that Nan would be back before I finished.

Then I tried another hundred. *Five* hundred.

I sat watching the minute hand tick round and round, and I could feel my heart inside my chest going *tick, tick, tick* too. It was eight o'clock now. Nan was always home by this time.

I couldn't sit still any more. I circled the kitchen table, I traipsed in and out of the bedrooms, I paced up and down the hallway. I opened the front door to see if I could see Nan coming along the road. There was no sign of her.

I kept breaking little pieces of bread off the loaf, dipping them in the jam, and stuffing them in my mouth. I ate and ate, though I felt sick. I decided Nan might come if I made her a perfect cup of tea, so I boiled the kettle and went through the whole perfor- mance, and poured out a cup, so that Nan could burst through the door and say, 'Oh my, I could murder a cup of tea!' and there it would be, waiting for her.

She didn't come. The tea grew cold. It was half past eight now, and I knew I should leave or I'd be late for school. But how could I go without knowing whether Nan was all right or not? Who was I kidding? Of *course* Nan wasn't all right or she'd be here with me.

I started to cry, nuzzling into Albert Trunk like a little baby. His sweet dusty smell failed to soothe me.

'Nan, Nan, Nan!' I mumbled, at a loss to know what to do next.

2

At ten past nine a police car drew up outside the house and my stomach turned over. I peered out of the window. I could see the big black boots of the policeman and a woman's old wedge shoes with worn-down heels. I knew Nan didn't own a pair of wedge shoes, but I ran to the door, going 'Nan!' even so.

It was a completely strange woman with her hair in a turban, though she was wearing a pinny just like Nan's. The policeman stood behind her, his face very pink and shiny, like blancmange.

'Oh dear, are you little Elsie, Vi's grand-daughter?' asked the woman.

I nodded.

'Let's go inside,' said the policeman. 'Is your mummy here, dear?'

'No, she's away. I live with my nan,' I said.

'Yes, well, that's why we're here, Elsie,' said the policeman. He fiddled with the strap of his helmet, wobbling his chin. He looked at the woman for help.

'Your nan's been taken poorly, dearie,' she said.

'I know,' I said. They stared at me in surprise.

'She didn't feel well last night. She shouldn't have gone to work. I said so,' I muttered.

'Well, she keeled over at work – she gave us all such a shock. There was all this blood—'

I gasped.

'But she's probably going to be all right, dear,' the policeman said quickly. 'They called an ambulance and they've taken her off to hospital.'

'Did she cut herself?' I whispered.

'No, she just coughed it up all over everywhere – it gave us such a fright. It was dripping all down her,' said the friend.

I rocked on my heels, horrified.

'We don't need all the details,' said the policeman, frowning. 'Anyway, your nan's quite poorly, Elsie, and I expect she'll be in hospital a while.'

'Nan hates hospitals,' I whispered.

'Yes, well, she's got no choice now,' Nan's friend said. 'That's when I thought of you, dear. I knew she looked after you. Always goes on about you, she does. She loves you to bits, your nanny. And I suddenly thought, who's going to look after you?'

I stared at her, shivering. 'I want Nan!' I whispered. I dodged round them and reached for my jacket.

'What are you doing, little 'un?' asked the policeman.

'I'm going to the hospital,' I said. 'I need to see Nan.'

'No no, dear, you can't go and see her, not just yet. She's too poorly. She needs to rest,' he told me.

'She needs *me*,' I said. 'I look after her when she's poorly.'

'Aaaah!' said Nan's friend. She nodded at the policeman. 'Isn't she a little love? Ever so old-fashioned!'

'Can she maybe stay with you then, just till we find out how her nan's doing?' said the policeman.

'What? Oh no, all my kiddies are long since grown up. I wouldn't know what to do with her,' said the friend, looking appalled.

'Just for a couple of days, maybe, until we can get something sorted?' said the policeman.

'I haven't got anywhere to put her. No, sorry, I'm afraid it's out of the question,' she said. 'In fact, I've got to get back home now. My hubby's got a bad back. I need to fetch and carry for him.'

The policeman looked at me in alarm. 'Well, what are we going to do with her then?' He lowered his voice and tutted. 'You say there's no dad, and Mum's not part of the picture . . . ?'

'Yes she is!' I said. 'I've got a mum, a *lovely* mum.' I didn't like Nan's friend any more.

'Where is she then?' asked the policeman.

'Vi says she comes and goes,' said the friend. 'It's more going than coming, if you ask me.'

'Nobody *is* asking you,' I said, which made her suck her teeth. 'My mum's very busy. She's a showgirl on the stage.'

'There!' said the friend, clearly disliking me back. 'No better than she ought to be!' she hissed.

'I'd better go and phone,' said the policeman. 'How can we get in touch with Mummy?' he asked me.

'I have her phone number,' I said, running to get Nan's little notebook. 'But you can't call her just yet. She'll still be asleep. She never gets up early.'

'Well, she'll just have to stir herself,' said the policeman. 'Is that her number, dear?' he asked me when I came back.

'I'll do it,' I said, but he wouldn't let me.

He turned to Nan's friend. 'Keep an eye on the kiddie while I go and give her mum a bell.'

'Look, I'm not a babysitter,' she said, but she sat down on Nan's chair, sighing, as the policeman went back out of the front door.

I waited, gnawing my thumb tip, while he went to phone Mum. I so hoped she wouldn't be too cross when she answered.

I stood staring at Nan's friend. She fidgeted uncomfortably, digging her elbows into Nan's special velvet cushion.

'That's my nan's chair,' I said.

'Yes, well, she's not here to sit in it, is she?'

I started crying.

'Oh don't. I'm sorry, lovey. I didn't mean it to sound like that. I'm sure your nan will get better, pet. She gave us all such a nasty shock, keeling over like that, and then bringing up all that blood. I thought she was . . . Well, never mind. Don't look so worried. There's worse things happen at sea. I'm sure the doctors will make your nanny better.'

I nibbled harder, biting at a hangnail.

'Don't do that now, you're hurting yourself.'

I sat down at the table, fingering the green chenille cloth instead. Nan's friend started making laborious conversation, asking me about school and which lessons I liked the most. I mumbled brief answers, barely listening. I kept thinking about Nan, picturing her lying on the floor in her pinny. She sometimes went out with her hair curlers still in place, hidden by a turban. She'd hate everyone seeing her with her curlers in, especially at the hospital.

She'd be calling for me now, I just knew she would.

I'm coming, Nan, I whispered inside my head. *I'm coming as soon as I can, and I'll comb your hair out for you and make you look pretty. You'll get better soon. You're going to be as right as rain, like you said.*

'Nice little flat you've got here,' said the friend. 'Cosy.' She looked around at the twin china crinoline ladies curtseying on the mantelpiece and the baby photos of Mum and me in matching silver frames. Mum was smiling, all over curls and dimples. I didn't have much hair at all, and I was scowling. 'Sweet,' she commented.

I scowled in real life.

'Ooh, there's a face! Watch the wind don't change, you'll be stuck like it,' she said.

I turned my back on her. We waited and waited.

'He's a long time, that bobby. Maybe he can't get hold of your mum. You sure you gave him the right telephone number?' she said.

I nodded. I was feeling sick with worry though. Mum's phone number kept changing. I thought I'd got the right one, but perhaps she'd moved on. She lived in so many digs while she was touring. Or she might be living with an uncle. I wasn't sure she had one at the moment, but you could never tell with Mum.

What if he really couldn't get hold of her? What would happen to me?

Sour water spurted into my mouth. I had to make a run for it.

'Hold on – where are you going?' Nan's friend asked.

'The lav,' I said tersely.

I only just got there in time. I threw up down the pan and then stood there trembling, blinking away the tears. I blew my nose on the toilet paper and took a gulp of water from the cold tap. I didn't want to go back and face the friend, so I sat on the edge of the bath, snivelling into a flannel.

After a little while there was a knock on the door. 'Elsie? Are you all right?' she called.

I didn't bother answering. Of course I wasn't all right! Nan was in hospital and I wasn't sure about Mum and I knew all too well what might happen to me. It had happened once before, long ago. I couldn't really remember it properly. It was when I was really little and living with Mum. I think she went out and left me and some landlady heard me crying. I ended up in a big Home that wasn't a bit like a home at all, with a lot of other children, and I didn't know anyone and I had to eat cabbage and I got smacked for wetting the bed. I still had nightmares about it, though I think I was only there for a few days. Nan came to get me and I went to live with her.

I was so scared I was going to have to go back to that Home. But then I heard the front door and the policeman's voice, and I went dashing out of the bathroom.

'Hey, hey,' he said when he saw my red eyes and wet cheeks. 'It's all right. Your mum's coming.'

She didn't come straight away. She couldn't come till the evening. She sent a message to say I should go to school, just like normal, but I didn't want to go. In the end I went to the police station with the policeman. I was scared he'd lock me in a cell, but he was very kind and sat me on his desk and took my fingerprints, and even let me play with a pair of handcuffs. Lots of the policemen came and talked to me and called me funny names like Tuppenny and Dandelion-and-Burdock. They gave me steak and kidney pie and chips for lunch, which was much nicer than school dinners. Then they gave me a newspaper with lots of photos, and I inked moustaches and beards on everyone, even the ladies. They played games with me too – Noughts and Crosses and Hangman. If I hadn't felt so anxious about Nan I'd have had a lovely time.

Then Mum arrived – and she wasn't cross at all. She looked beautiful in her best red coat, with her hair all loose and blonde and fluffy on her shoulders. All the policemen looked at her as if she were a film star.

'My poor little girl,' she said to me, and she gave me a big cuddle right in front of everyone.

We even got a lift home in a proper police car. I wanted to hear the siren, and they played it just once, as a treat. I thought we'd be going straight to the hospital to visit Nan, but we went back home instead.

'But we have to see Nan!' I said.

'It's too late now,' said Mum, putting the kettle on. 'Visiting hours are in the afternoon, two till four. I phoned and checked.'

'Oh, we've missed it! Nan will be so sad and lonely by herself! Did you speak to her, Mum? Is she all right? When can she come home?' I gabbled.

'Ssh now, calm down. I don't think she's staying in that hospital. They're talking about moving her tomorrow,' said Mum.

'Oh, she's coming home tomorrow!' I said, clapping my hands.

'No, she's got to go to a special blooming sanatorium.' Mum leaned against the wall, rubbing her forehead, her eyes closed.

'A sanatorium?' I said. 'What's that? What's wrong with Nan?'

'They think she's only gone and got TB,' said Mum, lowering her voice when she said the two initials, as if it were somehow shameful.

I'd vaguely heard of TB but didn't know much about it.

'Nan will get better though, won't she?' I whispered.

'How on earth do I know? Oh God, I could weep. Why didn't she go to the doctor's when she first started coughing? Maybe it wouldn't have turned into full-blown TB then! Oh Lordy, how are we going to manage now? We'll have to keep this quiet. I'll never get another job if it gets out there's TB in the family. They're ever so particular when you're in theatrical digs – you nearly always have to go for an X-ray to prove you haven't got it.'

'TB means she's really, really ill, doesn't it?' I said, and started crying again.

'Oh God, don't start that grizzling. My head's splitting as it is,' said Mum. 'What did Nanny do with that Christmas sherry? I need a tot of something to buck me up.'

'I can go and see her tomorrow, can't I?' I said urgently.

'What? No, you've got school. I'll go,' said Mum. 'I need to see how long this is going to take. I can't just walk out on my job, you know. I've got a pal to cover for me this week, though she doesn't really fit into the costume – but I have to get back as soon as possible.' She opened up all the cupboards and found the Bristol Cream.

I watched as she had first one tot, then another. 'That's *Nan's* sherry, Mum. She's saving it for Christmas,' I said.

'Mmm, well, Merry Christmas and ho ho ho,' said Mum. 'Now, make yourself useful, Elsie, and run down to the chippy for two fish suppers. I'm starving.'

I could see there was no point arguing. I kept as quiet as I could all evening. I slipped into Nan's room and wrapped myself up in her old bobbly dressing gown and then buried my head in her pillow, snuffling up the sweet Nan smell. I found a hankie tucked under the pillow, the one I'd bought last Christmas with N for Nan stitched in one corner. I folded it tight in my hand, fingering the stitches.

'Oh, for God's sake,' said Mum when she found me. She sounded horrified. 'Get up, you stupid girl. Go to your own bed if you're sleepy. Come on, I need to strip that bed.'

'Why? Don't take Nan's sheets off!' I said as she started pulling them onto the floor.

'They'll be crawling with germs! I'm sleeping in with you tonight!' said Mum, pulling at the sheets viciously.

I hoped she'd leave them in a pile in a corner of the bedroom, but she took them to the bath and put them to soak in soapy water. She even washed Nan's dressing gown. I clung tightly to the hankie, hiding it as best I could.

When Mum had scrubbed and pummelled the sheets and gown and strangled the water out of them, she hung them up over all the doors, so that it rained inside for hours, the whole flat a fug of damp that made my nostrils hurt.

She wasn't finished even then. She washed all the curtains too, swept all the floors, polished all the windows, moving round the flat like a whirlwind, her beautiful hair tied up in a turban and her dress tucked up out of the way in her knickers as if she were a little girl about to do a handstand.

She toiled madly far into the night, and then came crawling into my little bed. There was hardly room for one, let alone two, and neither of us slept properly.

She insisted on me going to school the next day.

'I *can't*, Mum! I've *got* to go and visit Nan!' I said.

'You're not staying off school and that's that. Hospitals are no place for kiddies,' said Mum.

'Oh Mum, please, I can't bear it if I can't see Nan!' I said, starting to sob.

'Now cut that out! Haven't I got enough to cope with? Look, I'll take you to see Nanny on Saturday – *if* you're a good girl.'

There was no arguing with her. I trailed to school wishing Mum were in hospital instead of Nan. Marilyn Hide and Susan Bradshaw kept picking on me, mocking my hairstyle and my old tunic and my boy's shoes, but for once I just stared at them dead-pan, not really bothering. Then they started saying horrible things about my mum. I didn't really care, because I didn't like Mum that much either, but then they said something about my *daft, smelly old nan*. I kicked them hard with my boy's shoes and they ran off screaming to tell our teacher, Miss Roberts.

I did get a bit worried then, because I liked Miss Roberts a lot. I loved her fluffy hair and her even fluffier angora jumpers. She was usually very kind to me, and once she gave me a gold star for one of my stories. I didn't want her to be cross with me.

My heart thumped when she beckoned to me from the other side of the playground. Marilyn and Susan sauntered off smugly arm in arm, nodding their heads at me.

I trailed miserably over to Miss Roberts.

'Oh dear, Elsie. I hear you've fallen out with Marilyn and Susan again,' she said.

'Yes, miss.'

'They said you kicked them?'

'I . . . I couldn't help it,' I said. I looked down at my shoes as if they had a will of their own.

'Did they kick you first?' asked Miss Roberts. 'You were limping as you walked across the playground.'

I tried to stand up properly. 'Sorry, miss.'

'You're the one who's hurt, Elsie, not me,' said Miss Roberts. 'I know full well Marilyn and Susan tend to gang up on you, dear.'

'Well, they didn't exactly *kick* me, Miss Roberts,' I said, hovering near the truth.

She thought I was protecting them and gave me a little pat on the head. 'Are you all right, Elsie?' she said. 'You've been a bit dreamy in class and you're looking a bit peaky. Weren't you very well yesterday?'

I fidgeted uncomfortably. I so wanted to tell her all about Nan and how worried I was, but Mum said I wasn't to breathe a word.

'There'll be hell to pay if they find out about the TB. We don't want anyone poking their nose into our affairs,' she'd said. 'You don't need to blab about Nan. *I'm* your mum – and don't you forget it.'

There wasn't much chance of that. I decided I couldn't risk telling Miss Roberts, so I said I'd just had a tummy ache yesterday. She didn't look as if she really believed me, but she patted me on the head and said I could go indoors for the rest of playtime and read a comic.

Marilyn and Susan were lurking nearby, and they nudged each other in triumph when they saw me go in the girls' entrance, thinking I was in disgrace. I knew it was a privilege, not a punishment, to sit peacefully in the classroom reading 'The Bash Street Kids' and sucking at an old toffee paper. But I couldn't feel happy. My stomach was in knots and I thought of Nan with every beat of my heart.

3

'Did you go to see her, Mum?' I asked, the minute I'd got indoors from school.

'Yes, yes, of course I did. I took her a clean nightie and dressing gown, and her hair rollers and brush, and a stick of 4711 eau de cologne – I bought it specially,' said Mum. 'I packed up a little case for her. They were taking her in an ambulance to the sanatorium this afternoon.'

'Will she get better there? Can she come home soon?' I gabbled desperately.

'No, of course not. She's still very poorly and she's got to stay in bed there and not budge for weeks,' said Mum. 'She has to get that cough better. And I don't know what I'm going to do. Who's going to look after you? You can't come and live with me – they don't take kiddies in theatrical digs, and anyway, there'd be nobody to keep an eye on you. Oh Gawd, what a shame you're not a bit older, eh?' She sucked in her breath through her teeth.

'Mum?'

'Shut it now, Elsie. I'm trying to think.'

'Mum, Nan isn't going to . . . to die, is she?' I whispered.

'What?'

'She promised me she wouldn't, but *can* you die of TB?' I persisted, starting to cry.

'Stop that,' said Mum, but then she put out her arms and gave me a hug. I breathed in her Coty L'Aimant talcum smell and sobbed harder.

'Nanny's a fighter, you know that. Of course she'll get better. Look, we'll go and visit her at the weekend, and you'll see for yourself,' said Mum, pulling me properly onto her lap.

'I'll be able to see her on Saturday? You promise, Mum?' I said, sniffing.

'Oh, for Gawd's sake, wipe that nose. I don't want snot all over my best blouse. *Yes*, I promise,' she said.

So on Saturday I marched along beside Mum, and inside my head I chanted, *See Nan, see Nan, see Nan*, as I put my left foot down and then my right, determinedly marching.

'Stop limping, Elsie!' said Mum.

I stared down at my skinny legs. I pulled a face at my grey socks and brown Clarks lace-ups. 'It's these shoes,' I said. 'They're too small now. They're hurting my toes.' I wanted new shoes – shiny black patent ones, or bright scarlet with a strap.

Mum bent over and prodded my feet through the ugly brown leather. 'Nonsense, you've got heaps of room.'

'Couldn't I have them anyway? I hate these. They're boy's shoes!'

Nan had found them for a shilling at a jumble sale, barely worn and my size, worst luck.

'What do you think I am, made of money?' said Mum, standing up and giving me a tug to hurry me along.

'They all tease me at school because I've got boy's shoes,' I said mournfully.

'Stop that whining,' said Mum. 'I've told you, you've got to learn to stand up for yourself. Now come on, or we'll miss the bus. And *stop* limping, it's driving me mad. You're walking along all lopsided.'

'My leg aches.'

'Oh, you're full of aches. Headaches, belly aches, all-over aches. Just pull yourself together. And you're to give Nanny a big smile when you see her. I don't want her worrying, it'll only make her worse,' said Mum.

I scurried along beside her, making such an effort to walk properly that I couldn't do it naturally at all, and developed kipper feet.

'Mum, look, I'm like Charlie Chaplin,' I said, waddling, and doffing an imaginary bowler hat.

Nan always laughed at my imitations and said I was a proper caution. Mum just looked irritated.

'Stop messing about this instant or I'll send you back home and visit Nanny by myself,' she said, in that snippy tone that meant she wasn't joking.

I walked left-right, left-right, like a little soldier, though my leg ached worse than ever. We got the bus to the hospital – *two* buses – and although I usually thought a bus ride was a treat and liked chatting to the conductor, this time I kept quiet and nibbled my lip anxiously the whole way.

'For heaven's sake, Elsie, leave that lip alone! You're making it bleed. No one will ever want to kiss you if you've got chapped lips,' said Mum.

I decided I didn't care and went on nibbling. I didn't want anyone to kiss me, only Nan, and I knew she wouldn't mind a chap or two.

I was surprised by the sanatorium. It wasn't like a hospital at all – more like a bleak holiday camp, but without any rides. It took us ages to find Nan, but eventually we were directed to a kind of Nissen hut at the end of the complex.

I was suddenly frightened, and hung back, clinging to Mum, even though I was so desperate to see Nan.

'Don't be such a baby,' Mum said, but her own palm was clammy too. She wrinkled her nose. 'I hate the smell of hospitals.'

There were twelve ladies lying down flat in bed, six on one side and six the other. I thought they'd all be quite old like Nanny, but most were Mum's age or even younger. They all looked very white, as pale as their pillows, and huddled shivering beneath their thin blankets. It was hard to tell whether they were awake or asleep – or even dead.

'Nan?' I quavered.

'Blooming heck, it's like an iceberg in here,' said Mum, peering around at all the wide-open windows. 'There's Nanny, right at the end. You smile at her and say hello nicely like a good girl.'

I don't think I'd have recognized Nan if Mum hadn't pointed her out. She was lying on her back like all the others, and her mouth was sagging open. She didn't have her false teeth in. I averted my eyes quickly, knowing Nan would hate me seeing her empty mouth.

'Come on, chin up,' Mum hissed behind me. 'There now, Mother, I've brought our Elsie to see you. What are they trying to do, freeze you to death?'

'It's meant to be good for us – fresh air,' said Nan, her voice oddly muffled. 'But all it's doing for me is giving me chilblains. Where's my best girl, then?'

I was hiding behind Mum, suddenly stupidly shy of Nan. She looked so different. Something had happened to her hair. She usually had it in a roll at the front, and then pulled back in a neat bun at the back. But the bun had gone missing now. Someone had chopped Nan's hair off at ear level. It stuck out wildly in every direction, every follicle clearly in shock. It made her look crazy.

'Hello, Nan,' I whispered to the mad old lady in the bed pretending to be my dear warm nanny.

'What's that face for, darling?' she asked. 'Don't look so frightened, poppet. I'm still your nanny, even if they've cut off my crowning glory.'

'And made a right mess of it too,' said Mum. 'What did you let them do that for? It's like a prison haircut!'

'They don't have the time to wash long hair so they cut it for convenience.'

'Well, they could have given you a decent perm while they were at it. And what in God's name's happened to your teeth? They haven't taken them away for convenience too?'

'No, no, they just thought they needed to be sterilized. I've asked the nice nurse and she's going to try and find them again for me,' said Nan. She was peering round Mum, holding out her arms to me. 'Hey there, Elsie!'

'Now you can't go cuddling her, Mum,' said my mum.

'I know, I know, I'm not going to breathe all over her. I just want to hold her hand,' said Nan.

'Oh Nan, here!' I said, darting forward and latching onto her dear knobbly fingers. 'You're cold!'

'Yes – daft, isn't it. I need a pair of big furry gloves to keep me warm.'

'Perhaps I could make you some?' I suggested. I could knit – Nan herself had taught me – but I had so far only managed meagre little plain-stitch scarves for my two dolls and Albert Trunk. I hoped my great love for Nan would spur me on and give me new skills and perseverance.

I hung onto Nan's poor cold hand, pulling on it like a bell ringer. 'Don't you worry, Nan, we'll make you warm and cosy. Oh dear, I wish you could come home!'

'So do I, pet, but I'm not better just yet. I *will* get better, like I promised. All these ladies are getting better, see?' said Nan.

I wasn't at all sure she was right. Mum wasn't convinced either.

'They look at death's door to me,' she hissed. 'I'm sure you'll get worse, breathing in all their germs too. It'll make your TB run rampant.'

I gave a little gasp.

'Don't be so silly, Sheila,' said Nan sharply. 'Now, what's in that bag of yours? Have you brought something for the poor invalid? I hope it's not grapes – you know I can't cope with the pips.'

'We've got you chocolate, Nan – a bar of Fry's Chocolate Cream, your favourite. I chose it for you! And a bag of sherbet lemons too, and a bottle of Tizer in case you get thirsty.'

'Oh my, it's like Christmas and birthday all in one go!' Nan blew us both kisses, leaned out of her bed, and tucked her goodies in her locker, right at the back behind her spare nightie. 'Don't want anyone helping themselves,' she said, hauling herself upright again and then coughing.

'I thought no one was allowed out of bed,' said Mum.

'It's them nurses. They're like gannets!' Nan gasped between coughs.

'There now. Lie still, can't you,' said Mum, because Nan was leaning over again, reaching for a little enamel pot on the top of her locker. She coughed again, then bent her head and spat copiously into the pot.

'Mum! Do you have to?' said my mum, shuddering.

'Yes, I *do* have to,' Nan gasped.

'It's disgusting, spitting like that. You're like an old man on a bus. It turns my stomach.'

'I don't do it for *fun*,' said Nan, wiping her mouth. 'We have to. And we're all given these little pots, see?'

'Still, you shouldn't do it in front of Elsie,' said Mum.

'I don't mind a bit, Nan,' I said quickly.

'It's not . . . bloody, is it?' said Mum.

'No, no – there was just a wee bit one day, and then the awful haemorrhage the next – oh my God, it gave me such a fright.' Nan put the lid back on her pot and set it carefully on her locker top.

'I think it's very sensible to have your own little spitting pot,' I said supportively.

'Nobody asked *your* opinion, madam,' said Mum. She looked around the bleak room. 'This place gives me the creeps. What do you *do* all day, Mum?'

'Lie here. Take my medicine. Have a little doze. Maybe dream about Elsie,' said Nan, patting my hand.

'Oh Nan,' I said. 'Yes, dream about me! I know, we'll *both* dream, and then it'll be like we're really seeing each other. Let's dream tonight that we're going down the park and feeding the ducks together.'

'That's a lovely idea, dearie! And then, when we've fed the ducks, we'll come home and we'll squash up together in my old armchair and I'll read you a story, and then you can maybe read me one – you're a grand little reader.'

'And tomorrow night we'll dream we're going to the seaside together, and we'll go paddling and you'll buy me a big ice cream and I'll buy you a stick of peppermint rock,' I said. 'And we'll go to the country some dreams, or we'll go up to London – oh yes, we'll go to London to see the Queen.'

This was the wrong thing to say.

'Oh, the Coronation!' said Nan, and she gave a little moan.

'Don't worry, Nan, it's months yet,' I whispered, hoping Mum couldn't hear. 'I think you'll be absolutely better by then, and we'll still be able to go, you and me. We'll camp out all night and then we'll watch the big golden coach go by, and we'll cheer and wave, and the Queen will see us and wave back. "There's Nan and Elsie!" she'll say. "Oh, I'm so glad they can make it on my special day."'

Nan had her lips pressed together. She was trying not to cry, but a few tears leaked down her cheeks.

'There, you've upset her now,' said Mum, giving me a poke in the back.

'I'm sorry, Nan. Look, would you like a piece of your chocolate? Can you manage without your teeth? I could maybe have a little tiny bit too?' I tore off the chocolate wrapper, took a quick nibble, and then held the rest out to Nan. She couldn't bite, but she sucked at it a bit, like an ice lolly.

'That's it – you like it, don't you?' I said. 'Oh, I made you a special Get Well card!' I peered into Mum's shopping bag. It had got rather crumpled. 'Oh dear, and I spent ages on it . . .' I tried to smooth it out.

They had better crayons at school than mine at home, so on Friday I'd asked Miss Roberts if I could use the class crayons for a special private project. Oh, Miss Roberts was magic! She didn't ask any questions, she just smiled at me and said I was to stay in after lunch and she'd see what she could do.

She didn't just give me the tray of class crayons – she lent me her own special box of Derwent crayons, all the colours of the rainbow, with wonderful sharp points.

'I know you'll be very careful, Elsie, and not break any of them,' she said. 'Do you need paper too?'

She didn't give me sugar paper. She gave me a sheet of smooth white cartridge from her own sketchbook.

'You are the kindest teacher in the whole world, miss,' I said.

I folded the paper very carefully and drew Nan a card. I coloured her a thatched cottage in the countryside with red and yellow roses round the door. Nan had stayed in a thatched cottage on her honeymoon with Grandpa and she always said she'd give anything to live in one now. Grandpa had gone off to heaven even before I was born, but Nan had me now. I drew the two of us together in the garden, with orange marigolds and yellow daffodils and purple pansies all around our feet in the carefully shaded green grass. I didn't draw Mum, but I supposed she could always come on a visit.

We had our pets in the garden: my three chocolate box kittens, some fluffy bunny rabbits so Nan could comb them and make me an angora jumper, and baby Brumas the polar bear, because we had been to see him at the zoo and had fallen in love with him. I'd made him a special blue pond to swim in if he felt hot.

Inside the card I printed:

To dear Nan,
Please get better very soon.
I love you very much.
From Elsie
xxxxxxxxxxxxxxxxxxxxxxxxxxxxxxxxxxxxxxxxxxxxxxxxxxxx

I was just doing the kisses when the bell went for afternoon school and Miss Roberts came into the classroom. She didn't try to peer at my picture, but I held it up to show her.

'It's a card for my nanny,' I said. I didn't tell her what the card was *for*. It could be a birthday card for all she knew.

'Oh Elsie, it's simply lovely,' said Miss Roberts, smiling.

I hid it in my satchel quick, not wanting Marilyn and Susan to clap their beady eyes on it. I hadn't shown it to Mum either. She always said I'd done the hair the wrong colour or put the feet on sideways or crossed the eyes whenever I drew a person, and I could see for myself that my cottage was a bit skew-whiff – it looked as if it would collapse any minute and crush the kittens, the rabbits, and baby Brumas.

Nan didn't have any complaints. 'Oh Elsie, it's wonderful! Bless you, darling, there's you and me and our special cottage,' she said at once.

'You're good at guessing,' said Mum. 'So what are all those weeny wriggly things in the grass – mice?'

'Oh Mum,' I said, hurt.

'No, no, you always get mice in those old cottages,' she said, pretending to be serious.

'Of course it's not mice!' said Nan sternly. 'It's Elsie's kittens, all three of them, and – ooh, we've got rabbits too – look at their lovely ears! And how sweet of you, darling, you've given us a little puppy too.'

I decided it didn't really matter if Nan mistook baby Brumas for a little dog. It would certainly solve quite a few problems as he got older. Perhaps we'd be better off with a puppy – and we could *all* swim in the little blue pond.

'I'll put my lovely card on my locker,' said Nan. 'And I'll look at it every day and wish I was there with you, Elsie.'

'You will be one day, Nan. When I'm grown up I'm going to buy us that cottage and we'll have the flowery garden and all the pets.'

'What about me?' asked Mum. 'I'm the one who pays all the bills! Don't I get to come to that cottage of yours?'

'Yes, of course, Mum,' I said out loud, but inside my head I shouted, *No, you don't!* Mum couldn't hear, but she gave me a funny look all the same.

'Oh well, maybe I'll meet my Mr Wonderful at last, and I'll have a blooming great palace up the road, with all mod cons, white carpets and lovely sofas and one of them big sunken baths you see in Hollywood films, and I'll come and visit you two once a week, how about that?' said Mum.

'What's happened to what's-his-face – was it Sam?' asked Nan.

'Tim! No, he's history. He had very funny little habits that weren't *my* cup of tea,' said Mum.

I'd only met Uncle Tim twice, and I didn't like him either time. His hair was all sticky with Brilliantine, and his hands were sticky too when he picked me up for a kiss, as if I were a little baby. I was glad he was history.

'No one else on the horizon?' said Nan.

'Fat chance,' said Mum. 'And how am I going to meet anyone likely now? I'm up the creek without a paddle, aren't I? I'm going to lose my engagement up north if I'm stuck down here any longer.'

I looked at Nan and she looked at me.

'Well, Nan will get better soon, and then she can come home and you won't be stuck then,' I said quickly.

'I'll do my best to be home with you as soon as possible, my little lamb,' said Nan, not looking me in the eye. She started coughing again and had to reach for her little enamel pot. I made to pick it up for her.

'Don't touch it, don't touch it – watch the germs!' Mum screamed.

My hand halted in mid-air while I imagined little maggoty germ creatures swarming out of the pot, wriggling up my cardigan sleeve and nestling in my armpit. I shrank back. Nan's eyes looked so sad and ashamed as she clutched the pot herself and did her very best to heave herself round in the bed. She turned her back on us as she spat into the pot.

'I'm sorry, Nan. I'm so sorry,' I said.

'No, dear, no. Your mum's right. Better you don't get near it. I don't know how infectious I am yet. I'd kill myself if I gave it to you, Elsie,' Nan gasped. She put the pot down and lay back weakly on her pillows.

'Charming,' said Mum. 'What about me? We'd all be in Queer Street if *I* caught it. Lucky I stay clean and healthy.'

'You've got to get yourself checked out, though, Sheila – and our Elsie too. The doctor was most insistent. You've both got to be tested. Anyone living at the same house, that's what he said. You must go and tell Miss Godden and that Irish couple on the first floor.'

'Do you think I'm daft?' said Mum. 'They'll go blabbing to the landlord and we'll all be out on our ears. They won't have got it – they never come down to the basement, do they? And I'm hardly ever at the house, so I'm all right, thank God.'

'But Elsie—' Nan said urgently.

'Look at her – she's right as rain, aren't you, Elsie?' said Mum, giving me a nudge. 'She's always been a bit on the skinny side, it's just natural – and she hasn't got a cough, has she?'

'No, she hasn't,' said Nan. 'But promise you'll take her for this test.'

'Yes, yes, don't fuss about it.' Mum looked at her watch. 'We'd better get going soon.'

'No, Mum, we've only just got here!' I protested. 'I want to stay with Nan all afternoon.'

'That old bag at reception said we're only allowed ten minutes on this ward – and you're not supposed to be here at all, Elsie. They're just turning a blind eye as we've come all this way,' said Mum.

'All right, then. Best get going,' said Nan. 'But you'll come back next Saturday, won't you?' She looked anxiously at Mum.

'We'll do our best, though those Green Line buses are only one an hour from town and they go all round the moon, and then the nearest stop is a good mile away from this dump.' Mum peered at her shoes, frowning. 'I've worn down my heels at the back, look! We need to kit ourselves out with hiking boots to get here.'

'But we'd come even if we had five miles to walk, Nan. No, fifty miles. We'd come if we had to walk through mud up to our ankles – up to our knees – up to our *chins*,' I said.

'Button it, Elsie. You're just being silly now,' said Mum, standing up. 'Right, we'll bring you some more sweeties next time, Mum. We can all make pigs of ourselves now rationing's over! I'd offer to do your laundry, but you'd better let the hospital boil it up, because of the germs. You take care now.'

Nan's mouth drooped, though I could see she was struggling to control it. I wanted to throw my arms round her, but I knew it wasn't allowed now. She looked so little and lonely in her strange neat bed.

'Here, Nan,' I said, bending down and then pretending to pick up a furry handful. 'You have Snow White and Sooty and Marmalade all week. They'll bounce about on your bed and keep you amused.'

'You what?' said Mum – but Nan smiled, though her eyes were watering again.

'*Thank* you, darling,' she said, stroking thin air. 'I'll look after them ever so carefully. Whoops! Watch it, Marmalade – don't fall off the bed.'

'You two are a right pair of loonies,' said Mum. 'OK, we're off then. Ta-ta, Mum.'

'Bye, Nan. Oh, I'll miss you so. Bye-bye,' I said.

I blew kisses to Nan – and then I had to kiss Snow White and Sooty and Marmalade. It made Nan laugh but it made Mum sigh heavily.

'Come on, Elsie, quit acting daft,' she said, tugging at me.

It felt terrible walking out of the ward. I kept peering round to wave to Nan. She started to cough, but she kept her mouth clamped shut, her eyes popping, so she wouldn't have to spit again while we were watching.

I kept seeing her face all the way home. I started to cry a little – just quietly, no noise at all.

'Stop that snivelling now,' said Mum.

'But I'm so sad for Nan,' I moaned.

'Crying in the street and making a public spectacle of yourself isn't going to help her, is it? Now pull yourself together.'

We just missed our Green Line bus home, even though we ran for it. We had to wait a whole hour for the next. I kept trying not to cry, but I couldn't help the odd sniff and snort.

'Oh dear, what's up with you, tuppence-ha'penny?' asked a fat woman waiting with us. 'Have you been naughty? Have you had a telling off?'

'My nanny's ill,' I wailed, though Mum's fingers dug into my shoulder.

'Oh dear, I hope it's nothing serious,' said the woman. 'You been to visit her then?'

I nodded, though Mum's fingers pressed harder.

The fat woman paused, her beady eyes darting from me to Mum and back again. 'She's not in the sanatorium, is she?' she said, nodding in that direction.

'No, she's not,' said Mum forcefully.

'That's a relief,' said the fat woman. 'It's a disgrace

they built it there, right in a residential area. They say it's not catching, but you can't fool me. It's a wonder we haven't gone down with it. We all breathe the same air, don't we? Mind you, I don't want to sound uncharitable. I feel sorry for the poor souls stuck in there. They go in – but you never see them coming out. They say you can cure TB now, but I think they all fade away.'

I gave a little gasp.

'Do you mind? You're upsetting my little girl,' said Mum, and she steered us several paces up the pavement.

I shook with suppressed sobs while Mum dabbed at my face with her hankie.

'Don't take any notice of that nosy old biddy,' she muttered.

'But she said—'

'Yes, and *I* say she doesn't know what she's talking about. She's just making mischief. Don't take any notice.'

'But—'

'No buts. You take note of what I say. I'm your mother, aren't I?'

I knew she was my mother whether I wanted her to be or not. I snuffled against her and she patted me, the two of us together, united against the fat woman. Mum even started up a game of I Spy to pass the time. We had M is for Mum and T is for tree and N is for nylons and BS for bus stop and NV for nail varnish, and then I spied something beginning with VFL and Mum was stumped. I whispered, 'Very fat lady,' and we both got the giggles.

We were getting on famously, but then I spoiled it all on the long bus journey home. The driver kept stopping and starting, jolting us backwards and forwards.

'Mum, I feel sick,' I whispered.

'Don't you dare!' said Mum, but I couldn't help it, and we didn't have a carrier bag with us either.

4

I missed my kittens badly on Sunday. I had their picture on the chocolate box but they wouldn't come alive for me. Of course, I knew they weren't real, but they'd been real in my head, and they left a big gap. Still, I was happy they were playing with Nan now. They'd be romping all over her bed with their little paddy paws, and then diving under the covers whenever a nurse came near. They'd curl up on Nan, one round her neck, one tucked into her armpit and one on her tummy, and then they'd all three go to sleep.

Nan could stroke their soft fur – oh, they'd be better than furry mittens.

I was glad I'd given them to Nan, but my own little couch felt cold and empty without them – and I had no one to play with all day. Mum slept late and I had to creep about the flat so I wouldn't disturb her. I made myself some bread and jam and didn't put the kettle on because it had a noisy whistle. I tried to make a pot of tea using hot water from the tap but it didn't work properly, and I had to pour it all away.

I read my old *Girl* comic, though I'd read it from cover to cover already. I liked 'Belle of the Ballet' best. I tried tying my hair back like Belle's and pretending it was blonde instead of brown. I wished I had real ballet shoes. Laura Totteridge went to ballet classes. She changed into her special ballet outfit in the girls' toilets before she went off to her after-school class. She wore a black tunic, with matching black satin knickers, and an angora bolero – pink to match her ballet shoes.

I *wished* I could be Laura. Well, I wanted to keep my own nan, but apart from that I wanted to swap. Laura had a big brother who watched out for her and gave her piggybacks, and she had a little sister who hung on her hand and giggled at everything she said. She had a kind soft mother who came to meet her from school every day, and I'm sure she had a gentle big father who told her she was his pretty princess.

I'd told Nan all about Laura.

'Why don't you make friends with her, Elsie? She sounds such a nice girl,' she suggested.

I loved Nan more than anyone else ever, but sometimes she made me sigh and roll my eyes. As if a girl like Laura would ever be friendly with a girl like me.

'Go on, *try* to make friends with her,' Nan urged.

'I don't know how,' I said pathetically.

'Give her that lovely smile.'

I had tried flashing my teeth at Laura when we were in the toilets together – but she stepped back nervously as if she thought I was going to bite her.

The next day Nanny gave me a tuppenny bar of chocolate for playtime. 'Share it with Laura,' she said.

It was hard work tracking her down this time. I eventually spotted her over by the bicycle sheds with Melanie and Pat and Joan, all of them practising handstands. You can't give someone a piece of chocolate when they're upside down. I lurked nearby, wanting to get Laura on her own. I was so anxious I nibbled the chocolate for comfort, and then realized I only had one piece left to offer her. I wrapped it up quickly and hung onto it. I waited until the bell went, and Laura and the other girls righted themselves and untucked their skirts from their knickers. Then I went charging up to Laura.

'This is for you,' I said, thrusting the piece of

chocolate into her hand. I'd been clutching it so hard I think it might have melted. It was certainly un-pleasantly warm.

She looked at it as if I'd slipped a slug into her hand. 'What's this?' she asked suspiciously.

'It's a present,' I said.

'Well . . . thank you,' she said, because she was really a very nice girl, but when we went into the classroom I saw her throwing it in the wastepaper basket.

I lied to Nan and said Laura had eaten up all her share of the chocolate and said 'Yum yum,' and then shared her own banana sandwich with me. Nan usually knew when I was lying. Perhaps she believed me simply because she wanted it to be true so badly. I kept up the pretence for weeks, inventing all sorts of best-friend scenarios for Laura and me. I even had us swapping desks so we could sit together in class. We exchanged books and comics, we told each other secrets, we went around arm in arm together at play-time. I invented so many telling details I almost started to believe it myself. Then Nan unnerved me utterly by suggesting I invite Laura home for tea.

'No! No, I don't want her to come!' I said, panicking.

'But she's your friend. I'm sure you'd both have a lovely time together. I'll do you a slap-up tea, darling. We can have tinned peaches and evappy milk.' This was our favourite tea-time treat, which we usually only had on Sundays.

'I still don't want her to come, Nan,' I said.

Nan looked at me carefully, her eyes squinting. 'You're not ashamed of us, are you, Elsie?' she asked.

I *was* a little ashamed, because we lived in a rented basement flat that smelled funny, whereas Laura lived in Elmtree Road, where all the big black and white houses had neat little hedges and geranium, alyssum and lobelia in their front gardens in a patriotic red, white and blue floral display.

I was ashamed because I was Weird Elsie, the girl with a home-made tunic and boy's shoes, the girl who muttered to herself when she played games, the girl who didn't have a dad.

'I'm not ashamed of *you*, Nan,' I said. 'But please please please, don't make me ask Laura to tea.'

I should have realized Nan wouldn't let it alone. She went right up to Laura and her mother after school one day, while I was still only halfway across the playground, doing up one of my wretched laces. I saw her and charged over, but I didn't get there in time. I saw Laura and her mum walk away from Nan. Laura peered round worriedly.

Nan was looking puzzled. 'That *is* Laura, isn't it – the dark girl with the pink ribbons?' she said.

I thought of lying again, but then Nan might

interrogate every girl in my class, trying to find the right Laura. I nodded miserably.

'The Laura who's your best friend?'

'Well, she's not actually my *best* friend,' I mumbled.

'Her mum says you're not friends at all. You don't ever play together,' said Nan. 'You don't even sit together in class.'

'Well . . . I did give her some chocolate,' I said madly.

'Oh Elsie,' said Nan. 'Was it all a story then? Have you been fibbing to your old nanny?'

I nodded, not daring to say any more in case I burst out crying. Marilyn and Susan were standing nearby while their mothers were chatting. If they found out they'd have a field day.

I must have been going red in the face.

'Come on home then, ducks,' said Nan.

I was scared she might be cross with me for fibbing, but she didn't tell me off at all. *We* had tinned peaches and evaporated milk for tea, just the two of us. Nan didn't mention Laura again, so neither did I.

I waited in suspense the next few days at school, but Laura didn't tell anyone. She gave me nervous little smiles when we passed each other in the corridor. Once she dropped a Merry Maid Caramel on top of my desk. I wasn't sure if it was an accident or not. I wondered if she could possibly want to be friends after all, but she never made any other overtures and I didn't dare.

Now, while I waited for Mum, I drew a picture of Laura and me in a dancing display, both of us wearing white tutus. I copied our ballet positions from the 'Belle of the Ballet' strip.

When Mum got up at last, I showed her my drawing and she nodded and said, 'Very good' – but she didn't really look at it properly. I asked if we could go to see Nan again that afternoon, but Mum sighed at me.

'We've just this minute seen her! We'll go again next week. Now stop hanging around with those big moony eyes – you're getting on my nerves. Go and play.'

It was hard finding something to do with Mum glaring at me. She hated it when I played pretend games. She said I looked gormless gesturing to myself and mouthing words. She didn't like me playing with my paper dolls either. She didn't mind so much when I was cutting out their clothes, snipping carefully round every white tag, but when I'd got them all dressed up and chattering happily, ready to go out, Mum said I looked loopy shaking bits of paper about. She was even less thrilled when I took Albert Trunk for a trundle across the carpet. Once she caught him doing a little pile of red plasticine dung and smacked me for being dirty.

'Play a proper *game*, Elsie,' she said, tapping the

sideboard where Nan kept the Ludo and Snakes and Ladders and our pack of Happy Families.

'Will you play too, Mum?'

'I've got too much to do. I've got to mend the armpit of my best silk blouse and press my suit,' she said.

'Why?' I said, not really concentrating.

'*Why?*' Mum said, taking hold of me and shaking me hard. 'Because I can't go back to my job up north on account of the fact I've got to look after *you*.'

'I'm sorry, Mum!' I stuttered, my teeth rattling. 'Look – you go back to your dancing job. I'll be fine. I can look after myself, really. I can make tea and cheesy beanos and all sorts.'

'Oh yes – if I leave you for just one blooming evening, then someone will blab and you'll be whipped into care quick as a wink. And if you don't stop annoying me I'll start to consider it a tempting option,' said Mum.

I clamped my mouth together, and when she let me go I ran outside. I found a stump of chalk in my pocket and played a game of hopscotch on the pavement. I hummed under my breath, pretending I was feeling just fine, though my heart was hammering inside my chest.

Mrs Brownlow from next door came bumbling along, her massive bulk squeezed into her huge scarlet coat. She looked like a London bus and certainly seemed intent on running me over.

'What are you doing, Elsie Kettle?' she asked.

'Playing,' I mumbled.

'On a Sunday?' she said, sniffing. 'You been to Sunday School today?'

'We don't go to church, Mrs Brownlow,' I said, hopping. My right leg was aching so I had to hop with my left and I was much clumsier.

'I know that mother of yours wouldn't set foot in a church,' she said. 'She's no better than she ought to be.'

That was what Nan's work friend had said. Mrs Brownlow often used this mysterious phrase when she talked about Mum.

'I feel sorry for poor Mrs Kettle, her Sheila bringing shame on the family,' Mrs Brownlow went on.

I knew *I* was the shame. I turned my back on her, trying not to care.

'Where *is* your grandma, Elsie? I nipped round to borrow half a pint of milk for a custard the other day and I couldn't get any answer.'

'She's poorly,' I said warily.

'Oh dear. In bed, is she? I'll pop round tomorrow then, see if she needs any shopping.'

'No, she doesn't,' I said.

'And I'll bring her my *Woman's Home Companion*. It's a good read, that,' said Mrs Brownlow. 'I'll fetch it now.'

'No, you can't come in. Nan isn't here.'

'What? She's never in hospital, is she?' said Mrs Brownlow.

I nodded.

'What's wrong with her then? It's nothing really serious, is it? Elsie, I'm *talking* to you. What's the matter with your nanny?'

'I'm not allowed to say,' I mumbled.

Mrs Brownlow looked even more interested. 'Is it women's troubles?' she hissed.

I didn't have a clue what she meant, but it seemed a good idea to nod.

'Oh, the poor thing. She'll never be the same again,' said Mrs Brownlow.

'Yes, she will. She's going to get better. She said,' I retorted, turning my back on Mrs Brownlow and hopping. I used my right leg and staggered a little.

'What's up with your leg then?' she asked.

'Nothing!' I said, and hobbled indoors.

It did ache a lot though. I knew it irritated Mum when I limped – but perhaps if I exaggerated it, she might take it more seriously. She might even let me stay off school.

Mum was in her petticoat in the living room, ironing all her clothes, humming along to *Family Favourites* on the wireless. She had an insistent, high-pitched hum, almost as if she were playing a

58

tune on a comb with a piece of toilet paper. I wondered if she was trying to be brave too.

'Mum?'

She frowned at me, mid-hum.

'Mum, my leg hurts really badly. Look, I'm limping,' I said, parading around the living room.

'Well, stop it,' she said.

'I can't help it,' I said. 'Ouch, it really, really hurts.'

'Then stop marching about and sit down, you silly fool,' said Mum.

'I think I really wrenched it playing hopscotch,' I said. I rubbed my leg gingerly. 'I can hardly bear to walk. Maybe I've broken it!' I was warming to this theme. I'd always wanted a limb in plaster. People wrote little messages all over the hard white surface and made a big fuss of you. I stomped harder with my bad leg, trying to make it worse.

'Do pack it in, Elsie,' said Mum. 'I've got enough on my hands without you playing silly beggars too. If I don't get another job, we'll be in Queer Street, I'm telling you.'

'My *leg*!'

'You're just putting it on to get attention.'

'No I'm not. Mrs Brownlow saw and asked me what was wrong with it,' I said.

'Mrs Brownlow? That nosy old cow! What have you been saying to her? You didn't tell her about Nanny, did you?' Mum asked, suddenly giving me her full attention.

'No, I didn't. Well . . .'

'Elsie!' said Mum, catching hold of me.

'I didn't say about the TB, I swear I didn't. I said Nan had women's troubles,' I said, wriggling.

Mum stared and then burst out laughing. 'Good for you,' she said.

She stayed in a good mood after that. We played Beauty Parlours when she had finished her ironing. She let me brush her hair after she'd washed it, and then buff her nails – her toes as well as her fingers.

'You're so pretty, Mum,' I said enviously.

'I just know how to give Nature a little helping hand,' said Mum smugly.

She let me stay up with her all evening, singing along to the music on the Light Programme. I did my best to be useful, making her cups of tea and running for a fresh box of matches and emptying her ashtray.

'You're a good little soul really,' said Mum, giving me a pat. 'Maybe we'll get on together OK, you and me.'

'You bet,' I said, but my chest went tight again. 'Mum, Nan *is* going to come home, isn't she?'

'Yes! For pity's sake, you're like a broken record,' said Mum.

'And if my leg's really bad tomorrow, can I stay off school?' I asked.

'No you can't, so stop going on about it. Now go to bed.'

I could try wheedling with Nan, but there was no point arguing with Mum.

She sent me off to school extra early the next day, because she wanted the flat to herself to prepare for her job interview. I stumped along the road, exaggerating my limp. I pretended to be a pirate with a wooden leg. I hunched my left shoulder because I had a parrot perching there, pecking my ear affectionately and crooning, 'Pieces of eight! Who's a pretty girl? I'm Polly Parrot and I love Elsie.'

Then I caught sight of myself in a shop window and blushed because I looked such a fool. I stepped out properly, marching left, right, left, right, but I'd got into such a limping habit it was more like left, hobble, left, hobble.

I hoped at the very least to get out of doing PT today. It was now my absolutely worst lesson. I hated it even more than mental arithmetic. I wasn't *bad* at PT – I could run quite fast, limp or no limp, and I could do all the silly arms-stretch, knees-bend exercises, and I could catch a ball neatly and throw it high in the air with one deft flick of my wrist. It was my new knickers that were the problem. We were supposed to wear regulation navy school knickers with elastic legs. I didn't have the right knickers.

'I'm not wasting my money on hideous school bloomers!' Mum had told me.

She'd bought me a pack of three from the market. They were pink, pale blue and lilac, with a white lace frill at the back.

I was pleased at first and thought they were pretty, but when I took my tunic off at school, all the children collapsed, laughing and pointing. I had a new nickname now: Frilly Bum.

I tried to find the old navy knickers I'd had ever since the Infants, but Nan had already cut them up for dusters. I begged Mum to buy me more proper knickers, but she refused. She was adamant, particularly after Miss Roberts sent a polite letter asking if Elsie could wear school underwear on PT days in future.

'No, our Elsie blooming well can't!' said Mum. 'She can't tell me how to clothe my child. It's none of her business. I don't tell *her* what kind of knickers to wear!'

I was terrified she might say something of the sort to dear dignified Miss Roberts. At home I kept quiet about the Frilly Bum teasing. Nan might have understood and tried to save up for a proper pair of knickers – but she wasn't here now.

I decided I couldn't face another day of giggles and cat-calling. I wouldn't go to school at all today! I hadn't had the opportunity to bunk off school before because Nan nearly always walked there with me, then went to the shops on her way home. But now I could run straight past the school gate. I could go all the way into town and look round the big shops. I could look at the filmstar photos outside the Odeon and make up the story of the film. I could go to the park and play I was in the countryside. I could go paddling in the duck pond and pretend it was the seaside.

My heart soared. I skipped down the road in my boy's shoes, my limp vanishing. I didn't go over the crossroads and join the little troop of mothers and children hurrying down the road to Millfield Juniors. I turned quickly up Burnley Avenue, heading for freedom.

A big Rover car was turning into our doctor's surgery at the end. It was Dr Malory himself, smiling at me and waving me past. Then he suddenly wound down his window.

'Hey, you're the little Kettle girl, aren't you?'

I froze. He was still smiling but I was sure I was in trouble. I wanted to run, but he was out of the car now.

'Hang on a minute! It's Evie, isn't it?'

'Elsie,' I mumbled.

'Oh yes. And your grandma's in the sanatorium now. They wrote to notify me,' said Dr Malory, in his great booming posh voice. He might as well have been shouting through a megaphone. I didn't know what to do. Everyone could hear, and yet I couldn't shut him up or contradict him, because he was a doctor.

'Have you been to visit her? How's she getting on?' he asked.

I had been trying hard not to think of Nan too much because it made me want to cry. I could already feel my eyes burning and my throat tickling. 'She's all right,' I said quietly, my head down.

Perhaps Dr Malory was more sensitive than he seemed, because he patted me gently on the head.

'Now listen, Elsie. I sent a message to your mother that you two, and anyone else who lives in your house, must come and have a chest X-ray and a little skin test, to make sure you haven't contracted tuberculosis too. I dictated the letter to my secretary the moment I heard about your grandma. Hasn't your mother mentioned a letter?'

I shook my head anxiously. Mum didn't always bother to read the letters that came when she was home. If they looked official, she was likely to toss them straight in the bin.

'Well, it's very important. TB can be very contagious. Now, you be a good girl and remind your mother, otherwise I'll have to inform the authorities.'

The word *authorities* was like a blow to the stomach. I didn't know who they were, but they sounded frightening. I saw men in black uniforms and jackboots marching to our house and arresting everyone.

'You'll make sure you'll do that, Elsie?' said Dr Malory.

'Yes, sir,' I muttered.

He suddenly focused on me, looking at my clothes. He saw the school badge Nan had sewn onto my cut-down navy jacket – I didn't have a proper blazer either. 'You go to Millfield Juniors, don't you? So why aren't you going to school?' he asked.

My heart hammered behind my telltale badge. I couldn't possibly admit that I was intent on playing truant. He'd maybe send for those authorities straight away. I had to find an excuse – any excuse.

'Please, sir, I'm going to the d—' I started gabbling like an idiot. I managed to gulp back the word *doctor's* before I said it. I repeated the 'd' again, as if I had a stammer. Where could I be going? The dancing school? The draper's? The doll shop? Then it came to me.

'The dentist's,' I said, tapping my teeth.

'Oh dear! Well, I hope it doesn't hurt too much. Off you go then – and tell your mother to bring you along to my surgery tomorrow.'

'Oh, for pity's sake, Elsie,' Mum exploded. 'Why did you have to go hanging round the blooming *doctor's*? What were you doing there anyway?'

'I – I got a bit lost on the way to school,' I stammered.

'What are you – a halfwit? You were in a day-dream, weren't you, playing some baby game and muttering away to yourself like a loony!' said Mum.

I nodded meekly, glad that she was giving me such a good alibi. She'd get even crosser if she knew I'd bunked off school all day. It hadn't been worth it. I'd been so worried about Dr Malory and the authorities that I hadn't enjoyed a single moment. In the end, I didn't dare go round the shops because my wretched school uniform was so noticeable. I'd lurked in the park all day instead.

I was very bad at mental arithmetic, but even I knew there were only seven hours between nine and four. There had seemed to be seventy-seven hours in this day. I nearly wore out the soles of my boy's shoes trailing miserably round and round the park. I went on the swings until I saw the attendant hobbling towards me. He was famous for having been wounded in the war – he had lost a leg. He seemed to have permanently lost his temper too, and was forever yelling at children.

I ran away quick and hid in the bushes. I watched him stumping along, worrying that my own limp might get as bad. I crouched in the bushes until I got cramp, and then I trudged right to the other side of the park and hung about by the duck pond. I was so hungry by now I helped myself to a couple of crusts the ducks had ignored. I was thirsty too, but I drew the line at duck-pond water. I did paddle for a little while because my feet were rubbed sore inside my shoes, but the pond was as cold as ice and I stepped on a tin can and cut my foot. It was only a little cut, but it bled and I worried about that too.

I sat on a park bench waggling my foot in the air, and an old man in a greasy raincoat came and sat beside me. He offered me his hankie for a bandage, but there was something furtive about him and he was sitting much too close to me, so I grabbed my shoes, stuffed my feet inside, and ran for it.

By the time I eventually dared go home I was exhausted. Mum was out after all that. I ate five slices of bread and jam, one after the other, drank two glasses of orange squash, and then curled up on Nan's chair and went to sleep.

Mum came home at six, equally dispirited. She kicked off her high heels and smoked two cigarettes in succession, tapping the ash impatiently. There was no point asking her if she'd got the job. It was obvious she hadn't.

We had Spam and chips for tea, which I usually enjoyed, but I already had my five slices of bread churning around in my stomach. I knew I had to tell Mum about Dr Malory.

I only screwed up the courage to do it at bedtime. Mum was furious, as I'd expected.

'It's not *my* fault, Mum,' I whined. 'I'm just passing on the message.'

'Well, you've passed it on. Now button your lip about it,' she snapped. 'Off to bed.'

I hovered. Whenever Mum told me off like that I imagined the big maroon buttons on Nan's winter coat. I saw them sewn along my top lip and firmly attached to little slits in my bottom lip. I knew how important it was to keep them in place. But somehow tonight I couldn't stop them unbuttoning of their own accord.

'So can I stay off school tomorrow or will we go after?' I said.

'What? Go where?'

'To the *doctor's*,' I said, wondering if Mum had been listening after all. Sometimes I'd talk to her for half an hour and she'd say yes and no in the right places, but then stare at me blankly when I asked a final question, clearly not having heard a word.

'We're not going to the doctor's tomorrow or any time soon. In fact, I don't think we'll see Doctor Malory ever again, because he's such an old nosy parker,' said Mum.

'But he said—'

'I don't *care* what he said.'

'We *have* to have these tests and get our X-rays.'

'There's nothing wrong with us! We're not coughing, are we?'

'No, but—'

'And we're not tired out and getting all scraggy like Nanny, are we? Well, I'm not – and you've always been skinny, so it doesn't count.'

'But why can't we have the tests? We'll pass them and everything will be all right.'

'Oh no it won't, Miss Clever Clogs. As soon as anyone gets wind of us going for chest X-rays, they'll guess – and then they'll act like we've got the plague. The mums at that school of yours will fuss about you being a carrier and won't want their kiddies playing with you.'

They didn't play with me anyway, but it didn't seem the right time to point this out to Mum.

'And I'll never ever get a job, because they'll think I'll infect all the other girls. And if I don't work, how are we going to pay the rent, because if I tell all the other tenants your nanny's got TB and they've all got to be tested, they'll snitch on us to the landlord and we'll be kicked out into the gutter.'

'They'll kick us?' I said, so worried I couldn't get my wits together.

'Oh, for pity's sake, I don't mean literally. Stop gawping at me like a bally goldfish, you're driving me insane. Go to bed!'

I went to bed, and after a very long time snuffling into Albert Trunk I went to sleep – but then I started dreaming. Dr Malory loomed in front of an army of authorities, and they were seizing hold of me and kicking me along the gutter like footballs while they chanted the two terrible initials, *'TB! TB! TB!'* over and over again.

'Elsie! For God's sake, wake up! You're screaming! You'll wake the whole blooming house!' said Mum, shaking me.

I clung round her neck, breathing in her sweet powdery smell. 'Oh Mum, don't let them take me away,' I sobbed.

'Don't be so daft. No one's taking you anywhere,' she said, but she slipped into my bed and cuddled me close. 'There now, calm down. It's all right, Mummy's here.'

'Oh Mum, it was so awful!'

'It was just a silly dream.' Mum stroked my hair and pulled me onto her lap so we were lying like spoons. 'So you didn't want to be parted from your old mum in this dream of yours?' she said. 'Why was that?'

'Because – because I love you,' I said.

'I thought you were a right old nanny's girl,' said Mum.

I *was*. I loved Nan a hundred times more than I loved Mum, but for once I was wise enough not to say this out loud. I just nestled against Mum's soft silky petticoat, and I think she went on holding me tight long after we were both asleep.

She was gentler than usual when we got up in the morning.

'I've been thinking, Elsie – maybe we *will* pop

along to silly old fusspot Malory. We'll take his test and get our chests X-rayed to stop him kicking up a fuss. But we won't tell the O'Henrys upstairs or Miss Godden, or that weird Mike in the attic flat. Dr Malory's not necessarily going to know they live in the house with us. He'll have hundreds of patients. I'm sure he won't know where most of them live. I'll come and meet you after school – but don't you breathe a word about it, OK?'

I felt very relieved, though now I worried about this X-ray and test. I knew an X-ray was a photo of your insides, but I didn't know whether it would hurt or not, and I didn't want to show my frilly knickers to anyone else. I went to school, thankful that we didn't have PT on a Tuesday.

'Where did you get to yesterday, Elsie?' Miss Roberts asked.

'Oh, I had to go to the dentist's, miss,' I said, not quite looking her in the eye.

'You were at the dentist's all *day*?'

'Yes, miss. I had to have lots and lots of fillings,' I said.

'It must have hurt dreadfully,' said Miss Roberts.

'Oh yes, it did,' I agreed.

'But at least you've got it all over now. You won't have to go to the dentist's again for a very long time, will you, Elsie?' she said.

'No, miss,' I said, daring a quick glance.

Her eyebrows were raised quizzically. Did she *know*? I slid away to my desk and sat there, heart banging. She didn't need to warn me not to bunk off again. I'd sooner do PT all day long than hang about that park again.

School wasn't too much of a trial. In English we had to write about our favourite hobby. I didn't really have a hobby. I was sure knitting scarves didn't count. I pretended I did ballet lessons instead. I'd picked up quite a lot of terminology reading 'Belle of the Ballet' so avidly. I wrote about practising the five positions and doing pliés with my back straight. I imagined little authentic details, saying I loved to dance on my points even though it rubbed my toes and made them ache.

Miss Roberts marked our English books at lunch time and handed them out in the last lesson before home time.

'Well done, everyone. What an interesting selection of hobbies! I thought I'd get some of you to read your compositions out loud. They're very entertaining and it might inspire some of you to take up a *new* hobby.'

She picked Andrew Clegg, which didn't surprise anyone, because Andrew was the class swot and always came first. Andrew's hobby was experimenting with his chemistry set. He read his composition earnestly, his glasses gleaming, rattling off all the chemical names with the greatest of ease.

Then Madeleine Keyes was asked to read out her composition about bird-watching. She had her own little pair of binoculars and had ticked off every entry in her I-Spy *Book of Common Garden Birds*. Everyone got the giggles when she talked about great tits and little tits, and Miss Roberts sighed and shook her head at us.

Then she asked Micky Smith to talk about his conjuring – and he actually did a couple of card tricks for us too. He took up quite a lot of time, so when Miss Roberts picked Marilyn, we thought she'd probably be the last before the bell went.

She started off in her affected voice: 'I have got a rather unusual hobby . . .' I knew *exactly* what it was: tormenting Elsie Kettle. But apparently her other hobby was cake decorating. She went on and on about icing sugar and buttercream and marzipan, showing off like anything. I wanted to take one of her cream cakes and shove her face in it.

'Well done, Marilyn,' said Miss Roberts, glancing at the clock. 'Now, time for just *one* more composition.'

She'd picked boy, girl, boy, girl, so all the boys sat up expectantly, some of them putting up their hands and mouthing 'Pick me, miss!' She didn't pick any of them. She picked *me*!

'You read out your composition, Elsie,' she said, smiling at me.

I stood up and started talking, my hands trembling so much my exercise book wobbled. I could hear Marilyn and Susan behind me whispering, 'What a load of rubbish!' before I'd even read the first paragraph. Someone else giggled, and I felt an ink pellet spatter on my neck. I trailed to a halt.

'Go on, Elsie. It's very interesting,' said Miss Roberts.

So I read my whole composition, and gradually the class quietened down. Even Marilyn and Susan listened as I read out my account of dancing the Sugar Plum Fairy at a special Christmas concert (just like Belle).

'Well done, Elsie, that was really good,' said Miss Roberts. 'You must tell me when you're going to be in another concert. I'd love to come and watch you.'

I smiled at her shyly, almost believing I really *would* be dancing in a concert. The bell went – and Laura came up to me as we were putting our chairs on the table.

'I never knew you did ballet, Elsie! Which dancing school do you go to?'

'Oh, it's . . . it's Madame Black's,' I said, making the name up on the spot.

'I've never heard of it,' said Laura.

'No, you wouldn't. It's up in London. I have to get the train,' I sighed. 'I go twice a week and it takes ages to get there, but it's worth it. I love it at Madame Black's.'

'Let's see you do a little dance then, Elsie Kettle,' said Marilyn.

'Yeah, up on your points,' said Susan, tiptoeing around stupidly.

'Yes, go on, Elsie,' said Laura, in a friendly way. 'Can you really do the dance of the Sugar Plum Fairy already? You must be brilliant at ballet.'

'I – I'm not *that* good,' I said, blushing.

'*Dance*, then!' said Marilyn.

'I wish I could,' I told her. 'But I've strained all the muscles in my leg and I've got a bad limp. I can't dance at all at the moment. Now I've got to go – my mum's waiting for me.'

I hobbled out of the door, across the playground. Mum was there at the gate, smoking a cigarette, wearing her best suit and her white high heels. Her blonde hair curled to her shoulders and she wore full make-up, so she had bright eyes and pink cheeks and glossy red lips. She seemed so different from all the other mums in their headscarves and old coats. I couldn't help feeling a thrill of pride. She looked just like a film star. I rushed up to her.

'Stop that limping, Elsie! You're walking all lopsided,' she said.

'Sorry, Mum. It's my shoes,' I said quickly, clenching my aching leg and trying to make it work properly.

'Who's that with Elsie Kettle?' Marilyn said behind me.

'She said it's her mum,' said Susan.

'Her mum's much older and she's got grey hair,' said Marilyn.

'No, silly, that's her nan,' said Laura. 'So that lady must be Elsie's mum. Isn't she pretty?'

'No, she's not a bit pretty. She's common.' Marilyn had lowered her voice but I could still hear. I glanced up at Mum, terrified, but she seemed oblivious.

'Come *on*, Elsie. I've made an appointment for us and we're going to be late,' she said.

'Where are they going?' asked Susan.

I turned round. 'We're going to Madame Black's and I'm doing a special audition for *Swan Lake*,' I said, forgetting all about my strained leg muscles.

'You what?' said Mum, pulling me along. We were out of earshot now.

'I just said we were going to see my dancing teacher,' I said.

'You little fibber!'

'Well, you said not to talk about going to the doctor,' I protested.

'Yes, I suppose I did,' Mum said.

'Mum, if I really went to dancing lessons, it wouldn't be a fib. *Could* I go? *Please*?'

'What do you think I am, made of money? Dancing lessons cost a fortune.'

'*You* had dancing lessons when you were a little girl,' I persisted.

'Yeah, well, Dad paid,' said Mum. Her voice always softened when she mentioned my granddad. She'd clearly been a daddy's girl.

'Able to twist him round her little finger,' Nan always said.

I ached at the thought of Nan, and had to blink hard to stop myself crying.

'What are you doing, twitching like that? You look like a rabbit. Stop it!' said Mum.

'If I had dancing lessons I could do a rabbit dance,' I said, squatting down and doing little rabbit jumps along the pavement.

'Stand up properly and stop showing off,' said Mum. 'You're not starting dancing lessons and that's that. I'm not forking out and staying up half the night sewing your costumes.'

'Nan can make them for me,' I said.

'Well, Nanny's not here any more, is she?'

'But she *will* be. She will get better, Mum, won't she? You promised she'd get better and come back home!' I said, my tears starting to spill now.

'Stop that! Yes, yes, of course Nanny's going to get better,' Mum said, but she didn't sound certain.

I cried all the way to the doctor's. I couldn't stop, even though Mum threatened me with a good smacking. When we got to Dr Malory's, the receptionist peered at my red eyes and crumpled face.

'Oh my, are you feeling really poorly, dear?' she said. The waiting room was half full. 'Perhaps you'd better see the doctor first.'

'Well, yes please, that's very kind,' said Mum, who hated waiting for anything. She opened her handbag and got her hankie out to wipe my eyes and runny nose. 'There now, Elsie. Pull yourself together.'

I gave a great sniff and clamped my lips shut.

'Oh, what a brave girl,' said the receptionist.

She was wearing a lilac angora jumper and I thought she looked lovely, though she had very big teeth.

'*She* looks the spitting image of a bunny rabbit,' Mum murmured as we sat down.

I sniggered guiltily, hoping the receptionist hadn't heard, especially when she'd been so sweet to me. Mum never had a kind word for any other woman. The receptionist seemed to be looking at us reproachfully. I fidgeted on the hard seat uncomfortably, until a patient came out of the doctor's room clutching a prescription.

Dr Malory called 'Next?' and the receptionist beckoned to us, not bearing any grudges. Mum swept past, but I grinned at her.

Dr Malory sat behind his desk, holding his hands as if he were praying, his chin resting on the tips of his fingers.

'Ah, it's little Elsie – and Mrs Kettle?' he said.

'Miss, actually, but I'll go along with Mrs if you like,' said Mum, sitting down and crossing her legs with a rasp of stockings. She never seemed in awe of any man, not even a doctor.

Dr Malory shuffled his files of notes. 'Your mother's recently been diagnosed with pulmonary tuberculosis,' he said. 'And you've come along to be tested, as requested. Are there any other members of the family living at home?'

'Just Elsie and me,' said Mum.

'No other tenants of the house?'

'No, no, just us.' Mum pressed her lips together, her lipstick very bright in the dull beige consulting room.

'Well, I'll give you both a special Mantaux test,' said Dr Malory, opening a drawer and bringing out a needle.

Mum and I winced at the sight of it.

'Don't worry, it won't hurt at all – just a little scratch,' he said. 'If you get no reaction after a few days, then you're absolutely fine. But if your skin goes red and inflamed, then it's a sure sign you have the tuberculosis bacilli in your blood.'

'We won't, you know,' said Mum, rolling up her sleeve so he could do the test on her wrist. 'We're as fit as fiddles. We don't ever cough, do we, Elsie?'

I felt a tickle in my throat right that instant, but swallowed hurriedly, knowing I'd get a thump afterwards if I let her down. My arm shook as I held it out to Dr Malory, but it really didn't hurt much. Then he gave me a Smartie out of a little jar. It was pink too, my favourite.

'Here, don't *I* get a Smartie?' said Mum.

Dr Malory raised his eyebrows but passed her the jar too. Then he started writing on some forms.

'You both need to go and have an X-ray too,' he said, looking at his watch. 'If you pop along to the hospital quickly, the X-ray department should still be open.'

'But we're fine, you can see that,' said Mum. 'And we've just had that test.'

'Tuberculosis is infectious, Miss Kettle. We must be vigilant. You don't want to risk Elsie's health, do you?' said Dr Malory. He handed her the forms.

'What a palaver!' said Mum, sighing. She stood up

and trit-trotted out of the room in her high heels while I scurried after her.

'Elsie?' said Dr Malory, when I'd got to the door. 'Are you limping?'

'No!' I said. 'Well, it's my shoes.'

I hoped he might tell Mum they were totally unsuitable and she had to buy me new shoes at once, preferably shiny black patent – but he seemed to have lost interest, and was looking at the notes of his next patient.

I stared at my arm in horror. I looked as if I'd been bitten. My wrist was deep pink with little raised bumps that itched. I could feel them like the pimples on plaice skin. I pulled my cardigan sleeve down almost to my fingertips, desperate to hide them.

Mum didn't notice for a while – but then frowned at me. 'Don't mess around with your sleeve like that, Elsie. You'll pull the wool all out of shape.'

I let the sleeve go and quickly put my arm behind my back.

'What are you looking like that for?' said Mum.

'I'm not looking like anything,' I said, my heart thumping.

'Yes you are. You look all furtive. Come here!'

I backed away instead.

Mum grabbed hold of me – by the wrist.

'Ouch!'

'What? That can't have hurt you,' she said. Then she took a proper look at my wrist. 'Oh my God!'

'I'm sorry,' I wailed, starting to cry.

'What have you *done* to it?' said Mum. 'Have you been messing around trying to light the stove?'

'No!'

She peered at it more closely. 'Have you fallen in stinging nettles?'

'No, Mum. I haven't done anything to it. It just . . . came.'

'Come over to the light so I can see it properly.' Mum pulled me across to the window. 'You've been picking at it, haven't you? Scratching it like mad, so it's all inflamed?'

'No, I haven't touched it,' I sobbed.

Mum was silent for a moment. We both stared at my alien skin. Then we looked at each other. We were both shaking.

'It's that test, isn't it?' Mum whispered.

I nodded. We'd both known it all along, but it was just too dreadful to admit.

'*My* wrist's all right,' said Mum, rubbing her own smooth white skin. She peered at mine again. Then she took a step backwards. 'But this looks like you've got it too!'

'I haven't! I'm not coughing. I feel perfectly OK,' I said, though I was starting to feel awful.

'How *can* your nanny have given it you?' said Mum. 'What was she *doing*, coughing all over you? Why couldn't she keep her rotten germs to herself?'

'It wasn't Nan's fault, Mum!'

'She had that cough for ages. I found six different bottles of cough medicine in the bathroom cabinet. If she'd only got herself to the doctor sooner!'

'You didn't want *us* to go to the doctor's, Mum.'

'Oh shut up, will you, Elsie! Trust you to take your nan's side even now when she's given you a mortal illness!'

'What does mortal mean?' I asked fearfully.

'Nothing. I didn't mean it,' said Mum, looking flustered.

'Oh Mum, am I going to die?'

'No, no, don't be silly, of course not,' said Mum, but I saw the fear in her eyes.

I was terrified – but I suddenly felt weirdly, blackly *glamorous*. I wasn't just odd Elsie Kettle who told stories and had no friends. I was the Child who was going to Die.

I saw my funeral, the whole school attending, everyone dressed in black. Mum would have a black veil over her yellow hair and would cry into a white lace handkerchief, her mascara running. Poor Nan would be there in a wheelchair with a surgical mask over her face, insensible with grief. Miss Roberts would be crying too, telling everyone I'd been her brightest ever pupil. All my class would be weeping, even Marilyn and Susan. No, *especially* Marilyn and Susan. They'd kneel at my freshly dug grave and call down to my coffin, begging my forgiveness. Laura would throw white roses on top of me, telling me that I'd always be her best ever friend, and when she starred in a ballet on the stage she'd dedicate her dance to me.

But then I realized I wouldn't be there to see all this. Would I be an angel hovering in the air, flapping snowy-white wings? I'd like a white dress too – and if it got chilly in heaven, maybe we'd be kitted out in white angora cardigans?

'Oh dear Lord, Elsie, what are we going to *do*?' said Mum.

'I don't know!' I whimpered, suddenly yanked out of my own funeral.

'Perhaps – perhaps Doctor Malory can cure it at

this stage,' said Mum. 'After all, you haven't got a cough, have you?'

I felt the tickle in my throat again. 'I don't think so,' I said, struggling.

'And maybe you've made your wrist worse by scratching it,' said Mum, examining it again.

'I *didn't*!'

'You could have been scratching in your sleep. Anyway, we'd better get you to the doctor's.'

'Mum, if I *have* got TB—'

'Ssh! Don't go broadcasting it to all and sundry,' Mum hissed, though we were entirely alone.

'*If* I do, will I have to go to the sanatorium?' I suddenly cheered up immensely. 'I could be with Nan!'

Maybe they'd let me have a little bed right beside hers. We could chat to each other all day and play with my pretend cats, and then hold hands at night. I was so comforted by this idea that I skipped on the way to the doctor's, even though my leg ached.

'Ah, you've perked up, young lady,' said the receptionist, smiling at me.

She didn't let us jump the queue this time. We had to wait nearly an hour while Dr Malory called for everyone else in the room. I sat and read the *Beano*. I didn't like it as much as my precious *Girl* because the stories weren't as real, but it passed the time. Mum flicked through a very old copy of *Woman's Own*, but she didn't pause to read any of it – not even the problem page at the back. Then she simply stared into space, nibbling at a hangnail on her thumb. She always smacked me if she caught me pulling one of *my* hangnails.

We were called in at long last. Dr Malory was sitting in his usual position, hands praying.

'Ah, Elsie, and Mrs – Miss – Kettle. It's good news,' he said as we sat down on the chairs in front of his desk.

'*Good* news?' said Mum.

'The results of your X-rays. You've both got perfect pairs of lungs – not a hint of a shadow.'

'Oh, thank goodness! You're absolutely sure?'

'Absolutely,' said Dr Malory.

'There, Elsie! We were getting ourselves worked up into a state over nothing. You *must* have been scratching that wrist, you silly girl.'

'Elsie's wrist?' asked Dr Malory.

'It's gone a bit pink and puffy where you injected her – but obviously it's nothing to worry about now,' said Mum.

Dr Malory took hold of my arm and pushed up my cardigan sleeve. He stared at my wrist for a long time, looking grave.

'It can't mean she's got . . . TB,' Mum said,

whispering the dreaded initials. 'Not if her lungs are fine.'

'Her lungs *are* fine, there's no mistake there. But you can harbour the tuberculosis bacilli in many other parts of your body. Pop your jersey and dress off, Elsie. I'd like to examine you,' said Dr Malory.

'Oh Lord,' said Mum, dragging my cardigan off and pulling my dress over my head.

I bent over in shame, terribly conscious that my vest was grubby and I was wearing the awful frilly knickers.

'Stand up straight, Elsie. Don't be silly,' said Mum.

Dr Malory put a thermometer in my mouth and started gently but firmly feeling my spine and my arms and my legs. 'She's very slight,' he commented. 'Has she lost weight recently?'

'She's always been a skinny little thing. She takes after her grandma,' said Mum without thinking. Then she went, 'Oh!'

'And does she run around a lot with all the other kids, or flop about at home?' said Dr Malory.

'I try to encourage her to go out and play,' said Mum. 'She's shy. She doesn't make friends easily.'

I felt myself flushing scarlet. I tried to protest that I *did* have friends. Maybe Laura and I really might pal up one day? But I couldn't speak properly with the thermometer in my mouth.

'And what about a limp?' said Dr Malory.

'Well, she puts it on at times. She doesn't like her shoes.'

Dr Malory took the thermometer out of my mouth and peered at it. Then he put it in a little jug of disinfectant. 'Have a little walk around the room, Elsie,' he said.

I set off ultra-self-consciously. I didn't know if I was supposed to limp or not. Dr Malory squinted carefully at me. I moved stiffly round his desk, goose pimples prickling my arms.

'Yes, yes, I thought so. There's definitely a slight limp there – do you see, Miss Kettle?'

'Yes, but I tell you, it's her shoes. Take the shoes *off*, Elsie, and walk properly for the doctor.'

I unlaced my shoes and padded around in my socks. I felt even worse now because I had a hole in my sock and my big toe poked through.

'She's still limping,' said Dr Malory. 'Come here, Elsie.'

He got off his chair and felt each leg all over again. 'Ah!' he said triumphantly as he prodded my right kneecap. 'It definitely feels doughy.'

Mum and I looked at each other, baffled.

'It's a classic symptom. Look, it's a little swollen – and the right knee feels hotter too,' said Dr Malory.

We all stared at my knee as if it were a loaf of

bread starting to rise. I couldn't really see much difference between my knees. They were both knobbly and rather grubby because Nan wasn't there to tell me to give them a good scrub.

'Why are we looking at her knees?' said Mum. 'Surely you get TB in your chest?'

'This isn't pulmonary tuberculosis, Miss Kettle. I'm pretty sure Elsie has the bovine variety.'

We looked at him blankly.

'I think she has tuberculosis of the knee,' he said.

'So, can you cure it?' said Mum.

'She'll need complete rest in hospital,' said Dr Malory.

'With Nan in the sanatorium!' I said.

'No, no, we'll send you to a special orthopaedic hospital,' said Dr Malory, busy writing notes. 'There's a very good one with a children's ward at Miltree.'

'What?' said Mum. 'That's a good fifty miles away! Can't she go to the local hospital? Or can't she stay in bed at home if all she needs is rest?'

'No, Elsie's leg needs to be completely immobilized in a special splint, and once my diagnosis is confirmed she'll need daily injections too.'

'I don't like injections,' I mumbled.

'Yes, but you're going to be a good brave girl and not make a fuss, isn't that right?' Dr Malory smiled at me.

'Will I get Smarties every time they inject me?' I asked.

'I rather doubt it, but you can have one now,' he said, reaching for his special jar.

He gave me a dark brown one this time. It was my least favourite. I hated the colour brown and I didn't like dark chocolate very much, but I managed to thank him politely and popped it in my mouth.

'Now, Miss Kettle, you need to take Elsie back to the hospital for further X-rays straight away – just give them this note,' said Dr Malory.

'Oh, for goodness' sake, she'll start glowing in the dark with all these blooming X-rays!' said Mum. 'Aren't they supposed to be bad for kiddies?'

'Tuberculosis is worse – and we need to confirm the diagnosis. Then, as soon as Elsie's had the X-rays, you need to take her to the orthopaedic hospital. I'll phone ahead and tell them to expect you this afternoon.'

'Surely we can wait till you're certain sure she's got TB of the leg or whatever?'

'Elsie needs to be rested in bed under observation,' said Dr Malory.

'One day can't possibly make any difference,' Mum argued. 'I've got a job interview lined up for this afternoon. I can't go chasing halfway across the country looking for some bally hospital, not if I'm going to make the interview – and anyway, where am I going to get the fare for the two of us? I'm totally skint right this minute.' She looked at him hopefully, as if she expected him to take out his wallet and offer her a couple of pound notes.

'If money is a serious problem, take this note and show it at the National Assistance office,' said Dr Malory. 'Don't look so worried, Elsie. I have a feeling they *will* have a great big Smartie jar for good girls in the hospital.' He made little waving movements with his hands, clearly ushering us out.

'Well!' said Mum, out in the street. She peered warily at my wrist again, as if it were a time bomb. 'It looks like you've really got it then. Gawd, what a turn-up. We'd better hurry and get you kitted out with new pyjamas and a decent toothbrush.'

I didn't usually wear any pyjamas or nighties in bed – I stayed in my vest and frilly knickers. I couldn't help feeling excited when Mum took me into Woolworths, especially when I saw a pair of pink winceyette pyjamas patterned all over with *kittens*.

'Oh Mum, please may I have those ones? Oh Mum, please, please, please,' I begged, hanging on her arm.

'They're seven shillings and sixpence! It's daylight robbery,' said Mum – but she bought them, *and* a pink toothbrush, *and* a Muffin the Mule flannel.

'Are we using up all our money, Mum? Will we

have to go to the National Assistance?' I asked.

'Ssh! No, we will not! That doctor had a cheek suggesting it. We're not riff-raff,' said Mum.

She bought me a new *Girl* too, and a pastel sweetie necklace. 'You can eat it when you get sick of wearing it,' she said.

'Oh Mum, I do love you,' I said, and reached up to kiss her.

She pulled away from me. 'Watch out! I don't want your germs!' she said sharply.

I backed away in dismay, my hands over my mouth.

'Now don't look at me like that with those big Bambi eyes! There's no point me catching it too, is there? I'm the one who has to work to pay all the bills,' said Mum. 'Now come on – let's go and get those stupid X-rays done.'

We went back to the hospital. I had to lie down on a strange table this time and keep very still while they twisted my legs into odd positions. We'd been kept waiting a long time so it was nearly lunch time now.

'Tell you what, we'll go to Lyons for a treat,' said Mum.

Nan and I rarely went to Lyons, and never for lunch. If we went out, we went to the ABC and shared a currant bun and a milk-and-a-dash, and I had an extra sugar cube to suck.

'Are we having a bun, Mum?' I asked.

'No, we'll have a proper lunch,' she said.

I couldn't make up my mind in the queue so Mum chose for me: tomato soup with a roll and butter, fish and chips – under a plastic dome to keep them warm – and then strawberry mousse.

It was the most glorious meal I'd ever had, and yet somehow I didn't feel like eating it. I kept thinking of the germs wriggling around inside me. I could almost feel them tickling under the skin. I kept my sore wrist covered up with my cardigan sleeve and hid it under the table to make sure no one could even get a glimpse of it. I ate one-handed, trying hard not to spill the bright red soup.

Mum kept staring at me, shaking her head. 'I can't quite take it in,' she said. 'Eat up nicely now, Elsie.'

I tried hard but my throat seemed to have closed up. I couldn't even swallow the soft white roll, though I chewed and chewed. I ended up just sucking a few chips and eating a spoonful of mousse.

'What a waste,' said Mum, but she'd barely touched her own meal. She looked at her watch. 'Look, my interview's at two. Maybe we could trek all the way to this hospital afterwards. How do you feel about that?'

I wasn't really used to being asked how I felt. I shrugged my shoulders.

'That's it. That's what we'll do,' said Mum. 'After all, someone's got to pay the rent, eh? And it's going to cost me a fortune, going backwards and forwards to Miltree.'

'How long will I be there?' I asked. The roll still seemed to be in my throat, stopping me from swallowing properly.

'How should I know?' said Mum. 'Then I suppose I'll have to visit your nanny too, though she really doesn't deserve it, passing all her TB on to you.'

'Nan didn't mean to, Mum,' I said. A sudden overwhelming desire for Nan washed over me. 'I must see her!'

'Don't be silly, Elsie – you've only just seen her.'

'But if I'm going to be in this hospital, I need to say goodbye. Can I get the bus out to the sanatorium while you go for your interview?'

'No you can't! You're so gormless you'd never get the right bus. You'd be off to John o' Groats or down to Land's End. And it would be a wasted journey anyway. There's no visiting allowed on weekdays. Now, come on, we'll take you home and you can get packed up while I go to my interview. There's a good girl.'

Home still seemed so strange without Nan in it. It was a very small basement flat but now it seemed very big and very bleak. I wandered from room to room, playing a ridiculous game. If I held my breath and counted to twenty, then maybe, just maybe, I'd find Nan in her armchair, Nan standing stirring something at the stove, Nan having a doze on the bed, Nan on the toilet with her floppy pink knickers around her ankles. I looked for phantom Nans in each room, scarlet in the face from holding my breath, even though I knew she was in the sanatorium, imprisoned in that narrow bed as if her green coverlet were chain mail.

'Nan!' I wailed, and then I covered my mouth with my hand because my voice sounded so eerie in the silent flat.

I retreated to my bedroom, stood on a chair, and fetched my cardboard suitcase down from the top of the wardrobe. I packed my new kitten pyjamas and my comic. I didn't have a sponge bag so I put my toothbrush and toothpaste into an old sock. I tucked Albert Trunk's trunk into the other sock, pretending it was his nosebag. I thought he needed a little comfort, stuffed up in my suitcase.

I spent a long time picking over the rest of my toys, wondering if I should take any of them with me. There was a teddy I'd had since I was a baby, but he'd lost his glass eyes. Nan sewed new eyes on in thick black thread, but they changed his whole expression, so he looked incredibly bad-tempered. I decided he'd much prefer staying at home undisturbed.

I had a plastic duck and an enamel spinning top and a set of little coloured bricks, but they were all baby toys and I never played with them now. I had a book, *Treasure Island*, given to me long ago by Uncle Stanley. He said it had been his favourite book when he was a little boy. I was in the top set for reading and I liked books, but I couldn't get into *Treasure Island* – I wasn't very interested in pirates. I invented an island game for Nan and me instead. I still had a whole pad of drawings of our own special treasure island, with a mermaid lagoon and banana trees and beautiful shells, and a little house made out of twigs and palm leaves, just big enough for two. We found treasure, of course – a great tin trunk of rubies and emeralds and diamonds. I threaded them on neck-laces and we wore six each, our chests flashing red and green and sparkling white in the tropical sun.

I wondered about packing the drawing pad in my suitcase, but there were no spare pages left and my pictures seemed embarrassingly childish now, Nan and I gawky pin-people, and the yellow sand just smudged scribble.

I didn't have any other toys. I wandered into Nan's room instead. I touched her china crinoline lady and her lace doilies and her little pin pot in the shape of a strawberry. Then I picked up her button box with Snow White and Sooty and Marmalade on the front.

I gave them all a stroke, stretched an elastic band right over the box so it wouldn't come undone, wrapped it in my vest to muffle the clatter of the buttons, and packed it underneath Albert Trunk.

There! I sat back on my heels and played a little drum tune on my suitcase. I thought that if I acted in a jaunty manner, it might stop feeling so scary. 'Hey, it's all right, Elsie!' I said out loud. 'Maybe the hospital will be really nice and they'll give you lots of Smarties like Doctor Malory said. There will be nurses, and they'll all look pretty in their blue dresses and white aprons and funny white hats. They will tuck you up in bed and look after you until you are better. Nan will get better too and—'

I couldn't keep up the pretence any more.

'Nan!' I wailed, and I keeled over onto the cold lino and howled, my inflamed wrist tucked into my armpit. I cried for a very long time, until my whole face was slippery with tears and snot, and I'd made my new sweet necklace uncomfortably sticky. I fell asleep in a little sodden ball and didn't wake up until I heard Mum coming in the front door.

7

'Well, every cloud has a silver lining,' said Mum as we rattled along in the train. 'Imagine me, personal secretary to a managing director!'

I stared out at the little gardens flashing past. Two boys stood on top of an air-raid shelter, pointing. I wasn't stupid: I knew they were simply pointing at the train and then making a note of the number – two harmless little train spotters – but it felt as if they were pointing straight at me.

There goes germy Elsie with her TB! they might be writing. *Keep clear of her!*

'I'd really only gone for the receptionist's job – any girl with a pretty face can do that – but Mr Perkins asked about my typing and shorthand,' said Mum.

A large collie dog barked at the train. He barked right at me, and I had to hold tight to Snow White and Sooty and Marmalade, who hissed and squirmed in my arms. They'd wriggled out of a crack in my suit-case and were trying to comfort me. I gave them each a special stroke.

'Stop dabbing your hands about – you look gorm-less,' said Mum. 'Yes, I was a bit worried when I had to take dictation. I haven't done shorthand since I was at school and I was never that good at it, to be honest – but I looked him straight in the eye and said I was a bit rusty because I'd been pursuing a career on the stage, and he was ever so understanding.'

We passed a school and I could see all the heads of the children sitting at their desks. Some of them looked out at me. 'Did you hear about Elsie Kettle?' they whispered. 'She's got TB!'

I thought about my own school. Maybe they'd found out already.

'We always knew Elsie Kettle was dirty,' Marilyn and Susan said in chorus.

'Just think, I nearly made friends with her!' said Laura.

'Poor little Elsie, I hope I haven't caught her

horrid germs,' said Miss Roberts, washing her angora cardie just in case it was contaminated.

I gave a little moan.

'Yes, I think he rather liked the idea – said he'd always been very partial to theatre-going. He asked which plays I'd appeared in. I had to be a little vague – I doubt he's ever been to the Saucebox Follies! Though I don't know – there was a naughty twinkle in his eye for all he was so gentlemanly in his pin-stripe suit. Elsie . . . ? Oh Elsie!'

She'd seen the tears rolling down my cheeks.

'Cheer up, you silly sausage. You're going to be fine. They'll make you better in hospital. All you have to do is lie in bed and rest. Sounds good to me!'

I carried on crying. I was scared she'd get cross, but she cuddled me in close and stroked my hair with her long cool fingers.

'There now, little bunny,' she murmured.

She used to call me Bunny when I was very little and had a hood on my jacket with furry rabbit ears. I nestled against her and she didn't even tell me off when my nose dribbled onto her smart suit.

'What's up with the little moppet?' the woman opposite asked. 'She's going to hospital, you say?'

I felt Mum stiffen.

'Yes, she's hurt her knee,' she said quickly.

The woman launched into a long and harrowing

account of her son's stay in hospital when he was a little boy.

'Starved him, they did. Just gave him a plate of mashed potatoes and gravy for his dinner. I ask you, is that food fit for a growing lad? I should send your little girl in with a big tuck box or she'll fade away altogether. She's thin as a pin already!'

'She's naturally petite,' said Mum, a little huffily. 'There now, Elsie. Have a little rest, dear.' She cradled me closer.

The woman started talking again but Mum hushed her. 'Do you mind? I'd like her to have a little nap,' she said firmly.

I wasn't the slightest bit sleepy because I'd napped for a couple of hours that afternoon, but I shut my eyes and snuggled up to Mum. She was so different to Nan, who said herself she was all string and bones. Mum was soft yet firm, like a cushion, though her bosom and tummy were taut and I could feel the elastic ridges of her underwear. I knew for a fact that Mum's knickers were even frillier than mine, but they didn't look at all silly on her.

The train made a comforting *diddly-dum, diddly-dum* noise, over and over again. When it slowed down and stopped at each station, there were the same sounds too: slamming doors and whistle-blowing, and then judders and wheezes as the engine blew out steam. Perhaps we weren't going in a straight line at all. Perhaps we were on a gigantic circular track, like a toy train, and we'd be going round and round for ever, never arriving.

But suddenly Mum gave me a push and stood up, grabbing my suitcase. 'Come on, Elsie, we get off here!' she hissed.

'Good luck, dear!' called the woman. 'Chin up!'

I tucked my chin down into my coat and stumbled off the train. Mum was quizzing the porter and looking annoyed.

'For pity's sake, the bus goes every hour, and would you believe it, we've just missed one!' she said. 'We'll get you there by midnight at this rate – and then I've got to make the whole wretched journey back again! Come on, we'd better have a cup of tea.'

We went into the refreshment room at the station. I still wasn't hungry even though I hadn't eaten my lunch. Mum bought me a tuppenny iced bun, but I just licked the white topping off and then played cigars with the bun while Mum sipped her tea and crunched on a custard cream.

It wasn't very cold in the room but I seemed to be shivering. My teeth clanked against my glass of lemon barley water.

'Stop that,' Mum said.

I tucked my teeth behind my lips, which made

drinking difficult. A long dribble of lemon barley spurted down my coat.

'Your good coat!' said Mum – as if I had a whole wardrobe of *other* coats. She spat on the edge of her hankie and rubbed my coat vigorously so that I juddered up and down inside it. 'Honestly, I can't take you anywhere without you showing me up.'

'I'm sorry,' I mumbled. When she'd finished rubbing at me, I tried to nestle up to her the way I'd done in the train, but she sat me down properly on my own chair.

'Careful – you'll spill it again!' she said.

That was my mum for you, always blowing hot and cold. I saw her hot on the train, her face lipstick-red all over, her embrace like fire – and now I saw her freezing cold with snow in her hair and icicle finger-nails. She was tapping those nails on her cup, fiddling with the paper from the sugar cube, crossing and uncrossing her legs, all of a fidget. Maybe she was scared too.

We needed Nan to calm us both down, but she wasn't there. I trailed off to spend a penny and sat there on the toilet, praying to Nan as if she were God.

'Dear Nan, please let it be all right. Please don't let the doctors do scary things to me. Please let the nurses be kind. Please don't let the other children be horrid to me. Oh, please let me get better quick, and you get better too, so we can both come back home together.'

'Elsie? What are you *doing* in there?' Mum called, rapping on the door. 'You haven't locked yourself in, have you?'

I looked at the lock on the door and seriously wondered about keeping it bolted for ever. I could creep out every night and eat stale buns from the refreshment room and run up and down the empty platforms for exercise, and then scuttle back at dawn and lock myself away again . . .

'Elsie! Come out this instant!' Mum commanded.

I unlocked the door and shuffled out sheepishly. We went to wait at the bus stop outside the station. We waited and waited. Mum kept consulting the gold wristwatch Uncle Stanley had given her.

'Don't say we've missed the bally thing!' she said – but at last we saw the single-decker red bus looming in the distance.

'At last!' said Mum. 'This hospital's at the back of beyond. I'm sure Doctor Malory's sent you there on purpose, just to make life more difficult.'

We got on the bus and I stared anxiously out of the dirty window, looking for some large ugly Nissen hut like poor Nan's sanatorium. The bus hurtled down narrow country lanes for what seemed like hours.

'We must have gone past it,' said Mum, consulting

her watch again. 'Hey, conductor! I thought you were going to tell us when we got near Miltree Hospital.'

'So I will, duck, when we get there. In another ten minutes,' he sang out cheerily.

'Duck!' Mum muttered. 'Does he think I'm some daft old biddy? I'll give him duck!'

When the conductor announced the hospital at last, Mum swept past him haughtily, tugging at me to do the same. My leg had gone funny after all the sitting down. I stumbled and dropped my suitcase. It burst open, and my new pyjamas and underwear and Albert Trunk and the button box came flying out all over the deck.

'Whoops!' said the conductor, bending down and helping me. 'Don't want you to lose your frillies!' He flapped my terrible knickers in the air and half the bus sniggered. I was scarlet by the time I'd retrieved all my treasures and shot off the bus.

'Do you *have* to show me up?' said Mum, giving me a little shake. She looked around at the trees and hedges. 'I think that bally fool has turfed us out at the wrong stop. There's no sign of any hospital.'

There weren't even any proper pavements. We walked along the narrow strip of grass, Mum having to pick her way on tiptoe because she didn't want her high heels sinking into the mud. She peered over the hedge and then stopped.

'Hell's fire, is *that* it?' she said. 'I think it must be.'

I was too little to see over the top. 'Does it look horrid, Mum?' I asked.

'No, it's like a blooming palace,' said Mum. 'It's *huge* – and there's gardens all over – and, oh my Lord, a fountain! Here, breathe on me, Elsie. I wouldn't mind getting your lurgie if I can stay here too!'

I bounced up and down, but I had to wait until I came to a gap in the hedge before I could see for myself. It truly *was* like a palace in a fairy tale, a huge soft-grey mansion with a turret and towers, set in beautiful formal gardens.

'Oh Mum!' I said. Then, 'It *can't* be the hospital!'

'No, you're right, it can't be,' said Mum – but when we got a little nearer we both saw the sign: MILTREE ORTHOPAEDIC HOSPITAL. 'Oh my! Doctor Malory's turned up trumps after all.'

I was still scared stiff, but when the hospital was in full view before us, I stared at it in awe. I furnished it with red carpets and gold chairs and twinkling chandeliers. All the patients had four-poster beds in private rooms with little maids. *My* bedroom would be up in the tower. Maybe I would let my hair grow like Rapunzel, and I'd wear beautiful pink and blue and white silk princess dresses every day and my cat pyjamas at night . . .

I pretended all the way along the drive and up the

big stone steps – but the moment we stepped inside the big arched door I was slapped back to the real world with a vengeance. There was a horrible hospital smell of strong disinfectant, and no carpet, red or otherwise – just miles of polished brown wooden floor that made our shoes squeak horribly in the silence. The walls were painted cream and green, just like school, and there were no private rooms at all, just stark signs to all the different wards.

'Which ward will I be in, Mum?' I whispered.

'How on earth should I know?' she said.

There was a big reception desk to one side of the vast hallway but no one was sitting behind it.

'Excuse me?' Mum called into the air, but no one came. 'Oh well, we'll have to find out for ourselves.' She took my hand. 'Come on, Elsie.'

'I don't think we're allowed,' I whimpered, peering around fearfully. 'Shouldn't we wait till someone comes?'

'Don't be daft, there isn't anyone! Come on, I've got to get all the way home again. I can't hang around here, waiting.'

Mum set off up the corridor while I struggled along beside her. We turned a corner and were suddenly in a big bleak ward with rows of beds, all with green coverlets and pale patients.

'It's just like Nan's sanatorium,' I said. 'Oh Mum, I don't like it!'

'Stop whining, Elsie, it's getting on my nerves,' said Mum, peering around for an empty bed.

A nurse with a complicated white hat and a blue dress came bustling out of a side room and stared at us in astonishment. 'Whatever are you doing here? You're not allowed on this ward!' she said. 'You must leave immediately.'

'See!' I said, tugging at Mum's arm.

'But we've been told to come here,' she said, standing her ground.

'We only have visiting hours at the weekend, from two till four – and even then we don't allow children, except in special circumstances,' said the nurse crisply.

'This is Elsie,' said Mum, giving me a little shake. 'She's going to be a *patient*. The doctor sent us here.'

'We don't admit patients *now*. It's nearly five o'clock! You'll have to bring her back tomorrow at two, the proper time.'

'If you think I'm taking the kid all the way home on the bus, the train *and* the tram and then trailing her back here tomorrow, you've got another think coming,' said Mum. 'Who do you think you are, Mrs Hitler?'

There was a little snort of shocked laughter from the nearest bed.

The nurse flushed. 'You can't leave her *here*. This

is the women's ward, as should be obvious. The children's wards are in the annexe. You have to go out and round the back. But they won't admit her, not at this time,' she said.

'We'll see about that,' said Mum, and she marched us away.

'What a bossy little madam!' she muttered. 'It's the same old story – give them a uniform and they think they're it. Well, I'm not letting some jumped-up queen-of-the-bedpans tell *me* what to do.'

'Oh Mum. *Can't* we come back tomorrow?'

'No, of course we can't. I haven't got enough for the train fare all over again for a start.'

'Can't we just go home, and I'll rest there, like you said?' I begged.

'I can't leave you there on your own, day after day.'

'I wouldn't mind, not a bit.'

'Somebody's tongue would wag and they'd end up carting you off to a children's home. I tell you, it was touch and go when you were little, before we went to live with Nanny.'

'Mum—'

'Do shut *up*. You're not making this any easier. Don't look at me like that. It's not *my* fault. *I* didn't give you this dreaded illness, did I? Blame Nanny, coughing her germs all over you.'

That really did shut me up. I couldn't bear to

blame Nan. We tramped all the way round the side of the big grey building in silence, down a lot of stone steps at the back, and followed a path across the big lawn to a long low modern building with a veranda all the way round.

There was a sign outside:

MILTREE ORTHOPAEDIC HOSPITAL, CHILDREN'S ANNEXE.
BLYTON AND RANSOME WARDS TO THE RIGHT.
STRAIGHT ON FOR POTTER WARD.
TURN LEFT FOR CHRISTIE.

'Well, which are you, do you think?' said Mum. 'I suppose we'd better find someone and ask.'

The door to the annexe was closed. We had to ring the bell. My tummy was churning. Mum rang again, and knocked loudly at the door too.

'Mum!' I said in agony. 'They'll be cross!'

'*I'm* cross, hanging about here in the cold before they'll deign to let us in. You've got a serious illness. It's not good for you.' She knocked again – and the door opened at last.

Another nurse stood there, in an even stranger white hat with wings. It looked as if a starched seagull had landed on her head.

'What on earth do you want?' she said. Her voice was starched too, cold and crisp.

'I should have thought it was blooming obvious,' said Mum fiercely. 'My poor little Elsie has got TB and we've travelled for hours and hours to get here. She's an urgent case – the doctor says she's to be hospitalized straight away.'

'Did he not tell you our admission hours?' she said.

'I don't give a fig about your admission hours,' said Mum. 'We got here as soon as we could. Now, will you kindly tuck my little girl up in bed where she belongs. Call yourself a nurse!'

'I'm not a nurse, I'm the Sister here – and I'll thank you to keep a civil tongue in your head,' she said, but she stood aside and beckoned us in.

There was more green and cream paint, more polished floor. She turned right and we followed. She opened a door into a smaller whitewashed room with a sign saying BLYTON WARD, with two rows of beds.

'Oh my God,' said Mum.

I clasped her hand tightly. I almost snapped her fingers off. The children were nearly all buckled into weird pulleys and splints so that they couldn't move. Two were flat on their backs with their legs held apart in frames. One boy was encased in plaster like a rigid little snowman.

'What are you *doing* to them?' asked Mum.

'We have to immobilize their affected joints,' said the Sister.

'You're not doing that to my Elsie!'

'We will proceed as we see fit to make the child better,' the Sister told her. 'We shall keep her under observation for a day or two while the doctors assess her. You can visit her on Saturdays and Sundays between two and four. I'm afraid we can't have any visiting whatsoever at any other time. Now, come with me into my office so we can start your paperwork.'

'It's like a torture chamber in here – the poor little mites,' said Mum, still staring around.

'Keep your voice *down* – I don't want you upsetting my patients!' said the Sister. 'Come with me!'

I stumbled along between Mum and the Sister, peering back fearfully at a boy in the middle of the row, trussed up and tied down in a terrifying steel frame. He was lying so still and looked so waxily pale I wondered if he was actually dead, but then he crossed his eyes and stuck his tongue out at me.

'Will they strap me down too, Mum?' I whispered, tugging at her arm.

'Not if I can help it,' she said – but she didn't sound too sure.

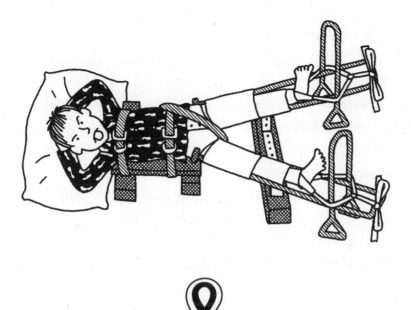

8

I sat on Mum's lap while the Sister filled in all the forms. I looked around all the shelves and worktops in her room, but I couldn't see a jar of Smarties anywhere. I was trying so hard not to cry that my throat felt as if it were stoppered with cotton wool, so maybe I wouldn't have been able to swallow one anyway.

'Elsie Kettle,' said the Sister, printing painstakingly. 'And *your* full name, Mrs Kettle?'

'I'm Sheila Alice.'

'And Mr Kettle?'

'There isn't one.'

The Sister sniffed. 'Can I have the name of Elsie's father, please?'

'It's none of your business,' said Mum. 'We don't have any contact with him.'

'Nevertheless, I need his full name and address for the sake of our records.'

'Well, you'll know more than me if you put his name and address down. I think his name's Frankie something but I haven't got a clue where he lives. I met him at a party in Fulham – and never saw him again,' said Mum.

I was momentarily distracted from my terror. I wriggled on Mum's lap excitedly. My dad was a man called Frankie! I had asked Mum many times, but she always said I didn't have a dad. I'd asked Nan too, but even she had just shaken her head, wrinkling her nose and pursing her lips in that *Don't-ask-me-dear* expression.

Frankie of Fulham. It wasn't much to go on. I screwed up my eyes to think as clearly as possible. I was pretty sure I'd never been to Fulham. I wasn't even certain where it was. The only time I'd heard the name was during the football results on the wireless: *Fulham two . . . Fulham one . . . Fulham nil.*

Frankie. There was a Frankie in my class at school. Well, he was Francis really, Frances Thorpe, but everyone called him Frankie. I didn't like him much. He wore such long underpants they hung down an inch below his short trousers, and he frequently picked his nose and then smeared it under his desk. I was always very glad I didn't have to sit next to him.

I pictured a grown-up version of Frankie, in grey-white underpants, picking his nose. I *couldn't* have a dad like that. Mum would never want that sort of a man for a boyfriend. I thought of all my uncles. They'd either been good looking or they'd had lots of money.

I suddenly thought of Frankie Vaughan the singer. Nan had one of his records, and there was a picture of him on the cardboard cover. He was good looking, and he must be rich if he was a famous singer.

Oh, what if I were Frankie Vaughan's daughter? I wasn't good looking, I wasn't dark, and I couldn't sing, but it suddenly seemed just a slight possibility. Mum was in show business, after all. Maybe she'd been one of Frankie Vaughan's backing dancers and they'd had a whirlwind romance? And perhaps she wasn't allowed to tell anyone because he was married, and famous to boot.

'Stop fidgeting, Elsie! Do you want to go to the lav?' asked Mum.

I did, but I shook my head quickly, embarrassed.

The Sister continued to fill in all the forms, copying now from a letter on her desk.

'Is that from Doctor Malory?' said Mum. 'What does it say?'

'It's confidential because it's a medical document. Please try to be patient, Miss Kettle. I have to do things properly,' said the Sister.

There was clearly not going to be a courtesy Mrs as far as *she* was concerned. When she had finished the forms at last, she asked Mum to sign at the bottom.

'What for? I'm not signing my kid away!' said Mum.

'It's standard procedure. We won't accept any child here as a patient unless their parent gives us full permission to proceed as we see fit. You want Elsie to get better, don't you?'

'Of course I do. But she's my kid, not yours. Just you remember that,' said Mum – but she signed her name.

'There!' said Sister. Then she looked at me. 'Say goodbye to Mummy, dear, and then I'll tuck you up in bed.'

I clutched Mum hard.

'Now, you're not going to be a silly girl, are you?' said the Sister.

I felt I was very silly indeed. The tears started welling in my eyes.

'Don't start bawling, Elsie, or I will too,' said Mum, giving me a quick hard hug and then tipping me off her lap. 'You be a good girl and I'll come and visit you on Saturday. All right?'

It was so not all right that I couldn't even start to protest. My mouth just opened in a silent *Oh*.

'Come on, now. Shut that little gob or the flies will get in,' said Mum, and she tapped me under my chin, kissed my forehead, and stood up.

'You'd better look after her,' she said threateningly to Sister, and then ran out of the room.

I could hear her high heels clop-clopping away into the distance. I stuck my knuckle into my mouth, trying to stopper the sobs.

'Now, now,' said the Sister, patting me on the shoulder. 'I'll get one of my nurses to take care of you. You'll get along very well, Elsie. All the other children like it here.'

I stared at her as if she were mad. She rang a little bell and a nurse appeared in the doorway as if by magic.

'This is the little Kettle girl. Her mother's only just arrived with her – but I suppose it's better late than never. Take her off and put her to bed please, Nurse.'

'Certainly, Sister,' she said. She held out her hand. 'Come along then, Elsie,' she wheedled in a loud clear voice, as if I were a little dog. 'There's a good girl.'

I didn't like her any more than the Sister, but I took her hand obediently. She was a tall, lumpy lady with wispy hair and sticking-out ears that didn't suit her nurse's cap. She was chewing busily.

The Sister raised her eyebrows.

'Sorry, Sister,' said the nurse, swallowing.

I had to trot along beside her.

'What a time to arrive!' she said. 'Right in the middle of my tea break! By the time I get you sorted, all the others will have scoffed the lot, and it's ginger cake, my favourite.'

She didn't take me back into the ward. She took me to a small bathroom instead. She sent me to the toilet in a little cubicle while she ran a scalding hot bath. 'Hurry up and jump in!'

'But I'm *clean*. I had a bath last Friday,' I said, emerging from the toilet.

Friday was always bath night at home. Nan lit the boiler specially, and I always had first scrub, and then ate a jacket potato supper in bed while Nan had a good soak herself. I realized that I actually hadn't had a bath on Friday – Mum never seemed to get us organized. Even so, I didn't want to have a bath right in front of the nurse with sticking-out ears.

'Come *on*, surely you can take your clothes off yourself?' she said impatiently.

I slowly took off my coat, my shoes and socks, my

cardie, my dress and my vest. I stood there in my frilly knickers, blushing.

'Take your knick-knacks off too, silly, and jump in the bath,' she said. 'Don't go all coy. Heavens, you'll soon learn not to be so shy here.'

That sounded very ominous indeed. I removed my knickers very reluctantly and got in the bath. She took a brand-new flannel and a cake of red carbolic soap and approached me.

'I can bath myself – I'm not a baby,' I said quickly.

'Very well, but get on with it,' she said. She watched me like a hawk, making me scrub every-where. She washed my hair herself, digging in hard with her fingertips while my head juddered up and down, and she didn't care when the soap got in my eyes.

'You're very mean,' I spluttered.

She just laughed at me. I had to rub myself dry, shivering, while she fetched a horrible white gown with no back to it.

'What's that?' I said.

'It's your nightie!'

'No, no, I've got my own pyjamas. They've got cats on them,' I said, running over to my suitcase to show her.

'Oh yes, very saucy – but you can't wear them just yet.'

'But my mum bought them specially!' I wailed.

'I dare say – but they have to be fumigated first. You'll get them back in a few days.'

'But I want to wear them now!' I said, opening up my suitcase and clutching my cat pyjamas. Then I saw Albert Trunk wearing his sock, and a terrible fear overcame me. 'I can have my elephant, can't I?' I said.

'Yes, dear, when he's come back from being fumigated,' the nurse told me.

'But I can't sleep without him. My nan gave him to me when I was a baby and I have to have him tucked up with me, else I can't settle.'

'I'll see if I can find a nice teddy from our toy box for you to cuddle,' said the nurse. 'Now stop getting yourself so worked up, it's not good for you.' She towelled my hair, pummelling my head, until it was almost dry, and then she gave me a parting on the wrong side, digging in hard with the end of the comb.

'I don't have a parting there,' I said.

'Stop it now. You're just being difficult on purpose,' she said. 'Look, we'll put a couple of Kirby grips in to keep the hair out of your eyes – you'll like that, won't you?'

'I don't like it one bit,' I muttered, but under my breath. I looked desperately at my suitcase, but she shut it up and labelled it. Albert Trunk bellowed miserably from the dark depths. All the cats swarmed off my pyjamas and ran round and round, terrified. Snow White and Sooty and Marmalade mewed piteously, scrabbling at the cardboard lid. All my friends in the *Girl* clamoured to get out too. Belle kept leaping up in frantic pirouettes, banging her head each time. They all called out desperately for me to rescue them, but I was helpless. Nurse Sticking-out Ears made me abandon them all.

She led me back into Blyton Ward with all the trussed-up children. They mostly couldn't sit up, but they craned their necks to stare at me. I was horribly embarrassed by my stupid hospital gown. I reached round and clutched it together at the back so they wouldn't see my bottom. There was only one empty bed – the one next to the boy who had stuck his tongue out at me.

The nurse pulled me towards it.

'Can't I sleep somewhere else?' I looked around wildly. 'Next to one of the girls?'

'I'm not trundling beds around at this time. You can go next to Martin. You'd like a bit of company, wouldn't you, dear?' she said cheerily to the rude boy.

'I want Robert back,' he mumbled.

'Oh dear,' said the nurse.

'Who's Robert?' I asked.

'Never you mind,' she said. 'Now then, Martin,

this is Elsie. Say hello nicely to her, everyone.'

'Hel-lo, El-sie,' they chorused slowly, the way you say good morning to your teacher at school.

'Say hello back, Elsie!' said the nurse.

I was busy staring around open-mouthed, peering at the various ways in which most of the children were imprisoned in their beds. The rude boy's contraption was particularly fearful – and I was very frightened by the poor little mummy boy encased in plaster. I backed away from the nurse.

'Elsie?'

'I don't want you to strap me up in those things!' I said. 'I especially don't want the plaster stuff.'

'Don't be silly, dear. These are all devices to keep you nice and still so that all your poorly parts can get better.'

'Robert didn't get better,' said rude Martin.

'Ssh now, Martin. Elsie! Hop into bed,' the nurse said, turning down the sheets.

'You promise you won't tie me up?'

'It's nothing to be afraid of. It doesn't *hurt*,' she said.

'Yes it does,' said Martin.

'It hurts ever so – I'm all sore,' said the big girl across from Martin.

'And it *itches*,' added another girl.

'Now now – don't all start! You've got to be good,

remember, or you won't get a story after supper.'

'Don't want a stupid story – not about daft *pixies*,' said Martin in disgust.

'You're not the only one here, Mr Grumpy. All the others *love* the story, don't you, children?' said the nurse. She smiled at me. '*You'd* like to hear a story, wouldn't you, Elsie?'

I considered. 'Do you know any stories about cats?' I asked.

'I think there's a lovely big book about a marmalade cat called Orlando in the library. If you're a really good girl while you're having your treatment, I'll read it to you,' she said. 'Don't look so worried. We're not doing anything to you just yet – you're under observation.'

I wasn't quite sure what that meant. Were they watching me? If I was really bad, would they tie me up and smother me in plaster? I jumped into bed quickly. It was so tightly made I had to fight my way into the cold sheets and my feet had to lie sideways.

'That's a good girl,' said the nurse. 'Now, I'll go and see about supper.'

The moment she was out of the room there was a clamour.

'What's your proper name – Elsie what?'

'How old are you?'

'What's wrong with you?'

'Where do you go to school?'

'Why didn't you come earlier?'

'Where's your mum?'

I blinked, not sure what to say first. 'I'm Elsie Kettle,' I said.

'Elsie *Kettle*!' said Martin, hooting with scornful laughter. 'What sort of name is *that*?'

I decided not to answer any more questions. I struggled further down into the bed and shut my eyes, pretending to go instantly to sleep.

'Hey, you, Elsie Kettle, we're talking to you,' said Martin. 'That's not really your bed, you know. It's my friend Robert's – only he *died.*'

I froze. 'No he didn't, you're just fibbing,' I said.

'He did die, last week, didn't he?' Martin said to the room, and there were murmurs backing him up. 'That's the Bed of *Doom.*'

'No it's not,' I said weakly. My skin started crawling. Did a boy really die in this very bed? 'What did he die *of*?' I squeaked.

'He had an infection and it went all up his leg and it went black and they were going to cut it off but he died before they could do it,' said Martin. 'I dare say *you'll* get an infection too, Elsie Kettle.'

'No I won't,' I said – but I imagined poor Robert's germs slithering towards me from all four corners of the bed. My toes were cold and crampy. Maybe they'd been attacked already? I struggled to peer down under the covers to make sure my feet were still pink.

'What's the matter with you anyway?' said Martin irritably. 'You look all right to me.'

I hesitated. Mum had drummed it into me that I mustn't tell anyone I had TB – but this was a hospital, after all.

'I've got something wrong with my knee. Well, they think I have,' I said. 'It's – it's very serious.'

'That's not serious! I've got tuberculosis of the hip, which is much worse – *and* I've got abscesses,' said Martin proudly.

I didn't have a clue what that meant, but it did sound awful, I had to admit. I looked around at the other children, especially the poor boy in plaster.

'Does it hurt being stuck in plaster like that?' I asked timidly.

'That's Angus. He's Scottish, but he doesn't speak,' said Martin. 'He's got TB of the spine. Maureen's got plaster too, but not all over.'

'It itches,' said little Maureen.

'She's Maureen. She's a sap – *all* the girls are,' said Martin.

'You shut up, Farty Marty,' shouted the big girl.

I sniggered, and some of the children laughed out loud. The big girl had blonde hair in a ponytail and she looked very pretty, even though she was scowling.

She seemed to be lying in a peculiar way, flat on her back, though she didn't seem to be trapped in anything like Martin and some of the others.

I sat up and looked at her properly – and then recoiled. She was stuck in some kind of steel frame that held her horribly rigid. She saw me staring, and she didn't like it.

'What are you looking at, Gobface?' she said.

'I'm – I'm just looking around,' I mumbled.

I was startled by these rude, scary children in their torture beds. I thought children ill enough to stay in hospital would be quiet and subdued, but Martin and Ponytail were far worse than Marilyn and Susan.

'Gobface!' they all spluttered.

I knew this would be my new nickname here. It was as bad as Frilly Bum. I'd always hated the word *gob*. I couldn't say it out loud when I chose a penny gobstopper in a sweetshop, I just had to point.

'Don't you dare call me names, you lot,' I said to the room at large. 'You're just a whole lot of *prisoners*!'

9

There was a little stunned silence. I was astonished myself. Then the nurse with the sticking-out ears came bustling back in with a food trolley. She had another nurse with her, a little one, with mad curly hair like Shirley Temple.

They had to lend a helping hand to each child. Nurse Sticking-out Ears had to sit beside Angus in his plaster and feed him carefully, spoonful by spoonful, because he couldn't move. I sat up in bed and nibbled my cheese on toast and ginger sponge and drank my cup of milk self-consciously.

When the nurses were up at the other end of the room, Martin whispered, 'Scoff away while you can, Gobface. Just you wait! You'll see what it's like.'

I was so frightened, the milk in my mouth curdled and I was suddenly sick all down my hospital gown.

'Really, Elsie!' said Nurse Sticking-out Ears. 'As if we haven't got enough to do! You must learn not to bolt your food.'

She mopped me up impatiently, and then fetched me another ugly immodest gown.

'It's not fair – *he's* got proper pyjamas,' I said, nodding at Martin.

He only wore them on his top. He had to make do with strange underpants on his bottom half because he was strapped up so thoroughly, but they were real pyjamas all the same. They weren't boring stripes either, they were navy, with little Dan Dares and green Mekons patterned all over, battling up and down his arms and across his chest.

'You'll get yours back when they've been through fumigation – I *told* you, Elsie. You're going to have to learn to *listen* while you're in here, so you can co-operate properly,' said the nurse, tying my new nightgown so tightly she practically strangled me.

As soon as they had trundled away the food trolley, the two nurses brought in a kind of walking washstand, with basins and jugs and strange sinister receptacles like large test tubes. Every child had to wash their face and hands and brush their teeth. That seemed a perfectly routine procedure, but then – oh *then* the nurses started toileting the children in full view of each other!

The boys were luckier because the test tubes fitted neatly over their willies. The girls had complicated bowls that slid under their hips. My heart started thudding. I had always been very shy and squeamish. I often waited all day long at school, my bladder bursting, because I hated making a trip to those smelly toilets where girls could jump up and see you over the top of the low door, or crawl on their knees and peer up at you from below.

I couldn't even go to the toilet in front of Nan when I was safe at home. If I had my way, I liked to banish her to the opposite end of the flat just in case she might be listening.

The sticking-out-ears nurse handed me a chamber pot. 'Here you are, Elsie. Nip out of bed and do a tinkle, dear,' she said cheerily.

I slid very slowly out of bed and stood beside it. Rude Martin was staring straight at me, grinning.

'I can't go in that, miss,' I said hoarsely.

'I'm *Nurse*, dear – Nurse Patterson. Of course you can go in the potty. You're not on total bed rest yet.'

'I'll go in that washroom place where you bathed me,' I said, starting to run up the ward in my bare feet.

'Hey, hey, slow down! You're not allowed to *run*!' she said, catching me. 'Goodness gracious, the doctors will have my guts for garters! And you're not allowed in the bathroom by yourself either. Now stop being a silly girl and use your potty.'

'But he's *watching* me, miss – Nurse,' I said in agony.

'Don't be so foolish, dear. There's no place for any little Miss Modestys on an orthopaedic ward. Don't worry, you'll soon get used to it.' And she pushed me hard down onto the pot with her big strong arms – so I was facing Martin. He was grinning right across his face now.

I spread the skirts of my horrid nightgown around me and shut my eyes tight. I couldn't go, not even a tiny dribble.

'Let's see now,' said nasty Nurse Patterson, hauling me up again and peering. 'Well, now you're being naughty and uncooperative.' She stuck me down again. 'Come along, Elsie, I'm waiting.'

'I can't go! I went before, you *saw* me. I can't go just like that! I'm not a tap you can turn on and off!'

Martin snorted with laughter.

'Very well, *be* awkward – but don't start calling for

a potty in the middle of the night, missy,' said Nurse Patterson. 'Get back into bed then, quick sharp.'

When she'd turned her back on me to assault the next child, I stuck my tongue out at Martin triumphantly. He stuck his out back at me, waggling it. We had a tongue-display duel, sticking them out to their full extent. The little boy on the other side of me had a fit of the giggles and then tried to join in.

'Michael, why are you pulling that ugly face?' said the little nurse with curls. 'Watch out! The wind might change and you'll be stuck like that. Stop it now, or I'll pull your little nose off.'

Michael squealed and waggled his tongue again.

'Ooh, you little monkey,' said Nurse Curly. 'Right then.' She pretended to pull off his nose and then held her fist in front of Michael's face, her thumb peeping out between her fingers. 'There – I've got your nose now!'

It didn't really look like a nose at all, but Michael's chuckles suddenly stopped. He lay there quivering.

'Oh darling, don't look so glum!' said Nurse Curly. 'Look, I'll stick it back on for you.' She pressed her thumb onto his little face. 'Here's your little nosy, back safe and sound between your rosy cheeks,' she said.

Michael chuckled happily.

'Come along, Nurse Curtis, it's not playtime now,'

said Nurse Patterson. 'We won't get any story time if we don't hurry up.'

'Story time, story time!' Michael sang out.

I hoped Nurse Curtis would read the story, but Nurse Patterson clearly considered herself the story-teller of the two. She fetched a chair and sat in the middle of the ward and read in a loud teacher voice, with a little too much expression. Martin was right – there were pixies and elves in the story. Nurse Patterson made her voice go high and squeaky, and I winced, though everyone else seemed to be enjoying it – everyone except Martin. He rolled his eyes, and snorted in disgust. I thought the story was a bit soppy too and sniggered myself.

'Ssh, you two! I want absolute silence or I'll stop reading. You're spoiling it for the little ones,' said Nurse Patterson in hurt tones.

I turned over onto my stomach so I couldn't see Martin any more. I wondered what it must be like for him, tied permanently onto his back. I wriggled extravagantly in the cold bed, trying to get properly comfortable, barely listening to the story now.

The children were climbing right to the top of a tree, then going up a mysterious ladder into another land entirely above the clouds. It was a Land of Toys, and all the children went to Santa Claus's castle.

'There now, isn't that a lovely story?' Nurse

Patterson closed the book and patted it fondly. 'We'll have another chapter tomorrow if you're all very, very good. Now settle down, everyone. Night-night.'

There were half-hearted murmurs from each bed. The curly-haired Nurse Curtis came dancing round to each child, tucking a sheet in here and there, giving everyone a little cuddle. She put her rosy cheek close to mine and whispered, 'Don't worry, Elsie. You'll soon settle in and get used to everything.'

I didn't usually like strange people touching me, but my arms reached up of their own accord and I clung to her.

'Oh darling, don't get too upset.'

'I want to go *home*,' I mumbled into her ear. 'I don't like it here. I'm not *ever* going to get used to it.'

'Oh dear, I know. It must be very frightening just at first, but we're not all ogres, you know. All the nurses are very kind.' She tucked the sheets in tight around me. 'Close your eyes and you'll go to sleep in no time.'

'No I won't. I need Albert Trunk!'

'Who's Albert, dear?'

'He's my elephant,' I blurted out.

She looked so surprised I had to add, 'He's my toy,' so she wouldn't think I was mad, but it felt like a terrible betrayal because Albert was so real to me.

'Oh, a *toy*,' she said, giggling.

'I had him all packed in my suitcase with my new cat pyjamas, but that other nurse won't let me have him. She says he has to be fumigated,' I wailed.

'Oh dear. Yes, I'm afraid it's a rule. But you'll get him back soon, I promise.'

'I need him *now*,' I said. I suddenly realized that Snow White and Sooty and Marmalade would have to be fumigated too. I wasn't quite sure what fumigation was, but it sounded terrible. I imagined a huge hot chamber and all my beloved pets herded inside and then gassed. It was such a terrible thought it became real and I burst out crying.

'Oh sweetheart, there now! They'll be back in a day or two. And meanwhile . . . Here, hang on a sec.' She ran up the ward, her flat shoes squeaking on the polished floor. Nurse Patterson remonstrated but she took no notice.

I lay there snivelling, ducking my head right under my sheets, but it was no use. I was hardly making any noise but Martin had ears like a bat.

'Cry-baby!' he said scornfully. He cleared his throat. 'Gobface is a cry-baby,' he announced to the whole ward.

Nurse Curtis came dashing back clutching something. 'Here, Elsie. He'll keep you company until you get your elephant back,' she said, and she thrust a large stuffed Donald Duck into my arms. 'He's from the little ones' toy box in Potter Ward, but I'll make sure you get to keep him as long as you need him. Night-night now.'

'Night-night, Nurse. And thank you – thank you very much,' I said, sniffing. I didn't like Donald Duck. He'd never been my favourite cartoon character. I didn't even care for his name. I'd had an Uncle Donald once when I was little, and he always tossed me up in the air or tickled me too hard. I'd been very glad when Mum got a new boyfriend to replace him.

This Donald Duck was old and faded and he smelled of hospitals. His felt skin made my nails twitch and his stiff beak stuck out rudely right in my face. Nevertheless I clung to him when Nurse Patterson switched the lights off. There was a desk light at the far end which glowed eerily in the dark.

'Hey, Gobface, still grizzling?' Martin called.

I didn't have the spirit to retaliate this time. I lay there on my back, the tears seeping down my face and dribbling into my ears, while Donald Duck pecked at me.

The others whispered to one another for a while, and then their voices faded away. I could hear someone snoring. I thought it was Martin, but then his voice came hissing through the air: 'Remember, Gobface, you're in the Bed of Doom.'

I put my hands over my ears, hating him. I knew

he was only saying it to frighten me, and yet this other boy, Robert, really *had* died in my bed, and recently too.

I wasn't sure what happened when you died. Nan said you went up to heaven and wore a white nightie with fluffy white wings to match, and walked in gardens and thought beautiful thoughts. Mum laughed at that idea and said she thought it would be too boring, and if that was the case she'd sooner go downstairs to the Other Place, which sounded much more lively. But they didn't seem *serious*, either of them. Maybe Robert hadn't gone up to heaven or down to hell. Maybe he was still trapped here in the hospital? I looked up fearfully in case he was hovering above his old bed. I couldn't see a ghost boy in the gloom, but maybe he'd been made invisible. Perhaps he was coming to take me away with him?

I hunched up in a little ball under the covers, not even daring to put my head on my pillow, but I must have gone to sleep. I dreamed of Donald Duck. We were paddling frantically on a choppy sea, trying to get away from the ghost who was going to get us. I could feel his cold hands pulling me down under the water. I kicked and struggled, and woke up fighting the sheets. I was still wet, though, as if . . .

Oh no. I lay in my sodden bed, my heart thumping. I'd wet myself! I hadn't wet the bed since I was a baby.

What was I going to *do*? What would Nurse Patterson say? She'd surely be cross, especially as I hadn't used her wretched potty. All the other children in the ward would know. Martin would have a field day tormenting me.

I lay very still, willing this all to be a terrible nightmare. If only I had enough willpower, perhaps I could make myself wake up in my own bed at home, with Albert Trunk safe in my arms and Nan coming in to give me a cuddle . . . I shut my eyes tight and clenched my fists and squeezed my knees together and *willed* it to happen – but I stayed wet and lonely in the Bed of Doom. I could hear footsteps now, *squeak, squeak* across the polished floor, coming nearer and nearer.

'Hello? Who have we here?' It was a soft, gentle voice. Not Nurse Patterson, not Nurse Curtis – but one peep showed me a white hat with wings. Another nurse. I lay as still as I could, eyes shut again, breathing slowly in and out, even snuffling a little to sound as if I were snoring – but she wasn't fooled.

'It's Elsie, isn't it?' she whispered. 'I think you're awake, aren't you, poppet? And I think . . .' Her hand slid under my covers and felt my damp sheet.

I held my breath, waiting for the slap, the shouting.

'Your sheets are in a bit of a tangle,' she said. 'You

need a nice new pair. Don't worry, we'll soon make you comfy.'

She walked off, checking each child as she went. She was walking stealthily now, almost on tiptoe, so that no one else would wake. I lay still, wondering if I might have imagined her – but then she was back with her arms full of clean linen. She didn't snap on my light. In the darkness she lifted me out of bed as if I were a baby, took my wet nightgown off, wrapped a blanket around my shoulders, and gently washed me with a warm sponge. Then she put the clean new nightie on, and tucked me back in the blanket.

'There, my little parcel!' she whispered. 'You wait there, sweetheart, and I'll have your bed made in a jiffy.'

She was like a conjurer, wafting a sheet here and there, and suddenly working magic. My wet sheets were soon lying in a little bundle on the floor, my bed was made with fresh new ones and, wonder of wonders, when she lifted me back into bed, I felt a hot-water bottle carefully wrapped in a towel.

'Newly made beds always feel a bit chilly,' she said. She took my hands and rubbed them. 'There, poor little frozen fingers! And who's this?' She took Donald Duck. 'Do you want him tucked in too?'

'Mmm . . .' I couldn't decide. I didn't like him, but perhaps he was better than nothing. 'I really want

Albert Trunk, but that other nurse took him away,' I said, in a tiny voice.

'Oh dear. I suppose he has to be fumigated. But he'll be back soon. Let's pretend he's gone on his holidays. Albert Trunk has *packed* his trunk. Has he got his pyjamas?'

'No, he's just got this little red felt saddle thing, but *I've* got pyjamas with special cats on, only that other nurse wouldn't let me wear them.'

'You'll wear your own pyjamas soon, I promise. Cats, eh?'

'Yes, white ones, with a pink background.'

'Very pretty – and *white* cats. Perfect!' she said. 'Hey – *purr*fect, get it?' She giggled very quietly and I did too. 'I shall look forward to seeing your cat pyjamas, Elsie, but meanwhile, you might just find you have a white cat on your hospital nightgown. Just one – but she's very, very big and soft and furry.'

I thought she was trying to help me imagine a cat, one stretching right across my shoulders, though it was a little hard turning crisply ironed cotton into soft fur. But I was grateful for the thought, and so deeply thankful that she'd been so kind and tactful about my damp sheets, that I flung my arms about her neck when she bent close to tuck me in.

'You're the best nurse ever,' I whispered. 'What's your name?'

'I'm Nurse Gabriel, sweetheart.'

It seemed the perfect name for her. I watched her walk up the ward, seeing feathery wings bursting out of her blue nurse's frock and a gold halo outlining her white cap.

I lay in my clean sheets, still a little lost and lonely, but immensely comforted. Then I felt something jump onto my bed. I stayed still, stunned, while it picked its way delicately towards my head. I put my hand out, trembling, and felt the softest fur, like thistledown. I stroked tentatively, and the cat started purring, rubbing her head under my hand, clearly telling me to keep on stroking. I held her with one hand and stroked with the other, from her head all the way down her body to the tip of her long tail.

She quivered, luxuriating, and turned round once, decided which way was more comfortable, then sat down on my chest, settling herself with a contented little sigh. I went on stroking her, not sure whether Nurse Gabriel had conjured her up out of nowhere or whether I was dreaming. I didn't care. I lay still and listened to the cat purr until I drifted off to sleep.

10

When I woke up to the clank of the washing trolley and the murmurs of my ward mates, I thought the white cat might just have been a dream. I wasn't even sure Nurse Gabriel was real, though I was certainly in a clean dry bed. I peered hopefully at the nurse scurrying from child to child with her washcloth and soap, but she wasn't remotely angelic. She was little and very fat, her elasticated belt stretched to the utmost, her bosoms like two huge blue balloons about to go pop at any moment.

'Hello, little funny face,' she said, rushing up to me.

I put my hands to my face, mortified. For a long time now I'd had a creeping suspicion that I was ugly. Mum often sighed when she brushed my hair and told not to *pull that face* – though I never knew quite what face it was I was pulling. Even Nan would push her thumb into one side of my mouth and her finger into the other, and go 'Cheer up, chicken!'

I screwed up my face even more, trying not to think about Nan.

'Hey, hey, don't look such a saddo,' said the fat nurse, pulling my hands away. 'What's your name, eh?'

'Elsie Kettle,' I mumbled.

'Well, I'm Nurse Johnson. Now, you're still under observation, so you can wash yourself like a good girl, as I'm all behind like the horse's tail,' she said. She gave me a bowl of warm water to balance on my knees. 'Don't you spill it, mind!'

I started to wash myself carefully – and then very nearly *did* spill the bowl when the beautiful blonde nurse came in with the food trolley. Her white cap sat neatly on her golden curls and her blue eyes shone as she smiled straight at me.

'Hello, Elsie!' she said.

'Oh Nurse Gabriel!' I said, overcome.

So she was real after all – and she truly *was* an angel. She behaved as if she were meeting me for the first time so that Martin and the others should not suspect a thing. She gave me my cornflakes with extra sugar and top of the milk, and she cut my toast into four neat quarters, just like Nan did.

She wasn't just kind to *me*, she was kind to everyone, even horrible Martin. He said he wasn't hungry and didn't want his very-rude-word breakfast. Nurse Johnson heard, and gasped and said, 'That child needs his mouth washing out with soap,' and she held her cake of carbolic up threateningly.

'It's OK, Johnson, I'll deal with the little monster,' said Nurse Gabriel. 'Little *green* monster, like the weeny man from space on your pyjamas, Martin Harwood.'

'He's not a monster, he's the Mekon,' said Martin scornfully. 'He's in the *Eagle*. Don't you know anything?'

'Oh, my head's full of dull stuff like my *Orthopaedics for Nurses* book and the problem page in *Woman's Own*,' said Nurse Gabriel, laughing. 'Maybe I'll give myself a spot of serious instruction just now. Do you have a copy of the *Eagle* handy, Martin?'

'It's in my locker, you know it is,' said Martin, but he didn't sound cross now.

'Well, here's the deal,' said Nurse Gabriel. 'I'll park myself beside you and we'll read it together. I'll find out all about Mr Mekon while you eat half your corn-flakes. Is that a deal?'

'I said, I'm not hungry,' said Martin – but when Nurse Gabriel shrugged and seemed about to turn away, he added quickly, 'But it's a deal.'

She shook his hand and then gave him his comic. It was hard for him to read flat on his back, so after a moment or two she started reading it aloud, acting it all out solemnly, doing a gruff masculine voice for Dan Dare and a weird squeaky voice for the Mekon. As she read, she spooned cornflakes into Martin as if he were a baby. His mouth opened and he chewed and swallowed automatically. He burst out laughing at one point, spraying cornflakes, and Nurse Gabriel laughed too, and wiped the slurp from his chin all in one quick move.

'You're spoiling that boy,' said Nurse Johnson, puffing past.

'No, I'm spoiling myself – this *Eagle* comic is truly super,' said Nurse Gabriel.

I watched her as she circled the ward, making almost every child laugh and eat with gusto. She was wonderful when it came to the dreaded toileting too, even constructing a blanket tent so that Gillian, the eldest girl with the ponytail, could have a little privacy.

I was starting to differentiate between all the other children too, so they weren't just blurs in beds. By the end of the day I knew everyone's name. In the row opposite were big Gillian with her ponytail, her whiny friend Rita, then two little girls who giggled together – Maureen with curly hair and little pink glasses, and Babette, with very short tufty hair as if some large grazing animal had been chewing on it. On one side of me I had Martin the rude boy, and on the other side was little Michael. Silent Angus in his plaster bed came last.

I looked hopefully at the girls, wondering if any of them might be my special friend. Rita hung on every word Gillian said, and often squeaked, 'Oooh Gilly, you are awful!' Maureen and Babette were much younger than me and didn't seem interested in anyone else anyway.

It didn't look as if I would have a friend here either – though I certainly had an enemy in Martin. All morning he whispered hoarsely about the Bed of Doom, even though I stuck my fingers in my ears and went, 'La-la-la-la, can't hear a sausage!'

Then a doctor in a white coat with a stethoscope round his neck came strolling into the ward with Sister Baker, the two nurses behind him – Nurse Patterson with her sticking-out ears, and curly-haired Nurse Curtis.

'Where's Nurse Gabriel?' I asked anxiously.

'She's on nights. She's gone off duty now. These are the day nurses. Don't you know *anything*?' said Martin.

'And that's the day doctor? What's his name?'

'Doctor *Torture*!' Martin hissed. 'Watch out, here he comes. He's going to get you now, Gobface.'

I slid right down in my bed, hoping that the doctor would walk right past – and when he stopped and pulled the sheets off my face, I shut my eyes tight, pretending to be fast asleep.

'Wakey wakey, little sleepyhead,' he said. 'I'm Doctor Tortel – and you must be Elsie.' He tickled me gently under the chin.

I was still very frightened of what he might do to me, but I couldn't be frightened of *him*. He examined my knee and the rest of my leg and my hip. Then he had me walk round my bed, humming softly as he watched.

'Mmm – a clear case,' he murmured. 'Lucky it was spotted. I'll confer with Sir David, but I'm pretty sure we'll put her in a Thomas's knee bed splint tomorrow.'

'In *Thomas's* one?' I said.

Dr Tortel and Sister Baker and the nurses all laughed at me.

'It's just a silly name, called after the man who invented it. It will be *Elsie's* bed splint,' said Dr Tortel.

'I don't want one,' I told him.

'You want to get better, don't you?'

'Yes, but not if I have to be tied up,' I said firmly. 'Not like the others.'

'It doesn't hurt, I promise. It's just a little uncomfortable at times. Isn't that right, Martin?' the doctor said, turning his head.

'No, it hurts terribly – *especially* her kind of splint,' said Martin.

'You're a bad boy,' said Dr Tortel, but he laughed. 'Don't you listen to Martin's tall stories, Elsie. I think you two must be a similar age. You'll soon be great pals.'

I stared after him as he walked down the ward. He might be a clever doctor but he was a very stupid man.

Martin clearly thought so too. 'He's mad. I wouldn't be friends with you in a million years, Gobface,' he hissed.

'Now then, Martin, we all know you're just missing Robert,' said Nurse Curtis. 'Look, will you lend Elsie your *Eagle* comic for a bit, sweetheart? I'm sure she'd like something fun to read while we're finishing the rounds.'

'*I'm* reading it,' said Martin, struggling with it.

'I don't like the *Eagle* anyway,' I lied. I'd never actually read it, but I liked the sound of the little green Mekon. I imagined him spinning down to Earth in his flying saucer, stepping straight into Blyton Ward, and zapping Martin with his evil ray-gun as he lay there helpless.

'I'd sooner read my own *Girl*,' I said firmly. 'Will it be back from the fumigator's yet, Nurse Curtis?'

'Not yet, lovey. Give it a few days,' she said.

I felt too depressed to look at the old *Chicks' Own* comic she found for me in little Michael's locker. It was te-di-ous ba-by rub-bish an-y-way, with all the words broken into little bits. I watched the toileting and then the terrible injections. My heart started thudding hard when Nurse Patterson came near me with that awful huge syringe, but she walked straight past and attacked Martin.

I hated Martin and I'd just commanded the Mekon to attack him with his ray-gun, but I couldn't help feeling sorry for him when he screamed.

I thought we might have a bit of peace till lunch time, so I was surprised when Nurse Patterson and Nurse Curtis seized little Michael's bed and started trundling it noisily right out of the ward.

'Where are they taking him?' I asked Martin.

'They're taking him away to the torture chamber – and *you're* next,' he said, his voice still jerky from crying.

'You're just telling silly lies. You're pathetic. You can't scare me,' I fibbed.

I decided the nurses were probably taking him to the bathroom to give him a proper bath, though I wasn't sure how his horrible frame and buckles and straps would all fit into the tub – but in a minute they came back without him.

'Nurse Curtis, where's Michael?' I whispered.

'Oh, we've just taken him to play in the sunshine,' she said. 'You're next, sweetheart.'

I stared at her. I was sure Nurse Curtis couldn't be a liar too – but what did she *mean*? How could Michael play outdoors when he was clearly very ill and strapped rigid on his bed?

The two nurses seized my bed and trundled me down the ward. Martin went 'Ha-ha-haaaa!' like someone in a horror film. I knew he was simply trying to wind me up, but it was *working*. I had tight knots in my stomach and I could hardly breathe.

'Nurse Curtis!' I gasped.

'What's up, pet? Are we pushing you too fast? You're not getting giddy, are you?' she said.

'You won't let anyone hurt me, will you?' I whispered it, but Nurse Patterson heard and snorted.

'Don't be such a silly sausage, Elsie Kettle. No one's going to hurt you!' She laughed mirthlessly at the idea – and yet half an hour ago I'd seen her reduce tough Martin to tears with her injection.

They pushed me through a set of double doors, out onto a veranda. Michael's bed was already there. He was huddled under his covers, shivering. There was a very watery smudge of sun between the clouds, but a chill wind was blowing and it felt desperately cold. It might be spring but it felt like January.

'It's cold out here,' I said plaintively.

'Nonsense! You're in your lovely cosy bed,' said Nurse Patterson.

It wasn't cosy at all. I had a sheet and one pale green thin blanket. I tucked the *Chicks' Own* comic over my chest, which helped a little. The nurses went off to collect the next child.

'Why are they shoving us out here?' I asked Michael. 'Have we been naughty?'

'We always come out here. It's to get fresh air,' he said. His face was blue-white and pinched with the cold. I felt so sorry for him I slipped out of bed and gave him back his *Chicks' Own*, tucking it under his little armpits.

'There now, that's a bit cosier, isn't it?' I said.

Michael gave me a sudden beaming smile. I grinned back at him and held his tiny frozen hand. He was much too little to be in hospital, tied up in this terrible manner. The covers were hiding his straps and buckles, but I could see the shape of all the little knobs through his blanket.

Then the nurses came back trundling Martin – and Nurse Patterson shouted at me.

'Get back into bed this instant, Elsie Kettle! You're on total bed rest, like the other children. Don't you *dare* start messing about.'

'But Michael was so cold. I was only trying to warm him up,' I protested.

'You have to learn to do as you're told,' said Nurse Patterson. 'We know what's best for you. It's essential that you all have lots of good fresh air. It will improve your general health, stimulate your appetite, and make you sleep better.'

'But I'm shivering!'

'Because you're out of bed! Now get back in before I smack your bottom, young lady.'

I got back in sharpish. Martin was giggling at me. When the nurses marched off to fetch the next bed, I pulled a face at their backs.

'I'll smack *her* bottom back,' I muttered.

Martin sniggered and Michael went into peals of laughter. 'I'll smack her bottom too!' he gurgled.

'No, Gobface can push our beds and we'll run her over. Watch out, Nurse Patterson, you're going to get *squashed*,' said Martin.

We warmed up a little inventing fresh ways of getting

even with Nurse Patterson, suddenly united. Big Gillian joined in when she was pushed onto the veranda with us. Our beds were pushed so close together they were almost touching, so it was much easier to talk. Angus didn't say anything at all when he joined us, but Rita and Babette and Maureen laughed too, coming up with inventive new ways to humiliate Nurse Patterson. It was still hard work remembering which of the two little girls was which, and I mixed them up.

'*I've* got straight hair and Maureen's curly – it's *simple*, Gobface,' said Babette.

I couldn't stop Martin, but Babette was just a little squirt of a girl and I wasn't going to let her insult me. 'I'm not Gobface, I'm Elsie. It's *simple*, Babette,' I said fiercely.

'Oh shut up, you small fry, I'm blooming *perishing*,' said Gillian, and when the nurses came back, she called Nurse Curtis. She clearly knew it was a waste of time appealing to Nurse Patterson.

'Look at all my goose pimples! Couldn't I at least have my cardie from my locker?' she said.

Nurse Curtis rubbed her own chilly arms. 'Yes, it is a bit nippy today. Tell you what – I'll see about hot-water bottles,' she said.

'It's *spring* now, Curtis,' said Nurse Patterson crisply. 'They're only allowed hot-water bottles in winter.'

'Oh, pish posh,' said Nurse Curtis. 'It'll only take ten minutes and then they'll be so much happier.'

'They're not here to be *happy*,' said Nurse Patterson. 'They're here to get well.'

'Only some of us don't,' said Martin.

'I'll thank you not to eavesdrop and interrupt, young man,' said Nurse Patterson, and vented her temper on him because Nurse Curtis had run off, doing a funny Charlie Chaplin kipper-feet routine that made us all laugh.

She came back with a whole trolley full of hot-water bottles, and they made such a difference.

'You're the lucky ones! For two pins I'd get into bed with you,' said Nurse Curtis, clapping her plump arms. They were rosy red with the cold.

'I don't know why you're all making such a fuss,' said Nurse Patterson. '*I* think it's quite mild today' – though her sticky-out ears were scarlet.

A new lady came puffing out onto the veranda. She was wearing a hat and a winter coat and a woolly scarf and leather gloves. She kept them on all morning, clearly agreeing with us that it was freezing. She was Miss Isles, our school teacher.

'I didn't know you had teachers in hospital,' I said, sighing.

She wasn't soft or pretty, and I was sure she didn't

have an angora jumper under her coat like dear Miss Roberts back at my proper school.

She'd be wondering where I was now. Marilyn and Susan would be peeved that they didn't have anyone to pick on. I wondered if Laura might miss me just a little bit.

Miss Isles gave me an ugly grey workbook and a pencil, though at school I'd used a pen for ages. She set me twenty sums, made me read an excerpt from a story and then answer ten silly questions, and then had me tackle endless IQ puzzles.

'*If beak is to bird, then whisker is to . . .*' I mumbled.

I hated these stupid tests. They were never specific enough. Whisker could well be to *Nanny* – she had quite a few growing on her top lip, and a couple on her chin too. Mum was always nagging her to tweeze them away. *She* tweezed her face so much she didn't have any eyebrows at all when she took off her make-up.

I thought of Nan now, imprisoned in the sanatorium, and a tear ran down my cheek, *plop*, onto the paper.

'Oh dear, don't cry, Elsie! Don't worry if you can't answer many of the questions. They're just little tests so I can see how clever you are,' said Miss Isles.

Everyone was staring at me.

'You don't *need* to do a test, Gobface,' Martin hissed. 'We can all see you're a right old Dumbo.'

I blinked fiercely. 'You shut up,' I said, and printed c-a-t in my best handwriting. Then I looked up, and there *was* a c-a-t – the big white one from last night. She was sauntering over the grass, as delicate as a daisy, and then she got to the veranda and ducked straight under Michael's bed at the end.

I stared. No one else seemed to have seen her. I was making her up again. But she seemed so *real*, lifting her paws so gracefully, her tail stretched out behind her. I was thrilled, but also a little frightened. I hadn't realized my imagination was so powerful.

I closed my eyes and tried to conjure up Nan, my old laughing funny nanny. I tried to make her come walking up in her old black strappy shoes with the bunion bulge at the sides – but she was very sketchy and vague and her face wouldn't go right. She kept bending over to cough, her thin hand covering her mouth.

Then something caught at my sheets, and suddenly there was the white cat, bobbing up out of nowhere, jumping right up onto my bed. She looked at me enquiringly. I held out my hand, hardly daring to breathe. She walked up my blanket, turned round once and then settled down happily right on my stomach. I started to stroke her and she purred, arching her back and rubbing against my hand with her head.

'Now then, Elsie. Stop playing with that cat and get on with your work,' said Miss Isles.

Miss Isles could see my imaginary cat! I was astonished for a second, but then common sense kicked in.

'She's *real*!' I breathed.

'Of course she's real! What sort of nutter *are* you, Gobface?' said Martin.

'She got right into the hospital and jumped up on my bed last night,' I said proudly, ignoring the abuse.

'She jumps up on everyone's bed. Here, Queenie! Come to Martin!' he said, patting his own bed and making little tutting noises with his tongue to encourage her.

'Queenie? Oh, what a lovely name!' I said.

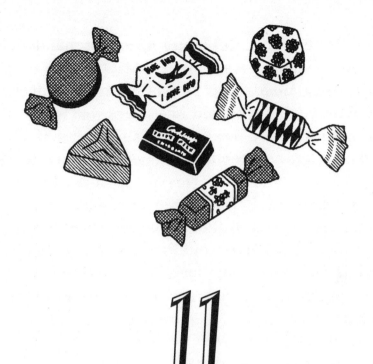

11

Queenie did look proudly regal, queen of all her domain. She even held her head up high as if balancing a tiny crown on top.

'But who does she belong to?' I asked Martin. 'And won't she get into terrible trouble if the nurses find her in the. ward because of germs and that?'

Nan wasn't necessarily a stickler for hygiene, but she didn't like me picking up stray cats in the street in case they had fleas.

I looked very carefully at Queenie's beautiful white

fur, but it seemed immaculate – not a trace of even one tiny flea. She had great green eyes and the sweetest rose-pink nose that sniffed me delicately. I seemed to pass muster, because she stayed where she was, purring gently, totally ignoring Martin.

'She belongs to our ward, stupid,' said Martin. 'We have Queenie, and she's the nicest of all the cats. Only the best for Blyton! Ransome's got Kitty, and she's boring, just an old tabby. Christie's got Samson – he's a big ginger tom – and Potter's got Puddleduck, and she's OK, I suppose. She's mostly white too, with ginger smudges, but she's nowhere near as beautiful as her mum.'

'So Queenie's her mum?'

'Yes, but they don't really get on very well now. If Puddleduck comes sniffing up to Queenie, she gives her a whack with her front paw, as if to say "Stop bothering me."'

'Like my mum,' I said without thinking.

'Does your mum whack you then?' asked Martin, sounding interested.

'Well . . . if I've been naughty.'

'My dad whacks, really hard. Does yours hit you?'

'I haven't got a dad,' I said, though I thought fleetingly about Frankie Vaughan. I saw him smile at me, open up his arms to embrace his long-lost daughter.

'That's daft. Everyone's got a dad,' said Martin.

'Yes, OK, but I don't *see* him. He doesn't live with us,' I said.

Gillian lifted her head, her ponytail flipping. 'Oh golly, are they *divorced*?' she said.

I hesitated. They hadn't ever been married so I wasn't sure they could actually be divorced.

'Don't worry, *my* mum and dad are getting a divorce,' said Gillian. 'It's because I'm ill. Dad hates seeing me like this. He says it's too upsetting. He's walked out on my mum.'

'Oh, I'm so sorry,' I said.

'It's OK. Mum and I don't need *him*. We're going to get our own flat, with my sister.'

'*My* mum and I have a flat, sort of, with my nan,' I said.

I felt thrilled to be having this adult conversation with Martin and Gillian. At school my unusual home was the subject of whispers and jeers, but here Martin and Gillian had a worldly-wise acceptance of these things. It almost made me part of their club. When Rita started gabbling that maybe her mummy and daddy were getting a divorce too because they always argued about who should put the dustbins out, the three of us just sighed and shook our heads at her silliness. And all the time Queenie sat on my lap and purred contentedly. I leaned forward and buried my face in her magnificent white fur and she purred even louder.

'Elsie! I told you already – stop playing with Queenie and get on with your worksheets. Martin, Gillian, stop chattering. You need to pay attention to your long division!' said Miss Isles.

I had to push Queenie gently to one side. She hovered at the edge of my bed, wondering about jumping off – but then she stretched out at the end, put her head on her front paws, and went to sleep.

I had to hunch my legs up so as not to disturb her. I felt very fidgety after a while, but I forced myself to keep still. I did the maths test, the English test, the IQ test – and then Miss Isles gave me a drawing board and a piece of blue sugar paper and some wax crayons and told me to draw a picture.

I tried drawing Queenie, but I didn't have a white crayon to colour her in. Next I drew Nan, but I couldn't make her look lovely enough. So in the end I did Mum, making her hair very yellow and her cheeks pink and her mouth bright red. I coloured in her best kingfisher-blue suit and tried to make her patent high heels look shiny. I even managed to draw her little gold bracelet round her ankle.

'Oh my, that's a very beautiful lady,' said Miss Isles, glancing across.

'It's my mum,' I said. 'Yes, she *is* beautiful.'

'You've still got lots of space on your paper. Why

don't you draw yourself beside her?' suggested Miss Isles.

I drew a scrappy little Elsie with spindly plaits and my best party dress. I gave myself patent shoes too. I certainly wasn't going to draw myself in horrible boy's lace-ups.

Then it was lunch time. I thought we'd be wheeled back to the ward, but we stayed where we were to eat our plate of mince and mashed potato and carrots and cabbage. I didn't like the taste of the cabbage. It was just like old face flannel, so I left it on the side of my plate next to a little pool of greasy mince.

Nurse Patterson shook her head at me. 'Come along, Elsie, this won't do. Think of all the poor little children in the world with empty tummies! Eat it all up like a good girl.'

'I don't like it, miss.'

'*Nurse!* How many times? Now eat it up at once. All the other children are eating theirs,' said Nurse Patterson.

'That's right, Elsie. Eat it up quick,' said Nurse Curtis. 'We're off to fetch the pudding now and you don't want to miss out, do you? It's jam roly-poly and custard!'

'Will they *make* me eat it?' I asked Martin, foolishly.

'Oh yes, they'll start spooning it in. They'll hold your nose to make you swallow – and if you dare sick

163

it up they'll make you eat that too,' said Martin, miming the whole revolting process.

My stomach heaved and I nearly *was* sick. I quickly tried offering my plate to Queenie. She sniffed at in disdain and jumped off my bed, deciding to go and forage for her own food.

I was left feeling desperate. I grabbed a great soft oozing handful of mince and cabbage, nipped out of bed, ran in my bare feet along the gravel pathway, and threw my meal into the middle of a rhododendron bush. I wiped my hand on the leaves and then sprinted back to bed just before Nurse Patterson and Nurse Curtis came trundling back with the pudding trolley. Martin and Gillian gave a cheer.

'What's going on?' asked Nurse Patterson suspiciously. 'Why were you cheering Elsie?'

I held my breath.

'Because she's finished her meal. She's eaten it all up, every bit,' said Gillian.

'Oh, good *girl*,' said Nurse Curtis. 'A big helping of roly-poly for you then!' She dug her ladle into the steaming metal dish. 'Ooh – lots of jam today . . . Mmm, blissful!'

I ate my roly-poly with relish, grinning gratefully at Gillian and Martin.

Then Nurse Curtis returned with a big box, which she rattled suggestively, grinning.

'What's in the box?'

'It's our magic sweetie box, Elsie. You can help yourself,' said Nurse Curtis.

'Only one, mind,' said Nurse Patterson.

'Oh, don't mind if I do.' Nurse Curtis unwrapped a Blue Bird toffee and popped it into her mouth.

'Don't you let Sister Baker see you or you won't half cop it,' said Nurse Patterson.

Nurse Curtis wrinkled her nose at her and chewed her toffee happily. 'Here you are, Elsie – choose,' she said, sticking the box under my nose.

'The liquorice pipes are *mine*. Don't you dare choose one of them,' said Martin.

I didn't push my luck. I chose a Quality Street instead, the purple one – chocolate and caramel and hazelnut. We always had a box of Quality Street at Christmas, and Nan saved all the purple ones for me because they were my favourite. I sucked my chocolate and caramel until I got to the hazelnut and twisted the shiny coloured wrapper around my finger, making myself a fairy wine glass.

After lunch we were supposed to settle down and have a nap. There were protests. Gillian said she wasn't the least bit sleepy and didn't want to take a baby nap. Rita echoed every word, but fell asleep almost straight away, snoring. Maureen and Babette giggled away, playing some little-girlie game, but soon fell asleep too. Soon they were all asleep, except for Martin and Gillian and me. I saw Angus's eyes fluttering, so maybe he was awake, but he never said anything so it didn't make much difference.

Martin started whispering dirty jokes. Then Gillian told even dirtier ones. I think they were trying to shock me, but I laughed boldly, though I didn't understand half of what they were saying.

'Go on then, Gobface – *you* tell us one,' said Martin.

I couldn't think of a single joke. At school, I'd never been in one of those little gangs where everyone whispered and sniggered together. But then I remembered Uncle Ivor, one of my mum's long-ago boyfriends, a fat little man with a very red face. He didn't tell jokes, at least not in front of me, but he did sing silly songs, and from the way Nan tutted I knew they were rude. So I softly sang a song about a lady with funny hair, and Martin and Gillian snorted with glee.

'Wow, that's really *filthy*, Gobface,' Martin spluttered. 'Teach it to me, go on!'

I wasn't sure of Martin's status now – whether he was still a deadly enemy or almost a friend. Gillian was also flatteringly impressed. I shyly said I liked her hairstyle, and she reached up and showed me how she fixed it, tying up the long strands and then wetting the straggly bits in front with spit so they went into kiss curls. I unplaited my hair and tried hard to copy her, though it was difficult without a mirror.

I was sure I wasn't sleepy, and I didn't want to lie back properly on my pillow because it would spoil my new hairstyle – but I think I nodded off in mid-sentence, because I suddenly opened my eyes, and there were Nurse Patterson and Nurse Curtis clanking round each bed, doling out bedpans. I didn't know what I was going to do now, so close to Martin. I felt myself going bright red with the horror of it, but to my enormous relief Nurse Patterson seized hold of my bed rails and trundled me along the veranda, back inside the hospital. She let me jump out in the bathroom and go to the toilet privately. I was so grateful I decided I might like her a little bit after all – not quite as much as Nurse Curtis, and certainly not like lovely Nurse Gabriel.

She didn't take me back onto the veranda. She pushed me down endless new corridors, her rubber-soled shoes squeaking horribly on the polished floor.

'Where are we going, Nurse Patterson?' I asked, sitting up.

'No, lie down, Elsie.'

'Where are you taking me?'

'Assessment,' she said, shortly and mysteriously, her teeth hissing on the four 's's like a snake.

'What's that?'

'You'll soon find out,' she said.

She took me to a waiting room, leaving my bed in front of a door that said SIR DAVID ROYALE. It sounded such a grand name that I stopped asking questions and hunched up small under the bedclothes. Even Nurse Patterson seemed nervous, biting her fingernails. I thought Sir David would be very big and imposing, with a shouty voice, but when he opened his door he was surprisingly small and thin.

'Come along in.' He flapped his hand in a welcoming gesture, as if he had invited us for tea. 'So you're Elsie. How do you do, my dear,' he said, shaking my hand. 'Hello, Nurse Patterson.'

She bobbed her head at him, blushing because he knew her name. Her sticking-out ears went painfully red.

He pulled my covers back and examined me carefully, his hands firm but gentle as he felt my hips and knees and calves. 'Up you hop, Elsie. Have a little march around my room,' he said.

I wriggled out of bed and pattered around, feeling very awkward in the silly hospital gown that showed my bottom. 'Please can I have my own pyjamas back soon?' I mumbled.

'Certainly, dear,' he said, peering at me and making notes.

'They've got cats on,' I said.

'Do you like cats then?' asked Sir David.

'I love them, especially Queenie,' I said.

'Ah, we all love Queenie. We'll put a little shrimp paste on your toes tomorrow, and then she'll come and give you little loving nibbles.'

I wasn't sure if this was a joke or not. He was staring at big shadowy pictures like photo negatives.

'What are those pictures?' I asked.

'They're pictures of you, Elsie – your poorly knee,' he said.

'Don't keep asking Sir David questions, Elsie,' said Nurse Patterson, giving me a little shake.

'No, no, I like the children to take an intelligent interest.' Sir David slid the pictures back in their big paper envelopes and beckoned to me. 'Come here, dear. I need to measure you.'

He very carefully measured round each of my thighs. I thought he must be making a mistake.

'It's my *knee* that's bad, Doctor,' I said, trying to be helpful.

'Sir David's not a *doctor*, he's a consultant,' Nurse Patterson hissed. 'And believe you me, he knows what he's doing.'

Sir David smiled. 'I'm glad you have such faith in me, Nurse, but certainly in this case I *do* know. I'm measuring your thighs, Elsie, because the muscles have wasted a little on your affected leg. And see here . . .' He touched my knee gently. 'See how it's swollen? But we've caught you early. Lots of rest and plenty of fresh air and you'll be a new young woman.' He pulled my ponytail. 'Pop back into bed, then you can wheel her away, Nurse.'

'So, will I get better?' I asked.

'Yes, you will, so long as you do as you're told,' Sir David said solemnly.

I whisked back under the covers. 'Does everyone get better if they rest in hospital?' I asked.

'That's what we hope.'

'Even old people with TB in their lungs?'

'Elsie!' said Nurse Patterson.

'Ah. That depends on the severity of the disease,' said Sir David.

I drooped. Nan was coughing up blood, and I knew that was severe. I felt my own throat grow tight and my eyes prickled. I managed to hold it in until I was back on the veranda, but then I couldn't stop the tears dribbling down my face.

'What's up?' said Martin. 'Have you been to see Sir David?'

I nodded, knuckling my eyes.

'Is he going to put you in a spinal frame like mine?'

'No, I'm not being put in any frame,' I said, sniffing.

'Yes you are, you poor sap. You've got TB, haven't you?'

'I haven't got *bad* TB. He said I'm going to get better,' I said.

'He says that to everyone, Gobface. He said it to my friend Robert, and look what happened to him,' said Martin.

'You shut up,' I said, and turned on my stomach to cry properly.

'Cry-baby! Well, make the most of it. You won't be able to wriggle about like that tomorrow,' said Martin. 'You'll be a prisoner too.'

'No I won't,' I said, and I buried my head in the pillow. I shut my eyes tight and tried to will myself far away, to be with Nan in her sanatorium. I rubbed her chest with magic ointment and spooned special medicine down her throat, and there she was, my nan, her old self again, so we could scurry back to our flat and get our old lives back.

I cried and cried because I knew this wasn't possible, no matter how hard I pretended. And then I cried some more, because I didn't know what else to do. Martin and Gillian and all the others were still there, and sooner or later I'd have to poke my head up and see them laughing at me and pointing and calling me a cry-baby.

At last I *had* to heave myself up to find a

hankie, because my nose was running so badly.

'Have you finished now?' said Martin matter-of-factly – and when my search for a hankie proved hopeless, Gillian told me to lean right over Martin and she'd lend me hers. I couldn't believe they were letting me off so lightly. At school, crying was the worst thing in the world – something you never ever did if you could help it because you'd get teased so badly.

'I wasn't crying just because of the TB,' I said, snuffling into Gillian's hankie. 'I was crying because of my nan.'

'Everyone cries sometimes,' she said.

'I cry lots and lots and lots,' said little Michael.

'I don't ever cry,' said Martin.

'You're a liar, Farty Marty,' said Gillian. I was sitting up so she raised her eyebrows at me. 'Boys!' she added witheringly.

'Yes, *boys*!' I replied, delighted.

I saw Queenie in the distance, trotting purposefully over the lawn towards a foolish little group of sparrows pecking for food. I imagined her tossing her head too and mewing, 'Boys!'

'Here, Queenie! Come here, Queenie girl,' I called, making little tutting noises with my tongue.

'She's not a *dog*, silly,' said Martin, straining up onto his elbows. 'She won't come to you – especially as she's about to have a massive helping of sparrow pie.'

'She doesn't eat *birds*,' I said uncertainly.

I couldn't imagine anyone as regal and white and fluffy munching on beaks and claws. Queenie surely dined on saucers of cream and lightly cooked fillet of sole. But then she made a sudden dash and pounced, though luckily the birds flew away before she could catch them. She tossed her head and pawed at the grass, tail in the air, pretending she couldn't care less.

'Come here, Queenie! Come on!' I called.

'You'd better start cheeping and flapping your arms – then she'll get interested,' said Martin. He started sliding back down, and then gave a little yelp. 'Hey, look. *Look!*'

'What?' said Gillian.

'Nurse Curtis has left the sweetie box on the steps at the back of the veranda!' Martin gasped.

'So?' said Gillian. 'Are you planning to hop out of bed and run and help yourself?'

'Oh, ha ha. We can't – but *she* can!' said Martin, nodding at me.

Gillian peered over at the distant sweetie box, then at me. She looked at the Timex watch on her wrist. 'Go on, then – but you'll have to be quick!'

They were all looking at me, the little ones giggling fearfully. My heart started thudding.

'But I'm not allowed!' I said pathetically.

'*I'd* go, if I wasn't strung up here,' said Martin. 'Go *on*, Gobface.'

I thought of Nurse Patterson. She'd be so cross if she discovered me out of bed. It wouldn't be a matter of jumping out and dashing back. The sweetie box was so far away I had to blink hard to keep it in focus. It would take a minute or more to get all the way to the steps, then another minute back. It was too risky. Nurse Patterson and Nurse Curtis had been gone a while. They might come back any minute – *this* minute.

'I don't want to,' I said.

'You little cowardy custard,' said Martin in disgust.

'You can call me any stupid names you want. I don't care,' I said.

Why should I take such a risk for Martin? He was my enemy. He'd done nothing but torment me since I got here.

But then Gillian started chanting 'Cowardy custard!' too, then Rita, then the little ones—

'Oh, shut *up*. I'm *not* a coward. OK, *watch*!'

I sat up and swung my legs out of bed. I stood up gingerly. My head felt a bit swimmy and my whole leg ached after Sir David's manipulations. I clenched my fists and ran, even so, while they all gave a little whoop as they watched me.

I staggered down the length of the veranda, the

stone floor cold and hard under my bare feet. I got to the end of the beds, ran on and on, reached the steps at last, gasping for breath, and crouched down by the sweetie box.

'Bring it back *here*!' Martin called. 'Give us each a sweetie!'

I knew that was far too risky. It would take for ever, and then I'd have to take the box all the way back. I'd almost certainly be caught. I whipped the lid off the box, grabbed two great handfuls of sweets, pushed the lid back in place with my knuckles, and then ran for it. I got back to my bed and jumped in – just as Nurse Patterson and Nurse Curtis came marching back.

I quickly put my hands under the covers and lay back, my feet stinging.

'What's going on?' asked Nurse Patterson, looking at our flushed faces. 'Come on, why do you all look so furtive?'

Babette and Maureen giggled nervously. The others stayed silent, but they couldn't help glancing at me.

Nurse Patterson narrowed her eyes. 'What have you been up to, Elsie Kettle?'

'She hasn't been up to anything, Nurse Patterson. She's – she's just been singing to us, because we're so bored,' said Martin.

'Well, you can stop that at once, Elsie,' Nurse Patterson snapped. 'This is a hospital ward, not a music hall. You're supposed to lie back in your bed and *rest*. That's the only cure for your condition – enforced, uninterrupted and prolonged *rest*.'

'Still, it must be boring for the poor kiddies,' said Nurse Curtis. 'So you sing, do you, Elsie? Perhaps you can give us one little verse? No more – Nurse Patterson's quite right – but it would be a treat to hear you just for two minutes.'

Nurse Patterson sighed irritably but planted herself at the foot of my bed, arms folded. 'Go on then,' she said.

I was stuck. I could only think of the uncle's very rude song, and I wasn't stupid enough to sing that.

They were all looking at me expectantly. I thought of all the songs I'd heard on the wireless but couldn't remember more than the first lines of any of them. Then I had a sudden painfully sweet memory of Nan singing hymns as she swept the carpet and dusted all her china lady ornaments, gesturing in both corners with her duster as she got to the end of the verse.

'Jesus bids us shine,
With a pure, clear light,
Like a little candle,
Burning in the night.

In this world is darkness,
So let us shine –
You in your small corner,
And I in mine!'

'Oh, lovely!' said Nurse Curtis, clapping.

Nurse Patterson nodded at me grudgingly. 'That's nicely sung, Elsie – but that'll do for today. Now let's get cracking on injections, Curtis.'

They pulled down the blankets one by one and examined each child's splint and brace and plaster to check they weren't rubbing their flesh raw. I didn't have any so my blanket stayed tucked under my chin – thank goodness, because I still had two fistfuls of stolen sweeties.

I had to wait a long time for Nurse Patterson and Nurse Curtis to go again. At long last they bustled off together, so I sat up and passed the sweets both ways until every child had one. Even Angus in his plaster bed moved his hand and hastily popped his sweet in his mouth. For a while we lay still, sucking contentedly.

Martin swallowed. 'I suppose you're OK really, Gobface – for a girl.'

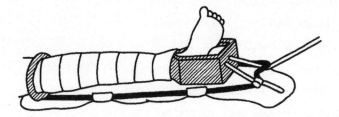

12

They came for me the next morning. They took me through the ward, down all the corridors, and I tried to tell myself that I was simply going to visit kind Sir David again – but they wheeled me right past his consulting room.

'Where are you taking me?' I asked.

Nurse Patterson looked purposeful, Nurse Curtis upset.

'Don't you fret yourself, Elsie. We're going to make you better,' said Nurse Curtis.

'But I *am* better. I'm not like the others,' I gabbled. 'I've just got a little limp and I don't mind it one bit.'

'You have a tubercular knee,' said Nurse Patterson, pushing so fast she was out of breath. 'If you leave it, all your bones will be eaten away and you'll lose the use of your leg.'

That shut me up. I started crying.

'None of the waterworks, now,' she said. 'You'll be as right as rain if you keep still inside your splint.'

'I don't *want* a splint!' I wailed, crying harder.

'Don't cry, darling,' said Nurse Curtis. 'It won't hurt. It'll just be a bit strange and uncomfy, that's all.'

'Please please please, don't do it to me. I'll stay in bed, I won't move a muscle, but don't tie me up in one of those awful things,' I said.

Nurse Patterson and Nurse Curtis took no notice. I saw a door right at the end, with TREATMENT ROOM in large red letters. It could just as well have been labelled THE MOUTH OF HELL.

I hunched up into a ball, tensing every muscle, and then tried to leap for freedom, but Nurse Patterson was too quick for me. She grabbed me by the shoulders and wrestled me back onto the bed.

'Oh no, you don't! You stay put, you naughty girl! Do you want to be tied up?' She held onto me firmly while Nurse Curtis pulled my bed forward – through the dreaded doors of the treatment room.

It was like a torture chamber, with splints and frames and leather belts and buckles laid out in chilling rows on shelves, but the man presiding over this terrifying equipment was rosy-cheeked and smiley, wearing a brown cotton coat that looked comfortingly ordinary amongst the starched white aprons of the nurses.

'Hello hello hello,' he said, like a comic policeman. 'And who have we here?'

'We've got Elsie Kettle, and she's a right handful,' said Nurse Patterson.

'She's just frightened, that's all,' Nurse Curtis explained.

'No need to be frightened of me, little buttercup,' he said. 'I'm Mr Dobbin. How do you do, Miss Kettle?'

I swallowed hard, barely able to talk normally. 'How do you do?' I whispered.

'Now, these kind, strong-armed nurses are going to lift you up and onto my special table here, and then we're going to sort that old knee out for you,' said Mr Dobbin.

'I don't want a splint,' I squealed.

'Of course you don't. But this isn't just any old splint, my dear. This . . .' He whipped a horrid contraption down from one of his shelves. 'This is a Thomas's knee bed splint, a very fine and aristocratic splint designed by Mr Hugh Owen Thomas of

Liverpool, who is the father of orthopaedic surgery. This wondrous little splint is going to sort your knee out for ever, so don't shrink away from it. Give it a little pat and say hello.'

I reached out fearfully and plucked at the leather ring at the top. 'Hello,' I whispered, and then I couldn't help giggling because I felt so ridiculous.

'Now, this particular Thomas's knee bed splint is simply longing to clasp you gently round your leg, but *first* we have to prepare you. Is this a clean leg, Nurses? Shall we give it another rub and scrub just to make sure?'

They washed my leg carefully and spent ages towelling it dry, patting my spongy knee very gently indeed. They put soft wool around my leg, and then Mr Dobbin stretched my knee out just so, and slipped the bed splint into place. The leather ring felt odd and the splints were strange, but it didn't actually hurt. They bandaged it all into place, and lifted me even more carefully back onto my bed.

'There now – is that comfy, Miss Kettle?' asked Mr Dobbin.

'I – I think so,' I said. I tried to wriggle. 'But I can't move it!'

'Exactly! That is the point. You must rest it absolutely. Rest all of that little body, Miss Kettle. But if you get restless' – he tapped my forehead – 'go for a run inside your head. Hop and skip and dance in your dreams. And *one* day you'll be able to do just that, in real life. Then you'll be able to kiss your Thomas's knee bed splint goodbye.'

I nodded solemnly, because I was good at making things up in my head. In fact it seemed to be the only thing I was any good at. But when I was wheeled back to the others, as trussed up and helpless as they were, it was hard to hang onto this.

'So you're a prisoner now too,' said Martin.

I closed my eyes and tried to clamber right up inside my head – but my leg was still tied up and I couldn't move. I kept my eyes squeezed shut but the tears started seeping out.

No one remarked on this, but after five minutes Gillian called, 'Here, Gobface, my secret supply' – and a sweet landed lightly on my chest. It was an orange cough candy, a medicinally flavoured sweet that I usually avoided like the plague, but I unwrapped it and sucked gratefully.

'That's not fair! I want one too,' said Martin.

'Oh, shut up,' snapped Gillian.

Surprisingly, he did. I lay still, breathing cough candy fumes, while my leg throbbed in its new prison. I couldn't move it at all, not even an inch either way. I thought of not being able to move day after day, week after week, month after month. Then I thought of poor darling Nan in a similar prison of her own flesh, and that made me start howling again.

Something poked me in the ribs. It was a folded-up *Eagle* comic.

'I don't mind if you have a read,' said Martin.

I gulped and nodded at him, and then opened up the comic. My eyes were too blurry with tears to read, but I blinked at the pictures. And then, out of nowhere, Queenie leaped up onto my bed. She padded up to me, delicately avoiding the bulk of my splint. She poked her head right up under the *Eagle*, trampled it out of the way, and curled up on my chest. She lay on me, her soft head under my chin, warm and sweet and beautiful. I stroked her very gently and she started purring. I stroked a little more firmly and her purrs grew louder in appreciation.

'Oh Queenie,' I whispered.

I had tucked the shiny yellow wrapper from a chocolate toffee under my pillow. I flattened it out of its goblet shape and tried to fashion it into a tiny crown. 'I hereby declare you Queen Queenie, Queen of all the Cats,' I whispered, balancing it on her white head.

She gazed at me with her beautiful big eyes, green as gooseberries. Then she bent her head and batted the wrapper away with one quick paw, telling me she didn't need a tacky paper crown to show her status.

I was scared she'd jump off the bed again, but she turned round and snuggled back, seeming to sense how much I needed her.

I wondered if they had cats in all hospitals. I hadn't seen so much as a whisker of one in Nan's grim ward, but perhaps they'd simply been hiding. I tried to will a cat up onto Nan's bed. I was sure she'd like it if it cuddled up close on her poorly chest.

I paid more attention to the story when Nurse Patterson read aloud to us after supper. I was getting the hang of the plot now. The children climbed up the magic tree, then up a little ladder right at the very top, and stepped through the clouds into a different land. I knew which land I was after. The Land Where Dreams Came True – and Nan and I would be together, living in our own cosy cottage. It wouldn't even matter if she was still very poorly. My land would have a special magic bed, and if Nan couldn't struggle out of it, I'd wheel her around. She'd looked after me when I was little, feeding me and washing me and dressing me, so I didn't mind taking my turn looking after Nan. We'd live in our cottage all by ourselves. Perhaps Mum might be allowed to visit occasionally, or maybe Laura could come to tea, but no one else. We'd have our very own pets. Queenie would leap up that ladder and stay with us.

I'd cook cheesy beanos and make perfect cups of

tea for Nan, and saucers of creamy milk for Queenie, and we'd have a big tin of sweeties all to ourselves. I'd wear my cat pyjamas every night, and I'd have a satin party frock for every day of the week with a fluffy angora bolero to match – pink, blue, primrose, lilac, mint green, apricot, and white on Sundays. And I'd never ever wear boy's shoes. I'd have pretty little patent shoes. I might even have *high heels*.

I went on telling my story to myself long after Nurse Patterson had finished her chapter, but then I was jerked rudely back into the real world by the terrible bedpan routine. It was so uncomfortable and embarrassing that I couldn't go for ages, and then, when I did, I was so heavy and lopsided now that my bottom tilted and the bedpan spilled.

'Oh you clumsy clot!' said Nurse Patterson, sighing heavily. She didn't really tell me off, just snorted a lot through her nostrils as she and Nurse Curtis struggled to change my sheets with me still in the bed, my leg immobile. Then at last they left me in peace. I tried to go back to my story, but Martin and Gillian and Rita kept whispering. I didn't feel like joining in this time.

'Gobface? Have you gone deaf or something?' Martin hissed.

'Leave her alone,' said Gillian. 'I expect she feels

fed up. I know *I* am. So pipe down, you two, and let us all have a bit of kip.'

They all seemed to go to sleep quite quickly, though I thought I heard sniffling right at the end, where Angus lay in his terrible plaster bed.

I lay staring up at the ceiling with ugly Donald Duck tucked in beside me. My leg started throbbing and itching and jumping because I so badly wanted to wriggle around and I couldn't. I always went to sleep curled up on my side, but that was impossible now. *Everything* seemed impossible.

I longed for Queenie to come back, but she was still outside, prowling in the twilight, moon-white in the shadows. Then I heard footsteps squeaking on the polished floor. Nurse Patterson and Nurse Curtis were going home, and – oh glory! Nurse Gabriel and Nurse Johnson were coming on night duty.

I hoped Nurse Gabriel would come straight over to me. She stopped right in front of my bed, but then Angus sniffled again and she went over to *him* instead. I was so disappointed I started crying again, forcing the tears a little, and making sad hiccupping sounds to be sure Nurse Gabriel heard – but she *still* didn't come.

I got Nurse Johnson instead, widdle-waddling over to my bed and bending over me with a strange squeaky sound.

'Are you having a little weep, Elsie?' She shone her torch in my face. 'Oh dear, yes. Let's mop those poor old eyes. I see you've got your splint on. It's not hurting you, is it?'

'*Yes*,' I said furiously.

'Where is it rubbing, pet?'

'*Everywhere.*'

'Hmm.' She pulled my covers down and very gently touched my leg, her fat fingers scrabbling about the bandages. 'I think it's all nicely wrapped up like a baby in a blanket. I don't think it's *really* sore, Elsie.'

'It is, it is,' I insisted. 'Please, take it *off*.'

'I can't do that, dear. It's got to stay on. It will help you heal.'

'It's awful. It's *torture*,' I declared dramatically.

'Now you're just being silly. And keep your voice down – you don't want to wake the others,' she said. She reached down for Donald Duck. I'd flung him out of bed in fury. 'Now then, let's cuddle you down with Donald.'

'I don't want Donald Dribbly Duck! I don't *like* him. I want my own elephant and my cat pyjamas and my leg back,' I sobbed.

'Oh dear, we *are* down in the dumps,' she said. 'I do understand. I know your leg feels a bit strange at first, but you'll get used to it.'

'No I won't! How can you understand? *You* don't

have a horrible splint,' I said, trying to wriggle away as she blew my nose.

'I've got *worse*,' said Nurse Johnson. 'Here, take a deck at these.'

She shone her torch on her own skirt and lifted the hem above her knees. She was wearing long knickers, the old-lady kind that Nan wore, but these seemed to be made of plastic. She moved her legs and they made that strange squeaky sound. I blinked at her, baffled.

'They're Stephanie Beaumans!' she said, plucking at them with distaste.

'They're . . . Stephanie Someone's?' I said, astonished that she was wearing someone else's weird rubbery bloomers.

'No, that's the *make*, silly,' said Nurse Johnson, giggling. 'Oh, you kids, you're so funny sometimes. No, look, I'm showing you because it's so uncomfortable wearing these shockers all day long – *much* worse than a splint, I reckon.'

'But *why* are you wearing them?' I asked, and then I felt myself blushing, because I suddenly wondered if they were acting as a kind of nappy.

'They're for my hips,' she said. 'They're special Stephanie Beauman slimming knickers. You wear them and they make you go hot inside and the inches melt away – at least, that's what the adverts say, and I jolly well hope it's true because they cost a fortune.

So, we're suffering together, you and me.' She gently pinched my nose and then waddled away, squeaking.

I stared after her, momentarily diverted. I wondered what would happen if she wore Stephanie Beaumans on her arms and legs too, or if she wore an entire Stephanie Beauman all-over suit like a space-man's. Would she be the incredible shrinking nurse, getting smaller and smaller every day, until she scurried around at ankle height like a mouse, still squeaking?

I couldn't help getting the giggles at the thought – and Nurse Gabriel came over at long last.

'Are you *laughing*, Elsie?' she whispered, smoothing my hair back off my forehead.

'Just a bit. I thought of something funny,' I said. I'd decided to be very cool and stand-offish as she'd chosen to go to Angus first and not me, but it was impossible now that she was beside me. I breathed in her soft sweet smell of soap and talcum powder and longed for her to cuddle me properly.

'You're being very brave,' she said.

'Not really,' I mumbled, because I'd been making an awful fuss all afternoon and half the evening.

She fiddled with Donald Duck, trying to get him to snuggle down with me.

'I don't like him much,' I said.

'Mm, I can see why. He's got a very odd expression.

Oh well, I think you'll probably get your own teddy back tomorrow.'

'He's not a teddy, he's an elephant – Albert Trunk,' I said.

'Ah yes, how could I forget? Then you can give Donald Duck here back to Potter Ward, where he belongs.'

I craned upwards a little, trying to look along the line of beds. 'Have any of the others got teddies or elephants?' I whispered.

I was very worried that Martin and Gillian might jeer at Albert Trunk.

'I think they've *all* got a soft toy somewhere or other,' said Nurse Gabriel.

'I haven't seen them!'

'Well, they're mostly nocturnal. Do you know what that means? They only come out at night.'

'Nurse Gabriel, has *Martin* got a teddy?' I asked.

'Ah, you'll have to ask him. I can't give away any-one's secrets,' said Nurse Gabriel loudly, in case Martin was still awake – but she nodded at me.

'Not *Gillian*?' I asked, because she seemed practically grown up, but Nurse Gabriel nodded again.

I peered down the row of beds. 'I can't see them,' I said.

Nurse Gabriel picked up my blanket and pointed

underneath, indicating that they were tucked inside, out of sight.

I heard Angus sniff again. 'And Angus?'

'Yes – although poor Angus can't really cuddle his teddy properly,' said Nurse Gabriel.

'Why is he in all that plaster?'

'It's to help his back straighten.'

'Does it hurt him?'

'I don't think it hurts too much physically, but he feels very unhappy about it.'

'He doesn't talk to any of us.'

'That's because he's feeling sad.'

'But he was talking to you, wasn't he?'

'We have special little chats, yes. Poor old Angus,' said Nurse Gabriel.

'Is he your favourite?'

Nurse Gabriel laughed. 'Nurses aren't allowed to have favourites, Elsie.'

I wasn't sure that was true. I was determined that *I* was going to be Nurse Gabriel's favourite.

13

I seemed to have been marooned in the hospital for many years. It was hard remembering that only a few days had gone by. I had almost stopped thinking about Mum. I never stopped thinking about Nan, of course.

Saturday seemed a very different day. It started with a much better breakfast: a fried egg and a rasher of bacon and two slices of toast.

There was no school on Saturday morning. After being wheeled out onto the veranda we were handed old comics and puzzle books. I was given a join-the-dot book of animals. Someone – many someones – had already joined the dots, but their efforts had been rubbed out until the paper had become fuzzy. I only had a stump of pencil to make the animals spring to life again, but I dutifully joined dot after dot after dot, and created an elephant and a giraffe and a monkey and a variety of big cats – a stripy tiger, a spotted leopard, and a lion. I drew a little cat on the end paper, with a tiny crown on her head. The writing underneath the lion said he was *King of the Beasts*. I wrote under my cat that she was *Queen of the Beasts*.

Queenie herself prowled from bed to bed. Martin tried to entice her by offering her a crust of toast, but she ignored him disdainfully and jumped up on *my* bed instead.

'Oh Queenie, you lovely cat! You like me, don't you?' I whispered, stroking her. She purred back that she liked me very much.

Then, after breakfast, just to make the day more special, Nurse Curtis came bustling along the veranda. She was carrying a large brown paper bag.

'Here's a parcel for a Miss Elsie Kettle,' she said, dropping it carefully onto my chest.

I opened it up – and there was Albert Trunk rearing up at me with desperate happiness.

'Oh, my Albert,' I said, so overcome I buried my face in his soft grey skin right in front of Martin and Gillian. But then I pushed him away, my nose wrinkling, because he smelled so *wrong* – dry and dead and chemical, and his skin was pale and dull as if he'd been very ill too.

'What's *happened* to him?' I said, holding him at arm's length.

'Nothing's happened. He's just been fumigated so he's not all nasty and germy,' said Nurse Johnson. She waggled Albert's trunk in a very familiar fashion. 'You're fine, aren't you, Jumbo?'

Albert Trunk gazed back dumbly, his small glass eyes bleary, as if they were full of tears. I tucked him down under my covers, wrapping the hem of my hospital gown around him. I wouldn't need it now because my new cat pyjamas were in the parcel too, though they didn't look new any more. They looked as if they'd been swirled in Nan's wooden washtub a hundred times, though they didn't smell *clean*. They had that same harsh chemical smell as Albert. But they still had their little white cats prancing on the pink material, and Nurse Johnson exclaimed at them too.

'Aren't they nobby!' she said. 'You really will look like the cat's pyjamas in them, Elsie! Shall I dress you in them?'

I could only wear the jacket now because the trousers wouldn't fit over my huge ugly splint. I pulled off the hospital gown and rolled the pyjama trousers round Albert Trunk instead.

'What else have you got in there?' said Nurse Johnson, shaking the big bag curiously.

I took out my *Girl* comic, and then Nan's kitten button box. I picked up Snow White and Sooty and Marmalade, all their buttons slithering and sliding inside the box.

Martin stuck his head up, peering hopefully. 'Is that all your money?' he said. 'You must have heaps!'

'I've got a piggy bank at home and it's so full it won't even rattle any more,' said Gillian.

'So have I,' said Rita immediately.

'Oh dear, you're not allowed to keep money on the ward, Elsie. You'd better give your money box to me for safe-keeping,' said Nurse Johnson, reaching out for my kittens.

'No! It isn't money – honestly. It's buttons,' I insisted, taking off the lid and showing her.

'*Buttons!*' Martin gurgled, and Gillian and Rita sniggered.

'What do you want all these buttons for?' asked Nurse Johnson.

'I collect them,' I said grandly.

I took out my last treasure – and this time the

other children were impressed. It was my little Coronation coach with its eight tiny horses. I worried that it might have got chipped or spoiled, but it was still perfect, the gold untarnished, and it smelled of its own special metallic tang.

'Oh look, she's got one of those Coronation coaches! You lucky thing, Elsie – *I* wanted one of them!' said Gillian. 'Let's have a proper look at it, Elsie, go on.'

I didn't want to relinquish it but I liked impressing Gillian. I leaned over as far as I could to pass my coach to Martin. 'Show Gillian,' I said.

Nurse Curtis had turned away to attend to the little ones, but now she came dashing back. 'Careful!' she said. 'You *mustn't* lean over like that! It's strictly forbidden. You could fall out and do yourself serious damage and waste all the good work of being in your splint.'

I'd only been in mine for a day, so it hadn't had a chance to do any good work yet, but I wriggled back meekly.

'Please could you show my Coronation coach to Gillian, Nurse Curtis?' I asked politely.

'That's better,' she said, picking it up. 'Oh, isn't it dinky? The detail!'

'Let me see it too!' said Martin. 'Is it just like the *real* Coronation coach?'

'It's an exact replica, but in miniature of course,'

I said proudly. 'My nan bought it for me. We were going to the Coronation together . . .' My voice suddenly wobbled.

'I was going too. My dad works up in London – he was going to take me,' said Gillian.

'I was going too,' said Rita.

There was an echoing wail up and down the beds.

'Now then, now then!' said Nurse Curtis. 'Don't get too upset. Maybe you won't miss the Coronation after all.'

'Nonsense, Curtis!' Nurse Patterson called, her sticky-out ears wagging. 'Come and help me with the injections and stop your nonsense.'

'Oooh!' said Nurse Curtis, pulling a face at us. She gave me my coach back and hurried off to Nurse Patterson.

'What do you think she was on about?' said Martin.

'Oh, she was just babbling,' said Gillian, tossing her ponytail. 'How on earth can we get to the Coronation?'

'Won't we be better by then?' I asked.

'Fat chance! We won't be better for months. You won't be better till next year at the earliest. *I'll* be better first, because I've been here for eight months already,' said Martin.

'Eight months!' I was so appalled I could barely breathe. '*I* won't be stuck here for eight months, will I?'

'Of course you will, stupid. Like everyone else,' he said. 'Don't you know *anything*?'

This new knowledge hurt even more than my streptomycin injection to cure my TB. It was so painful it made my eyes sting. The little ones, Michael and Maureen and Babette, all cried bitterly. Poor Michael went on sobbing, even though Nurse Curtis gave him a cuddle.

'Couldn't he have a sweetie out of the box?' I asked.

'You only have sweeties after lunch,' said Nurse Patterson, clicking her teeth.

'But he needs it *now*,' I said.

'Just you stop answering back and behave, Elsie Kettle, or you won't get any sweeties at all! You're a very greedy little girl,' said Nurse Patterson.

I thought this was very unfair of her as I hadn't been asking for a sweet for myself. I pulled a face at her when she turned her back, and Martin and Gillian laughed.

I lay with Albert Trunk under my armpit, stroking my button box kittens, with my little Coronation coach clutched in my other hand. My nose still prickled with the chemical smell, but I did my best to breathe shallowly.

Lunch was surprisingly good: two sausages and peas and a little mound of fluffy white potato, looking like a scoop of ice cream.

'Why is the food so much nicer today?' I asked, licking my forkful of potato.

'Because it's visiting day, silly. My mother and father always say, "What did you have to eat today, Martin?" You wait – your parents will say the same.'

'They won't,' I mumbled.

Mother and *father*. They sounded like people out of those reading books in the Infants. I hadn't properly realized before that Martin was posh, even though he told very rude jokes and called me Gobface.

I didn't think Gillian was posh, not when she wore her hair in a glorious ponytail like a teddy girl. I wondered if her mum had a ponytail too. I did hope so. I was sure she'd be pretty, like her daughter.

Wait till they saw *my* mum. If she came. She'd *said* she'd come and see how I was doing on Saturday, but I'd long ago learned not to trust my mum too much. She'd promised to come and watch me in the school play, and then in the carol concert, but she'd never turned up for either. I didn't really mind because Nan came instead.

Nan – oh, Nan. I wanted to bury my face in my pillow and weep, but my hateful splint made me lie flat on my back. But perhaps . . . perhaps Nan was better now?

I shut my eyes and willed her to sit up and look around and take notice. I made her poor lungs fill

with fresh air. I helped her slide her skinny legs out
of her hospital sheets. She stood up and stretched and
made the little soft smacking sounds with her lips as
she always did when she got up. She had her quick
lick-and-a-promise wash and then dressed herself:
shiny pink knickers down to her knees, with her
flappy vest tucked inside. I let her off her corset
because it was always such a struggle for her to get
into it. She kept her stockings up with garters, and
put on her best black dress with the little beady
pattern across the bust. I always got little indent-
ations across my cheek when I gave her a hug in that
dress, but I knew it was her favourite.

I made her walk right out of the sanatorium and
get the train and the bus over to me. I urged her along
every step of the way. I encouraged her up the driveway, round to the annexe, down that long polished
corridor, looking to left and right – looking for *me*. I
had her burst through the French windows, and there
she was, running in her best black shoes with the
buckles, calling 'Elsie, Elsie, Elsie!'

I heard her, I saw her, I felt her arms go round me
and hug me tight – but she wasn't *really* there. Real
people started arriving, making so much hubbub that
it was impossible to keep pretending. I hunched down
in bed, staring at everyone. Martin's mum and dad
were *very* posh, though his mum wasn't dressed up at

all. She was wearing a faded cotton dress with a drooping hem. She went kissy-kissy-kissy all over Martin's face. It was fun to see him squirming.

Gillian's mum was a disappointment too. She had very short hair, almost like a boy, and she wore slacks, very tight check ones. Michael's mum wore a skirt, but it was a very long swirly one, and she wore thick lisle stockings. Everyone had a mum to visit them, and most people had dads too. Angus's mum spoke with a Scottish accent, and seemed so old I wondered if she might be a granny instead. She looked very grey and lined, and I think she was crying, because she kept dabbing at her eyes with a handkerchief.

I kept looking up every time I heard footsteps, but the person was never Nan, never Mum. Then I saw Queenie sidling along in the shadows, head down, irritated by the noise and bustle.

'Here, Queenie. Come here, Queenie, *please*,' I called, clicking with my tongue in what I hoped was cat language. I held out my hand, dangling it over the side of the bed, and she came bobbing up and pushed her beautiful white furry head against my palm, wriggling and purring.

'Dear Queenie!' I said. 'Here, girl, jump up now. Come and see me.'

I patted my bed with my free hand and made

further encouraging noises. Queenie hesitated, turning this way and that, thinking about it. She looked around, seeing if any small snack were scuttling through the grass or flying about the trees – and then decided that she wasn't really hungry yet.

She looked up at me, tensed her haunches, and then leaped neatly onto my bed, landing softly on my pillow right next to my head.

'Oh Queenie!' I breathed.

She settled herself, leaned forward, and gave my face one lick with her raspy pink tongue.

'Oh Elsie!' she said. Well, she didn't actually *say* it with her little mouth, but I knew that was what she was thinking. 'I've come to visit you. How are you feeling today, dear? I'm sure your poor leg is very sore stuck inside that terrible splint. I would so hate to wear one and not be able to wriggle and stretch. You have my every sympathy.'

She flopped gently against me, and the moment I started stroking her she purred.

'There now,' she said. 'Oh, that's delightful, dear. I am becoming particularly fond of you. I shall visit you every day, not just at visiting times. I shall be your cat and you shall be my girl.'

'Oh Queenie, I do love you,' I whispered.

Martin's dad was looking at us. He had very bushy eyebrows and a moustache. His general hairiness made him look rather fierce, but he smiled when he saw Queenie and me. 'Look at that new little girl. She's really got a way with cats,' he said to his wife.

A way with cats! Oh, I did, I did! Snow White and Sooty and Marmalade jumped off their box and came tumbling beside us too. Queenie put up a paw to show them that she was the boss, but then let them lie beside her, curled up against this beautiful mother figure. They started purring too, kneading their tiny paws against her.

I closed my eyes and started breathing in time with their great cat chorus, inhaling deeply, trying to purr myself.

'Elsie! Are you asleep? Why are you making that weird noise? What's the matter?' It was Mum, here at last, bending over me so her hair tickled my face.

'Oh Mum,' I said. Then I craned my neck. 'Is Nan here?'

'No, of course not. What's up with you? Don't you remember Nanny's in hospital too? Dear God, I'm going demented visiting the pair of you.'

'She's still not better?' I asked.

'Well, of course not. You saw her, Elsie. She can barely speak, it's just cough cough cough. It's very upsetting seeing her in that condition. It upsets her too, and just makes her cough worse. I don't think it's good for her, having visitors.'

'But she'll be feeling so lonely! Oh Mum, can't *I* visit her, in a wheelchair or something?'

'Don't be soft, Elsie. How are you going to get a wheelchair on a blooming bus? And anyway, you're on bed rest now, they told me. So let's see this leg of yours.' She batted at Queenie. 'Come on – out of it, moggy.'

'Don't, Mum! That's *Queenie*,' I said.

Queenie stood up on her four paws, quivering with outrage at being called a moggy.

'Don't go, Queenie,' I said, trying to keep hold of her, but she wriggled out of my grasp and leaped off the bed. Snow White and Sooty and Marmalade tumbled off after her, landing in a squirmy heap. 'Oh Mum, she came and sat on my bed specially!'

'I don't know why they let cats lollop all over the place – it's not hygienic. You'll get fleas if you don't watch out. Oh my God!' Mum had uncovered my splint. 'What have you got this contraption on for? Just look at it! It's like you're a cripple – but you only had a little limp and I'm sure you were putting it on half the time. Isn't it *sore*?'

'It is – it's horrible. I can't move it at all – look,' I said, hoping for sympathy. 'And it rubs at the top of my leg.'

The nurses inspected it every four hours to make sure it wasn't rubbing too much, but I wanted Mum to feel sorry for me.

She shuddered and covered my leg up again. 'Sorry, dear, I've always been a bit squeamish. Poor little pet. Look, Mummy's brought you a present.' She fumbled in her bag and brought out a box of Rowntree's Fruit Gums and a large bar of Cadbury's Whole Nut.

'Oh Mum!' I was momentarily diverted. I'd only ever had a small tube of gums and a tuppenny bar of chocolate before.

'Go on, open the box and we'll scoff a few. And I'll snap you off a couple of squares of chocolate. Come on, you need to eat up. You're looking really peaky.'

'I don't think I'm allowed. We have to put all our stuff in the sweetie box and it gets shared out after lunch,' I said. 'I'd better not open them, Mum.'

'Don't be soft!' she said, ripping off both wrappers. 'They're just for you! I'm not spending a fortune on sweets to feed all them other kids. You eat up now. No one's going to stop you, not when I'm here.'

I peered around anxiously. 'Can I offer them to my friends, Mum?' I asked. I emphasized the word *friends* proudly. Martin was still sometimes an enemy too, but we seemed to have struck a truce at the moment. Gillian was always nice to me, and little Michael was everyone's friend.

'No you can't,' Mum snapped, glaring at the beds on either side of me. 'They've got their own. And they've all got fathers in work. I'm just on my own, providing for three. Well, two just now, I suppose.'

'*Three*. You, me and Nan,' I said.

'Oh Elsie. You saw the state she's in. I don't think poor Nanny's ever going to make it out of hospital,' said Mum, sniffing. She opened her handbag and dabbed her nose delicately with her powder puff. She dabbed my nose too to try to make me laugh, but I was too devastated to respond.

'She *must* get better, Mum. I can't live without my nan,' I declared.

'What? Come on now, you've still got me,' said Mum.

'She can't stay in hospital *for ever*,' I said.

'Well, if she recovers a bit, she might be able to go into a home,' said Mum. 'But I can't look after her, not with my job. I've started working with Mr Perkins already, Elsie. He was desperate. And we're getting along like a house on fire. I've taken to secretarial like a duck to water. I'm a bit slow on the typewriter and I can't always get the hang of the carbon copies — they get all crumpled — but he doesn't seem to mind. Of course, it's not the theatre, but beggars can't be choosers, and maybe I was flagging a bit when it came to chorus work. Most of the girls were still in their teens. I was like a mummy to half of them.' She paused. 'For goodness' sake, Elsie, buck up a bit. I've come all this way to see you. You might stop grizzling and sit up properly and give me a smile.'

'I *can't* sit up. I have to be propped,' I mumbled, knuckling my eyes. 'And I'm so worried about *Nan*.'

'Never mind Nan, you've got me now. I'm your mother. And I've changed my whole life round on your account so you might act a bit grateful, missy,' said Mum.

I sniffed and said nothing.

'Oh, sulking, are we? Look, I've got something else for you – lots of letters.'

'From Nan!' I said, wriggling upwards as best I could.

'*No*, silly – your nan can't write now. She's not well enough, is she? These are from all the kiddies in your class at school. I went in to tell that teacher of yours—'

'Miss Roberts! Oh, was she wearing her fluffy cardie, the blue one?'

'*I* don't know. I wasn't there to give her a clothes inspection. I just said you were very poorly and likely to be in hospital a while. I didn't say you actually had TB in case they thought it was catching. She seemed ever so upset. She must have told the kids because this came in the post next day.'

Mum fished out a whole sheaf of letters with illustrated margins and quite a few portraits of me wearing a nightie or pyjamas, my head lolling.

I leafed through them. Laura had sent me a special letter:

Dear Elsie,
I'm so sorry you're ill. I'm missing you. I do hope you get better soon.
Love from Laura
xxx

Kisses! And she'd drawn a picture of the two of us together, wearing pink ballet dresses. We were standing on our tippy toes, arms raised above our heads, doing a beautiful duet. She'd coloured it in very carefully too, pressing a little too hard, so that the dresses felt very smooth and shiny. I stroked them with one finger.

'This is from my *Friend* Laura,' I said. This time it was clear that she was a capital letter Friend.

They *all* seemed to be my friend. They must like me after all. There were letters from everyone, even Marilyn and Susan. They all said they were very sorry I was ill and they were missing me and they hoped I got better soon. They *all* said . . . The letters were practically identical. I suddenly realized that Miss Roberts must have chalked the letter up on the blackboard and told them all to copy it. They'd been free to draw their own pictures. I looked more closely at Marilyn's. She'd drawn herself with scribbles all round her head to represent hair and had given me two rat-tail plaits. We were standing together in a seemingly friendly way, but when I looked more closely I saw the Marilyn pin-girl was holding her smudge of a nose. She had written her own name in very tiny letters under the pin-girl. My name looked unfamiliar. I peered closely. She'd written two minute little words: *Frilly Bum.*

I stuffed the letters back in the big envelope – all but Laura's.

'Mum, can I write back to her? To my friend Laura?' I asked.

'If you really want to,' said Mum.

'Will you buy me the stuff – paper and envelopes and a pen and a stamp?' I asked.

'Oh, for heaven's sake! Shall I buy you a postman too, with his special sack?' said Mum. 'All right, all right!' She caught the eye of Martin's dad next door and raised her eyebrows and shook her head. He nodded back at her, looking mesmerized. I wondered if he'd wink at her too.

'Could you buy them for tomorrow, Mum? It's visiting again on Sunday, two till four,' I said.

'Oh dear goodness, I'll do my best – but I've got so much to catch up on at home. Nan's really let things slide the last few months. The flat is in a shocking state. What if I want to invite a visitor? I'm going to have to give it a good scrub from top to bottom.'

'Nan always kept it lovely,' I said indignantly.

'I'm not *blaming* Nan. I'm just saying it was clearly getting too much for her,' said Mum.

'I'm going to send a letter to Nan too,' I said, itching to start one right that moment.

'There's not much point, Elsie. She's not up to sitting up and reading stuff,' said Mum.

'Well, I could do lots of pictures for her. You could bring my crayons in for me,' I suggested.

'Hey, hey, stop giving me orders, young lady. Sit up just a bit. Let me look at you. Why have you got your hair dragged back like that?'

'I've got a ponytail. My friend Gillian showed me how to do it.'

'I see. Well, I know they're all the rage with teenagers, but you're just a little girl. Come here, I'll put it in plaits for you,' said Mum.

I wanted to keep my ponytail but I knew it was lopsided, and I liked Mum brushing my hair and twisting it neatly into plaits. She was good at it, even better than Nan, who couldn't always get her partings straight, so I ended up with one fat plait and one very thin one.

Mum kept pressing chocolate and fruit gums on

me so it was hard to talk with a sticky mouthful. *She* talked instead, telling me all about this Mr Perkins. She sounded so keen I wondered if he might become another uncle. But she also chatted to Martin's parents, particularly his father.

'It's such a strain, seeing your kiddy trussed up like this,' she said, shaking her head. 'And it's so far for me to come. I live right over Burlington way. I have to get the train and then that awful local bus that goes all round the moon, and you still have to walk miles. My feet are killing me.' She slipped a high-heeled shoe off and rubbed her slim white foot. Martin's mother frowned and looked at her own sensible fringed flatties, though she didn't comment.

Martin's father stared at Mum's foot. 'Perhaps we could give you a lift part of the way home in our car?' he suggested.

'To Burlington! We can't possibly go that far – and I thought you said we were low on petrol,' Martin's mother murmured.

Martin's father looked determined to give Mum a lift, even if he had to personally push his car every inch of the way.

'Oh, I wouldn't want to put you to any trouble,' said Mum.

He said it was no trouble at all, and could he at least drive her to the railway station? When this was agreed, he turned his attention back to Martin, making up mental arithmetic problems and getting him to shout out the answer. He even timed him with a stop watch, only giving him a minute.

'Why don't you join in too, Elsie – make a little game of it?' said Mum.

I thought this an appalling idea. I was nearly always bottom of the class at mental arithmetic. I shook my head firmly.

Martin didn't look as if he were enjoying the game either. His face went very red every time his dad barked '*Wrong!*' or '*Out of time!*'

Martin's mother objected softly, saying: 'Don't you think that's enough, dear? Martin's getting a bit tired now.'

'Nonsense!' said Martin's dad. 'He needs to keep his brain active. Just because his body's useless it doesn't mean his mind can go to sleep too. And it's *fun*, isn't it, Martin, old boy?'

'Yes,' said Martin, through gritted teeth.

Martin's mother was taking in that my male parent was missing. While there was an agonized wait for Martin to work out how much change he would get out of a pound note if he brought twelve Christmas cards at tuppence ha'penny and nine Christmas cards at a penny three farthing (extra time allowed), she leaned over towards *my* mother.

'Is your husband working today, dear?' she asked.

Mum flushed a little. I willed her to tell a quick lie – but she took a warped pride in telling the truth and disconcerting people. 'I haven't got a husband,' she said evenly.

'Oh!' said Martin's mother. 'Oh, I'm so sorry, dear!' She obviously jumped to the wrong conclusion. She lowered her voice to a sympathetic hiss. 'Did you lose him recently?'

Mum looked at me, then looked back at Martin's mother, arching her eyebrows. It was clear she was indicating that she didn't want to talk about it in front of me. Martin's mother nodded understandingly, and offered me one of Martin's Crunchie bars.

I was already feeling queasy from the fruit gums and chocolate, but I ate it all up even so.

When the bell rang for the end of visiting time, I waved to Mum until she disappeared. Then I lay very still, wondering how it was possible to feel so full and so empty at the same time.

14

It wasn't just me. Everyone seemed upset and restless after visiting time. Even sunny little Michael, who only ever cried when he was given his injections, started wailing fitfully, and deliberately knocked his milk mug over, so that his whole bed had to be changed.

Nurse Patterson and Nurse Curtis weren't really cross with him, but they did tut amongst themselves.

'It's always the way – and they'll be even worse on Sunday night,' said Nurse Patterson. 'If I had my way, parents would be banned. They just unsettle the kiddies.'

'And feed them too many sweeties and make them feel sick,' said Nurse Curtis, holding a pot under Babette's chin. She'd eaten three Mars bars in a row and was bitterly regretting it.

Nurse Patterson read us another magic tree story, but even that seemed to have the Saturday blues. The children climbed up the ladder into a scary new land where they were attacked by polar bears. Martin and Gillian and I weren't scared at all, but Rita started gasping like a goldfish out of water and had to put her head in a paper bag and breathe slowly until she felt better – and the little ones were all round-eyed with worry.

Nurse Patterson closed the book mid-chapter, in spite of a chorus of protests. 'What's the matter with you, you silly babies! You're frightened half to death,' she said. 'I can't possibly read any more – you'll get nightmares.'

'Pooh, it's not a bit scary. It's *soppy*. Who could ever be scared of polar bears? I *love* polar bears, especially baby Brumas at London Zoo,' said Martin.

'Go on, Nurse Patterson – *read*, please,' said Gillian.

'But look what the story's done to your poor little pal Rita,' said Nurse Patterson.

'Oh, Rita's a *baby*,' said Gillian unkindly.

'I'm not, I'm not – it's my asthma!' Rita gasped, still with her head inside the paper bag. 'Go on, Nurse Patterson, I want to hear the end of the story too.'

But Nurse Patterson was adamant. We had to make do with the half-chapter – and everyone blamed poor Rita.

I was mean enough to be secretly thrilled that she was now despised as one of the soppy little kids, even by her best friend Gillian – whereas I was now one of the big bold ones who had clamoured for more.

I waited until Nurse Patterson and Nurse Curtis were busy in the bathroom – and then I started.

'I'll tell a bit more of that polar bear story, shall I?' I said.

'No!' cried Rita.

'No, we've heard it all before, Gobface,' said Martin. 'It's a stupid baby story. Those children always get away in the nick of time and go back down the tree. Yawn yawn yawn.'

'I know a *different* story,' I said. 'Who's coming up *my* tree with me? It's quite a struggle to climb it. The branches are ever so far apart. The little ones can't climb it by themselves. I suppose we could give them a piggyback but it would be very, very dangerous.'

'You're daft – you can't climb. None of us can. We're all on bed rest,' said Rita sulkily.

'We can climb all we want in my story,' I said. 'Leastways, *I* can climb, and Gillian and Martin. I'm not sure about you.'

'I can climb if *you* can,' said Rita.

'But do you really *want* to? Remember the polar bears lurking at the very top of the tree, in the land beyond the clouds.'

'There aren't any *real* polar bears – Nurse Patterson promised. And there'll be another land at the top of the tree next time,' said Rita, but she sounded uncertain.

'Oh well, you and Nurse Patterson can stick in your silly storybook version. But Martin and Gillian and me are climbing up the tree, up and up. Whoops – a huge great bird like an eagle just flew out of its nest and very nearly got caught up in Gillian's ponytail!'

'No, it didn't!' said Gillian.

'That's right – it just missed and you were very brave and swatted it away,' I said.

'An actual eagle, with a hooked beak?' said Martin.

'This one had a *very* hooked beak, and it had a squirmy mouse hanging out of it.'

'Shut up, Gobface,' said Rita, and Babette and Maureen squealed.

'Ssh! We don't want a nurse to come. Just stop your ears up if you don't want to listen. *Now*, we're climbing the tree, right?'

'La-la-la, this is boring,' said Rita rudely.

'What other birds can we see? What about a buzzard? Or a kite?' said Martin, who obviously knew far more about birds than I did.

'I think one day there will be a whole *land* of birds up at the top of the tree – and we'll grow wings too and see what it's like to fly,' I said.

'Really? But that's not in the book. I told you, I've heard it before,' said Martin.

'Yes, and *I* told *you*, my story's different,' I said. 'Next time we'll maybe go to the Land of Birds, but *this* time it's polar bears – enormous white furry beasts with little mean red eyes and quick paws and very strong teeth. They're all up there, snapping and snarling in the snow because they haven't eaten for weeks and they're very, very *hungry*.' I wondered about snapping my own teeth or attempting a roar or two, but realized I might just sound silly and set them laughing, whereas now they were all listening, heads straining up off their pillows – except for Rita, who had her hands over her ears and was la-la-la-ing for all she was worth.

'Yes, the polar bears are *so* scary – even the little baby one with snowy-white fur,' I continued.

'That's Brumas,' said Martin.

'Can I pat him?' asked Michael unexpectedly.

I didn't have the heart to frighten him. 'Yes, you

can pat him. I was wrong – baby Brumas isn't dangerous yet, he's just sweet and playful and friendly. He's just big enough to give you a little ride in the snow, Michael. Would you like that?'

'Oh, yes please! And I won't fall off, will I?'

'No, but even if you do it won't matter, because it's so soft and snowy in Polar Bear Land – you'll just tumble around laughing. Brumas is such fun to play with. He likes to run right up to the top of this big hill, and then he slides all the way down on his bottom – and you do it too – we all do.'

'*Listen*, Rita, it's not scary now. This is a fun story,' said Gillian.

I blushed at the praise.

'No, it's not, it's a stupid story. Gobface is just making it all up. I can't be bothered to listen because it's all rubbish,' said Rita. 'I'm not a bit *scared*.'

Right. I decided to show her.

'Michael and Babette and Maureen stay playing with baby Brumas. They don't notice the pack of adult polar bears trekking silently through the snow towards us. *We* see them – and in a moment they're surrounding us, growling viciously. Oh, they're so hungry, showing their yellow teeth. The tallest one stands up on his hind legs, grunting with the effort. I can see all his muscles tensing, ready to spring. He's looking straight at me with crazed bloodshot eyes . . .

But guess what, I stand firm – well, as firm as I can manage because I'm shaking all over. I call out, "You don't want to eat me, Mr Polar Bear. You want to eat Marilyn Hide!"'

'Who's Marilyn Hide?' asked Martin, laughing.

'She's my worst enemy at school. I really, really can't stand her, she's the meanest girl ever – but I'm going to show her. As soon as I say her name, she appears, standing knee-deep in the snow, screaming her silly head off – which, as any fool knows, is the worst thing you can do when confronted by a pack of vicious polar bears. So the big polar bear springs – and Marilyn is knocked right over, splat in the snow, and then the bears' teeth snap, and within minutes there's not much left of her. We're all left standing clutching each other, hoping they're completely full up now. But they're still very lean and hungry. One gristly little girl like Marilyn isn't going to go far. Oh, look – another bear's standing up, sniffing the air. I think he wants a boy snack this time. Quick, Martin – he's about to pounce. Name someone – someone you don't like—'

'My dad!' said Martin.

We all gasped.

'You can't choose your *dad*. You don't want him to get eaten up, do you?' I said.

'Yes, I do,' Martin insisted. 'Oh, look, there he is!

He's running across the snow, going *"Help help help!"* but the bears are chasing after him—'

'It's *my* story – you can't do it too,' I said. 'OK, your dad is running like the clappers, but *whoops*, he trips, and the bears pounce. He *could* dig a hole in the snow and hide from them—'

'No, he's not quick enough, so the bears attack. They're eating him – gollop, gollop, gollop, he's all gone,' said Martin. 'I *like* this game.'

'My turn now, isn't it, Elsie?' said Gillian. 'I choose Miss Morgan – she's a teacher at my old school. She's the meanest old cow ever. When I didn't pass my eleven plus, she said, "Serves you right, Gillian Robinson. You'll never amount to anything." Well, I'll show her. Come and see the polar bears, Miss Morgan. Have they spotted her, Elsie? She's the fat lady wearing a grey suit, and when she walks, her podgy legs rub together and her nylon stockings make this awful raspy sound.'

'Yes, she's there. She's up and running, *squish squish, swish swish* – she's easy game. *Whoops* – she's tripped. She's sprawling in the snow with her skirts up round her waist showing her knickers. She's kicking those fat legs. Here go the polar bears: big fat pudding time – munch, crunch, slobber.'

'This is brilliant!' said Gillian. 'Listen, Rita! Take your stupid fingers out of your ears. Who do you want the polar bears to eat?'

'I'm not playing. I don't like it,' said Rita.

'Can I play?' said someone else.

I hauled myself up and craned my neck along the beds to see who was speaking. I didn't think it was any of the little ones. No one else seemed to be looking at me, just Martin and Gillian. We all wrinkled our noses in puzzlement.

'Who said that?' asked Martin.

'I did.' The voice was very quiet, but distinct. It came from right at the end of our row.

Our heads swivelled. I stared at the boy, immobile in his plaster bed. 'Did *you* speak, Angus?' I said, astonished.

I hadn't heard him say a single syllable before. I hadn't thought he *could* speak. He just lay there in his plaster coffin, staring up at the ceiling. He opened his mouth when the nurses fed him, and he grunted a bit when he was being washed or wiped, but he never spoke. He didn't join in any lessons with Miss Isles. She tried propping a board over his chest and balancing his books on top, but he didn't read or write in them. I'd forgotten he might be a real person. He just seemed like a big boy doll stuck in the end bed.

'Of course you can play, Angus,' I said quickly. 'Do you want the polar bears to eat anyone?'

'Yes,' said Angus. 'Nurse Patterson.'

We all gasped and then giggled.

'OK, Nurse Patterson it is!' I said. 'There she is, stamping in the snow, her ears going bright red with the cold. She doesn't like the polar bears, she thinks they're very naughty. She's waving a big thermometer at them and she's going to poke it right under their tongues like she does us – but the first polar bear bites the thermometer in two – *crunch* – and then he spits out all the little pieces of glass and raises his paw, and thwack – down goes Nurse Patterson, rolling over and over. Another bear lumbers up, and he thwacks her, and Nurse Patterson shrieks and rolls up into a little ball. The two bears are playing *tennis* with her, *thwack thwack thwack*. Oh dear, Nurse Patterson has lost her silly cap! She's telling the bears they're naughty, naughty boys, but *they're* telling her she's a naughty, naughty nursey. "Bad Nurse Patterson," they grunt, in bear language. "We're going to teach you a lesson, Nurse Patterson."'

I was so carried away, grunting and thwacking, that I didn't realize the others had gone silent. I blinked and focused, and saw Nurse Patterson herself at the end of the beds, towering over Angus.

'What's going on here? You're meant to be going to sleep! Elsie, why were you making that silly noise?'

'Oh! Oh Nurse Patterson, I – I've got a tummy ache,' I said. 'I was calling for you. It feels bad, my tummy.'

There was a little gurgle of laughter from under Martin's sheets.

'Stop that silly spluttering. I know you're all up to mischief, you can't fool me – and you're the ring-leader, Elsie Kettle.' She swished over to my bed and stuck her cold hand under the sheets onto my tummy. 'Where does it hurt?'

'There! And there and there and there,' I said, squirming as she prodded me.

'Nonsense! It feels fine to me. But just to make sure I'll give you a big dose of cascara. That will soon sort you out.'

'No!' I said quickly. I wasn't quite sure what cascara was, but I knew I wouldn't like it. 'My tummy's getting better now, honestly. I don't need any medicine.'

The threat was enough to shut me right up until Nurse Patterson went off duty. Then I hissed down the ward: 'The polar bears are still there and they are *gorging* themselves on Nurse Patterson – *chomp chomp chomp*. They're fighting over who gets to have her sticky-out ears as a special delicacy.'

Everyone laughed, even Rita and the little ones. Angus laughed most of all – great snorty chuckles that made him shake in his plaster bed.

Nurse Gabriel and Nurse Johnson came onto the ward.

'What's going on?' asked Nurse Johnson, bustling between our beds. 'Nurse Patterson *said* you were all in a very silly mood.'

'I think they sound very jolly, Johnson,' said Nurse Gabriel gently.

She started at Angus's end of the ward, sitting beside him for ages, murmuring to him. I hoped he hadn't actually hurt himself laughing so much. I thought I heard him saying my name. Was he telling tales on me? Oh dear, I'd sooner drink a whole bottle of Nurse Patterson's cascara than get into trouble with dear Nurse Gabriel.

I lay there fretting, still wide awake when she stopped by my bed at last – though I kept my eyes tight shut, hoping that if she thought I was asleep I might avoid a telling off.

'Hello, Elsie,' she said softly, tickling my neck so I had to wriggle. 'How are you doing, pet? How's your leg?'

'It feels funny,' I mumbled.

'Yes, it's going to take a lot of getting used to. But it will make such a difference in the end. You're going to get better again, I promise,' she said, holding my hand.

I had a sudden thought. 'Does wearing a Thomas splint make everyone better, Nurse Gabriel?'

'Yes it does, even though it takes a long time.'

'So, could it make a grown-up better too?'

'Yes, we use Thomas splints in the adult wards.'

'Then could my nan have one, do you think? She's got TB too, but it's in her chest. If she had a big splint to keep her still, would she get better quicker?'

'Oh sweetheart, they don't treat TB of the chest with splints. Is your nan in a sanatorium?'

'Yes, and I was only allowed to see her once. She was ever so poorly – she just kept coughing. She didn't really look like my nan any more,' I said, the tears starting to splash down my cheeks.

'Oh dear,' said Nurse Gabriel, gently dabbing at me with her handkerchief. 'Poor Elsie, you obviously love your nan very much.'

'I love her the best in all the world,' I said. 'So how *can* Nan get better?'

'She has to rest in bed, just like you. All you children are on total bed rest to stop your TB attacking the rest of your bones. Your nan will have special medicine and complete rest, and they might just collapse her lung for a little while.'

'And then she'll get better?'

'Some people with TB do get completely better, yes, darling.'

'But not everyone?'

'No, not everyone,' said Nurse Gabriel sadly.

'Mum says Nan can't do anything now. She says

it'll be a waste of time my writing to her because she won't be able to read my letter,' I said.

'Perhaps a nurse could read it out to her. I think she'd love to get a letter from you, Elsie. It would be a lovely surprise. I don't think she'll be able to write back, not if she's on complete bed rest. They have to be very strict with their patients in the sanatorium.'

'I don't mind. I just want to write to her.'

'Of course you do. Well, you write the letter and give it to Mummy. Is she coming tomorrow?'

'I think so!'

She hadn't promised, and I knew it was a very long way, but I so hoped she'd come all the same.

'And if by any chance she can't make it, then I'll post it for you.'

'Oh Nurse Gabriel, thank you!'

I was prepared for Mum to be tired and snappy and in a bad mood if she'd had to make the journey out to see me all over again. I'd begged Nurse Curtis to brush my hair into two neat plaits to please Mum, and I'd practised saying a couple of Martin's cleaner jokes to make her laugh. I thought if I prepared properly, it would somehow *make* her come. I even cajoled Queenie onto my bed and stroked her soft white fur and whispered into her delicate ears, 'Please make Mum come, Queenie.' She looked at me inscrutably with her green eyes, but purred encouragingly, as if she were definitely considering granting my wish.

But Mum wasn't there at the start of visiting time. I wondered if she'd missed the bus and would come tick-tacking in on her high heels, all out of puff. I waited and waited. But she didn't come at all. I was the only child on the ward without a single visitor.

'I don't care,' I said, and started to write my letter to Nan. I didn't have any writing paper or envelopes, so I used the back of an old temperature chart.

Dear, dear, ever-so-dear Nan,

I miss you so much and I hope you're not too lonely in that hospital. I can't visit you because I am in hospital too. I have TB as well, but mine's in my knee. I have to wear a horrid splint thing but it will make it better. Now listen, Nan – you have to try to get well too. As soon as my leg gets better I will come and see you, and that's a promise. And then I will take you home and put you to bed and look after you, and that's another promise.

Lots and lots and lots of love from Elsie

x x x x x x x x x x x x x x x x x x

I folded the paper up into quarters, and then wrote

on the back, even though there were lines zigzagging all over the page. I drew Snow White and Sooty and Marmalade, with little thought bubbles above their heads saying *We love Nan* and *Get better soon* and *You make us purr*. Then I drew a big portrait of Queenie. I wished I had a white crayon to colour her in properly. All I could manage was blue biro for her eyes. I tried shading to indicate her general furriness, but it made her look as if she'd been to the hairdresser's and had a blue rinse. I had to give her a large speech bubble:

Hello, Nan. I am Queenie, the Blyton Ward cat. I am REAL (but I'm not really blue, I am snowy white and ever so beautiful). I am Elsie's friend. I come to visit her every day.

Underneath I wrote: *Maybe you have a cat in your own ward, Nan? I do hope so.*

Then I spent the rest of visiting time putting a kiss into every single square on the page. I kept my head down so I wouldn't have to look at anyone.

Michael's mother leaned over me and offered me a packet of dolly mixtures. 'Go on, take a handful,' she said encouragingly, so I did.

Then Martin's dad stopped quizzing him about the rivers of the world and came and stood over me, casting a shadow on my page. 'That looks very pretty,' he said. 'What is it?'

I didn't want to tell him, and my mouth was still stuffed with dolly mixtures, so I just mumbled vaguely that it was a drawing.

'Where's your mother today then?' he asked.

I heard Martin's mum draw in her breath at his lack of tact and hiss at him.

'She couldn't come. She has to . . .' I said, and then I couldn't quite think what to say next, so I just chomped on my dolly mixture. They didn't taste right. I wished they weren't clogging up my mouth. My tummy churned uneasily.

'Well, that's a shame,' said Martin's dad. 'She's a very attractive lady, your mum. She brightens the whole place up a bit. Oh well, I expect she'll be here next week . . .'

'Oh yes,' I said – but I remembered all the times Mum disappeared for months. I tried to swallow, but couldn't. My tummy flipped right over. I was suddenly horribly sick – all over myself, my bed, and Martin's dad's sharply creased trousers.

15

It was obvious I'd been eating a lot of dolly mixtures because they were bobbing about in the sick in a truly ghastly fashion. Nurse Patterson told me off royally when she'd wheeled me away to the bathroom to clean me up.

'You mustn't eat so many sweets at a time, Elsie! And I don't think they were even your *own* sweets,' she scolded.

'Michael's mum gave them to me,' I whispered.

'Well, that's very kind of her, but you're a big girl –

you know the rules, even if Michael doesn't. You have just *one* sweetie at visiting time and then hand the rest in. You were told that clearly yesterday. It's very greedy to eat great handfuls at a time – and danger-ous too for all you bed-bound children. If you can't sit up properly, you could choke on your own vomit, and *then* where would you be? What would happen to poor little Angus if *he* tried to stuff sweeties down his throat?'

She went on and on and on. I tried to imagine the polar bears nuzzling round her knees, jaws snapping, trying to gulp great lumps of Nurse Patterson down their huge throats, and it helped distract me a little.

'Take that smile off your face, you naughty girl! I won't have this nonsense,' said Nurse Patterson, going pink.

She didn't slap me, but she sponged my face and chest a little too hard, her dabs so fierce they were almost like punches.

'There now! I hope you've learned your lesson,' she said when I was clean and dry again, in new sheets and a regulation hospital nightie. My cat pyjamas were in a soggy heap at her feet.

'I can have my own pyjamas back when they're washed, can't I?' I said.

'I don't know about that,' said Nurse Patterson triumphantly. 'They'll have to be sent to the laundry as your mother isn't here to take them. Oh dear!' she sighed, as if I might never see them again in that case.

'I think you're a very mean lady,' I said.

'And *I* think you're a very rude, spoiled little girl. No stories for *you* this evening,' she said.

She was as good as her word. When story time came, she wheeled me back to the bathroom in disgrace.

'I don't care,' I muttered, over and over again, but I *did* care, and it was particularly hard when Nurse Patterson came to take me back to the ward.

'Oh dear,' she said, pretending to be sad. 'You missed the Land of Birthdays, Elsie.'

When I was back with the others, Martin said, 'You didn't miss much, Gobface. I think it's a soppy book.'

'Yeah, but it's good, especially this last chapter,' said Gillian.

'It was *lovely*. They all had birthday presents, and there was a doll that could really walk and talk,' said Rita, sighing wistfully. 'I'd like a doll like that. I've got an Elizabeth doll at home, like the Queen when she was a little girl, but Mum won't let me have her here in hospital in case she gets mucky.'

I thought of Nan's plan to take me up to London to see the Queen's Coronation, and it hurt so badly I had to screw my face up to stop myself crying.

'Don't cry, Elsie. I'll tell you what happens,' said

Gillian, thinking I was fighting tears because I'd missed the story.

'It's OK. I'll tell you what happens in *my* Land of Birthdays,' I said quickly, sniffing. 'Who's coming up *my* tree, eh?'

'You're going to have them polar bears again and spoil it all,' said Rita.

'No, I *said*, it's the Land of Birthdays. And I'm climbing the ladder, stepping through the clouds, and suddenly it's brilliant sunshine, and so warm! All the ice has melted. There's not a claw or a whisker left of the polar bears, because this is Birthday Land. The trees are hung with those little lights you get on Christmas trees, with huge pink balloons tied to all the branches, and there are all these little people—'

'Fairies and pixies!' said Martin in disgust.

'No, they're like that, but they're *real* little special birthday people. They're all singing "Happy Birthday" and dancing round and round. I'm dancing too. I'm doing *ballet* dancing. I'm in a pink ballet dress, a satin top with tiny straps and a sticky-out skirt, and I've got pink satin ballet shoes with pink ribbons—'

'Pink, pink, pink!' Martin moaned. 'Pink *stinks*, Gobface.'

'It's what ballet-dancer girls wear, stupid. *You* don't have to wear it. You don't even have to come to my Birthday Land. It's *my* birthday, see,' I said fiercely.

'Can *I* come?' said Rita unexpectedly. 'Can *I* have a pink ballet dress too?'

I paused, wondering which way to play this. 'I'm not sure . . .' I said slowly. 'Can you do ballet?'

Rita didn't have the sense to fib. 'No, but I've always wanted to,' she said.

'Well then, *obviously* you can't have a pink ballet outfit,' I said.

'Ohh,' said Rita, sounding like a balloon deflating. She couldn't see that *none* of us could do ballet now in our splints and braces and plaster. We couldn't do it even if we were all little Margot Fonteyns. I didn't like Rita much, and I despised her for being such a stupid little copycat, but when I craned my neck and looked at her, I realized she was near tears.

'Only joking,' I said quickly. 'Of course you can have a ballet-dancer outfit, Rita. Do you want pink like mine? Or what about sky blue with blue satin ballet shoes to match? Or pure white, so you look like a little swan?'

That cheered her up, though she was flummoxed by the choices.

'Pink too. No, maybe blue. Or would white be better?' she burbled.

'We want pink!' said Maureen and Babette in unison.

'Yes, you will be all in pink. You can even have pink knickers,' I said, knowing Martin would groan again.

He did.

'What about you, Gillian?' I asked politely.

'I don't like all that fancy ballet lark,' she said. 'I like rock 'n' roll jive-type dancing.'

I wasn't one hundred per cent sure what this *was*, but I thought I knew the right clothes.

'You can have a sleeveless blouse and one of those huge great swirly skirts,' I said. Suddenly the magic finishing touch came to me. 'And you're wearing proper high heels – really high ones like my mum wears – but you don't wobble in them a bit.'

'That sounds smashing,' said Gillian. 'Red high heels! Can I have red, Elsie?'

'Yep, and you've got proper nylons too, with a seam going all the way up the back,' I said, inspired. I wanted to give her proper grown-up underwear too, but I didn't want to embarrass her in front of the boys.

Martin was growing increasingly restless. 'This is so *boring*, Gobface. I think the land's changing. The polar bears are coming back. It's getting much colder. You're all shivering in your soppy dancing clothes,' he said.

'Excuse me! This is *my* story. If you don't watch out, you'll be wearing a pink ballet dress and –

and . . .' I suddenly remembered the old taunt at school. 'And frilly pink knickers to match!'

Everyone snorted with laughter. Everyone except Martin.

'You shut up or I'll punch you, Gobface,' he muttered, though he was tethered in his bed, totally out of reach.

I knew I had to win him over.

'You don't have to join in any dancing, Martin,' I said kindly. 'This is just the beginning bit, anyway. This is the Land of Birthdays. Us girls are having a dance but the boys don't have to.'

'I'll dance,' said Angus. He said it very quietly but we all heard.

'Dancing's for *girls*, stupid,' said Martin.

'Not my kind of dancing,' said Angus. 'I'm doing Red Indian *war* dancing.' He made a sudden wonderful Indian war cry.

'Oh, that's brilliant!' I said.

'Shut *up*! Old Nurse Patterson Big Ears will hear you making that row,' said Martin. He was clearly in a grump because *he* hadn't thought of such a great idea.

'You can have a Red Indian outfit, Angus,' I said. 'With a full feather head-dress right down past your shoulders and war paint on your face.'

'Me too, me too,' said little Michael. He tried to do

a Red Indian whoop, but his tongue kept getting in the way. 'Show me how, Angus!'

Angus demonstrated, and Michael tried again, with little success but great enthusiasm.

'Idiots,' said Martin, but he sounded wistful.

'Why don't you be a cowboy, Martin?' I said. 'You could have one of those checked shirts and tight trousers with a gun holster round your hips, and a cowboy hat and cowboy *boots* – leather ones with tassels and those sticky-out things at the back . . . *you* know.'

'Nurse Patterson's ears?' said Gillian, and we all laughed.

'*Spurs!*' said Martin, and I could tell I'd got him hooked at last. 'And I don't exactly do a dance. Cowboys think all dancing is sissy, but I whirl my lasso around, whipping it through the air, and then I catch a Red Indian with it!'

'Catch me, catch me!' Michael said.

'Yes, I catch the littlest Red Indian and I *tickle* him,' said Martin. 'I tickle him till he squirms and begs for mercy.'

'Yes, yes,' Michael agreed happily, his chin on his chest, his arms flailing, giggling as if he really were being tickled.

'*So*, the music plays and all my little birthday people dance and sing the "Happy Birthday" song and we all join in, and then Rita and Babette and Maureen and I do a birthday ballet in and out of the lit trees while the others cheer and clap us. We dance, all four together, and then I do a solo in a special spotlight. It's called the Dance of the Roses, and I have a rose in my hair and I dance on rose petals. It looks lovely and it smells beautiful. At the end of the dance I pick up great piles of rose petals and shower them about. I smell of roses for the rest of the day.' I sniffed my hands, and just for a moment I thought I smelled a sweet soft rose scent instead of hard carbolic soap.

'We smell of roses too,' said Rita. 'It's *our* rose dance as well.'

'It's a *solo,* Rita. That means just *one* person does the dance, and that's me. But you can be my understudy, and one day, if I'm not feeling well, then *you* get to do the rose dance. You two can do it when you're a bit older, Babette and Maureen. *Now*, the music changes. It makes us all tap our feet and snap our fingers, and it's your turn, Gillian.'

'Yep, it's my turn, and I'm jiving with Bill Haley. We've got matching kiss curls. He's swinging me around like crazy,' said Gillian.

'But you don't wobble a bit in your high heels, and your ponytail bobs about and your skirt flares out—'

'Showing her knickers,' said Martin.

'You shut up, squirt. Yes, Bill and I dance and dance – jiving away. He flings me right over his shoulder—'

'And you land on your bum,' said Martin.

'Listen – you shut up or I'll give you a really good kick with my new high heels,' said Gillian.

'And now you and Bill Thingy sit down—' I went on.

'Can I sit on his lap?'

'Oh Gillian! All right, you're on his lap, and the music changes – it's all sort of thundery and we can hear horses' hooves, and it's the cowboy and Red Indian dance.'

'I don't dance,' said Martin.

'OK, you don't dance, you whip your lasso about, *crack crack crack*—'

'And I catch the Red Indians.'

'*No*, they're doing their war dance. You catch a horse, a wild golden palomino horse, and it leaps and bucks but you tame it and get on its back and trot round and round with it—'

'I gallop.'

'Look, who's telling this story, you or me? You can go galloping round and round in a circle, waving your cowboy hat, while Michael and Angus do their war dance. They've got red and blue war paint all over their faces and their hair hangs down in plaits.'

'*Girls* have plaits, not boys!' said Michael.

'OK, you can have short hair, with a band, and just one bright feather because you're still little, but Angus has his full head-dress.'

'Can I have a tomahawk in my hand?' asked Angus. 'And I'm stamping my feet in my moccasins, leaping up in the air, going *walla-walla-walla!*'

'Oh yes, that's a great war cry – but *softly*: we don't want Nurse Patterson to come.'

'Yes we do, because I shall scalp her!' said Angus.

'No, this is *Birthday* Land – no one gets hurts. Hey, guess what? All my little people have stopped singing now. They're rushing helter-skelter through the trees. Where are they going? We have to follow . . . We run behind them, crying, "Wait for us!" and then glimpse a beautiful garden with roses.'

'Pink roses?' said Martin.

'No, these are all different colours of the rainbow – red and yellow, but also bright emerald-green roses, and deep purple ones, and roses as blue as the sky. But never mind the roses – in the middle of the garden there's a long table spread with the most wonderful party food. There are great wobbly jellies and enormous blancmanges – *pink* blancmanges because they're raspberry flavour – and there are trifles with cream and cherries on the top, and ice cream all different flavours – vanilla and strawberry and chocolate – and there are cakes too – big fat sponges with cream and jam, and chocolate cake with chocolate buttercream – and lemon meringue pie with the meringue whipped into peaks, and fruit tarts – peach and cherry, with little rosettes of cream . . . And wait till you see the birthday cake right in the centre! It's huge, like a fairy castle covered in snow – that's the icing – and there are windows and doors made of marzipan, and little tiny sweetie figures too, and they're us – me and Gillian and Martin and Angus and Michael and Rita and Maureen and Babette. We pop them in our mouths, and they're like the best fruit gums you've ever tasted.'

'Does the birthday cake have candles?' asked Gillian, as absorbed as the others.

'Yes, the top of the icing castle roof has all these ridgy things, up and down—'

'Battlements!' said Martin.

'Yes, that's it, and there are candles all along the battlements, and we line up together and the little people sing us the birthday song, and when it's over they go "Blow! Blow out your candles!" in their little high-pitched voices, and so we all blow.'

They all blew obediently.

'And now we have to cut the cake and make a birthday wish!' I said.

'Oh please, let *me* do it and get the wish,' said Rita.

'One of the little people has one, two, three, four, five, six, seven, eight silver knives on a polished silver platter. One for each of us. The cake's enormous, so we all line up, and when another little man blows on a silver flute, we cut the cake together,' I said triumphantly. 'Then we all have a wish.'

'Oh, oh – what do we wish for?' said Rita.

'You wish *privately* or it doesn't come true,' I said. 'Shut your eyes and wish.'

I closed my eyes and wished so hard I thought I might burst.

I wish Nan would get better and I wish I could get better and we could live together again!

I wanted to keep on wishing it, over and over, but the others started clamouring to know what was going to happen next.

'We eat all the birthday tea, you sillies,' I said. 'We gorge ourselves on jelly and blancmange and trifle and ice cream and every kind of cake.' We were eating for England, though we'd all had our Spam sandwiches and tinned mandarins for hospital supper.

It didn't stop us playing party games. I let each child choose a game to keep them interested. Martin chose Murder in the Dark and insisted on being the murderer each time. Gillian played Kiss Chase and insisted that Bill Haley was playing too. Rita dithered because I insisted she choose a game of her own, and eventually said she wanted to play skipping. It wasn't a proper party game, but I let her have her way and gave an extra length of rope to Martin – 'To practise your lassoing – don't you go round hanging anyone,' I said sternly.

Angus chose Musical Bumps, and we all leaped up and down to the music. Michael opted for Hunt the Thimble and we let him find the thimble every single time. Babette and Maureen conferred and chose Squeak Piggy Squeak and then gave continuous little piggy squeaks in between fits of giggles.

'Shut up, you lot. You're being daft,' said Gillian. 'What game are you going to play, Elsie?'

'I think I shall play Pass the Parcel,' I said. 'Oh my goodness, the little people are bringing us the parcel, and it's *huge*. When we form a circle and the music starts, we have to *roll* it round the ring.'

'That's not right for Pass the Parcel. We played it at my last party and Mummy gave us just a little parcel,' said Rita.

'Yes, and what did you do with it?' I asked.

'Well, we unwrapped it. First there was brown paper, and then newspaper, and then wrapping paper, and eventually we got right down to this tiny little pink plastic doll. It was my party, so *I* should have got it, but this other girl snatched the parcel off of me and *she* got the doll, and when Mummy went back to

Woolworths to get me another one, they'd sold out,' said Rita.

'Do shut *up*, Rita, or I'll lasso you and tie you to a tree,' said Martin. His arms were attached to his brace in such a way that he couldn't move them freely, but he made swishing noises with his tongue.

'Yes, shush, Rita. You'll see *why* I need such a big parcel. Come on – we're rolling it round while the little people tootle and drum, and then they all stop. It's your turn to unwrap it, Martin – quick, scrabble with the paper, tear off the string. Whoops, what's this falling out? It's a present!'

'You don't get the present already,' said Rita.

'In my version you do – *that's* why the parcel's so big. It's got lots and lots of presents – and Martin finds a gun. A toy gun with caps.'

'Oh yes,' said Martin. 'And I seize it and shoot at everyone – *bang bang bang*, and my caps go *pop pop pop* and make that lovely fireworks smell.'

'And now the band starts up and we roll the parcel round again, and now it's . . . Maureen who has the parcel when the music stops. Tear at the paper, Maureen. I'll help you because your hands aren't very strong. Oh, your present's quite big!'

'Is it a big gun? I don't really like guns,' Maureen said anxiously. 'I don't like it when they go bang.'

'No, it's not a gun – it's far too big and bulky for a

gun. It's like a big solid rectangle, but there are lots of funny round things chinking inside the parcel too.'

'What is it? What is it?' Maureen squealed.

'It's a toy stove, with a little door that really opens and a dish you can put inside, and there's a whole set of silver saucepans, and all sorts of other cooking things, even a little wooden rolling pin, so you can make lots of dinners for all your dollies.'

'Oh, how *lovely*. I've wanted one of them for ages,' said Maureen.

'Now, let's get the parcel rolling again. It's a little bit lighter now – and hey, the music stops already. You've got the parcel now, Babette. Unwrap it quick before the music starts again,' I said.

'Do I have a present too? Is it a cooking stove like Maureen's?' Babette asked.

'Well, take a look, silly. Off with the paper . . . Here, I'll help – and what's this tumbling out? I don't think it can be a cooking stove, it's too small and soft. Pull the paper away. What's that? It's an *ear* – a long blue ear, and there's another one! It's a bunny, Babette. A blue toy bunny with a pink nose, and he's got a dark blue knitted jumper and bright red trousers with a little hole at the back for his fluffy tail to poke through. Do you like him?'

'Yes, I absolutely love him. I'll call him Bobs Bunny and give him carrots to eat.'

'Maureen can cook the carrots for him on her stove,' I said. 'Oh, the music's starting! Pass the parcel quick! It's still pretty bulky, but roll it round carefully – we don't want to break anything.'

'Is it my turn now?' asked Rita. 'The music's stopped and *I've* got the parcel—'

'No, they're still playing – can't you hear them?' I said firmly. 'You mustn't cheat, Rita. Pass the parcel to Gillian – OK, now it's stopped!'

'I'm a bit old for toys,' said Gillian.

'I don't think this is a toy. It's quite big, like a box, and you can feel a clasp through the paper. Can you guess?'

'Is it a chest to keep my things in?'

'Open it up and see!'

'This is a *weird* game,' said Gillian. 'OK, I've got the paper off.'

'Look – it's a blue box with a gold clasp and a handle sticking out at the side. Better open it, Gillian. What's inside? Oh goodness, it's not an ordinary box. It's got a round table thingy inside, and a little arm with a needle—'

'It's a gramophone!' cried Gillian. 'My own gramophone!'

'So you can play your dance records as often as you like. You play your Bill Haley records so much we all yell at you, but you don't care. You just dance to the music. Oh, the little people are starting up *their* music again.'

'It's my turn now,' said Rita. 'I want a gramophone too! Oh please, let me have my very own gramophone, Elsie.'

'It's not me that works the birthday magic, Rita. It's the little people – they decide when to stop the music. They want to give everyone a turn, but they don't like rude girls and boys begging for it to be their go. They might just decide to make you last now, *if* they've still got a present for you. I should shut up if I were you,' I warned her.

Rita did as she was told. She even put her hands over her mouth. I felt a bit mean, then – but it was a good feeling too, having such power over Rita, power over *everyone*.

'OK, there's the music. It's such a lovely tune, and we roll the parcel. Do you know, it's still *ever* so big. What on earth can be inside? Pass it round. Don't hang onto it, Rita! Round it goes. Oh Michael, the music's stopped and you've got hold of it. Quick, scrabble at the wrapping paper. Rip it off – use both hands, *that's* the way. Oops, watch out, here's something very heavy, and I can see shiny red, and there are wheels and a handlebar. Can you see what it is, Michael?'

'Is it a bike?' he whispered.

'Yes, it's a brand-new bike for you, Michael.'

'Is it a trike with three wheels like my one at home?' asked Michael. 'Or – or is it a big boy's bike?'

'It's definitely a big boy's bike, but it's a specially small size, so you can reach the pedals easily. Get on, quick! Let's see if you can ride it.'

'I won't fall, will I, like I fell off my brother's bike?'

'Of *course* you won't fall – and it won't matter if you do, because the grass in Birthday Land is so soft and thick it's just like jumping on your bed. You bounce straight up again. But you're not falling . . . you get your balance straight away, and off you go, round and round, so quickly we all get giddy – but *you* don't, Michael, you keep going. We all cheer you, and – oh my goodness, you raise your hands above your head and pump them up and down in the air. You don't even wobble then – you're a brilliant bike rider! You'll be riding the Wall of Death in a fairground quite soon. Speedy Mike, that's what we'll all call you.'

Michael laughed and laughed and went '*Wheeee!*'

'Now, the parcel's much smaller now, and lighter. We can just about throw it to each other. The music is quicker, and we pass the parcel in time to the beat. Sometimes it stops for a moment, and I tear at the paper—'

Rita gives a little moan.

'But the music always starts again before I can get the layer off. It stops for Martin—'

'It's not fair, he's had his go! He had his gun!' Rita wailed.

'And Martin scrabbles hard, but the paper is all stuck down with paste now and it won't tear off easily – and *goodness*, there's string around the next layer. Rita pulls at it when the music stops.'

'Oh!'

'She has to unpick the knots but she's too impatient. The music starts again. Around we go—'

'You're doing this *deliberately*, Elsie. You're being so mean,' said Rita. 'I'm not playing any more. I'm not listening. I'm sticking my fingers in my ears, see? La-la-la!'

'Oh dear, that's a shame, Rita, because I'm pressing the parcel right into your hands and the music's stopped.'

'La-la-la . . . You're just teasing, I know.'

'And you say you're not playing, but your hands are tearing at the wrapping paper. You simply can't resist, and then *suddenly*—'

'The music starts up again – how did I guess?' Rita snapped.

'No, no, the band is silent. All the little birthday people are staring at you, eyes shining. We're all waiting, and *there*, in your hands, is a shiny crimson enamel box – round, in the shape of an apple, with a dear little green stalk clasp. You shake the little box and it *rattles*. I wonder what's inside . . .'

'Old apple cores and apple pips?' said Martin.

'Go and play with your gun, you silly boy. Of course it's not. Open the clasp quick, Rita. We're all dying to see what's inside. Oh! Oh my goodness!'

'What? *What?*' said Rita.

'You're opening it – very carefully so nothing will spill – and it's full of jewellery . . . *real* jewels. There's a gold necklace with a little heart and the letter R picked out in tiny red rubies.'

'Rubies!' Rita whispered.

'And there are rings, one for every day of the week, set with different stones: a ruby to match your necklace, then an emerald, a sapphire, a yellow topaz, a pearl, and an amethyst – and a great big sparkly diamond to wear for best on Sunday,' I said.

'Here, why does Rita get all the jewels? They must cost heaps and heaps more than a toy gun,' said Martin.

'Because she wanted them more. And don't tell me you want to swap your gun for a lot of necklaces and rings.'

'No fear!' he said. 'I was only commenting.'

'Thank you *so* much, Elsie,' said Rita, her arm in the air, admiring her invisible jewellery.

'Don't thank me, thank the birthday people,' I said. 'We're still playing. The music starts—'

'What are you going to give yourself, Gobface? I bet it'll be pink,' said Martin.

'It might not be my turn,' I said. 'We're passing the parcel again, all of us. Come on, you lot. Stop playing with your presents. You've got to join in too, Angus, so put down your tomahawk for a moment.'

'Oh, I always forget Angus,' said Martin tactlessly.

'The birthday people don't forget him. In fact, they've got a special present in store for him. I wonder what it can be, because the parcel's quite small now.'

'It could be your turn, Elsie. Maybe you've got diamond jewellery too?' said Rita.

'That would be lovely but— Oh, the music's stopped, and we've both got our hands on the present. It's a big box with a skull and crossbones on it. I pull it and Angus pulls it, and we hear a little rattling inside, and one of the birthday people goes "Careful, children – that parcel's dangerous!" So I let go of it, a bit scared, but Angus hangs onto it and opens the lid, and it's a chemistry set with lots of little test tubes and bottles and jars, and a tiny book telling you how to do all these experiments. Angus, you can make itching powder!'

'I can sprinkle it all over Nurse Patterson!' he said.

'And you can create your own fireworks. You can even make a bomb!'

'Yes, you can blow her up too!' said Martin. 'Can I have a go with your chemistry set? I'll let you have a shot with my gun.'

'Can you make powder with your chemistry set, Angus? Powder and lipstick? I'll have some of them if you can,' said Gillian.

'OK. And maybe there's a way to crystallize rocks. If so, I'll make you some more jewellery, Rita,' said Angus. 'What can I make for you, Elsie?'

'You can make me some rose perfume. That would be lovely,' I said.

'It's your turn with the parcel now, Elsie,' said Gillian. 'Get them little people to start up the music.'

'Yes, they're playing, and we send the parcel round and round again. We can toss it one-handed, it's so light – almost *too* light. Maybe we've had all the presents and there's absolutely nothing left?'

'Oh no!' said Babette.

'No, no,' said Maureen. 'That's not fair. You *must* get a present, Elsie. Or you can share some of my saucepans. You can even have my little rolling pin.'

'She'll have her own present – won't you, Elsie?' said Gillian. 'Go on, the music's stopped. Open it!'

'Yes, all right. The band plays a long final chord, and as the music fades I scrabble at the parcel. It's difficult because I've got bitten nails – look – but I very carefully nip the last bit of paper with my teeth, and then the tiniest little ornament tumbles out.'

'What's a ornament?' asked Maureen.

'It's a boring china thingy like a crinoline lady,' said Martin. 'My mum has some in a cabinet. What did you want one of them for, Elsie?'

'This isn't a china crinoline lady! This is a teeny weeny golden Coronation coach pulled by eight pearly grey horses stepping out grandly, each little leg the size of an eyelash.'

'But you've already *got* one of them. What do you want another for?' asked Martin.

'I haven't got one like *this*. I hold my palm out flat, and the little coach and horses glow and glow, so brightly it's like I've got the whole sun in my hand. It's burning me, so I set it down very gently on the ground. It's started *humming* now, and as we watch, we see the horses' legs start to *move*, making the tiniest clacking sound with their weeny hooves – and then the coach and horses start getting bigger and bigger. In a flash they're life-size – and I peer into the coach, and there's this smiley lady wearing a crown.'

'The Queen!' Rita gasped.

'Yes, it's the Queen, in a white dress with that blue ribbon sash, and she's got a gold crown set with diamonds on top of her brown curls. She's waving at me – she's waving at all of us. We'd better curtsey – and you boys bow.'

There's a lot of bashful giggling going on.

'Ssh! You have to pay the Queen some respect!' I said sternly. 'She's leaning out of the window. She's beckoning to me. "Hello, little girl!" she says, in such a posh voice. "Would you like a lift in my carriage?"

'So I bob another curtsey and say, "You bet, Your Majesty," and I open the gold door and climb into the carriage beside her.

'"We've room for one more," says the Queen.'

'Me! Oh, take me!' said Rita.

'I wish I could take you, but the Queen says it has to be a relative to look after me.'

'Are you taking your mum?' asked Martin.

'No fear! I'm taking my nan. There she is, running in her best coat and hat. She tries to do a curtsey too, but it's a bit wobbly. The Queen doesn't mind a bit though. She says, "How do you do, Mrs Kettle. I've been longing to meet you. Kindly hop up into my carriage."

'So Nan gets in beside me, and the Queen says, "Right, let's go to my Coronation!" and off we go!'

16

'I hear you tell very good stories, Elsie,' said Nurse
Gabriel.

I looked up at her anxiously. Now I was for it.

'Nurse Patterson and Nurse Curtis couldn't hear
me, could they?' I said.

'No, no.'

'So who told you?'

'Oh, just a little bird.'

I frowned at her. I hated it when grown-ups played
that 'little bird' trick. I thought it was beneath Nurse

Gabriel. I knew Martin and Gillian and Rita and Michael hadn't told on me, because they were within earshot. Babette and Maureen might have blabbed, but they both seemed fast asleep by the time Nurse Gabriel came on duty, worn out playing with their toy stove and bunny. That just left . . .

'It was Angus,' I said. 'He snitched on me.'

'He didn't *snitch* – what a terrible word, Elsie! He just couldn't help telling me what a wonderful story-teller you are. He thinks the world of you,' said Nurse Gabriel.

I lay there fidgeting, trying to take it in. I had thought I'd be in trouble for making up stories. Even kind Miss Roberts at school shook her head when I went rambling on, and said reprovingly, 'Oh Elsie, you're such a storyteller.' I knew it drove Mum nuts. Even Nan sucked her teeth at me sometimes, her eyebrows raised, and went, 'Yatter yatter yatter – how about saving your breath to blow on your porridge?'

'So you're not cross with me?'

'I'm very, very pleased with you, you silly girl. You've cheered everyone up – and you've made my little friend Angus very happy. You're the best medicine he could possibly have. He's been very down since he had his treatment. We've all been worried about him.'

'But *I've* made him better?'

'Yes, you have. You've cheered him up enormously.'

'I've written a letter to my nan,' I said. 'I'll give it to my mum when she next comes. I'm keeping it under my pillow so that no one else can read it.'

'Well, I can post it if she doesn't come next weekend – but no one else will read it – it's yours and your nan's. It's private,' said Nurse Gabriel.

She was being so kind that I felt my lips trembling and my eyes filling with baby tears.

Nurse Gabriel misunderstood. 'Oh dear, it's so difficult for all of you, when you can't be private at all in hospital.' She seemed really distressed herself. 'I nursed in Potter before here – that's for the babies, and somehow it doesn't seem quite so bad for them. Often they're not old enough to wash or dress themselves or be potty-trained, so it's not such a shock. But it's so hard for you older ones being trussed up in bed, isn't it?'

'Yes!' I said. 'And – and I'll have to stay here weeks and weeks, won't I?'

'Perhaps months and months,' said Nurse Gabriel gently. 'But then you will be better.'

'And Nan will get better too?'

She hesitated. 'I really hope so.'

'I do love my nanny,' I said.

'Of course you do,' said Nurse Gabriel.

'It isn't really *her* fault . . .'

'What's that, Elsie?'

258

'She didn't *mean* to give me TB. Mum says it's all her fault and she'll never forgive her for giving it to me, but Nan couldn't help it, could she?' I said.

'Oh Elsie, your nan didn't give you TB, darling. You have tuberculosis of the knee. If your nan's in the sanatorium, she must have TB of the lungs. That's entirely different. You don't catch TB of the bone from a person. Yours is *bovine* TB. You got it from a cow. You must have drunk infected milk at some time.'

'Are *you* telling a story now, Nurse Gabriel?'

'No, I promise you.'

'But it seems so weird. I got ill straight after Nan.'

'You probably had it quite a long time before it was diagnosed. How long were you limping?'

'I don't know. Can't remember.'

'It was such a good job you went to get checked out by your doctor though. If it had gone undiagnosed, it would have eaten its way right through the bone and you'd have been in a terrible state.'

This new knowledge seethed in my head all through the long week. It washed over me when Nurse Patterson subjected me to her sloppy bed baths. It scraped me during my toileting. It stung me when I was given my horribly painful injections. It threatened to choke me when I ate my breakfast and lunch and supper. It distracted me during Nurse

Patterson's story time and overwhelmed me when I tried to tell my own story afterwards. It wasn't my poor dear nan's fault that I had TB. She hadn't given me her germs. As soon as I could, I got out my letter and scribbled in big capitals on the back: *IT'S NOT YOUR FAULT, NAN, HONEST*. Then I put it safely under my pillow again.

I couldn't wait to tell Mum when she came on Saturday. She wasn't there at two o'clock with all the mothers and fathers, and I began to be horribly scared that she wasn't coming.

'All on your ownio again?' said Martin's father.

I ducked my head, not wanting to give an answer.

'Poor little scrap,' his wife whispered. 'What kind of a mother *is* she?'

I pretended to be absorbed in my *Girl* comic. I'd read it again and again but I had nothing else. I tried to join Belle on the stage doing a *pas de deux*, but my feet were leaden. Then I heard *clip-clop, clip-clop*, the heart-warming sound of high heels – and there was Mum, picking her way along the veranda, wearing tight white slacks and an apricot jumper with her best white high heels.

'Gordon Bennett, here comes Diana Dors!' said Martin's dad.

'Oh Mum, you're here after all,' I said, fighting back tears.

'Well, of course I'm here! Haven't you got a nice smile for Mummy when I've come all the way to see you?'

I tried very hard but my lips wobbled. 'You were late – I thought you weren't coming,' I mumbled.

'For God's sake, *I* can't drive the blooming bus and make it come any quicker, can I? It's all right for the other parents – they can all roll up in *cars*.' Mum sniffed and sat down on the side of the bed, crossing her legs. She saw that her stocking seam was twisted and wriggled it round, emphasizing her shapely calf as she clasped the slippery nylon. Martin's dad was practically drooling.

'Mum! Mum, wait till I tell you,' I said, tugging at her sleeve.

'Careful, Elsie, I don't want your grubby little mitts all over my jersey! Do you like it? I got it in Dorothy Perkins, five and six. I had my first wages on Friday. Six pounds, ten shillings – not bad, eh, when I'm just sitting at a desk going, *Yes, Mr Perkins, No, Mr Perkins, Three bags full, Mr Perkins*. I think I've been a bit of a mug toiling away in the chorus all these years. I've never earned more than a fiver a week there.'

'Mum, listen! It's *not* Nan's fault. I didn't get my TB from her,' I blurted.

'You what? Don't be daft, Elsie – who else could have given it you?'

'I was talking to Nurse Gabriel.'

'What a name! Has she got wings and one of them gold plates stuck to her head then?' Martin's dad heard and chuckled appreciatively. Mum looked up at him slyly through her blonde waves and waggled her foot at him. I hated it when she was in this sort of mood, so cock-a-hoop and cheeky. She usually acted like this when she'd met a new uncle.

'Nurse Gabriel said I got my TB from a cow,' I said.

Mum burst out laughing. 'The things they come out with!' she said to Martin's parents. 'I thought you were meant to be bright, Elsie. How could you catch it from a *cow*? When have you ever been hob-nobbing with a herd of cows? Are they out there mooing away up and down the alleyways and dancing round the gasometer? You've hardly ever *seen* a cow. We've never been to the countryside – it makes me depressed because there's nothing there.'

Martin's dad laughed uproariously. His wife barely responded, just twitched her lip in brief acknowledgement.

'No, I can't quite see you walking through a ploughed field in those shoes,' said Martin's dad. He'd laughed so much he had to dab the spit off his mouth with his handkerchief. 'Still, your little girl's right,' he added.

'What?'

'That's how all the poor little things got TB – dodgy milk. TB's rife in cows, and they can carry the infection in their milk. Mad, isn't it? My wife was always on at Martin to drink his pint a day, thought it was so good for him – even bribed him to drink more by adding chocolate – and what was she doing? Infecting him with this beastly disease.'

'Don't. Please don't,' said Martin's mum weakly. She looked as if she might start crying.

'You're having me on,' Mum said uncertainly. 'So you think Elsie caught it from *milk*?'

'Yep. Never touch it myself – terrible stuff. I prefer a drop of whisky any day of the week,' said Martin's dad.

'Well, I'll second that,' said Mum. They held imaginary whisky glasses in the air and clinked them together.

Martin's mother muttered something, stood up, and walked down the veranda.

'Uh-oh,' said Martin's dad. He groaned and stretched. 'Better go after her. She can't take any banter nowadays. She's grown very sensitive since our boy got ill.' He sighed at Martin as if it were all his fault, and lumbered after her.

'Sorry!' I mouthed at Martin.

He shrugged, seemingly quite happy to be shot of both parents for the moment.

'Milk!' Mum muttered.

'So you see, Mum, it's just coincidence that Nan has TB too. She didn't give it to me – so you won't still be cross with her, will you? You *will* go and see her and tell her? And I've got a letter for her – you can take it to her, can't you?'

'Do stop nagging, Elsie. Calm down now. Dear goodness, what's the matter with your *lip*?'

I nibbled at it anxiously, while Mum put her hand under my chin to look properly.

'Stop *doing* that! You've got a nasty-looking cold sore, that's what you've got! And no blooming wonder, keeping you out here all the time when it's been arctic this spring. It's all right getting a bit of fresh air, but this is going too far. I'm going to have a word with one of them nurses.'

'Oh please don't, Mum. I'll get into trouble. I'm not cold, really I'm not.'

I had a sore on my mouth because I kept licking it anxiously. Nurse Patterson had noticed and smothered it with horrible grease, so that my mouth tasted funny all day and I couldn't nuzzle into Albert Trunk at night because I'd smear him too. I was sure I had a sore on my bottom too because Nurse Patterson wiped it so fiercely, but I was keeping quiet about that.

'Your hair needs a good wash too. It's ever so greasy,' said Mum, her nose wrinkly. 'You must ask them to wash it more often, Elsie, especially as you've got a fringe. You'll be getting spots on your forehead if you don't watch out.'

I lay there feeling ugly, as if spots were popping out all over my face as she spoke.

'I still think it's mad keeping you lying here in hospital all the time. It doesn't look like it's making you *better*. You must buck up, Elsie, and make an effort,' said Mum. 'Look at me – I lost my job, didn't I, with fat chance of getting another dancing job round here. I'd have had to go up to London and they always want younger girls. Some of them are only fifteen and sixteen, still silly little kids. But did I lie on my back feeling sorry for myself? No, I went right out and got myself an office job, which was maybe a bit premature – I *could* have gone back to the show up north and finished the season, seeing as you're stuck here. Still, it's an ill wind, and all that, and Mr Perkins and I are getting on like a house on fire. And I've got to think of the future. My legs aren't quite what they were.' She stuck them out one at a time to see if they still passed muster. Then she suddenly lifted my blanket to peer at *my* legs.

'Mum!' I said, pulling my pyjama top down to make sure I was decent. I hoped Martin wasn't looking.

She tutted at my splint. 'And look at *your* poor little leg,' she said. 'It'll wither away, trapped in that thing. I hope they know what they're doing, that's all I can say. What if you end up crippled? What are we going to do then? You were perfectly fine just a fortnight ago, running around like any other little kiddie. If only your nanny hadn't infected you.'

'Mum, I *said*. And Martin's dad. Didn't you listen? It's nothing to do with poor Nan,' I said.

'Hey, hey, no need to take that tone, young lady. I still think it's pretty rum, your nan getting ill and then you going down with the self-same disease.'

'How *is* Nan, Mum?'

'You know how she is. We trailed all the way out to see her.'

'But can't you go and see her *again*? Here's my letter,' I said, fishing it out from under my pillow. 'You'll give it to her, won't you?'

She took it and put it in her handbag. 'How can I be in two blooming places at once, answer me that! I'll go tomorrow, if I can manage it.'

'And tell her that I'm all right and it isn't her fault. If you don't go and see her, can you post it to her for me? I just hate the idea of her fretting. Oh Mum, I miss her so,' I said, starting to cry.

'Oh dear, not the waterworks again! Stop it now or you'll start me off. I can't bear to see you like this. Here, have some chocolate. I bought you a Fry's Five Boys bar. You look just like the little boy grizzling in the picture! Come on – eat it all up now. I don't hold with you having to hand your sweeties in to those nurses. I bet they just help themselves.'

'Can I give a bit to Martin and Gillian – and Angus?' I asked.

'No, you eat it up yourself. I'll have a chunk too. I just had bread and dripping for lunch.'

'I tell everyone stories, Mum,' I said proudly, my mouth full of chocolate.

'Well, you're a naughty girl,' she said. 'Your tongue will go black.'

'No, I don't mean I tell fibs. I tell proper bedtime stories and everyone listens and *likes* them. I made up this story about a magic land up at the top of a tree.'

'That's not your story, that's in a book.'

'Yes, but I do it *better* than the book. I make it real, and everyone likes it,' I said. 'Nurse Gabriel says I'm a brilliant storyteller.'

'Well, that's nice, dear,' said Mum. 'But don't start boasting now. I expect she was just being kind.'

It was no use. I so wanted her to be proud of me, but it was clear that I was failing dismally in every respect. I longed for Nan. She always made me feel as if I was her best girl, perfect in every way. I still wasn't sure Mum would go and visit her tomorrow. I wanted to beg her again and to remind her about my letter, but I knew the more I pushed, the more it would irritate her.

I felt horribly fidgety, as if my legs wanted to run off to Nan's by themselves. It was so awful to be tethered all the time, trapped on my back no matter how I strained. My legs itched and I started scratching, especially round the leather band keeping the brace in place.

'Elsie! Stop that! Goodness me, *scratch scratch*. People will think you've got nits.'

'I *itch*, Mum. It's all *sore*.'

'Let me see,' she said, pulling the covers away. '*Where* is it sore? Is this awful contraption rubbing you?'

It wasn't really sore at all, but I wanted Mum's sympathy.

'Yes, it's *very* sore,' I said, and I winced and shivered when Mum tried to edge her finger under the leather.

'This is ridiculous,' she said. 'What are they playing at? They're rubbing you raw, you poor little mite.'

All four nurses examined my leg scrupulously every day, and washed and dried and powdered it under the ring so that my skin stayed baby smooth – but I couldn't help getting sucked into Mum's tirade.

'It really hurts, Mum,' I said, and I snivelled convincingly.

'Well, it's simply not good enough,' she said. 'I'm

not standing for it. Where's that nurse? I'm going to have a few words.'

My stomach lurched. 'No – don't, Mum,' I gabbled, panicking. 'It's not really *that* sore.'

'It's really hurting you, I can see that. You need proper attention. Heaven knows what could happen if that sore takes a hold. You could end up losing your flipping leg!' said Mum, working herself up. 'I'm going to put in a complaint.'

'No, Mum!'

'It's not right if they blooming well neglect you. I'm going to have my say. *I'm* not a negligent mother.' She was off like a shot before I could stop her, curls bouncing on her shoulders, high heels ringing on the stone veranda.

'Is your mother off already?' said Martin's dad. 'I could have given her a lift to the station.'

I didn't reply. I lay there, miserably scratching, praying that Mum wouldn't be able to find any of the nurses – they usually had a long tea break during visiting hours. But, to my horror, Mum returned triumphantly a few minutes later with *Sister Baker*. I shut my eyes and lay very still, wanting to die.

'Elsie?' said Sister Baker. She spoke very quietly, but even so she made it plain she wasn't messing about. I had to look at her. She was smiling in a very crocodile kind of way, all teeth – rather as if she wanted to take a bite out of me. 'Your mummy says your leg is hurting you, dear.'

'Not – not really,' I mumbled.

'You said that leather thing was rubbing you raw!' said Mum. 'You take a look, Nurse.'

'I'm Sister Baker, Miss Kettle,' the Sister said, still carefully pleasant and polite, though the look on her face made me shiver. She pulled back my blankets and examined my poorly leg, running her finger expertly underneath the leather. 'Is this where it's sore, Elsie?' she asked.

'Yes. No. I don't know,' I gabbled, in a cold sweat.

'It's too tight, that's what it is,' said Mum. 'Can't you unbuckle it a bit?'

'The splint has to be reasonably tight to be effective,' said Sister Baker. 'But we examine it scrupulously every four hours, checking for any discomfort. Which nurse last washed your leg, Elsie?'

'Nurse Patterson,' I whispered, truthfully enough.

'Well, your leg feels a little damp. Perhaps she didn't dry you properly. I'll have a word with her,' said Sister Baker.

She took the towel from my locker, and dried and powdered my sweaty leg. 'There now. Is that more comfortable?' she said.

'Yes – yes it is,' I said eagerly.

Mum nodded, tossing her long hair, pleased that

she'd fought for her daughter and obtained satisfaction.

'There you are!' she said, when Sister had marched off purposefully. 'Happy, now? Your old mum's fixed it.'

I wasn't at all sure I was happy. My tummy was in a tight little knot of anxiety. I'd more or less told a lie – and even Nan hated liars: 'You can be as naughty as you like, Elsie, so long as you own up to it. I can't stomach liars,' she always said.

I told endless stories but I never told downright lies – at least not to anyone that mattered. I hadn't *intended* to lie to Mum. It just slipped out of my mouth without me thinking properly.

'What's up *now*?' Mum said, frowning at me. 'Why the long face?'

'I – I'm a bit scared, Mum. My leg wasn't really *that* sore. I shouldn't have made a fuss,' I said in a sudden burst.

'Of course it was sore. Any fool could see it was rubbing. Like that Sister said, it hadn't been dried properly,' she said. 'I hope she gives that nurse a right ticking off!'

'I don't want anyone to get into trouble,' I said.

'Nonsense – that's how all them nurses learn. They can't get away with shoddy treatment, especially when they're dealing with little kiddies. Don't you worry, Elsie, I'll see you're all right. You tell your mum if you're sore anywhere else, right?'

271

I felt rubbed raw all over right that minute, but I kept quiet. I hardly said a word the rest of the visit, and Mum got bored and started chatting to Martin's dad again. At the end of visiting time she went off with Martin's parents, very chipper because she was getting a lift.

'Toodle-oo, little darling,' she said to me, blowing me a kiss.

'Your mum doesn't half pong,' said Martin as all the parents disappeared. 'I can still smell all her flowery scent stuff.'

'It's Californian Poppy,' I said. 'My uncle gave her a big bottle.'

'Fancy your mum going and getting Sister!' said Gillian. 'What was all that about?'

'Oh, she was worried about my splint,' I mumbled.

'You said your leg was all sore and it was Nurse Patterson's fault!' said Martin, who had sharp ears.

There was a collective gasp and a lot of giggling.

'I didn't say it like that exactly. I won't get into trouble, will I?' I asked anxiously.

'Nurse Patterson will!' said Gillian. 'I bet Sister Baker is laying into her right this minute.'

'Oh no,' I said.

'Sister Baker can get ever so cross if she thinks the nurses aren't doing their job properly. Remember that time she caught Nurse Johnson pinching a sweet out of the tin, Rita? She really hit the roof,' said Gillian.

'She went absolutely nuts,' said Rita. 'Nurse Johnson cried buckets.'

'I didn't mean for Nurse Patterson to get into trouble,' I said, nibbling my sore lip.

'Don't worry, Elsie. Who cares about Nurse Patterson?' said Angus. 'She's not very nice to us, is she?'

'I know, but I still didn't mean her to get into trouble with Sister.'

I waited in dread for the nurses to come bustling in. Nurse Curtis came along at last, very pink in the face, her lips pressed tightly together. There was no sign of Nurse Patterson.

'Right, we'd better get you indoors,' she said, seizing hold of Babette's bed and trundling her off. Maureen started wailing. Babette and Maureen loved to be pushed along together, the nurses working in tandem while the little girls played they were in cars and turned imaginary steering wheels, racing each other. There was obviously going to be no fun or games this afternoon. Nurse Curtis trundled backwards and forwards by herself, her face getting pinker and pinker.

'Where's Nurse Patterson, Nurse Curtis?' Gillian dared ask.

'She's . . . not very well,' said Nurse Curtis. She looked straight at me and gave a sniff of disgust.

I didn't risk saying a word to Nurse Curtis when she pushed me back to the ward. I didn't even speak when she pushed me right past my usual bed-space, down to the end of the room – out into the corridor and straight into the little bathroom. It was clear that I was in total disgrace.

I waited fearfully to see what would happen next. I waited and waited and waited, with only a dripping tap and a stack of bedpans for company. I wondered if I was going to miss out on supper, but Nurse Curtis brought me a tray of tomato soup with an egg sandwich. I looked at it doubtfully, wondering if she might have spat in the soup.

'What's the matter, your ladyship?' she said snippily. 'Isn't the food up to scratch? Are you going to complain about that too?'

'I *didn't* complain, not really. Mum misunderstood,' I said.

'Well, you and your blessed mum have scuppered poor Patterson good and proper,' said Nurse Curtis.

'Oh dear, has she got into trouble with Sister?'

'Oh, you make me sick, acting so naïve. Of course she's in trouble. You've only gone and accused her of negligent nursing, and that's the one thing Sister Baker will never forgive. You could come on the ward with your apron on backwards and a potty on your head, and Sister would tick you off and tell you not to be such a silly fool – but she wouldn't hold it against you for long. But if she thinks you're not giving proper nursing care to all you kiddies, then, oh my goodness, you're for it, good and proper. How could you be so wicked, Elsie? You know full well we all wash and powder your wretched leg with scrupulous care – and Patterson always takes particular pains.'

'I know, I know,' I said, cowering under my covers. I accidentally spilled tomato soup all over my tray. 'I'm sorry!' I was scared she might think *that* was deliberate too.

She just sniffed at me again and flounced off. I was left with my unappetizing tray. The soup pooled in a corner, looking unpleasantly bloody. It had even spattered the egg sandwich. I left it altogether and nibbled round the edge of the sandwich. Nobody came to take the tray away when I was finished. With my leg stuck up to my hip in a splint, I couldn't manoeuvre the tray off my chest onto the floor. I didn't dare throw it off. So I had to lie there with the soup congealing in front of my nose, its scent so powerful I felt I was swimming in it.

I heard footsteps – Nurse Curtis's light tread, but then a heavier march on thickly soled rubber heels. Nurse Patterson! But neither came into the bathroom.

I heard the rattle of the washing trolley, but no one came to wash me. Then the ward went quiet, except for the faint buzz of Nurse Patterson's over-emphatic voice. She was telling them all the bedtime story.

Well, I didn't care. I could make up my own story. I tried to make one up there and then. I took myself up the tree, climbed the little ladder through the clouds and stepped out into . . . Grandma Land. It was peopled with hundreds of soft, sweet, grey-haired grandmas, all living in separate tiny thatched cottages, all loving and all very lonely because there didn't seem to be any children in Grandma Land.

'Oh, come and be *my* little grand-daughter, Elsie,' each grandma begged. 'I'd give anything to have a little girl just like you.'

They tried to clutch hold of me with their knobbly little fingers to give me a hug. They shook toffee tins at me and tried to adorn me with hand-knitted cardies and mittens and bobble hats. I was very gentle and grateful with all of them, but I carried on along the twisting path that connected all the cottages until I reached the very last house up a little hill. It was especially lovely, with roses and honey-suckle growing round the door, and a big white cat like Queenie sunning herself on the doormat. I knocked on the yellow door and the grandma inside opened it. She was my own dear nan in her best beaded black dress, her china rose brooch pinned to her chest.

'Oh Nan!' I cried.

'Oh Elsie, my own Elsie!' said Nan, and she hugged me so tight the china rose stuck straight into my cheek, but I didn't care because I was just so happy to be with her at last.

I closed my eyes to keep the image of Nan and me together safe in my head.

'Oh, so we're asleep, are we?' It was Nurse Patterson looming over me, her sticking-out ears in alarming silhouette.

I jumped, and my tray slid dangerously sideways.

'We've taken to spilling all our food now, have we?' said Nurse Patterson. 'I suppose that's my fault too?'

'No, no, I didn't mean to. I didn't mean to do *anything*,' I said. 'I just said to Mum . . . but she took it the wrong way . . . and then Sister came . . .'

'Yes, Sister came, and you told her I didn't wash and powder you properly under your splint,' said Nurse Patterson, stepping backwards, her arms folded. I could see her eyes were very red now, the lids puffy.

'I didn't say that, exactly,' I said. 'I'm really sorry. It was all a mistake.'

'You're the mistake, Elsie Kettle,' said Nurse Patterson. 'A great big mistake.'

I hated the way she said it. People sometimes called me a mistake when they wanted to be nasty to me. They meant I was a mistake because Mum hadn't been married to my dad. Mum herself called me that, 'My little mistake' – as if she'd much sooner I hadn't happened.

I felt my eyes filling with tears.

'Oh, that's right, start boo-hooing, you little cry-baby,' said Nurse Patterson, snatching the tray from me and seizing a towel. She dabbed at my face fiercely. 'Better dry you quick before you say your face is sore.' She wiped so hard she nearly knocked my nose off.

'You're a cry-baby too!' I said, struggling to turn my head away from her.

'Yes, and no wonder! Sister said such dreadful things to me. She'll hold it against me for ever. God knows what she'll put on my report. And it's so *unfair*. I'm a good nurse, I know I am. I'm especially good with children. I take such pains to jolly you all along. I even read you a special bedtime story! I'm scrupulously careful when I wash you, you *know* I am. I've tried particularly hard with you, Elsie.'

I wriggled. I knew it was true. But I also knew it was all pretend. She didn't truly like any of us children – and she *especially* didn't like me.

'I'm going to wash you now, and don't you *dare* say I don't do it properly,' she said.

She washed me thoroughly, rubbing a little too

hard, as if I were a dirty mark and she wanted to get rid of me altogether.

'Now for your wretched leg . . .' She spent a good ten minutes soaping and rinsing and wiping and powdering. 'There – is that good enough for Madam Muck?' she said at last.

'Yes, thank you,' I said. I was trying to be polite, but it seemed to infuriate her further.

I had to endure the whole toileting process, and then she powdered my bottom too, as if I were a little baby.

'Why are you doing that?' I asked.

'Because madam's clearly got such sensitive skin. We don't want any sores whatsoever,' said Nurse Patterson. 'If Sister sees so much as a spot on you, it's clear I'll get the blame. She could get me referred. I could even be thrown out altogether, when I've wanted to be a nurse ever since I was six years old.' She looked as if she might burst out crying again.

I squirmed in embarrassment. 'I'm sorry. I'm really sorry,' I mumbled.

'Yes, well, it's easy enough to say sorry, but it's too late,' said Nurse Patterson, and she switched off the light and flounced off.

I was left lying in the dark. I wondered if Nurse Curtis might come and trundle me back to the ward, but she didn't come near me.

'I don't care,' I said aloud, in case Nurse Patterson was listening. 'I *like* it here all by myself.'

But it was very dark and very lonely and very quiet, apart from the steady drip of the tap. I had always found the snores and sighs from the other sleeping children irritating, but now I longed to hear them.

I tried to imagine myself back into Grandma Land, but I couldn't do it properly any more, and the thought of Nan herself made me cry now. I told myself to hang on. The nurses changed shifts soon. When my dear Nurse Gabriel found me lying there, all forlorn, she'd be kind and comfort me.

I waited and waited and waited. At last I heard more footsteps and murmurings. *Thump thump thump, patter patter patter* – 'Goodbye, Nurse Patterson' . . . 'Hello, Nurse Gabriel'! She'd give me a cuddle, let me have a private little weep, and then wrap me up tenderly and push me back to the ward with all the others. Yes, she'd put her head round the door . . . There she was! She'd shake her head at me sorrowfully – *yes*! And then – and then . . .

'Oh Elsie!' she said softly, and *she walked straight out again*. She left me on my own, in disgrace.

I couldn't bear it. I thought she might come back in five minutes, or maybe ten, just to teach me a little lesson. Maybe she'd come back when she'd checked on everyone else. She didn't. Nurse Johnson didn't come either.

I cried and cried so the tears dripped into my ears. And then someone pattered ever so lightly across the floor, steadied herself, and leaped onto my bed.

'Oh Queenie, it's you!' I said.

'Yes, it's me,' she purred, and she walked delicately up my covers until she got to my face. She put her own soft head down, nuzzled under my chin, and felt my wet tears.

'Dear dear dear,' she purred sympathetically, and she put out her pink tongue and carefully licked my salty skin to give me a wash. Her tongue was a little raspy and tickled, but I lay there gratefully, still as a statue. Then she rubbed the top of her head against me, acting like the softest towel, and settled herself around my neck like a white fur stole.

'Oh Queenie, you darling,' I whispered. 'You're the best little cat in all the world.'

'And you're the best little girl,' she purred. 'Take no notice of those silly nurses. We'll be fine together, just you and me, my Elsie.'

'My Queenie,' I said.

I whispered and she purred long into the night. A nurse might have looked in on us once or twice, but we took no notice. We had our eyes shut, fast asleep.

17

Nurse Gabriel was still a little cool with me in the morning.

'Poor Patterson. She was distraught. You probably didn't *mean* her to get into serious trouble, Elsie, but it's very naughty to complain like that, especially when you know it isn't true,' she said reproachfully as she pushed me back to the ward.

'I *didn't* mean to,' I said. I meant to sound sorry but it came out sounding sulky.

'Now then, missy,' said Nurse Gabriel, making

little tutting sounds as she slotted my bed back between Martin's and Michael's.

'I say, you're in *serious* disgrace,' Martin told me, sounding awed.

'You've certainly got them all in a tizz,' said Gillian. 'Nurse Patterson was booing her eyes out.'

'Good,' said Angus. 'Serves her right. She acts all nicey-nicey but she's horribly mean in lots of little ways. It was horrid of her to shut you away in that scary bathroom all night long.'

'I didn't mind,' I said. 'I had company.'

'You what?' asked Martin.

'Queenie,' I said proudly. 'She's my friend.'

'She's friends with *all* of us,' said Gillian.

'Yeah. Queenie comes to Gillian whenever she calls her, so ya boo sucks to you,' said Rita.

'You wait. Queenie will come to *me*,' I said. 'So ya boo double sucks to you, Rita Rubbish.'

Queenie was out on her morning round of the garden, threading her way stealthily through the shrubberies and lying down for a little snooze under a peony bush. But she wandered back at lunch time, lured by the smell of food. She wasn't really supposed to have any lunch – just a dish of mashed-up whiting for breakfast and again for supper. Queenie clearly felt that this wasn't enough and came on the scrounge.

We only had fish for lunch once a week, but Queenie wasn't too faddy an eater. She was partial to boiled egg or a little liver, and she loved milky puddings. I leaned as far out of bed as I could with my splinted leg and enticed her with titbits. Soon she came running straight to me even if I had only bubble and squeak to offer her, a dish we both detested.

She didn't talk to me in front of the others, but when she lay on my pillow, she rubbed her soft head against my ear and purred gently. It was plain as can be that she was saying, *I love you.*

'And I love you too, dearest Queenie,' I said, stroking each of her ears and tickling her neck so that she wriggled with pleasure.

Sometimes I carefully raked her furry back with my fingers, pretending to be a brush, and she purred so loudly then that my whole bed vibrated.

I tried using my real brush, but Nurse Patterson swiped it from me.

'Stop that, you stupid little girl. Do you want to get fleas?' she said.

'Queenie doesn't have fleas, she's absolutely squeaky clean,' I said indignantly.

'Don't argue with me, you cocky little madam,' said Nurse Patterson. She took the brush and didn't give it back. 'I've sent it off to be thoroughly disinfected,' she told me.

I asked for it the next day. She looked me straight in the eye and said, 'I don't know what you're talking about.'

It was only a grubby hairbrush, a pink baby affair with a cartoon lamb on the back, but it was *my* hairbrush, one of my few remaining pieces of home, and I cried at its loss.

'Don't show her you care, or she'll pinch something else of yours,' said Martin. 'She's really got it in for you now.'

I kept a very careful eye on Albert Trunk and my kitten button box and my Coronation coach, clutching them all in bed with me at night just in case Nurse Patterson tried to steal them out of my locker. It was as well to be vigilant. One evening I spilled cocoa down my cat pyjamas and Nurse Patterson took the jacket 'to soak the stain away'.

I waited twenty-four hours before confronting her. I did it in front of Nurse Curtis so she could act as a witness.

'Please can I have my pyjama top back?' I asked.

'Which pyjama top, Elsie?' said Nurse Curtis.

'The cat one. My special one,' I said.

'Well, what have you done with it, chickie?' said Nurse Curtis.

'I spilled cocoa on it and Nurse Patterson took it

away to be washed and she didn't bring it back,' I said.

I looked Nurse Patterson straight in the eye as I said this. She pulled a silly face, a cartoon of puzzlement.

Nurse Curtis frowned. 'Oh Elsie, are you telling naughty stories again?' she said.

'No, she *did* take it,' I insisted.

'I think you've got a bit muddled, dear,' said Nurse Patterson. The way she said 'dear' made it sound as if she meant the exact opposite. 'I don't do the laundry.'

'I think maybe your mummy took it home after visiting,' said Nurse Curtis. 'Don't look so worried. You've got a hospital nightie.'

I didn't want a wretched hospital nightie. I wanted my own dear cat pyjama top.

'Just you wait till my mum comes,' I muttered.

But Mum didn't seem that interested when I told her the next Saturday.

'Typical!' she said. 'Hospitals are hopeless. They always lose stuff. When I was in the maternity ward having you, someone pinched my pearl powder compact right out of my handbag.'

'That nurse took it. She doesn't like me because she got into trouble about my leg. You know, when you got Sister.'

'Yes, how *is* that sore leg? Any sign of it getting

better?' Mum peered under the covers gingerly, as if she might find a mouse under there. 'It looks just the same to me. I don't know, here's you stuck in here, and your nanny in the sanatorium—'

'Did you go and see her last Sunday, Mum? Did you give her my letter?'

'What's this, the Spanish Inquisition? I told you, she's not well enough for visitors. Cough cough cough, every time she tries to talk, and spitting all the while into that little pot. It really turns my stomach.'

'Oh, *poor* Nan.'

'Stop that – there's no point upsetting yourself.'

'Mum, could you get me new cat pyjamas?'

'All these demands! I can't help feeling you're getting a bit spoiled, lying back here like Lady Muck, being waited on hand and foot. I'm not made of money, you know, but I'll do my best to get you another pair,' said Mum.

'*Will* you? Pink ones from Woolworths, with white cats all over them? Oh Mum, wait till I tell you! I'm still Queenie's favourite. I am, I absolutely am – ask any of the others. She jumps right up on my bed every day and gives me such a lovely cuddle,' I said.

'I thought I told you to pack that lark in, it's not hygienic. Oh my Lord, Mr Perkins is a *stickler* for hygiene. I made him a cup of coffee the other day and he noticed this teeny smudge of lipstick on the rim.

Someone else must have used it, probably me! I'd just rinsed it clean under the tap. He nearly hit the roof, acting like lipstick was deadly poison or something. I had to take the coffee away and scrub that cup till I damn near broke it. Goodness me, what a palaver! He has this thing about germs. He's always washing his hands. He leaps up to do it right in the middle of dictation. I thought he had a bit of trouble with his waterworks and was just going for a wee, but this is really just washing his hands . . . Lovely hands, they are, with very clean nails, not like most blokes. He's clean all over. His *shirts*! They look so crisp and white it's like each one's fresh out the packet. And he's got this lovely clean lemony smell about him. He never pongs even when he gets het up.'

I listened to Mum sing the Perkins praises for a full ten minutes without drawing breath.

'Is he going to be another uncle?' I asked eventually.

'What? No! Good Lord, he's much too posh and rich. He's Perkins Ballpoint Pens Manufacturing, silly. They sell all over the country – all over the *world*. Think of it, all those Froggies and Eyeties scribbling away with their Perkins pens. I'll see if I can bring you some – they'll be good for your drawing. Mr Perkins is right out of my league – not to mention the fact that he's got a snooty wife with a voice like she's sucking acid drops. She's forever phoning up about this and that. He's got two kiddies too. There's a photo of them on his desk. He lives in one of them houses up the hill – you know, the huge ones with big gardens. Ever so posh, they are. Seven bedrooms and just as many bathrooms. He can wash his hands in a different room every day of the week.' Mum laughed uproariously at her own remark, tossing her hair about.

Martin's dad was staring at her. So were the other dads. She was wearing her last year's pink blouse with little puff sleeves and her pencil skirt. The blouse looked littler than I remembered. I was worried Mum was going to burst right out at the top.

'What?' she said.

'Are you getting a bit fatter, Mum?' I asked.

'You *what*? Cheeky little devil! Still, I must admit this waistband's a bit tight. I'm used to two hours' dancing practice and a long show every night – and I've eaten fish and chips every supper time because I can't be bothered to cook for myself. Oh Gawd, I *am* getting fatter, aren't I?'

'You could always wear them Stephanie Beauman knickers. Nurse Johnson wears them,' I said.

'No blooming fear!' She sat up straight, sticking out her chest, smoothing her hands over her stomach.

'*Am* I getting fat?' she said again, glancing coyly at Martin's dad.

He looked eager to reassure her, but one glance at his own wife made him keep quiet.

'Your mum!' said Martin, when visiting time was over.

'What *about* my mum?'

'Showing all her chest like that!' he said.

'It's the fashion,' I said fiercely.

'That's not fashion,' Gillian muttered to Rita. 'That's dead common.'

'Yeah, *my* mum calls her the blonde floosie,' Rita whispered.

'I *heard* that! You shut up about my mum. *Your* mums are just jealous because she's so pretty,' I said, burning.

I wouldn't talk to anyone for the rest of the day. I called for Queenie, but she was out hunting in the grounds. I tried to pretend her, but it wouldn't work. I was so used to her soft warm weight that I couldn't conjure her up convincingly. I tried imagining Snow White and Sooty and Marmalade, but I hadn't played with them for a while and they suddenly seemed like a baby game. I was so jangled up inside I couldn't play *anything*. If only Nan could visit me instead of Mum.

I almost wished Mum wouldn't come visiting at all

– but when she didn't come the next Saturday, I was devastated. I craned my neck for two whole hours, until I felt my head would snap right off and roll under the bed. I couldn't help thinking something bad had happened and it was all my fault for being ashamed of her.

I plucked up the courage to ask Nurse Curtis if Mum had sent a message to say she couldn't come.

'I'm sorry, dear. Maybe she'll come tomorrow,' she said, and she sat beside me and chatted for five minutes, telling me silly stories to distract me.

Even Nurse Patterson wasn't quite so cool when she washed me ready for bed that night. She didn't comment on my tear-stained cheeks, but when she'd finished me, patting me drier than the Sahara, she said, 'Chin up, chicken.'

I kept my chin right down on my chest until Queenie came to see me. I'd been too distracted to save her any titbits, but she was very forgiving. She walked all round me, purring, and then curled up beside me, nestling into my neck.

'Oh Queenie, what's happened to my mum?' I whispered.

'Nothing's happened to her, dearie,' Queenie purred. 'You know what your mum's like. She's a busy lady, especially now she's got this new job with old Mr Perkychops.' She yawned, clearly bored silly just at the mention of his name. 'Tell you what, Elsie! I expect she went shopping. Yes, she'll have gone to Woolworths and bought you another pair of cat pyjamas – very fetching, those jim-jams, with all those beautiful white cats.' She preened herself, knowing that if there were a talking mirror in Cat Land, it would declare that *she* was the most beautiful of them all.

'Do you *really* think she went to get me new pyjamas? So will she come with them tomorrow?' I asked her.

'Yes, of course,' Queenie purred. 'Now lie still and stop fussing so we can both go to sleep.'

I woke up convinced that Queenie was right – but I started to doubt as Sunday morning moved on. I was in a terrible state by visiting time. I so hoped Mum would be first in the queue of visitors, rushing out onto the veranda the moment the bell rang – but she wasn't there.

I had to lie trapped in my bed all alone for the next two hours while all the other parents chatted to their children.

'Where's your mum this weekend then?' asked Martin's dad.

'Oh, she's – she's had to work this weekend. She's a top secretary, you know, and her boss is very demanding,' I said.

'I'll bet,' he said. 'Here, our Martin, give us that Mars bar back. We need to share it with the little lass.'

I thought Martin would object, but he didn't even murmur when his dad broke it in half. I usually thought Mars bars a great treat. I liked to nibble along the top until I got to the wonderful sticky caramel part – but this time I ate it properly. It tasted of cardboard. I was glad to brush my teeth that night to get rid of the taste.

I didn't want to talk to anyone again. I pretended to be asleep when Nurse Gabriel and Nurse Johnson came on duty – but my dear Nurse Gabriel wasn't fooled. We were friends again now, though neither of us risked referring to Nurse Patterson.

She sat on my bed and held my hand.

'My mum didn't come!' I mumbled.

'Yes, I saw the visitors' book.'

'And she didn't come yesterday either.'

'Poor Elsie.'

'Do you think she's . . . all right?' I asked.

'Yes, I'm sure she is. You mustn't fret, Elsie. But listen, why don't you write *her* a letter? I'll post it for you.'

'Oh, *would* you? Can I write it now?'

'If it's just a little letter and you're very quick.'

'And can I write to Nan again too?'

'You can write to your nan tomorrow.'

'Do you think she really got my last letter? She hasn't written back.'

'I don't think she'll be allowed to, not if she's really poorly,' said Nurse Gabriel. 'Now, let's get this letter written, lickety-spit.'

Dear Mum,

I hope you are all right. I missed you on Saturday and Sunday. Please come to see me.

Love from Elsie.

P.S. And please could you bring me some new cat pyjamas as I hate the hospital nighties.

'There now,' said Nurse Gabriel. 'I'll fetch you an envelope and you can write the address. Better print it to make it really clear.'

'I'm not a very good writer, am I,' I said, looking at my scrawl. My letters were wobbly and tipped uncertainly backwards and forwards.

'Maybe you're not so hot at writing things down – but I know you're very good at making up stories in your head. I hope you'll carry on with your story-telling, Elsie. The other children are missing their night-time treat. Poor Angus is quite upset.'

'I'll tell a story again tomorrow,' I said.

'That's a good kind girl. Now, let me settle you

down for the night.' She turned my pillow over so I could have the cool side and plumped it up carefully. She smoothed my hair out of my face and tucked the sheets under my chin.

'Night-night, sweetheart,' she said softly, stroking my cheek.

'Oh Nurse Gabriel! I wish *you* were my mum,' I whispered.

She seemed startled, but she smiled at me sweetly. 'And I wish you were my little girl, Elsie,' she said.

I tried to dream that Nurse Gabriel really was my mum and we lived in a lovely house with a special bed for poorly Nan, and Queenie came to live with us too, and we all lived happily ever after. But when I fell asleep, everything got mixed up and terrible. Nurse Gabriel ran away and didn't come back, and Queenie hissed at me, and poor Nan lay very still and grey in her bed, and she wouldn't open her eyes no matter how hard I tried to wake her . . .

I didn't get a letter back from Mum – but she came the next Saturday. She was right at the front of the queue in her pink blouse and tight white trousers, flip-flapping her way down the veranda in new high-heeled mules – and she had a carrier bag in her hand.

'Oh Mum!' I said, and I burst into tears.

'Well, *there's* a nice greeting! Come on, stop that silly bawling. Look, I've got a present for you.'

'Is it – oh, is it new cat pyjamas?' I said.

'You have a little look,' said Mum, thrusting the carrier bag at me.

There was a flat box tied with ribbon and the name of a fancy department store written again and again, the way I scrawled *Elsie Kettle* hundreds of times on my school jotter.

'But this isn't a Woolworths box,' I said.

'This is none of your Woolworths rubbish, silly. Take a look!' said Mum.

My hands trembled as I undid the ribbon and opened the box. I had to scrabble amongst the tissue paper before I brought out my surprise. It didn't seem to be pyjamas after all, just a blouse top with puff sleeves and yet another pair of terrible frilly knickers.

'Well?' Mum demanded. 'Aren't they absolutely darling?'

'Yes, but – but I can't wear proper clothes while I'm in hospital.'

'They're pyjamas, silly! Baby-doll pyjamas. They're the latest thing. Don't tell anyone, but I've bought a pair for myself! As soon as I saw them I knew they'd be perfect for you. I *had* to buy them even though they cost a fortune.'

'Are you *sure* they're pyjamas, Mum?'

'Yes, silly. Jayne Mansfield's wearing a pair in my latest copy of *Picture Show*. And they're ideal for you because they've got the panties, see. I know you can't get pyjama legs over that awful brace thing. How is your leg? Let me have a look.' She peered under the blanket, tutting.

I stared at the baby-doll pyjamas. 'They've got little red hearts on,' I said flatly.

'Yes, aren't they cute?' said Mum.

They might be cute, but they weren't *cats*. I wondered if I dared beg Mum to return the baby-dolls and buy the right pyjamas – but I was pretty sure I knew what her reaction would be. I bit my lip instead.

'I don't know how that leg's going to get any better if they don't give it any treatment. It'll wither up if you stop using it altogether. I think you'd be much better off hobbling around to make it work again. I need you to get better and be a good strong girl. I want to show you off to Mr Perkins, and he's very particular. He's got a horror of hospitals and cripples. He says it makes his stomach turn over. He can't even look at that little plaster boy with a surgical boot that stands outside the chemist's shop – you know, the one where you put your money in the slot in his head and it goes to some sick kiddies' charity.'

I knew and loved that plaster boy. Nan always let me put a penny in him when we went to buy cough sweets and milk of magnesia and sticking plasters. I called him the Penny Boy and pretended he was real.

He stumped along beside me when we went to Woolworths, and I let him choose a toy from the penny counter and shared my packet of lemonade dip with him.

Now I burned with indignation on his behalf as much as my own. 'Mr Perkins sounds silly,' I muttered.

'What was that? Don't you go bad-mouthing him! He's my boss and he's a very important man,' said Mum.

I looked at her. 'He *is* your boyfriend now, isn't he?'

'Stop that cheek or I'll give you a good slapping,' said Mum indignantly. Her cheeks were as pink as her lipstick. Who did she think she was kidding? Of course he was her boyfriend.

'Where were you last Saturday?' I asked. 'Why didn't you come to see me?'

'Gawd, another Spanish Inquisition! I was *busy* last weekend. I had to do overtime. We had a sudden big order and it was all hands on deck.'

'So you were with Mr Perkins?'

'There's no need to say it in that way. I *told* you, he's just my boss and I've got to do my best to keep in with him. He's not a bit like the sleazy riff-raff you get in show business. You should see his suits! They're all bespoke, Savile Row – and his shoes are so highly polished you can see your face in them. He wouldn't be seen dead in suede. Now listen, I'll do my best to trail over here to visit you—'

'And Nan.'

'Well, she's not up to visitors, so stop giving me your orders, Miss Saucebox. Apparently she's taken a turn for the worse,' said Mum.

'Oh no!'

'Now now, no need to act like a little tragedy queen. They've collapsed her lung.'

'What? Why did they do that?'

'*I* don't know. All these medical experts do this and that, but none of it seems to make any sense. All I know is she's got to have complete rest and peace and quiet and no visitors. Maybe it's just as well. TB is very catching. She's already given it to you.'

'No she *didn't*! Nurse Gabriel said—'

'Oh, I know, but nurses will say any old thing. Fancy coming out with that cow fairy story! As if you could catch TB from a glass of milk! If Mr Perkins knew that, he'd never have a cup of tea again, which would make my life a lot easier. I have to make him a fresh cup at least five times a day. *Anyway*, we can't afford for me to catch it too, else we'd all be in Queer Street. Do stop looking at me like that, with those big eyes. You're starting to *look* like a cow now. You'll be mooing next.'

I shut my eyes tight.

'And don't go to sleep on me either! I thought you were desperate for me to visit you, writing me little letters! You love your mummy really, don't you, you funny little kid?'

I nodded obediently.

'I can't wait to see you in your new baby-dolls. You'll look so sweet,' said Mum.

I saved wearing them till the next Saturday, so they'd be clean and uncreased. Nurse Curtis cut the ribbon round the box in half and tied each piece round the end of my plaits.

'There, you look as pretty as a picture,' she said.

But our efforts were wasted. Mum didn't come at all that weekend.

18

I had learned not to count on Mum coming. She'd might say she'd see me next week, but that didn't mean she'd actually turn up. She stayed away the next two weekends too. Nurse Gabriel asked if I'd like to write another letter, but I didn't want to.

Mum turned up the next week. She came loaded with gifts: a violet soap and talc set, a new blue brush and comb, and a little gilt brooch with the Queen's head on it.

'You'll want to smell nice and keep fresh and tidy

while you're stuck here in bed – and I thought you'd like the little brooch. It's cute, isn't it? You know who the lady is, don't you?'

'It's the Queen,' I said. A fresh wave of missing Nan overwhelmed me.

'What's up *now*?' said Mum, looking cross. 'If you don't like the brooch, I'll have it back.'

'No, I do, I do. It's just I was remembering – Nan and I were going to the Coronation,' I said mournfully.

'Oh dear, yes. And here you are stuck in your beds. Well, I don't know whether to tell you this, Elsie. It seems a bit mean under the circumstances – but I'm hoping to be able to go myself.'

'*You're* going to the Coronation?' I said.

'There's a chance I might be able to watch it in comfort,' said Mum. 'Mr Perkins has a very good friend who works in an office ever so near Westminster Abbey. We're going to watch from his office window. We should have a wonderful view.'

'You lucky thing,' I said flatly.

'Well, you could always try and get better and then you could come too,' said Mum.

'I *am* trying, Mum,' I said.

I asked Nurse Gabriel that night if she thought I had any chance at all of getting better by the Coronation.

'I'm afraid not, pet,' she said, taking hold of my hand.

'When *will* I get better?'

'Perhaps . . . perhaps by Christmas?'

'But that's ages and ages away.'

'Yes, I know.'

'And I've been here ages *already*.'

I knew it was only a couple of months or so, but it felt like a century. It was hard to imagine myself in my old life now. I knew I'd once walked to school and played hopscotch and run down to the shops on errands for Nan, but it seemed like something I'd made up in a story. I'd lift the blanket and peer down at myself. My good leg now seemed just as useless as my bad leg in the splint. I wasn't sure I'd ever remember how to walk properly again. Perhaps I'd end up in a wheelchair – but then who would push me?

I clutched Queenie in panic that night.

'Calm down, dear,' she purred. 'You must keep on feeding me titbits and then I'll grow and grow. By Christmas I could grow as big as a tiger, and then you could climb on my great strong back and I'd carry you anywhere you wanted.'

'Oh Queenie, yes please!' I said.

I started saving her a good half of each meal until Nurse Patterson caught me feeding her my entire portion of battered cod.

'What is the *matter* with you, Elsie Kettle? How dare you waste good food like this! You children are given the best of everything to build up your bones and make you fit and strong. What's the point of us giving you your injections and taking such care of your splints – *yes*, Elsie! – when you wilfully throw your food away,' she ranted.

'I'm *not* throwing it away. I'm giving it to Queenie.'

'And just look at her! She's not exactly starving, is she? The cook boils a whiting for her every day. She doesn't *need* your fish. You'll only make her sick if you give her any extra.'

'Yes, Nurse Patterson. No, Nurse Patterson. Three bags full, Nurse Patterson,' I said sullenly – and ended up spending hours by myself, banished to the bathroom.

'I hear you've been in the doghouse again, Elsie,' said Nurse Gabriel when she came on duty that evening.

'The *bath*house, Nurse Gabriel,' I said.

'You're a shocker, Elsie. You plague the life out of poor Nurse Patterson. Can't you try to be a good girl just for the next week?'

'Why a week?'

'That's when our tour of duty finishes. We'll be off to other wards then.'

304

'Nurse Patterson is *leaving*?' I said, not properly concentrating.

I'd assumed the nurses were permanent, as much part of the hospital as the beds in the ward.

I felt a rush of happiness that we'd be rid of Nurse Patterson at last – and then my stomach turned over at a new and terrible thought.

'*You* won't be going, will you, Nurse Gabriel?' I asked, my throat so dry that my voice came out all croaky.

'I'm being transferred to one of the men's wards in the main hospital,' she said.

'Oh no! I'll miss you so!' I wailed.

'And I'll miss you too, Elsie. I'll miss all of you. But when I'm on nights I'll pop in and visit during the daytime if you like,' said Nurse Gabriel. '*If* you're a good girl, Elsie.'

'I'll be like a little sunbeam,' I said, remembering another of Nan's favourite hymns.

Nurse Gabriel laughed and gently pinched my nose. 'You're a caution, you are.'

'You really *will* come back and visit me when you're no longer on the ward?'

'I promise.' She crossed her fingers and grinned. 'Cross my fingers and hope to die if I tell a lie.'

Miss Isles suggested we all make farewell cards for the nurses in our art lesson. I spent ages and ages on Nurse Gabriel's card. I drew a picture of me lying in bed waving. Queenie was on the bed too, waving her front paw. I still didn't have a white crayon, so I couldn't colour her in, but I did her outline very carefully, making tiny jagged lines to indicate her fluffy fur. I did every little red heart on my baby-doll pyjamas, and then I drew more, in a little trail up to the top of the page, where I draped them over my printed message: *I will miss you so, Nurse Gabriel*.

'Are they *hearts*?' said Martin, peering. 'It's a good-bye card, not a blessed Valentine, Gobface.'

'Oh, does it look silly?' I said, stricken. I didn't want to embarrass Nurse Gabriel.

'You shut up, Farty Marty. You're just being mean because you can't draw as well as Elsie,' said Gillian.

I left out the elaborate hearts on Nurse Johnson's and Nurse Curtis's cards, though I tried hard with them both because I liked them. I didn't try at all with Nurse Patterson's. I drew a pin-girl me and I didn't give her a smiling face. I was very tempted to write at the top: *Goodbye and good riddance, Nurse Pyjama-stealer*, but in the end I wrote *Sorry* in very tiny letters.

Nurse Patterson was trying hard to be nicey-nice to all of us. She sometimes *sang* as she went about the ward or pushed us up and down the veranda. She was going to a maternity home. 'I shall be nursing all the mums and their lovely little new-born babies,' she said happily.

Perhaps she had been really worried Sister wouldn't recommend her to anyone else.

'I hope she wipes the babies' bottoms more gently than she wipes ours!' Angus hissed. He didn't like her any more than I did. None of us thawed towards her, even though she gave us double sweets her last week and read us a chapter a night from a new story about a silly man called Mr Twiddle. I invented my own Elsie version, renaming him Mr Piddle, and made everyone snort with laughter.

On her last day Nurse Patterson came into the ward carrying a little paper parcel. She came up to my bed. 'Here, Elsie,' she said. 'Look what I found crumpled in a corner on the laundry floor. It must have been there for weeks. I washed and ironed it for you myself.'

I opened the paper parcel and felt the soft pink of my dear cat pyjama top. I looked up at Nurse Patterson. She had gone very pink too.

I wondered what to say. And then I decided to say nothing at all. I just slipped the pyjama top safely under the sheets – and all the little white cats jumped off the pink material and nuzzled against my bare skin.

The nurses all kissed us goodbye on their last day. Nurse Patterson actually had tears in her eyes.

'I'll miss you so,' she said to everyone, though I was absolutely certain she wasn't going to miss me. I wasn't going to miss her either. I wouldn't care if I never saw her again. Still, I was glad she'd found somewhere else to go – I didn't want to think of her being out of work because of me.

I cared desperately about Nurse Gabriel – but she was as good as her word. She came and visited me on Sunday. Some days she came in her tea break too. Other days she came in specially after night duty. She said she was coming to visit everyone, and she *did* have a little word with each of us – but she always came to sit by *my* bed.

'She's *my* special friend,' I boasted to the others.

'She only sits by you because you never have any visitors on a Sunday,' said Martin. 'She's sorry for you.'

Mum didn't come that Sunday.

'Why *doesn't* your mum come round?' Martin asked.

I had my suspicions. I looked like I had a new uncle . . . called Mr Perkins.

'My mum's just busy,' I said.

'What does your mum do? My dad says she's such a looker she ought to be in films,' said Martin.

'Yes, well, she used to be in show business, but now she's like this very senior secretary, ever so posh,' I said.

'My mum doesn't think she's posh. She says she thinks your mum looks very common.'

'Well, I don't care what your mum or your dad thinks, so shut your face,' I said fiercely.

I knew he was just jealous because he'd far sooner have a visit from Nurse Gabriel than his mum and dad. She looked lovely for a start. I hardly recognized her the first time she came, when she wasn't wearing her funny white nurse's cap and her blue dress and apron. Her lovely fair hair swung over her ears in a little bob. She kept it from falling in her eyes with a little butterfly hair slide, so she looked sweetly childish. She wore different dresses – candy stripe and polka dot and a flowery one I liked the most, but always on top she wore a fluffy blue angora bolero!

'I *love* your bolero, Nurse Gabriel,' I said, shyly stroking her shoulder.

'I made it myself,' she said. 'Can you knit, Elsie?'

'My nan showed me how to do plain and purl, and I did a scarf for Albert Trunk once,' I said.

'Well, maybe you could have a go at a bolero. I could ask Mrs Rhodes to help you,' said Nurse Gabriel.

Mrs Rhodes was a sort of teacher, like Miss Isles, but she taught us to make things. They were all pretty *useless* things: Michael and Babette and Maureen had to make plaited mats, and Rita and Martin and Gillian and I were labouring over cross-stitch purses. They certainly made *us* cross, especially Martin, who took great exception to being forced to do girlie sewing.

'What would I want with a flipping purse, anyway?' he grumbled.

'It will make a lovely present for your mother,' said Mrs Rhodes.

I didn't know about Martin's mother, but I knew my mum wouldn't want my big ugly cross-stitch purse. I had tried to pattern it with cross-stitch cats, but they looked very unnerving, like robot animals. I wondered if Nan might like it, even though the seams were very loose and wobbly so it wouldn't be sensible to store money in it. Maybe she could tuck her hankie inside?

Sometimes I almost forgot that Nan was stuck in the sanatorium. Whenever I dreamed of her she was at home, sitting in her armchair sucking pear drops or fast asleep in bed with her mouth open, her teeth grinning in a glass beside her.

I wondered if she dreamed of me. Maybe we could somehow jump into each other's dreams? I went to sleep thinking of Nan. I dreamed that we walked hand in hand all the way to London – no cough, no limps, the two of striding out, singing 'God Save the Queen'. When we got there, it was terribly crowded. We were pushed here and jostled there, but Nan kept tight hold of my hand and helped me climb right up some railings. We balanced there, and cheered when the Queen went past in her golden coach pulled by eight grey horses. They all tossed their heads and neighed at us, and then the Queen herself stuck her head out of the window and shouted, 'Hello, Nan, hello, Elsie! Thank you for coming!' while the crowd roared.

It was such a wonderful dream I told it to the others at breakfast time, but they laughed at me.

'You're absolutely bonkers, Gobface. As if the Queen would ever talk to you!' said Martin, chortling.

'It's so unfair. I'd give anything to see the Queen,' said Gillian.

'I wish we could go to London,' said Rita.

'*Pussycat, pussycat, where have you been? I've been to London to visit the Queen,*' said Michael, making us all laugh.

'Maybe you *will* see her!' said Nurse Bryant.

She was the best of the new nurses. She was tall and she had a long, thin, superior face like a camel's – but she was surprisingly good fun. She liked playing little tricks. One day she brought in a whoopee cushion, which made a spectacularly rude noise when you leaned against it. Another day she put a pretend plastic dog poo right in the middle of the ward, which made Nurse Smith squeal.

We all laughed and laughed. Martin in particular adored Nurse Bryant.

We thought it was just one of Nurse Bryant's elaborate tricks when, on the day of the Coronation, she came bustling into the ward with a big parcel. It was clearly heavy because Nurse Smith had to help her – and Mr Dobbin came too, to supervise as they unpacked.

We all craned our necks, waiting in suspense. When the wrappings were off we could see a square shiny brown box.

'What *is* it, Nurse Bryant?' Martin asked, giggling in anticipation.

'It's your own little Coronation,' she told him, grinning. 'The coach is inside, and all the horses, and the Queen herself in her splendid robes.'

We all blinked at her.

'Watch out when she takes the lid off,' Gillian warned, expecting an elaborate jack-in-the-box.

But Mr Dobbin was now twiddling knobs and waving a strange metal shape in the air. Suddenly we saw a grey and white picture flash across the front of the box and heard the sound of cheering!

'Oh my giddy aunt!' Gillian exclaimed. 'It's a television set!'

We had all heard of televisions, but none of us had one at home. But here was one of these magic boxes in our own ward – so we could watch the Coronation!

'It's all due to Sir David, bless him,' said Nurse Bryant. 'He's ordered a set for every single ward, so that none of the patients should miss the Coronation. And we can see it too, eh, Smithy? Isn't it marvellous?'

'We'll be able to watch it all?' I said.

'It'll be just like being up in London,' said Nurse Bryant. 'In fact, you'll have a much better view!'

A sudden hope made me shiver. 'Oh Nurse Bryant, is every hospital having a television – even a sanatorium?'

'It depends if they've got a consultant as generous as Sir David,' she said. 'I wouldn't think so.'

I would. I willed there to be a television in Nan's ward with every fibre of my being. 'And we'll watch the Coronation together, Nan, just like we planned,' I whispered, shutting my eyes tight and clenching my fists, making the strongest wish I could manage.

'Elsie? You won't see anything with your eyes shut, silly,' said Nurse Bryant.

For the first day ever we weren't pushed out onto

the veranda. Our beds were crammed together, mattresses touching, in a little line in front of the television. Angus was put at an angle to help him see better. The nurses propped the rest of us up with extra pillows, so that we felt a little dizzy and disorientated. We all stared at the tiny grey picture, straining to hear the commentary.

'That's Richard Dimbleby talking,' said Nurse Bryant, showing off her knowledge to Nurse Smith. 'I've heard him on the radio. He's very good.'

He was telling us about all the lords and ladies going into the great big church.

'That's Westminster Abbey,' said Nurse Bryant, determined to give us her own commentary.

We stared at all the posh people in their stiff outfits. Michael waved to them and we all half expected them to wave back. Hundreds of posh people crammed themselves into Westminster Abbey, while thousands and thousands of ordinary folk cheered outside in the rain. I narrowed my eyes, concentrating fiercely, searching the grey crowds – madly looking for Nan and me.

The commentary went on and on, and grew just a little bit boring. Where was the Queen? She was the one we all wanted to see.

Then, at last, we saw the coach.

'The golden Coronation coach,' said Nurse Bryant

– but it was a disappointing grey on the screen. The horses were all whitey-grey. The Queen herself was pale grey, even her curls and lipstick. I couldn't help feeling terribly disappointed.

The others pointed and called enthusiastically, still enchanted by the little television picture. I was interested when we went inside the abbey with the grey Queen, and I liked the grand music – but there was so much talking in between. Nurse Bryant and Nurse Smith still watched, absorbed, but we children all started fidgeting and whispering amongst ourselves. Then, eventually, a man in a long robe held the crown high above the Queen's head and solemnly lowered it, cramming it down on her forehead. A voice rang out: 'God save the Queen!' and soon the whole abbey was echoing it.

'God save the Queen!' said Nurse Bryant and Nurse Smith, standing up in deference.

We couldn't stand, of course, but we all said 'God save the Queen' too, though Babette and Maureen went into peals of giggles afterwards.

Queenie came wandering into the ward, clearly wondering why we weren't out on the veranda. She eyed us all warily, alarmed because our beds weren't in their usual positions.

'Here, Queenie,' I said, clicking my tongue at her encouragingly.

She hesitated, not quite sure what she wanted to do, but then readied herself and jumped up onto my bed.

'There, darling Queenie,' I said, reaching for her.

She butted her head against the palm of my hand, wanting me to make a fuss of her.

'God save our Queenie,' I said, and Martin and Gillian and Rita and Angus all said it too.

'Elsie! Show some respect,' said Nurse Bryant, but she wasn't really cross.

We watched the Queen make her way slowly out of the church, holding her head very stiffly and carefully, and then she got back into her coach while the crowd outside cheered and cheered. She smiled a little now, and gave elegant waves as if she were languidly fanning herself. We all waved back now, Martin messing about, fluttering his eyelashes and pursing up his lips.

Then all the posh people filed out of the abbey into the rain, and the solemn voice told us who everyone was all over again. They all looked the same except for the large black Queen of Tonga, Queen Salote. She got a really big cheer because she kept the roof of her carriage down so everyone could see her.

'Oh my, what a treat!' said Nurse Bryant, rushing round giving us all a hug.

There was another treat for supper too. We were all given a wonderful plate of creamy chicken.

'It's special Coronation chicken,' said Nurse Bryant. 'The recipe's been in all the papers. Oh, God save our cook as well as our Queen!'

I'd only ever had chicken at Christmas before. It was white and tender and it didn't have any fat at all. I decided it was my absolute favourite food. It was a bit of a struggle saving some for Queenie, but worth it when I did. She ate it up with immense relish, mewing for more.

We thought Mr Dobbin would come and pack the television back in its box. It was such a thrill when we realized that it was here to stay. We were pushed in early from the veranda now, our beds crammed together at five o'clock so that we could watch *Children's Hour* on the television.

We thought it was all wonderful, but I liked the puppet Mr Turnip best, with his little dancing walk. I begged some wool from Mrs Rhodes and tied long strands to Albert Trunk's legs, but no matter how I pulled he couldn't get the knack of walking. I got cross with him and gave him a little tap. I only meant to give him a tiny smack for being uncooperative, but he tumbled right off the bed and disappeared.

'Oh Albert Trunk!' I said, reaching out desperately with my arm.

'Whoops! You've lost him now, Gobface,' said Martin. 'Oh dear, I can just see him upside down on his silly head. Watch out he doesn't get swept up with the rubbish.'

'Stop it! He won't be swept up,' I said, wriggling myself inch by inch to the edge of my bed.

'Oh yes he will,' said Martin. 'He's rubbish now, all dust and gunge. They'll throw him away.'

'No they won't. They'll just send him off to be fumigated,' Angus called, trying to comfort me.

It only made me more agitated. I knew they probably wouldn't throw Albert Trunk away. Even Nurse Patterson had given my pyjamas back eventually. But they were so strict about dirt and germs, they *might* just take Albert Trunk off to be fumigated – and then he would come back smelling horrible again.

I looked around for Queenie. She was right at the other end of the ward, pacing the empty spaces where our beds were when we weren't watching television.

'Queenie! Over here, Queenie girl. Fetch! Fetch Albert Trunk for me,' I called.

Queenie looked up and gazed at me balefully. 'Don't try to treat me like a silly little dog,' she said, and stalked off.

'Then I'll fetch him myself,' I said determinedly.

I edged slowly across my bed, taking hold of my splint and dragging my bad leg along with me.

'Don't!' said Gillian. 'You're not supposed to do that! You'll bust it!'

'I have to get Albert Trunk,' I gasped, sweat prickling under my arms with the effort.

'The nurses will come along soon. They'll pick him up,' Gillian told me.

'But then he'll be fumigated.'

'No he won't! They only do that for our stuff when we first get here in case we've got bugs from home,' said Gillian.

'I didn't *have* any bugs!' I said indignantly.

The rush of anger gave me a little strength. I shoved hard, and then I was teetering on the very end of the bed. There were barely two inches between my bed and Martin's – just enough room for me to slide my arm down and fish up poor Albert Trunk.

'*Don't*, Gobface.' Martin was sounding a little panicked now. 'You can't reach him and you'll only hurt yourself.'

'No I won't,' I said, with one last thrust – and then my body shifted into thin air, and the whole of me went hurtling downwards and landed with an almighty thump on the floor.

'Nurse! Nurse! Nurse, come quick! Elsie's fallen!' Gillian shrieked.

I lay very still.

'Oh no! She's killed herself! It really *is* the Bed of Doom!' said Martin.

I was so stunned I couldn't work out whether he

was right or not. Was I dead? I couldn't seem to move. I couldn't see anything. My ears seemed to be the only bit of me that was working. Perhaps I was a ghost now. Was heaven a land above a magic tree? But how could I climb the ladder? My poorly leg was far too heavy – and my *other* leg throbbed too. No, it didn't just throb, it hurt unbearably – and it seemed to be crumpled in an odd way, kicking out weirdly at the knee as if I were trying to do the Charleston.

I heard a weird slithering noise. I opened my eyes and saw Nurse Bryant propelling herself towards me underneath my bed.

'Oh my Lord, Elsie Kettle! What have you done to yourself?' she gasped.

Nurse Smith frantically pulled the beds to one side so they could get at me properly. I was so scared I tried to roll away from them, but a terrible pain shot right up my leg – my *good* leg – to my hip.

'Please don't be cross,' I whimpered. My voice seemed to have broken too. It was just a tiny whisper.

'I'm flaming *furious*,' said Nurse Bryant, but she was touching me very gently and tenderly all over, tutting when she got to my legs. I hoped she would twist my good leg back into place for me, the way I manipulated my celluloid dolls' legs when they got stuck the wrong way, but she didn't even touch it.

'My leg hurts,' I said.

'I dare say it does. You've clearly broken it,' said Nurse Bryant. 'Better run for Sister and Sir David, Smithy. Someone senior needs to assess this little jobby. Heaven help us if the tubercular leg is broken too. Oh Lordy, they're going to have our guts for garters.'

'It wasn't your fault!' I said. I couldn't bear the thought of getting any more nurses in trouble, especially not Nurse Bryant, who was my second favourite after Nurse Gabriel.

'It's our job to look after you and to stop you flinging yourselves out of bed. Whatever possessed you, child?'

'I was trying to reach my elephant! He tumbled out of bed because he wouldn't walk like Mr Turnip,' I said, starting to sob.

'God save her, she's not making any kind of sense. Is she delirious?' asked Nurse Smith.

'No, this one's always mad as a hatter. Will you run for *help*, Smithy,' said Nurse Bryant, but she fumbled for Albert Trunk under the beds and sat him on my chest. 'There now, here's Jumbo Doo-Da come to cheer you up.'

'He's Albert Trunk,' I sniffed, clutching him fiercely.

'Lie still now. No moving at all until you're properly assessed,' said Nurse Bryant. 'Especially don't try to move your head.'

'Has she broken her neck, Nurse Bryant?' Martin asked.

'Oh Elsie, we *told* you not to do it,' said Gillian.

'Yeah, we told you,' echoed Rita.

'Maybe you're *all* broken and you'll have to be in a plaster bed like Angus,' said Martin.

'No she won't,' said Angus. His voice was quavery but he spoke as clearly as he could. 'Don't worry, Elsie. You'll be all right. And if you *do* have to go in a plaster bed, it's not too terrible. It just gets a bit itchy, that's all. Don't get upset, please.'

I swallowed hard. 'Thank you, Angus. You are a true friend,' I said hoarsely.

'Now now, Elsie, don't try to speak,' said Nurse Bryant. 'But you're right, Angus is indeed a true friend. Plaster beds aren't so very dreadful, but I don't think you'll need one. As far as I can see, you've simply broken your good leg, though heaven help us if your bad leg is broken too.'

Nurse Smith came scurrying back with reinforcements, including Sir David himself, in his shirtsleeves. I got really scared again, but he was so gentle, feeling me all over and then supervising the nurses as they lifted me back into bed. I was wheeled along to be X-rayed in the main hospital, my splint taken right off. Oh, the joy of getting that leg free again, though it looked alarming, like a little white

322

matchstick. My other leg was even more worrying, kicking out at its new awkward angle.

'Clean break, thank goodness,' said Sir David.

They operated the next morning. I was told to breathe into a horrible rubber mask.

'I don't want to!' I protested, but someone held it hard over my nose and mouth, and I suddenly slipped into a dream world. There was Nan, her arms out-stretched, sitting me on her lap and giving me a big hug. She told me again and again that I was her own special girl and she loved me so, in spite of my legs – and when I looked down, I saw they'd both grown enormously into huge crooked giant legs stretching right across the carpet, the feet pressed hard against the wall, terror legs that made me scream.

'Now now, Elsie, calm down, my little love,' said Nan.

Then her voice changed. 'There now, Elsie, it's all right. Calm down, dear.'

I opened my eyes, and there was *Nurse Gabriel*, her white nurse's cap outlining her head like a halo.

'Is it really you, Nurse Gabriel?' I mumbled. 'You've got your uniform on.'

'Yes, because I'm on duty in the men's ward, but I came haring across in my lunch break to check on you. I heard you'd been wilfully flinging yourself out of bed, you daft banana!' She gently poked me on my nose.

'Oh, my legs!' I said, starting to cry.

'Oh dear, do they hurt dreadfully?' asked Nurse Gabriel.

'No, but they've got so *big*. I won't ever be able to find socks and shoes for them,' I wept.

'Yes you will, you funny little moppet! Look – they've not got any bigger.'

She held up my blanket and I peered down. My right leg was back in its splint, fitting it perfectly. My left leg was encased in white plaster, which made me gasp a little, but I could see my foot poking out at the end, and it looked its own normal size. I blinked at them. They didn't grow at all.

'It was just a *dream*,' I said, laughing as well as crying, which sounded very spluttery.

'Yes, I think the anaesthetic gives you very vivid dreams, so heaven help you, Elsie, because you've got such an over-active imagination already,' said Nurse Gabriel.

'Is that a good thing or a bad thing?' I asked.

'It depends,' she said. 'It's good if you can comfort yourself telling stories. It's not so good if you tell those stories to the others and frighten them all into fits!'

I had a new story to tell now. I pretended to Martin that I'd really died.

'That's silly, I can *see* you. You're not one bit dead,' he said.

'No, but I *was* – for about five minutes. When I was on the floor, before they lifted me up,' I told him.

'You were talking to Nurse Bryant, I heard you,' he said.

'Not at first. I tell you, I *died*, Martin. I was in the Bed of Doom, right? Your friend Robert died, and so did I.'

'What was dying *like*, Elsie?' asked Angus.

'It was *so* scary. I just jolted right out of my body. I could see myself lying on the floor, my leg all twisted, and you peering and crying, but I wasn't in my body any more, I was just floating like a ghost, drifting along right up underneath the ceiling.'

'That isn't true, is it?' said Rita. 'Shut *up*, Elsie. You're giving me the creeps.'

'No, go on! Did you stay under the ceiling or did you get out?' said Angus.

'I found I could float right through the ceiling. It was the weirdest sensation.'

'But then you'd be in the attics,' said Gillian.

'No, I floated up through the attics, through the roof, up into the sky,' I said.

'Wearing your cat pyjamas?' said Gillian, giggling.

'You can laugh! It was most extraordinary,' I said. 'I looked up, and there was this blinding bright light, and a beautiful deep voice seemed to be calling me. *Elsie – Elsie . . .*'

'Was that your daddy?' asked Maureen.

'No, it was God, wasn't it, Elsie?' said Babette.

'I don't know who it was. I just hovered helplessly in the air. I wanted to fly upwards into the light, but I struggled too, because I wasn't really ready to die. I cried a little and called for my nan, and she climbed out of her bed and reached right out of the window and pulled me back, saying, "No, my Elsie, I can't let you go. You're my own baby." I turned and put my arms round her and promised I wouldn't go, not yet. Then I was pulled down, down, down again, and I ended up with a bump on the floor, with Nurse Bryant gasping and crying.'

'You wouldn't have had *time* to see your nan. You were only out cold for a minute or two,' said Gillian.

'There's no such thing as time in ghost worlds,' I said grandly. 'It's like when you dream. All sorts of amazing things happen in just a minute or two – *see!*'

Gillian tutted at me, clearly not convinced by my little act, but the others were hanging on my every word. I even had Martin hooked.

'So when you saw this bright light and heard the voice – was there anyone else around?' he asked.

'Hmm. I wasn't really looking, but I think there were some children up above me. Yes – there was this one boy waving at me, calling something. I think he was calling your name, Martin,' I said.

326

Gillian snorted but Martin took no notice. His head strained upwards, his eyes shining. 'It was Robert. He was calling for *me*!'

'Better watch out then, Martin. Your turn next!' said Gillian.

'Really?' said Martin, looking stricken.

'Of course not! I was just stringing you along – and so is Elsie. Pack it in now, Elsie Kettle, or you'll send them all nuts. They believed every word.'

'I don't believe it. Elsie's just a lying storyteller,' said Rita.

'I didn't believe old Gobface! What do you take me for?' said Martin.

But that night he lay awake long after the others were asleep. I was awake too, both my legs throbbing.

'Elsie?' he hissed.

'Yep?'

'Elsie, I know you were kidding, sort of – but when you were unconscious, *did* you see a bright light and hear a voice?'

I hadn't, but I'd imagined it so intensely I wasn't ultra-sure. 'I think so,' I whispered back.

'So *did* you see a boy – you know, calling for me?'

'I – I don't really know,' I said.

'Oh. Well, never mind,' said Martin. He sounded relieved but very sad.

'I think he *could* have been your friend Robert,' I said. 'What colour hair did he have?'

'He had this crazy ginger hair. I used to call him Ginger at first and it drove him daft,' said Martin.

'Well, *my* boy had bright red hair, all sort of tousled,' I said. 'And he was wearing striped pyjamas.'

This was an easy guess. All the boys in the ward wore striped pyjamas except for Martin in his Dan Dare nightwear.

'Yes! Oh goodness, it *must* have been Robert!' said Martin. 'Listen, Gob— Elsie. If you dream it again, or get knocked unconscious, will you tell Robert I miss him and we'll play that game of marbles together one day?'

'I will,' I said.

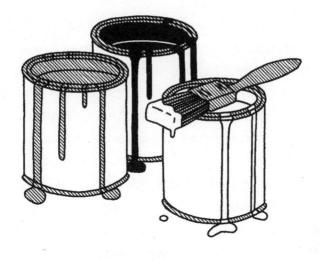

19

The children stayed a little in awe of me after that, but the nurses sighed and stuck me in a new bed with little sides so that I couldn't possibly roll out again.

'And if you try, we'll tie you to the bed sheets,' said Nurse Bryant.

I thought she was joking, but I couldn't be sure. I lay obediently in the middle of my bed, and when my broken leg itched and prickled in its plaster, I tried not to moan too much, because I knew it was my own fault.

Mum was appalled when she discovered I'd broken my other leg.

'What do you *mean*, you fell out of bed?' she said, looking at my plaster in horror. I'd been wearing it a couple of weeks now and it had got a bit grubby. I'd written my name and drawn a portrait of Queenie on it in smudgy blue biro. 'How could you be such an idiot? Were you trying to get up?'

'I was trying to reach Albert Trunk, Mum. He'd fallen on the floor.'

'Oh, for goodness' sake! I don't know what you're doing with that awful moth-eaten old elephant anyway. You're getting too big to play with stuffed toys – you look *simple*,' said Mum impatiently. 'What are you trying to do, permanently cripple yourself? You'll be limping on *two* legs now, and everyone will stare at you and you'll never get yourself a decent man when you grow up.'

'I don't *want* a decent man,' I said defiantly. 'I'll stay at home with Nan.'

'Oh for heaven's sake,' said Mum. 'Are you living in Cloud Cuckoo Land, Elsie? Your nanny's very poorly, you know that. She's not always going to be around.'

'Yes she *is*. I *know* she'll get better and she'll look after me.'

'But if she doesn't, *I'll* be looking after you, and you need to get yourself sorted. I have a feeling

Mr Perkins and I might be together in the future—'

'I *knew* he was your boyfriend!'

'You be quiet. You mustn't say anything to anyone just now, because Mr Perkins is a highly respected married man with a family. Now the thing is, I haven't told him all the facts about *my* family. He thinks I'm a little younger than I really am. It'll be a shock to him knowing I've got a great lolloping schoolgirl daughter – especially one who's poorly. He has a horror of anything unhealthy. So you have to get completely better, do you understand? Stop playing silly beggars and falling out of bed, do you hear me?'

Mum came to visit me that Sunday too. I stared at her agitatedly as she clip-clopped along the veranda. I already *had* a visitor – my dear Nurse Gabriel. She'd brought in a ball of pink angora wool and a pair of knitting needles, and was trying to show me how to follow a pattern for a simple bolero. I'd managed a couple of rows, but as Mum approached my needles jerked and I dropped half my stitches.

'Mum! What are you doing here? It's Sunday,' I said.

'I've come to see how you are, you silly sausage. Checking you haven't broken any more limbs overnight,' said Mum. She sat down heavily on the edge of my bed, flicking her hair back over her shoulders, peering at Nurse Gabriel. 'And who's this?' she asked.

'It's Nurse Gabriel, Mum. You know,' I hissed, embarrassed.

'You're one of Elsie's nurses?'

Nurse Gabriel smiled politely. 'I used to be. I'm on the men's ward now. How do you do, Miss Kettle.'

'So what are you doing here now?' said Mum. She sounded rude and I blushed, but Nurse Gabriel kept smiling.

'Oh, Elsie and I have become old friends,' she said. 'Here, Elsie, let me pick those stitches up for you.'

'It's a waste of time you teaching our Elsie to knit,' said Mum. 'She's got two left hands, this one. And now two blooming limpy legs.' She stuck her own shapely bare legs out at an angle. She'd drawn eyebrow pencil up the back of each leg to look like stockings.

'Elsie will have lots of physio. She won't necessarily have any kind of a limp,' said Nurse Gabriel smoothly. 'Here, Elsie. Show your mum how nicely you can knit a row.'

She gave me the knitting, each dropped stitch carefully retrieved. I tried hard to impress Mum, but it was a losing battle.

Mum sneezed. 'Oh Gawd, it's that fluffy wool. It always gets right up my nose,' she said, delving around in her bag for a hankie.

I sniffed deeply, loving the powdery smell of her handbag. I saw a glimpse of a picture postcard in amongst the compacts and combs.

'Oh, let me see your card!' I said, thinking it might be from Nan.

'No! Get off. It's a personal card from Mr Perkins,' Mum said. She gave Nurse Gabriel a sharp look. 'He's my employer. He owns Perkins Ballpoint Pens. He's on his holidays in Bournemouth.'

So *that* was why Mum was free this particular Sunday. I hoped she would shut up about Mr Perkins to Nurse Gabriel. I especially hoped she wouldn't say that he was her boyfriend, not when he had a Mrs Perkins and little Perkins children too.

I hoped Mr Perkins wasn't on a very long holiday. If Mum started coming on Sundays on a regular basis, then maybe Nurse Gabriel would stop coming, and that would be dreadful.

But Mr Perkins came back, and was obviously more demanding of Mum's company because she didn't come for ages after that. I persevered with my angora bolero, but Mum was right – I truly couldn't get the knack of knitting. Nurse Gabriel frequently had to unpick all the rows I'd done in the week because I'd dropped so many stitches. I couldn't make the rows lie smooth and even. They puckered up terribly, and my hands grew hot and damp as I knitted, so that the pink wool started to turn grey. In the end Nurse Gabriel took pity on me. She took the wool and needles away with her – and brought back a finished fluffy bolero within a fortnight.

'Oh Nurse Gabriel, I love it! And I love you!' I said, flinging my arms around her neck.

I wore my bolero every day after that. It looked a little odd with my cat pyjamas, but it suited my baby-dolls beautifully. I found I took after Mum, and angora wool made me sneeze, but I didn't mind a bit. It felt weird to be divided into two very different halves – my top delightfully adorned in my heavenly pink bolero and fancy pyjama top, and my bottom so horribly encased in splint and plaster.

The splint stayed on, of course, but after six weeks the plaster came off. They took it off with a little saw, which was frightening, because I was scared they might get carried away and saw my leg in half while they were at it.

It didn't look like my leg when it was freed. It was an ugly white matchstick that looked as if it might snap at any moment. I was introduced to Miss Westlake, the physiotherapist. She was very bouncy, her salmon-pink arms rippling with muscles. She had a very big chest, almost as impressive as Mum's.

'Now then, little Miss Kettle, let's get cracking on

that silly old leg,' she said, flexing her frightening arms.

I couldn't get up to see if I could walk on it because my other leg in its splint still needed complete bed rest. I had to lie flat on my back while Miss Westlake massaged my matchstick and then made me push down hard into her cupped hands with my limp foot.

'It hurts,' I said.

'Good, it's meant to hurt,' she said. I had to keep pushing while she pummelled, until the sweat was standing out on my forehead, making my fringe sticky.

I'd never been so glad to see the back of someone in all my life. To my horror, she came back the next day, and the next, and the *next*.

'We'll get that leg sorted if it kills me,' said Miss Westlake, attacking it with renewed vigour.

'You're going to have a super-leg by the time she's finished with you,' said Martin. 'The rest of you will stay all thin and weedy, but that leg will get bigger and bigger and bigger. It'll grow twice the size of the other one, with a calf muscle like a beach ball, and you'll hop all over the place, *boing, boing, boing*. You'll be so good at high jump, Elsie. You'll jump over houses and trees and church steeples and take right off into the sky, and people will stare up at you, shading their eyes, and go "There goes Super-leg!"'

'Ha ha, very funny,' I groaned as Miss Westlake commanded me to push harder.

'You watch your lip, young Martin,' she said, kneading my calf as if it were a lump of dough. 'It will be your turn next.'

'I haven't broken my leg,' said Martin.

'How long have you been here? I think your brace is due to come off soon,' said Miss Westlake.

We all stared at Martin. We all knew that our braces and splints and plasters would come off one day. We knew that Martin had been on Blyton Ward longer than anyone. But it still seemed incredible that he was actually going to be released from his terrible frame soon.

'You lucky thing, Martin,' said Gillian.

'Yeah, hurray for me!' he said. 'Just you watch me, you lot. They'll take off my brace and I'll stride off, just like a cowboy.'

They took Martin away to have his Jones spinal frame removed. We waited for him to come striding back along the veranda, but when he appeared he was still in his bed, his legs stretched wide apart as if he were still attached to his brutal frame.

'What's the matter, Martin? Why aren't you walking?' asked Gillian.

Martin didn't answer. He stared up at the ceiling, ignoring her.

'He'll be walking soon,' said Nurse Smith. 'Mr Dobbin's going to fix him up with one more little splint and a crutch.'

'It'll take a bit of practice, but you'll get there,' said Nurse Bryant. 'Don't worry, Martin.' She gave him a little pat on the shoulder. He'd normally shy away if the nurses ever tried to cuddle him, but now he just lay there. I saw a tear seeping sideways down his face.

He wouldn't talk to any of us. He wouldn't even join in my new story session. Nurse Bryant had started reading us a whole series of adventure stories about four children and their pet parrot, so I invented our own one about eight children and their amazing white cat, Queenie. The children captured robbers galore, generally helped by Queenie, who tracked down stolen jewels or banknotes like a sniffer dog.

I let Martin play a leading role in solving tonight's mystery and had him round up the dangerous armed robbers just by clever use of his cap gun – but Martin didn't react at all. It was as if they'd removed his ears as well as his horrible frame.

The night nurses were especially kind to him, bringing him a milky cocoa in the middle of the night when they found him wide awake. I liked them both, Nurse Robinson and Nurse Macclesfield – though they still couldn't hold a candle to my dear Nurse

Gabriel. They looked rather alike, with light brown hair curling fetchingly beneath their nurse's caps. I might have got them muddled, but Nurse Robinson usefully had very red cheeks, just like a robin red-breast. They called each other Robin and Mac and were very jolly together. But they couldn't jolly Martin out of his gloom – and after they'd squeaked off down the ward in their sensible shoes, I heard him sniffing.

'Martin, are you crying?' I whispered.

'No!' he said furiously, though it was obvious he was lying.

'Oh please, don't cry,' I said. I tried to manoeuvre myself a little nearer so I could perhaps reach out and take hold of his hand.

'What are you *doing*, Gobface? Keep *still* or you'll tumble out and break your wretched leg all over again,' he said.

'Chance would be a fine thing. I'm stuck with these stupid sides to my bed. I feel like I'm trapped in a coffin. Martin . . . what's up? Did they hurt you when they took you out of your frame?'

'No. Well, a bit, twisting me here and there.'

'So haven't you mended?'

'I don't think I can have done. They X-rayed my hip again, and they say it's fine, but that's stupid, because I can't blooming well walk, can I?'

'Not a bit?'

'I can't even stand. They tried to sit me up, but I felt so giddy I screamed. I had to beg and beg them to lie me down again. I can't do anything! I'm like a little baby. I shall be stuck on my back like a great big stag beetle for ever!' Martin declared, and started sobbing again.

I was scared. If Martin couldn't get better, maybe there was no hope for any of us. Maybe we were all stuck here simply because no one really wanted us any more, and we'd just have to lie here till we were wizened little old men and women. It was such a bleak thought that I started crying too. Queenie had been lying across the end of my bed, warming my toes. My shaking made her lift her head enquiringly.

'Oh Queenie,' I said, gently tapping the space beside me to get her to creep upwards, where I could stroke her. Then I decided that Martin's needs were more pressing than my own. 'Jump across to Martin, Queenie darling. He needs a cuddle,' I said, pushing her gently.

'Queenie's not a *dog*, Gobface. You can't tell cats to do stuff,' said Martin.

'Yes you can,' I said – and to my surprise Queenie decided to cooperate.

'I much prefer you to Martin, Elsie,' she purred. 'He's such a loud, rude, fidgety boy – but I can see he's really upset so I'll do my best to comfort him.'

She leaped neatly down over the side of my bed, pattered across the floor, and jumped right up onto Martin's pillow.

'Watch out, Queenie!' he said, his voice muffled. It sounded as if she'd landed right on top of him. I thought perhaps he'd push her off, but then I heard him crooning softly, 'There, girl. Good Queenie. Who's a lovely cat, then?'

'*I* am,' Queenie purred. 'Calm down now, Martin. I'm sure you'll be able to walk again soon.'

Martin didn't speak cat language, but he seemed comforted all the same. And Queenie was right. It took a few days for him not to feel very dizzy whenever he was lifted into a sitting position – but in the meantime Miss Westlake worked determinedly on his legs. The first time they helped him right up onto his feet with his crutch, he actually fainted. He was only out for a few seconds, but he actually gloried in his moment of drama.

'I died too, Gobface,' he boasted when he was brought back to the veranda. 'I saw the bright light. And you'll never guess who else I saw!'

'Your friend Robert?' I said.

'Yes! How on earth did you know that?' Martin sounded genuinely astonished. 'He came running up to say hello, and he looked really well – no splint, nothing. He thumped me on the back and I thumped him, and then we laughed and laughed. We were all set to play a game of marbles when I heard all these voices saying, "Come back, Martin," and "You can't play with Robert just yet," so I waved goodbye and gave him all my best marbles, even my big swirly rainbow one, and then I was whizzed back and I was in hospital again, with Nurse Bryant putting something smelly under my nose to bring me back to life.'

I stared at him. I thought he was making it all up just to match my story about being dead, but it was a remarkably detailed account and I wasn't sure Martin had that vivid an imagination.

'Honour bright, you actually saw your pal Robert?' I asked.

'Honour bright,' said Martin proudly. 'I hope I faint again tomorrow – it was fantastic!'

To his disappointment he couldn't manage to repeat his fainting trick. He stayed upright, and very soon was taking his first few steps, hobbling with his crutch.

'Watch me, watch me, you lot!' he shouted when he came back from his physiotherapy session, and he swung his legs out of bed.

'You just stay put, young Martin,' said Nurse Bryant.

'But I want to show them what I can do!' he said.

'Oh please, dear Nurse Bryant, let me just walk two little steps.'

'Just two, then – and I'm going to be hanging onto you tight in case you decide to do yourself a mischief,' she said.

She helped Martin out of bed, and he wobbled upright, leaning heavily on his crutch. He lurched forward.

'Watch it now, Martin, you're still not very strong,' said Nurse Bryant.

'Yes I am!' he insisted. 'Look at me, everyone.'

He took one step forward – and then another. He walked more like a clockwork toy than a cowboy, but it was walking all the same, and we all gave him a big clap.

'I'll be walking right out of here by the end of the week,' said Martin, flopping back into bed, exhausted.

'I dare say – but I should wait until the week after next if I were you,' said Nurse Bryant.

'What do you mean, Nurse Bryant?' asked Martin.

Her dear droopy camel mouth wrinkled into an enormous smile. 'Just you wait and see!' she said. 'We're going to have a very important visitor.'

'Who's coming?'

'Aha! It's a surprise. I'm not allowed to tell you yet,' she said. She put her fingers to her big lips. 'I have to keep shtoom.'

'Oh go on, Nurse Bryant, tell us,' we chorused.

'Oh well, you'll suss something out soon. We've got the decorators coming in tomorrow. Oh my Lord, it's going to be action stations here. Wait till you know who it is!'

We stared at her.

'*Who?*'

'I can't tell you.'

'*Nurse Bryant!*'

Queenie came pitter-pattering along the veranda. She rubbed herself against Nurse Bryant's ankles. Nurse Bryant bent and picked her up, slinging her carefully over her shoulder like a white fur stole.

'*Pussycat, pussycat, where have you been?*' Nurse Bryant chanted the old nursery rhyme. '*I've been to London to visit the . . .*' She opened her eyes wide, her head on one side. When we still didn't respond, she cupped her hand behind her ear as if she were deaf. '*To visit the . . .*'

'Queen!' said Michael.

Nurse Bryant silently mimed clapping. We stared at her.

'The *Queen's* coming here on a visit?' said Martin.

'I didn't tell you. I didn't breathe the royal name. But *I* can't help it if you've worked it out for yourselves,' said Nurse Bryant. She rubbed her hands together, her eyes sparkling. 'Isn't it exciting?'

'But why is the Queen coming here?' said Gillian.

'Has she got to have a splint?' asked Rita.

Nurse Bryant whooped with laughter. 'No, you silly! She's inspecting the whole hospital. Sir David's won some award for pioneering work in the ortho-paedic field and so we're having a royal visit.'

'Will we *see* her?' I asked.

'This is all still top secret, and I'm not going to say another word, but a little bird told me Her Majesty particularly likes visiting *children's* wards,' said Nurse Bryant.

We still couldn't take it all in. The Queen lived in Buckingham Palace with Prince Philip, Prince Charles, little Princess Anne, and a pack of corgis. We all knew that. She might journey out occasionally, probably in her golden coach, but she went to grand cathedrals and palaces and Parliament. She didn't visit sick children in hospital.

But it seemed she did. A whole team of decorators in brown overalls came marching into the hospital the very next day. We were all desperate to watch, but we were wheeled out onto the veranda as usual, even though it was cold and windy. In the afternoon it started to rain heavily. The roof of the veranda was meant to shelter us, but the wind blew the rain in so that it sprayed our faces and soaked the sheets.

'There won't be any children left for the bally

Queen to visit,' said Gillian, crossly patting her drooping hairstyle. 'We'll all have caught pneumonia and died off.'

When we were wheeled back at long last, we gazed around the ward, transfixed. We were so used to the dingy cream and green walls that we never even noticed them. But now they had been transformed. They'd become pale . . .

'*Pink!*' said Martin in disgust.

There was a grass-green frieze stretching right along the pink walls, with butterflies and little bees and fluffy lambs.

'How old do they think we are, *five?*'

'I *am* five!' said Michael.

'It's pretty. I love it,' said Babette.

'I especially like the lambs,' said Maureen.

Gillian and Martin rolled their eyes at each other. I wasn't bothered about the décor. I was peering around for Queenie. She was usually waiting to jump up on my bed when we came back to the ward, but she was nowhere to be seen.

'Where's Queenie?' I asked.

'They've probably painted her pink to match the walls,' said Martin.

'She's gone off in disgust. She doesn't like the disturbance, or the smell of paint,' said Nurse Bryant.

Queenie seemed even more disgusted than Martin.

She didn't come back all night long. I had to make do with Albert Trunk as a comforter. He wasn't the same as a real live purring cat. I still loved him – but he felt very stiff and solid, and it was hard work trying to make him speak to me. I still liked holding him close, hanging onto him by his trunk and breathing in his dusty smell. There was still just a whiff of Nan and home in his sawdust.

Oh Nan, I thought. *You'll never guess what. I'm going to meet the Queen!*

The parents were all thrilled when Martin and Gillian and Rita and Angus and Babette and Maureen and Michael told them about the Queen's visit. They came back on Sunday with so many parcels it looked like Christmas. They'd all bought their children new nighties and pyjamas. I stared wistfully at them all – especially Rita's. Her mum had bought her a brand-new pair of pink cat pyjamas.

'They're *my* pyjamas!' I said.

'No, they're not. My mum bought them for me,' said Rita.

'But you copied me. I bet you *asked* her for cat pyjamas!'

'No I didn't,' said Rita, but I could tell she was lying. 'Anyway, there's no law says *I* can't have cat pyjamas too.'

'It's not fair,' I wailed, and had to fight not to burst into baby tears.

My mum hadn't bought me anything because she hadn't come, either on the Saturday or the Sunday. But dear Nurse Gabriel came – and she had a tiny flat parcel for me. I couldn't help hoping that it was new cat pyjamas, even though the parcel wasn't even big enough for *doll's* pyjamas. I opened it with shaking fingers and found two beautiful pink silk ribbons.

'They'll match your bolero, Elsie,' said Nurse Gabriel. 'You can wear it over your baby-doll top. I'll see if I can nip in that morning and do your plaits for you. The other nurses probably won't have time.'

I was a little bit disappointed. Gillian had started putting her hair up in a wonderful elegant chignon, just like Belle of the Ballet, and I'd hoped she might show me how to fix mine in a similar fashion. I had started to worry that plaits were very babyish, but I didn't want to hurt Nurse Gabriel's feelings – and the ribbons were very soft and satiny.

'That will be lovely, Nurse Gabriel! Thank you very much. You're so kind.'

She kept her word too, rushing over to Blyton while we were still being toileted. My hair had been washed specially the night before, and was almost as soft and silky as my new ribbons. Nurse Gabriel brushed it until it crackled and then scraped a parting and plaited it very neatly. My fringe had grown so long that Nurse Robinson had started clipping it back with a slide, but Nurse Gabriel combed it into place and then cut it carefully with her nail scissors. She brushed the little locks of hair away, gently blowing on my nose where some were stuck.

'There now, you look an absolute picture, Elsie,' she said.

The Queen wasn't due until eleven o'clock, but I held my head unnaturally still and didn't flop back on my pillow, determined not to make my plaits untidy. I was very careful when I ate my breakfast so that I wouldn't spill toast or cornflakes down my bolero.

Queenie came walking fastidiously down the ward, still twitching her nose at the fading smell of paint.

'Here, Queenie! It's a very important day,' I said. 'The real Queen is coming. Are you going to say hello to her?'

Queenie considered. She arched her back, stretching, and then jumped up onto my bed. I didn't have any choice titbits for her, but I ran my finger over my toast and then let her lick it, because she liked the taste of butter.

'You're more special than any real queen,' I whispered to her, and Queenie purred in agreement.

Sister Baker came bustling into the ward, in such an excessively starched white apron that she walked as if she were wearing armour.

'Get that cat off the bed!' she said. 'Robinson, Macclesfield, I want all these breakfast trays cleared and the children in immaculately made beds in fifteen minutes flat. Do I make myself understood?'

'Lordy, Lordy, what a flap-doodle,' Nurse Robinson muttered to Nurse Macclesfield. 'Anyone would think the Queen was coming!'

We were all ready and out on the veranda by eight o'clock – and then had to wait three whole hours. Miss Isles gave out storybooks and comics, but we couldn't settle to reading. I had had Albert Trunk forcibly removed and imprisoned in my locker because he was getting so shabby, but I clutched my little Coronation coach firmly in my hand.

Sister Baker, Nurse Smith and Miss Isles were called away to a meeting in Sir David's office.

'To practise their curtsies,' said Martin, giggling.

I told the others a Queen story as I drove the Coronation coach up and down my sheets and along the long rugged road of my splint.

'The Queen's going to walk along the veranda, and she'll say hello to all of us, even you, Martin, but she'll stop at my bed and she'll put her royal head on one side, her crown nearly tipping off, and she'll say, "Oh my goodness, what's that you've got in your hand, Elsie?" and I'll say, "It's your Coronation coach, Your Majesty." She'll say, "Excellent! I was wanting to go home to my palace right this minute. Would you care to accompany me, Elsie?" I'll say, "But I'm stuck here in bed with my gammy leg," and she'll say, "Oh, you poor child. Don't you know about my corgis? They have magical tongues. Come to the palace with me and they'll lick you better in a trice."'

'Oh yuck!' said Gillian.

'Can corgis *really* lick you better?' asked Rita.

'Tell us *more*, please, Elsie,' said Angus.

'Well, I'm not going to miss a day out with the Queen, am I?' I started.

'Can we come too?' asked Michael.

'Oh, I wish you could – but look, there's not room in the coach, is there? Still, I'm sure the Queen will come back another day and take you on a trip, Michael,' I said reassuringly. '*Anyway*, I drag myself out of bed and stand on my good leg—'

'But you're not *allowed*!' Rita fussed.

'Oh Rita, it's a *story*,' I said. 'OK, there I am, out of bed, doing my best to curtsey with only one blooming leg that will bend. I set the Coronation coach down on the floor of the veranda and it starts growing and growing until all your beds slide into a corner, and there's the coach, huge and gold and glittering. The eight horses are tossing their manes and stamping their hooves, impatient to be off. Sister Baker opens the door for the Queen, bowing so low her apron cracks right in two, and then Nurse Bryant lifts me up into the coach next to the Queen, and it's really comfy inside, with red velvet cushions, and I can prop my legs up. The Queen shifts up a bit to make room for me. And then we're off! You lot are waving goodbye.'

The little ones waved!

'The Queen sticks her royal head out of the window and shouts, "Your turn next, Michael," and then the coachman clicks his tongue to the horses and shakes the reins and we're off – along the veranda, out through the gardens, right up the path onto the road, then all the way to Buckingham Palace, quick as a wink.'

'I've been there once. My dad took us,' said Babette.

'Yes, but you haven't been *inside*. Oh, it's simply gorgeous, with those huge twinkly lights hanging from the ceiling—'

'Chandeliers,' said Gillian.

'Yes, chandeliers, and there's red carpet everywhere of course, and lovely sofas and chair, but the Queen has her own throne, real gold with purple cushions, and she tells me to sit right next to her on a golden stool. She gets her lady-in-waiting to take off my splint, and then she throws back her royal head and whistles loudly, and all these corgis come woofing into the room – six of them, all with their tongues hanging out. "Here, boys, go over to Elsie and lick your hardest," the Queen commands. They all rush over to me, their big pink tongues hanging out, and they go *lick lick lick lick lick lick* – that's the six of them, all licking away like billy-o. It's amazing. It feels all wet and slobbery and tickly. I can't say I *like* it, but my leg is all tingly, as if something truly magic is happening. When I stand up, it's fine. I can walk just like that! The Queen takes me to her own personal X-ray machine in a side room, and we stick my leg under, and it's completely better, no TB at all. I'm cured! "Well, that's jolly good, Elsie, because I'm holding a ball tonight," says the Queen. "Would you like to come?"

'"Yes please, Your Majesty – but I haven't anything to wear. I've just got my baby-doll pyjamas and my bolero."

'"Oh, don't trouble yourself about that," says the Queen. "Have a poke around in my wardrobe and see if there's anything that takes your fancy." So the lady-in-waiting takes me to the royal bedroom, and there's this huge wardrobe with hundreds of frocks inside – pink ones and blue ones and white ones with long sticking-out skirts, and some have got embroidery and some have got lace. I choose a sky-blue dress with little red rosebuds embroidered all over it and a sticky-out skirt with its own frilly petticoat underneath.'

'And frilly knickers to match,' Martin sniggered.

'Shut up, Martin. Don't spoil it. Go on, Elsie,' said Gillian.

'So I go to the ball, and I'm a bit nervous at first because no one comes to ask me to dance.'

'Uh-oh! There's going to be a handsome prince any minute,' said Martin.

'There's Prince Philip, but he's the Queen's husband, and there's Prince Charles, but he's too little. No – do you know why everyone's waiting? They're waiting for the Queen, and she comes over to me and holds out her hand and says, "Do you know how to polka, Elsie?" And I do, of course, so I take the Queen's hand, and then we polka round and round the ballroom, ever so fast – so fast the Queen's crown tumbles right off her head, but a courtier runs forward and catches it quick, and she pops it back on her curls again.'

'Is it all going to end when the clock strikes twelve?' asked Maureen.

'That's *Cinderella*. No, this is *my* story, and I go on dancing with the Queen all night long.'

'Do you *really* know the Queen?' asked Babette.

I almost felt as if I *did* know her. I couldn't wait to see her in real life. At five minutes to eleven Nurse

Smith came flying along our row of beds on the veranda, checking us for running noses or rumpled sheets. Then, on the dot of eleven, the Queen herself came out – the real Queen, walking between Sir David and Sister Baker. She wasn't wearing her crown, which threw us all. Her head looked bare without it, even though she was wearing a little lilac hat. She wore a lilac coat too, the sort that would show every scrap of dirt, but it looked brand new and beautiful. The Queen's shiny patent shoes looked new too. I hoped she wouldn't slip going along the veranda. Her face was so weirdly familiar she really did seem like a friend or an aunty – but there was a scary queenliness about her even without her crown. Sir David was chatting away easily enough, but Sister Baker looked terribly shy and flustered, and was walking sideways like a crab so she could face the Queen respectfully at all times.

The Queen stopped by Michael's bed and smiled at him. Michael blinked back at her nervously.

'Hello, dear,' she said. 'I've got a little boy about your age at home.'

'Does he dance at the ball?' Michael asked.

The Queen looked surprised. 'Charles *plays* ball,' she said, a little uncertainly. She moved on to me.

I smiled at her hopefully, sitting up straight, my shiny ribbons on the end of my plaits. I felt very hot and itchy in my pink bolero, but I wouldn't have taken it off for the world.

'Hello, dear,' said the Queen, and passed on.

I couldn't help feeling disappointed. She said hello to Martin, she said hello to Gillian, but she didn't pause. Then she got to Rita.

'Hello, dear. My, what pretty pyjamas!' she said.

I wanted to jump out of bed and punch Rita. They were *my* cat pyjamas. Well, my own cat pyjamas were now past their best. The pink had faded and the little white cats were grey and limp with hospital boiling.

'I like the cats!' said the Queen.

'Yes, I do too,' Rita said smugly. 'We've got a white cat on Blyton Ward.'

'Say *Your Majesty!*' Sister Baker prompted.

'Yes, Your Majesty, we've got a white cat called Queenie. She jumps up on my bed sometimes,' said Rita.

'No, she doesn't! She jumps on *my* bed!' I said furiously.

Sister Baker turned and gave me a terrible glare. 'I can assure you it's all very hygienic, Ma'am, and therapeutic for the children,' she said.

'Oh, I think it's a lovely idea,' said the Queen. She gave Rita a dazzling smile. 'Queenie, eh? Did you name her after me?'

'Yes we did,' said Rita, another flat-out lie.

The Queen moved on to Babette and Maureen,

stopping in between their beds. She asked them how they were feeling. They clearly weren't sure. Babette put her thumb in her mouth and Maureen started giggling.

'Answer nicely, girls,' Sister Baker hissed, but they were beyond speech.

The Queen didn't seem to mind. She nodded at both of them in a kindly fashion and moved on to Angus. 'Oh my goodness,' she said, peering at his plaster bed. 'That must be very uncomfortable.'

Angus grunted.

'Do you have to stay in plaster all the time?' the Queen asked.

'He has a severe spinal condition, Ma'am, but we're very pleased with his progress,' said Sister Baker.

'It must be very tiresome not even being able to sit up,' said the Queen sympathetically. 'Can you read at all?'

'I can a bit,' said Angus. 'But Elsie tells lots of stories, and that's better than reading.'

Sister Baker stiffened, looking alarmed. She made helpless little gestures to the Queen, trying to hurry her along.

The Queen stood her ground, smiling at Angus. 'What sort of stories does Elsie tell you?' she asked.

'Wonderful stories! I liked her story about the magic tree, when we all had birthday surprises,' said Angus.

'Yes, dear,' said Sister Baker. 'That's nice.' She took a firm step forward. 'Perhaps we can offer you some light refreshments, Ma'am?'

'Elsie told us a story about *you*, Your Majesty,' said Angus.

'Really?' said the Queen.

'Yes – you took her for a trip in your golden coach, and then you danced the polka with her at the ball.'

'That's enough now, Angus,' said Sir David firmly, while Sister Baker flushed – but the Queen threw back her head and roared with laughter.

'So which one of you is Elsie?' she said, looking back at all of us.

I swallowed. 'I'm Elsie, Your Majesty,' I said. She came tip-tapping back to my bed, Sir David and Sister Baker in reluctant attendance.

'So we danced together, did we, Elsie?' said the Queen.

'Yes, we did,' I said. 'I thought you'd be an excellent dancer, Your Majesty.'

'Now now, Elsie, that's quite enough,' said Sister Baker. 'We don't want any of your cheek.'

But not even Sister Baker could shut me up now.

'You wore a lovely dress in my story, Your Majesty – and your crown, of course.' I looked pointedly at her.

'Yes, children are always disappointed when I don't wear my crown,' she said.

'Well, never mind, it gives your head a rest,' I said. 'I can't believe I'm actually talking to you. Me and my nan were coming to see you on Coronation Day. Nan gave me this little replica of your coach.' I held it out and showed her.

'Ah yes,' said the Queen. 'The real one's very similar, but much bigger, of course.'

'But then Nan got ill and I did too, and we couldn't go to your Coronation after all,' I said.

'Well, never mind,' said the Queen. 'Perhaps some day, far in the future, you'll be able to go to Prince Charles's Coronation.'

I thought about it. 'Nan won't be able to come then,' I said.

'No,' said the Queen. 'And neither will I!' She burst out laughing, and then she stepped forward and pulled one of my plaits. 'You're a real little character, Elsie. I shall remember you.'

'I shall remember you too. I shall remember this day for ever and ever,' I said.

The Queen turned at last, Sir David and Sister Baker swivelling round too. As I stared at the retreating royal back, I knew exactly what I had to do. I took a deep breath.

'God save the Queen!' I shouted.

21

Nurse Gabriel said I was the talk of the entire hospital.

'Trust you, Elsie!' she said. 'It sounds as if the Queen took such a fancy to you.'

'I think she liked the ribbons on my plaits,' I said. 'Wait till I tell my mum!'

But Mum didn't come the next weekend either, though all the other parents came flocking to hear all about the royal visit. I decided I didn't care. I had Nurse Gabriel instead.

'And I'll write to Nan and tell her all about it,' I said.

I wrote her a really long letter, recounting almost everything I said and the Queen said – though I left out the part about Prince Charles's Coronation because it didn't seem tactful.

I made Nan a picture too. I drew our beds all along the veranda, with me sitting up in the middle in my bolero talking to the Queen. I gave Her Majesty a crown instead of her lilac hat to make it clear to Nan who she was.

'That's a really *lovely* picture, Elsie,' said Nurse Gabriel.

'I'll draw you one too if you like – but this picture's for my nan,' I said.

'Of course it is,' she agreed.

'I need Mum to come so she can give it to her,' I said. My voice went a bit wobbly. 'Do you think she'll come *next* week, Nurse Gabriel?'

'I hope so.'

'I wish Nan could have my letter right now,' I said, sniffing.

'*I'll* post it for you, sweetheart,' said Nurse Gabriel. 'I'll put it in a nice white envelope.'

'My nan's name is Violet Kettle— Oooh!' I wailed. 'I don't know her address at the sanatorium.'

'That's all right. I'll find out the right address.

Don't worry. Hand it over, sweetheart.'

'You are so *lovely* to me, Nurse Gabriel. I'll always love Nan most, but you're definitely my second-best person in the whole world,' I said.

I was so glad I had Nurse Gabriel because I kept losing everyone else. Nan was in the sanatorium, Mum had disappeared – and now Martin was gone too. He couldn't walk really properly yet, but he could shuffle along using his crutch. Sometimes he stood on both legs and aimed his crutch at everyone, pretending it was a machine gun. They said he had to have a lot more physiotherapy, but he could live at home now.

His mum and dad came to collect him. Nurse Bryant helped him put on his outdoor clothes. His jersey sleeves were much too short and his trousers showed a lot of bare leg.

'Oh darling, I didn't realize just how much you've grown,' said Martin's mum, starting to cry.

'We'd better get you some long trousers, old chap,' said Martin's dad.

'Really? That would be so wizard,' said Martin. 'Can we go now?'

'Say goodbye to all your friends, dear,' said his mum.

'Goodbye,' said Martin, giving a lordly wave.

'Martin! Say goodbye *nicely*.'

So he hobbled round to each of us.

'Cheerio,' he said to Angus. 'Don't let all these soppy girls get you down.'

'Ta-ta, small fry,' he said to Babette and Maureen.

'Toodle-oo,' he said to Rita.

'See you later, Miss Kiss,' he said to Gillian.

I waited. He went to his locker. He was meant to have cleared it, but he still had a whole pile of *Eagle* comics.

'You can have this lot, Gobface,' he said.

'*What* did you call her, Martin?' asked his mum.

But I knew Martin meant it kindly, and I took the comics from him gratefully.

Little Michael was crying because he looked up to Martin so. Martin didn't say anything at all to him, but he gave him a quick hug.

Then he stumped hurriedly down the veranda. It looked as if he were trying hard not to cry himself.

I needed Queenie badly that night. She was missing Martin too, clearly puzzled by the empty bed, stripped down to a bare mattress. She circled it twice, and then jumped up beside me for reassurance.

'I know, Queenie. It's weird, isn't it? I never thought I'd miss old Farty Marty, but I do,' I whispered. 'Still, we should be pleased. He got better. I'm going to be better one day.'

My broken leg was fully healed and I could waggle

my toes and tense my calves at Miss Westlake's command, though my poorly leg was still a wizened dead thing in its hateful splint. Sometimes at meal times I took my knife and played cutting it off at the hip. I didn't press hard, it was just pretend, but it felt as if I'd really left my useless leg behind in the bed. I'd jump down and hop about the ward like a lopsided frog, free at last.

Martin's bed didn't stay empty for more than a couple of days. A big girl called Ann came to join us. She was only a year older than Gillian, but she wore lipstick and had a proper lady's figure under her nightie. She had long thick wavy hair that she set in pin curls at night. She looked very pretty, even when her head was all over metal grips. I saw she walked with a bad limp when she went to the bathroom the first night – she utterly refused to use a potty.

'I'm not weeing with all these kids watching me!' she said firmly.

I admired her enormously and hoped she might be my friend, but it was clear she looked down on me. The only one of us she talked to was Gillian – and in a day they were best friends.

'What do you want to be friends with *her* for?' said Rita when Ann was wheeled off to have her surgery in the main hospital. She had to have an operation because her limp was so bad.

'I think she's really, really nice,' said Gillian, smacking her lips together and then pouting. Ann had let her borrow her lipstick.

'But you're *my* best friend.'

'I can be best friends with both of you, silly,' said Gillian.

Rita didn't look convinced – with good reason. When Ann came back from the main hospital, in plaster instead of a splint, she was very distressed, especially when she couldn't sit up properly to fix her make-up or do her hair.

'Can't you do it for me?' she asked Nurse Smith.

'I should cocoa!' she said. 'I've got my hands full as it is. And you shouldn't be wearing make-up and having a perm at your age! You're still only a little girl.'

Ann called Nurse Smith a very rude word indeed. Nurse Bryant was more sympathetic, and did try to pin Ann's curls into place that night, but she wasn't very good at it.

'You're doing it all *wrong*,' said Ann ungratefully.

'I'll do it! I know exactly how to do it. I'm going to be a hairdresser when I'm grown up,' said Gillian. 'Nurse Bryant, if you'd please push my bed right up close to Ann's, then I can reach over and pin it up for her. Go on, there's a darling.'

'Girls girls girls! I'm here to *nurse*, not play

Musical Chairs with the furniture!' said Nurse Bryant – but she pushed the beds right up close even so.

Gillian did Ann's hair for her that night, and combed it out beautifully in the morning.

'Do *my* hair, Gillian,' Rita begged.

'Don't be daft, Rita. Yours is just a kiddy's bob cut. It just needs a quick brush. You can do it yourself,' said Gillian.

In a few days Ann had learned to hitch herself upright gingerly and do her own hair, but she begged to keep her bed pulled right up close to Gillian's. The nurses separated them whenever Sister Baker came on a round of inspection, but they were allowed to stay squashed up together at all other times. They lay whispering and giggling all day long.

Rita tried to join in, but she was too far away to hear properly.

'Besides, we're talking private big girls' stuff,' said Gillian. 'You don't know about film stars and fashion.'

'Or boys,' said Ann, and they both started giggling again.

'I do *so* know,' Rita lied, and then started crying.

She was so miserable that Nurse Bryant tried pushing my bed next to hers when we were out on the veranda.

'There! You two can keep each other company,' she said.

I didn't really fancy keeping Rita company at all, but I did try to be friendly to her. I even told her a private Queenie story as a very special favour.

'Did you know Queenie came padding very quietly up to my bed last night, and when I reached out to stroke her, I felt these strange fluttery, feathery things coming out of her back,' I started.

'What?' said Rita. 'Had she been catching birds again?'

'Well, *I* wondered that at first, but then the moon suddenly came out behind the clouds, and it was like Queenie was in an eerie spotlight and I saw she had grown *wings*, Rita – wonderful white wings to match her white fur.'

'She never!'

'Oh yes she did! I watched in wonder, and she flapped those wings, and they grew bigger and bigger, and then she purred to me, "Come for a ride on my back, Elsie. We'll fly into the night sky, right up to the moon and stars."'

'What?' Rita repeated. 'Piffle! Cats can't fly. They can't talk either. You're barmy, Elsie Kettle. Just shut up. I'm sick of you and your silly stories.'

It was obvious we were never going to get along. When Babette went home, a new girl called Moira took her place. She was a funny little girl with bright red curls. She had a silver bracelet with fantastic dinky charms dangling from each link. The best one was of the Queen's Coronation coach. You could tug at the top with your fingernail so that the roof lifted up on a tiny hinge, showing a minute silver Queen sitting inside.

'We've *met* the Queen, Moira,' I said. 'I had a long conversation with her and she told me all about her coach.'

'You fibber,' said Moira.

'No, it's true – really, cross my heart. Tell her it's true,' I said, and everyone confirmed it.

'I'll let you hold my Coronation coach if you let me try on your bracelet,' I bargained, but Moira said she wasn't allowed to take it off her wrist.

It had to be removed when she went to have her operation, and Moira cried, though the nurses promised to look after it and keep it safe for her.

'I want my *bracelet*!' she yelled. 'I'll tell my mum of you. Give me back my bracelet!'

'Oh dear, what a little spitfire!' said Nurse Smith.

Nurse Bryant tried harder, and gave Moira a cuddle.

'There now, darling, don't take on so. You'll be back in the ward in no time, wearing your pretty bracelet. You can't wear it while you have your operation though. It's against the rules.'

'I don't *want* an operation,' Moira sobbed.

'Yes you do. You want us to make your poor old neck better, don't you?'

Moira didn't have TB like the rest of us. She had a wry neck, so that her head poked to one side. Moira didn't seem to care. She was still screaming for her bracelet when she was wheeled away.

When she came back, she was in plaster. I felt really sorry for her then. All the charm bracelets in the world couldn't make up for being stuck there like a mummy, unable to sit up or take notice. They put her next to Angus so that he could encourage her, but Moira didn't feel like talking to him.

Rita was just starting to be allowed up. She shuffled over to Moira's bed and chatted to her every day. It was very *boring* chat, a drippy monologue about her mummy and her daddy and her baby sister and Harry and Billy. I thought they were baby brothers, but it turned out Harry was a hamster and Billy was a budgie.

Moira didn't say much, and I was sure she thought Rita as boring as I did – but when her own mum and dad came visiting, she announced that Rita was her friend.

'*See!*' said Rita, nodding at me.

Moira still didn't let her borrow her bracelet though.

Our beds were rearranged all over again. Rita was

put next to Moira, Maureen was tucked up beside Michael, Gillian and Ann stayed side by side, and I got to be next to Angus.

'You can tell me stories all you want, Elsie,' said Angus in his quiet Scottish burr.

So that was when a whole new series of stories started, just for Angus and me. I made them up each night for our own private consumption. We climbed up on Queenie when it was dark and circled the moon.

'We'll land there, on Moon Mountain,' I said.

'We'll need special spacesuits and heavy lead shoes, because the moon hasn't got any gravity,' said Angus.

'What's gravity?'

'No gravity means there's no Earth's pull – that's what it says in *The Boys' Book of Space*. You can't stay on the ground, you just bounce around in the air,' he said. *'Boing boing boing.'*

'Well, we go *boing boing boing*, all over the moon, the three of us. It'll be like jumping on the biggest mattress in the world. And when we get hungry, we'll break off a piece of moon rock and nibble on it. It's cold, like an ice lolly, but when we've sucked it inside, it's all freezing and tingly like lemonade powder. Then, when we're tired of bouncing on the moon, we jump back on Queenie and she flies us to one of the other planets.'

I wasn't sure what they *were*, but Angus had read his space book and filled me in on the details. I especially liked the sound of Saturn, with the rings running right round it.

'They'll be just like a gigantic slide at a fun fair,' I said. 'We'll sit on one and push off, and go whizzing round at top speed – *wheeee wheeee!*'

'*Wheeee wheeee*,' said Angus.

'For goodness' sake, how old are you – *three*?' said Gillian. 'What's all this boring *wee wee* rubbish?'

'They're just silly little twerps,' said Ann.

'Who cares what *they* think,' I said to Angus. 'Now, we've slid all the way back to Earth – and Queenie's ready for another adventure. "Climb on my back, dear twerpy ones," she purrs. We're still a little chilly from the icy planets, but her fur is lovely and warm. She's like a great big hot-water bottle, but we're still a bit shivery all the same. "I think I'd better take you somewhere warm," she says, and she leaps up in the air and we fly right over the sea. The sun starts to get very hot, almost burning, but we're OK in our pyjamas. I've got new cat pyjamas, *much* better than Rita's, and you can have tartan pyjamas seeing as you're Scottish. We see all this dense green land underneath us, with immensely tall trees, and we hear the strangest animal noises – a lot of roaring and birds calling and monkeys chattering.

Come on, Angus – be all the animals in the jungle.'

Angus joined in obligingly, extra loud to annoy Gillian and Ann.

'That's right, and now we hear another noise – it echoes right through the trees.' I took a deep breath. '*Arh-arh-arh-arh-arh-aaarh!*'

'Tarzan!' Angus whooped delightedly. 'Oh, let me be Tarzan!'

'OK, you're Tarzan, but I'm not that soppy Jane. I'm Elsie the lion tamer – all the lions and tigers and leopards just circle me lovingly, wanting to be stroked, and Queenie's queen of all the big cats, and they all bow down to her. They hold a big feast for us.'

'What sort of feast? Lions and tigers and leopards eat zebras and wildebeests,' said Angus.

'They make us a special vegetarian feast – lots of fruit from the trees, and nuts and birds' eggs, with creamy milk for Queenie, and then, when the moon comes up, Queenie stands there glowing white, and all the big cats throw back their heads and *roar* . . .'

Angus roared so loudly that Nurse Bryant came running, convinced he was urgently yelling for help.

Angus's mum and dad started to bring *me* sweets and little toys on Saturdays.

'You've been so kind to our wee boy. He thinks the world of you,' said his mum.

I'd almost given up on *my* mum – but she suddenly

appeared one Saturday, her hair longer and lovelier than ever. She was wearing a powder-blue costume, the jacket very low cut at the front so that you could see the pink lace of her petticoat. The skirt had a big split at the back. I thought she'd had an accident and said straight away, 'Mum, you've torn your skirt! Look – it's showing all your *leg.*'

'Oh, for heaven's sake, Elsie, don't be so thick. It's supposed to be like that. It's French tailoring, absolutely tip top – see the fit?' She smoothed the material that stretched tautly over her round hips. 'Anyway, what a way to say hello! Aren't you pleased to see your mummy after all this time?'

'Yes, Mum,' I said. She was acting as if it were *my* fault she hadn't visited for ages.

'I've been very, very busy. I've had a promotion! I've even done a little travelling abroad!' Mum said proudly. 'One trip to Paris and another to Amsterdam, seeing if their stationery shops wanted to stock Perkins Pens. I *flew* there, Elsie!'

I stared at her, for one mad moment imagining that she'd grown powder-blue wings to match her costume and flapped her way across the Channel. Then common sense took over. 'You went on a *plane*, Mum? Weren't you frightened?'

'You bet I was. Absolutely terrified. I clutched Perky's arm so hard he had bruises all over it the next day.'

'Perky?'

'Oh, it's just my little nickname for Mr Perkins,' said Mum, giggling.

He was definitely an uncle now.

'In fact, I'll be going on another trip with Perky soon – a really, really big one. Guess where, Elsie!' said Mum.

I shrugged my shoulders. 'I don't know.'

'Oh, for goodness' sake, *guess*, I said. I'll give you a clue . . . Think maple leaves! Think Mounties!'

I stared at her blankly.

'Oh Elsie! Your brain's addled because you've been in hospital so long,' she said impatiently. She lowered her voice and hissed, 'I'm going to Canada!'

'Canada!' I declared, astonished.

'Yes, only keep your voice down. You mustn't tell anyone. It's all very hush-hush. I'm going with Perky, see. He wants to open up a new factory there – start a new line. He's going global!' Mum giggled. 'And so am I!'

'Is Mrs Perkins going too?'

'No, that's the whole point. *I'll* be Mrs Perkins in all but name once we're out there,' said Mum.

'What does Nan say?' I asked. Nan usually said a great deal when Mum went off with anyone.

'What sort of fool do you think I am? I've not told her. I haven't seen her. I told you, she's too poorly for visitors. Poor Nanny,' said Mum, but she didn't look too sad. 'Don't pull that silly face, Elsie. Nanny's an old, old lady and I don't think she can get better now, not with her lungs all over TB.'

'She will get better, she *will*!' I said, tears dribbling down my cheeks.

'All right, if you know best, miss, of course,' said Mum. 'Now stop that silly fuss and see what I've got you.' She snapped open her handbag and brought out a little thin box, the sort you kept jewellery in. I stared at it through blurry eyes. I was still sobbing my heart out for Nan, but I couldn't help wondering what it was. Could it possibly be a silver charm bracelet like Moira's?

It wasn't a charm bracelet. It wasn't any kind of jewellery. It was a silver Perkins pen.

'It's our deluxe edition, the very best,' said Mum. 'See, I've even had your name engraved on the barrel. They've done it all fancy with flourishes, Elsie. Well, what do you say? Isn't it lovely?'

'Yes,' I said, in a very small voice.

'What was that?' said Mum, cupping her ear.

'Yes, thank you, Mum.'

'That's better. You're a very lucky girl. Those pens aren't made for children, you know. You've got a notebook, haven't you? You can write down all your stories now. And write to me if you like, though I haven't got an address sorted out just yet. We'll stay in a hotel first, and then Perky will probably rent a place. Hey, come on now. Are you crying because I'm going away?'

I nodded.

'Well, don't worry, it's not going to be *permanent* – just for a few months, till Perky gets the new business up and running.'

'A few *months*?' I said, suddenly frightened.

'Yes, but there's no need to fuss. You're safely looked after here in hospital, aren't you? It's the ideal time for me to take this opportunity.'

'But – but what will happen to me when I get better?' I said.

'I'll be back by then,' said Mum. 'Oh, you're in a right mood today. Cheer up! I thought you'd be happy for me. You mustn't be selfish, Elsie.'

'You *will* come back, won't you, Mum?' I said.

'Of course I will. I promise.' She said it looking straight into my eyes – but she'd broken heaps of promises before.

22

Rita started to get better next. She was surprisingly quick to be up and walking, and it wasn't long before they told her she could leave the hospital. She looked so different in her going-home clothes. Her mum had bought her a new blue Vyella dress with smocking, a beige tweed coat and a beige velour hat to go with it. She even had new matching footwear: pale blue socks and big beige shoes like boats to keep her upright. I couldn't help being glad that her beautiful outfit was a little spoiled by her orthopaedic shoes – and then I felt deeply ashamed because Rita clumped over to my bed in her new shoes and handed me a soft little parcel folded round and round like a Swiss roll.

'It's my cat pyjamas. I don't want them any more,' she said.

I gave her a hug and wished I'd been a better friend to her. I wondered if I should try to be a good friend to Moira, who was missing Rita terribly – but the moment little Michael went home she palled up with Maureen. I was relieved, because I didn't really *like* Moira much. I was very happy to stay best friends with Angus.

He was a truly good friend, my third favourite person ever. Nan was still my number one, and Nurse Gabriel second. I loved Queenie too, very much indeed. Sometimes I rearranged Nurse Gabriel and Angus, and had Queenie second after Nan. Mum didn't get a look in now.

I wasn't prepared for *Angus* to get better. Somehow I'd assumed he'd have to stay immobile on his back even when they cut him out of his plaster cast. He'd always seemed so much worse than any of us. He had regular X-rays, and Sir David told him that the bones in his spine were starting to heal. He was allowed out of his plaster bed at long last, though he had a splint instead. Miss Westlake got to work on his legs, and he actually started to walk. He could only manage little jerky robot steps, inches at a time – but he was definitely mobile.

'Well *done*, Angus! Hey, you'll be running soon. Playing football. Doing your daft Scottish dancing. All sorts,' I said, and I clapped him until he blushed scarlet.

'Good girl, Elsie,' Nurse Gabriel murmured on Sunday. 'I know you must envy Angus terribly. You'll really miss him when he goes home.'

'I will,' I said, my voice wobbly.

'Still, never mind, dear. It'll be your turn soon,' said Nurse Gabriel. 'I've had a look at your latest X-rays. That naughty old knee looks much healthier. Not too long now.'

This news set my stomach churning.

'Cheer up, sweetheart! You're doing really well. You'll be home before Christmas, just as I promised,' said Nurse Gabriel.

'But maybe Mum won't be back then,' I whispered.

'What's that?'

'She said not to tell,' I said.

'You can tell me,' said Nurse Gabriel, taking hold of my hand.

'Mum's gone to Canada.'

'*What?* Canada! Are you *sure*?'

'It's all hush-hush. You won't tell anyone, will you, Nurse Gabriel?'

'When's your mum coming back from this holiday then, Elsie?'

'It's not a holiday, it's work. I don't know when she'll be back. I don't really mind – it's Nan who always looks after me, but now Mum says Nan's too poorly. Mum acts like Nan's never going to get better.'

'Don't you worry about it, Elsie,' said Nurse Gabriel, putting her arm round me. 'I'm sure your mum will be back long before you're ready to go home. But perhaps you should write to her, so she knows you're making really good progress.'

'I would write, but she's never sent me her address,' I said.

'Oh dear, oh dear,' said Nurse Gabriel. 'Well, never mind. I'm sure she must have left a forwarding address with someone. Maybe she's written to Sister Baker and told her. Don't dwell on it, Elsie.'

She gave me a purple chocolate nut caramel from the sweet tin, my favourite, and when the bell went for the end of visiting hours, she scooped Queenie up and popped her onto my bed. 'There – you give Queenie a little cuddle,' she said.

I held Queenie close, burying my head in her soft white fur. 'What am I going to do, Queenie?' I whispered. 'What if Mum never comes back? And what if Nan never gets better? Who will look after me?'

'There there,' Queenie purred. 'You can look after yourself, Elsie. You can clean and do the washing and the shopping and cook cheesy beanos. You'll manage just fine and dandy, dear.'

'But they won't let me,' I said. 'They don't allow children to live by themselves.'

'You can come and live with *me*!' Angus hissed.

I hadn't realized he'd been listening. I was so taken aback I couldn't even reply.

'It would be absolutely wizard. We could play together every day, and you could go to my school and we could sit next to each other in class. You could share my bedroom. I'll ask Mum to get us bunk beds. You can even have the top one if you like.'

I swallowed hard. 'Oh Angus, it would be smashing,' I said. 'But your mum and dad wouldn't want me.'

'Yes they would. They like you lots because I like you. And they've always wanted a little girl. I've just got two brothers, and I bet they've got a bit bored with boys. You wait, Elsie. I'll ask next week, and they'll say yes, and then when you get better you can stay with us until your mum comes back.'

'I wish I could. I wish I could stay with you for ever,' I said. 'But they'll say no. You wait and see.'

And of course they did say no, though they sounded upset, and they hated it when Angus pleaded.

'No, son, it's simply not possible. Now don't take on so. Don't be silly – of course we like Elsie, she's a lovely wee girl, but she's not *our* wee girl, don't you see?'

I saw, but Angus wouldn't. He kept on nagging, and ended up crying bitterly, which made his mother cry too.

'*Don't*, Angus. You don't need to worry about me. I'll be fine,' I lied. 'My mum will come back.'

But she didn't.

'You're absolutely certain she didn't tell you where she was going?' said Nurse Gabriel on Sunday. 'She didn't say which part of Canada? Was it Toronto perhaps? Or Vancouver?'

'She didn't say either of those places. She was just going with her boss, Mr Perkins, of Perkins Pens.' I showed her my silver limited edition. Then I lowered my voice. 'He's got a wife but I think he's also Mum's boyfriend now.'

'Oh goodness.' Nurse Gabriel tucked her hair behind her ears, looking very embarrassed.

'It's OK. My mum has had lots of boyfriends,' I said, to show her that I was used to this situation, but that only seemed to make her more flustered.

'Oh Elsie,' she said, squeezing my hand. 'Well, perhaps in a few weeks, if your mum's still abroad, we'll have to contact her via her work.'

'She'll be really cross with me then. She said I wasn't to tell anyone,' I said.

'But she'll be delighted that you've made such good progress. She'll come rushing home and she'll be thrilled to see you and . . . and . . .'

I waited for Nurse Gabriel to say we'd live happily ever after, but she didn't go quite that far.

She kept it up for a while. Angus went home, and I missed him so badly I wouldn't eat properly and didn't want to talk to anyone. I would only whisper to Queenie, stroking her for hours.

'Come on, Elsie! Buck up, dear. No more silly moping,' the nurses said.

They were another new set now – Nurse Appleton and Nurse Finchley during the day, and Nurse Moore and Nurse Mitchell at night. I decided I didn't like any of them. I only liked Nurse Gabriel – and I didn't always like her when she went on about Mum because it just made me worry more. She tried hard to talk about other things when she visited. She brought me little presents – *Girl* comics, and *School Friend* and *Girls' Crystal* too, and two pink butterfly hair slides, and a little felt mouse in a red spotted dress, with a tiny red ribbon on the end of her cord tail. I read my comics from cover to cover, and kept my hair out of my eyes with my new slides, and hid my little mouse under my pillow whenever Queenie was around.

It was very kind of Nurse Gabriel to make such a fuss of me. I started to dare hope that if she really, really liked me, maybe she might want me to be her little girl, and then I could go and live with *her* when I was better.

'I know you live in the nurses' hostel, Nurse Gabriel, but wouldn't you sooner have a home of your own? Couldn't you rent a flat – just a little one? And then I could maybe keep it tidy for you. I could come and stay sometimes. Well, if you *really* liked, I could live with you. I wouldn't even need my own bed. I could curl up on the sofa, and then I'd make you a cup of tea when you came back tired from doing all your nursing.'

'Oh Elsie,' Nurse Gabriel said softly.

'I can cook too. I can make all sorts of things. Have you ever had cheesy beanos?'

'Elsie, sweetheart, I can't afford a little flat. It's against the rules for nurses to live out anyway. And even if I did, I couldn't take you in, much as I'd like to.'

'Don't you like me enough?' I said.

'Of course I do! But I couldn't possibly look after you. You know what a nurse's life is like. I'm either on duty or sleeping. If you were my little girl, I'd want to stay at home and play with you and teach you things and read to you. I know you're very grown up in lots of ways, but you're still only a little girl. You need someone to look after you.'

'But if Mum doesn't come back and Nan's too sick in the sanatorium, then I haven't *got* anyone,' I said.

Nurse Gabriel put her arms round me and gave me a cuddle, but I was too miserable to enjoy it.

Two weeks later Sister Baker came bustling purposefully along the ward when we were all watching children's television, our beds lined up together.

'I'd like a little word, Elsie,' she said.

I felt my stomach lurch as she took hold of my bed and wheeled me away, right up to the other end of the ward.

'Oh, I was watching *Whirligig*!' I said.

I didn't really care about the television programme. I just desperately wanted to avoid talking to Sister Baker.

'I think we need a little private chinwag,' she said.

I wondered if I was going to be sick.

'I haven't done anything wrong. I haven't told stories or been naughty to the nurses,' I said.

'Mmm,' said Sister Baker. 'I'll take that statement with a big pinch of salt. But I'm not here to tell you off, Elsie. I just need to get a few facts straight. You're doing surprisingly well medically. The knee seems to be healing nicely. You're a shining little advert for our nursing care.'

I bared my teeth at her in a false grin.

'It's early days yet, but we need to start setting up provision for your home care. Now, I believe Mummy hasn't been to see you recently.' She checked a folder. 'Mmm, not for many weeks. And you think she's now in *Canada*?'

I nodded.

'With a Mr Perkins?'

Oh dear, Nurse Gabriel had filled her in on all the details.

'Yes, Mr Perkins of Perkins Pens,' I whispered.

'Well, not any more. I've had the secretary try to make contact, but apparently Mr Perkins has sold his company. Presumably he's starting up a new business in Canada – with your mother.'

'Oh,' I said. There didn't seem anything else I could say.

'A children's officer has also been to 3a Franklin Lane, Elsie – the address your mother gave us. That is the right address, isn't it, dear?'

'Yes, it's where I live with Nan,' I said.

Sister Baker hesitated, and then actually took hold of my hand. 'The flat has now been rented out to someone else.'

I stared at her. 'Nan's flat?'

'It was in your mother's name, but now she's stopped paying the rent.'

'But – but where will Nan live when she gets better?' I asked.

Sister Baker looked grim.

I burst into tears. 'She will get better, I know she will! Don't you dare tell me my nan's too poorly.' And then the worst thought of all wouldn't stop ringing in my head like an alarm clock. 'She isn't dead! I won't believe she's dead. She can't possibly be dead. She's my nan.'

'Now, now, Elsie, try not to work yourself up into such a state. It's not good for you. I truly don't know whether your nanny has passed away or not. We will find out. But don't you have some other relation – an aunty or an uncle, perhaps?'

I'd had many uncles, but not the sort Sister Baker meant.

'There's no one else, just Nan and me,' I said.

'Well, you mustn't get upset about it, dear. I dare say your mummy will come back quite soon – and if she doesn't . . .'

'I'm not going to a children's home,' I said flatly.

She looked surprised. 'Well, yes, a children's home is certainly one option, but you mustn't look so worried. It's a lovely happy place with lots of other girls and boys to play with.'

'No it's not! It's horrid. I was there when I was little and I absolutely hated it and I'm not ever going back, so you can put that in your pipe and smoke it, Sister Baker!'

Sister Baker let go of my hand abruptly. She shook her head. 'What am I going to do with you, Elsie Kettle?' she said.

She whisked me back to the ward and I lay there, crying, while the others watched the end of *Whirligig*.

'Are you crying because Sister Baker told you off, Elsie?' asked Moira.

'No, I told *her* off,' I said.

'She's crying because her mum's done a runner and she'll have to go to an orphanage when she gets better,' said Gillian.

'I'm not an orphan. I've still got a mum – and I've got my nan too,' I said.

Queenie jumped up on my bed to remind me that she was part of my family too.

'Don't take on so, dearie,' she purred. She gently butted me with her soft head until I stroked her, and then she wriggled happily, stretching herself out beside me. I felt for the hairbrush on my locker and started brushing Queenie from head to tail. This was strictly forbidden, but Queenie and I didn't care.

'Oh, that's heavenly, Elsie,' she purred. 'More! Please more! Oh, divine!'

I brushed her until she was the softest, sleekest, silkiest cat in the world, as light as thistledown.

I climbed on her back and we ran away to Happy-Ever-After Land. There was dear Nan welcoming us home. We all curled up in bed together, Nan and Queenie and me.

'There now, this is home!' Queenie purred.

'Yes, it's home, and I'm here, and I'm going to look after you for ever,' said Nan.

I started crying again because I was so happy. Then someone started stroking my shoulder and whispering in my ear.

'Wake up, Elsie!'

I opened my eyes, and there was Nurse Gabriel. It wasn't night-time – it was supper time.

'I don't want to wake up,' I mumbled, and I tried to slide back under the covers where Nan was still waiting for me.

'Elsie, I need to talk to you *now*,' said Nurse Gabriel. 'I've been to see your nan!'

'She's in Happy-Ever-After Land in my dream,' I said.

'Come on, Elsie, listen. This isn't a story. I've really been to see your nan.'

'But she isn't allowed any visitors.'

'I know, but I'm a nurse, remember. I went in my uniform and I explained your situation to the Matron there, so she let me into the ward.'

'And Nan was really there? You saw her? She's not dead?'

'No, she's not dead. She *has* been very ill. I think at one time the staff expected her to die. She'd given up herself. She told me that straight. She felt so badly because she thought she'd given you TB too.'

'But I *told* her it wasn't her fault! I wrote her a letter!'

'I know you did, darling, but she never got it.'

'But I gave it to Mum. She promised she'd post it!'

'Well, I'm sure she did, and the letter must just have got lost. But never mind that first letter, Elsie. She got your *second* letter, the one about the Queen, and she was so happy for you and yet so worried too, wondering how you were getting along. She hasn't seen your mother for a long while. She started to worry who would look after you when you got better. So she knew it had to be *her*. She said she lay there, day after day, talking to you inside her head, telling you not to worry.'

'Oh Nan! I talk to her too! But why didn't she write back to me?'

'She wasn't allowed to. She had to have complete bed rest, flat on her back. She wasn't even allowed to read, let alone write – but now she's made such good progress she's on a different ward, with privileges – and look . . .' Nurse Gabriel felt in her apron pocket and handed me a folded piece of lined paper, ragged at one end because it had been torn out of a notebook.

I saw the word *Elsie* written in small, spidery pen-cilled letters, and my heart flipped over. I knew my nan's writing.

I opened the note, my fingers trembling.

Dear Elsie,

Take care, little darling. Fancy you and the Queen! I'm going to get better and look after you, just you see.

Love from Nan xxx

'Oh!' I said, and I clasped the letter to my chest and started crying. 'My nan! My nanny's going to get better and look after me.'

'You must remember she's still quite poorly. She's still going to take a while to get completely better, so that she's not infectious any more – and she *is* quite elderly.'

'No, she *will* get better, she will! And I won't – not until I hear my nan's as right as rain,' I declared.

'Now you're absolutely *not* going to take that tack! I'm going to *make* you better no matter what, little Miss Elsie Kettle,' said Nurse Gabriel.

I couldn't stop myself healing, even though I was determined to hang on in hospital as long as I could. In another month they actually took my splint off – and I had two legs again, although neither of them was working properly. The nurses eased me up, and I felt so sick and dizzy I had to shut my eyes while Blyton Ward whirligigged round me.

They held me firmly, a hand under each armpit, but when they tried to make me walk, I was terrified.

'I can't do it. I've forgotten how!' I shouted, my legs flip-flopping uselessly.

'Come on, Elsie, *try* – just one step!' they urged.

'No. No, I can't!' I said, tottering – but then an image of Nan holding out her arms to me long ago popped into my head. I was just a baby then, shuffling around on my bottom, but when Nan called to me, I pushed myself upwards and staggered towards her.

'That's my little darling!' I heard her say.

So I tried and tried, first one foot, then the other.

'That's it, Elsie! Well done, sweetheart! That's the way,' the nurses said, but I wasn't listening to them. I only heard Nan inside my head, urging me onwards. My good leg tottered forward half a step, and then my bad leg followed.

'Hurray! Good for you, Elsie! You're walking!' they cried.

I managed two tiny steps more before I was in Nan's arms. I wouldn't open my eyes for ages because I so wanted to believe she was really there.

Miss Westlake worked on my legs every day, and Mr Dobbin came and fitted me for a calliper with a pair of shoes.

'New shoes!' I said. 'Oh please, can they be shiny black patent, Mr Dobbin? Or maybe red with a button? Or white with an ankle strap?'

Mr Dobbin chuckled as if I were joking. The joke was on me. The new walking calliper was a hideous contraption with a leather ring round my bony hip and two sets of straps and buckles at my knee. The shoes weren't proper shoes at all, let alone black patent or red or fancy white. They were brown boots – huge sturdy brown boots that rubbed my ankles raw and clomped noisily as I staggered up and down the ward. They made the boy's shoes I'd worn long ago before I got ill look positively dainty.

'I hate them! I won't wear them! They're too ugly!' I protested to Mr Dobbin.

'Stop that nonsense, missy. I'm not here to turn you into a little fashion plate. I'm here to help you start walking properly,' he said.

Nevertheless, he took the boots away and lined the edges with soft silky stuff, and he threaded them with new laces – bright red ones. 'There! I've prettified them as best I can, you fussy little madam,' he said, grinning.

This time I minded my manners and gave him a grateful hug.

Nurse Gabriel bought me new red hair ribbons to match my laces – and a new frock too, because I was much too tall for the old blouse and skirt I'd worn to the hospital when I first came. It was a pink and blue checked pinafore dress, with two little white puff-sleeved blouses to wear with it, one on and one in the wash. My pink angora bolero fitted over the blouse beautifully and I could wear pink ribbons or red ribbons, whichever I fancied. Sometimes I wore a pink ribbon and a red ribbon together to make people smile and pull my plaits.

I drew a picture of myself in my new outfit and sent it to Nan. I wrote to her every single day and collected all the letters and drawings up to be posted off in a big envelope once a week. I always wrote *G. B. S.* in swirly initials on the back of the envelope, meaning *Get Better Soon!*

23

Nan wrote that she was doing her very best to get better as soon as possible – but it wasn't quite quickly enough. I was soon walking around almost normally, ready to go home. I tried pretending to limp, but it's quite hard to fool nurses. I made myself incredibly useful on the ward and veranda instead. I pushed the beds backwards and forwards, I trundled the meals trolley about, I did the wash round, and I took over the story after supper.

'You're our special little baby-nurse,' they said, and

sometimes, for a laugh, they dressed me up in one of their uniforms, pinning a proper nurse's cap to my hair and letting the blue frock trail on the ground.

Sister Baker saw me every day, but she simply smiled at me. 'Adjust your uniform, Nurse Kettle, you're looking a little scruffy,' she said, and walked me down the ward.

I thought I might really be allowed to stay here in the hospital until dear Nan was ready to go home, but one day Sir David came onto the ward with a visiting consultant – and they stared at me in astonishment.

Sir David called Sister Baker over. 'What is that child doing on Blyton Ward?' he asked, pointing at me dramatically.

'That's Elsie Kettle, Sir David,' said Sister Baker, looking terribly flustered. 'Take that nurse's cap off, Elsie!'

'I'm fully aware that she's Elsie. I'm also aware that the child has made a full recovery and should have gone home some weeks ago,' said Sir David.

'Yes, Sir David, I know, but you see, there are difficulties about where she is to *go*,' said Sister Baker. 'I'm afraid she can't go home to her grandma just yet.'

'I appreciate that. I do know the circumstances. But we cannot keep her here, no matter how much we might wish to. Elsie is taking up a bed she no longer needs. There are many truly sick children needing her place. Really, Sister Baker, I'd have thought you'd behave like a proper nursing professional rather than a philanthropic ninny,' Sir David said reprovingly.

Poor Sister Baker went painfully red and hung her head. I couldn't bear it.

'Sister Baker is *ever* so professional, Sir David. She just felt sorry for me because my nan's not better yet and I don't want to be shoved into one of them rotten children's homes,' I said. *'Please* can't I stay here at the hospital? I'm ever so useful, truly I am. And I won't take up anyone's bed. As long as I have a blanket and a pillow I can sleep on the floor.'

'Don't be silly, child,' said Sir David. 'Hospitals are for the sick – and we have cured you.' He turned to Sister Baker. 'You know what you must do, Sister.'

'Yes, Sir David,' she said. 'I will make arrangements for Elsie to leave tomorrow.'

I started howling. I went down on my newly healed knee and begged Sir David to keep me for just a few more weeks. He backed away from me hurriedly, talking to his colleague, doing his best to ignore me completely.

Sister Baker walked with them down the ward, but the moment they were gone she ran back to me. She didn't try to lift me up. She knelt down beside me, her starched apron crackling, and put both her arms round me. 'There now, Elsie,' she said, rocking me.

'Oh Sister Baker!' I wailed. 'I *can't* go to that children's home, I just *can't*. I'll run away!'

'No you won't – you'll simply have to put up with it, just for a little while, and then if your grandma has made a full recovery, there will truly be a chance you can live with her.'

'*If*?' I wailed. 'Only a *chance*?'

'I can't promise you that it will happen, dear, though I wish I could. But I *do* know that if you try to run away and behave in a wilful manner, the authorities will never let you live with an elderly lady in frail health.'

I clung to Sister Baker. 'Then I will be good,' I said. 'As good as gold. I will be like one of those saints and martyrs and walk round with a holy expression even if the other kids are horrible to me.'

I tried to look holy, raising my chin and fluttering my eyelashes. I wanted to impress Sister Baker, but I made her snort with laughter.

'Do you know what, Elsie Kettle? You're a real card! I shall miss you enormously when you're gone.'

'And I shall miss you too, Sister Baker. And I shall especially miss Nurse Gabriel,' I said, and I started to cry again. 'I won't even be able to say goodbye to her!'

'I'll telephone the main hospital to see if she's on

duty now. Perhaps she can slip across to see you some time today,' said Sister Baker.

Dear Nurse Gabriel appeared at supper time.

'Oh Nurse Gabriel, did Sister Baker tell you?' I said.

'Yes she did. Oh Elsie, I'm so sorry you're going! But I'll come and visit you in the children's home whenever I have a day off.'

'I'm not sure you're allowed visitors.'

'Just let them try and stop me!'

'And will you still post my letters to Nan?'

'Of course I will. And before you know it your nan will be better, and then you can go and live with her at last,' said Nurse Gabriel.

'You really think I will? You're not just kidding me along? Sister Baker didn't seem really sure,' I said.

'Sister Baker has to be cautious and use her head. I'm using my heart.' Nurse Gabriel tapped her chest. 'Mine's going *thump thump thump*, saying Elsie and her nan will live happily ever after.'

I tapped my own chest. 'Yes, I can feel my heart too! It's going *thump thump thump* just like yours. It's saying Nan truly is going to get better – and listen, it's saying something else. It's saying Nurse Gabriel will always be my friend too!'

'Of course I will, Elsie,' said Nurse Gabriel. She was laughing, but she had tears in her eyes too.

We had the biggest hug ever – and then she had to run back to the main hospital. I helped the other nurses wash everyone and then told one last story.

'I'm leaving the hospital tomorrow, but you don't have to worry about me. Maybe you heard Sister Baker saying stuff about a children's home, but that's not actually true now. I'll tell you where I'm *really* going until my nan gets better, though you must all solemnly swear you won't tell anyone, OK? You know I met the Queen when she came to the hospital? Well, she phoned up the other day, asking how I was. "She's a real card, that Elsie," that's what she said, and Sister Baker said I was having to go to a children's home until my nan gets better – which she *will*, I know she will. And the Queen said, "No, no, I'm not having Elsie shoved into one of those horrid homes. She can come and stay with me. I've got at least fifty bedrooms going begging. Elsie can take her pick. She can keep herself busy polishing all my crowns and taking my corgis for walks up and down the corridors, and she can play with Prince Charles and Princess Anne in their special Wendy house." So that's where I'm going. Aren't I *lucky*? And whenever we decide to have a day out at Windsor Castle, we'll go in the Queen's special golden coach, and while the Queen's doing all her public duties *I'll* get to feed the horses and ride each one all round the castle and back again.

So don't you feel sorry for me. I'll be having a wonderful time with my friend the Queen, OK?'

I managed to keep this up till bedtime. I went on whispering the story in the dark, but after a few minutes I could tell by all the steady breathing that everyone else was asleep. I suddenly felt terribly alone, but with wonderful timing I heard a soft patter of paws along the ward.

'Here, Queenie, come here, darling!' I called.

I'd saved her my supper bread so that she could delicately lick the butter off. She leaped up, purring noisily.

'Thank you, dearie. I'm very partial to a lick of butter,' she said, snuggling against me.

'Oh Queenie, I wish I had a whole pack of butter, and you could lick it all. Though perhaps you shouldn't – if you don't mind my saying, you're getting quite stout.' I stroked her big tummy while she squirmed happily on her back, not at all bothered by her increasing girth. 'It's a good job Nurse Johnson isn't on the ward any more. She'd put you in a weeny pair of Stephanie Beauman knickers,' I said.

'You can mock, treasure, but I am greatly admired for my curves in the feline world,' said Queenie. 'All the other hospital cats adore me!'

'I know, I know, you're the Queen of all the cats – and I'm going to miss you so much. You don't want to run away with me, do you? Maybe you could come to the children's home with me? I'd give you treats every day and cuddle you every night,' I said.

'Bless you, dear – but my home is here, not with a lot of unruly children who might try to grab my tail or chase me. At least the children here are tethered to their beds.'

'Well, some nights will you come and find me – in my dreams? And take me riding on your back up to the moon and stars?'

'Such a fanciful girl!' said Queenie. 'Well, I'll do my best, dear. I'll miss you too. None of the other children are as generous with my little treats as you, Elsie.'

We cuddled up together most of that long night. Queenie slept soundly, her ears twitching as she dreamed of tasty little mouse and vole and shrew snacks. I hardly slept at all, clutching her tight.

I had one dream about Nan: she was lying in her bed in the sanatorium, very white and frail, clutching her little spitting pot.

'Oh Nan, I thought you were getting better!' I wailed.

'I'm trying, Elsie – but I'm so tired,' she gasped, closing her eyes.

'No, wake up, Nan, please. Get better for me. We're going to live together, you and me. We have to live happily ever after, like the storybooks,' I said, and I seized Nan's crooked little hands and squeezed them tight. I woke up still feeling her hands with their knobbly knuckles and ridged little nails.

I held hands with Nan all that long scary day. A lady children's officer came to collect me from the hospital. I said goodbye to everyone – Queenie, all the children, the nurses, Sister Baker, Miss Isles and Miss Westlake, even Mr Dobbin. I didn't say goodbye to Sir David because he was sending me away.

Then I went off with the officer. It was cold outside and I didn't have a proper coat, but she'd brought one with her. I didn't think much of it: a boy's navy windcheater. I felt very ugly in my boy's coat and my sturdy boy's shoes. At least I had a pretty pinafore dress and an angora bolero and silk ribbons. I also had my frilly knickers, and I was dreading bedtime at the children's home. I was dreading *everything* at the children's home.

But it wasn't actually quite as bad as I'd feared. I wasn't sure if it was the same home I'd been in when I was little, or a different one. It was a big dark building with lots of domes and towers, like a haunted fairy castle, and certainly the Matron in charge was like an old witch – but some of the staff were quite kind, though none were anywhere near as loving as Nurse Gabriel.

She came to visit me, just as she'd promised. She

brought me sweets and a notebook and some new crayons, and pale pink writing paper and envelopes with a separate little sachet of stamps. She also bought me several balls of new angora wool – dark purple this time so it wouldn't get too grubby. I'd gone off knitting, but I thought the needles might come in useful for poking the other children.

They thought Nurse Gabriel was my mum. I was very happy to let them think that. I didn't expect to get along with any of them, but the big fierce ones mostly left me alone. They found out I'd had TB and they were scared of catching it from me. There were a few Marilyn and Susan type girls of my own age, but I didn't take much notice of their teasing and they soon got fed up with it. I got on much better with the little ones. They flocked around me like sparrows, wanting cuddles and silly games and endless stories. They especially liked my Queen stories – though everyone thought I was making it up when I told them about the day the Queen came to the hospital and had her very long conversation with me.

There were no cats in the children's home. This was the biggest disappointment of all. I missed Queenie terribly at nights, when I couldn't sleep.

I spent Christmas there, and it wasn't too terrible, because we had a big Christmas tree with fairy lights, laden with brightly wrapped presents. I got a chocolate mouse, a Knitting Nancy set and a magic painting book. You didn't need any paints – you just used a wet brush and dabbed at the paper and the picture coloured itself in very pale pastels.

Before Christmas, Nurse Gabriel gave me a big white toy cat just like Queenie. She also brought a present that had been sent to me at the hospital – a parcel from Canada. It was a very big box, but quite light. Inside was a pink satin party frock, all over bows and flounces. There were matching knickers and a pair of beautiful pink satin shoes, one and a half sizes too small for me. There was a jolly Santa Christmas card from Mum too. Inside, she'd written: *This is for when you get better! Love from Mum xxx.* There was no address – just a Canadian postmark on the wrapping paper.

'What a lovely present,' said Nurse Gabriel.

I shut the outfit back in its box, shoes and all. 'I like my white cat best,' I said.

But on Christmas Eve I was given the best present ever ever ever. We were all gathered at the window after dinner, looking out for cars. A few very lucky children were going away for Christmas – to aunties, to grandparents, to kind friends.

They arrived in relatively modest Morris Minors and Fords – but then an enormous shiny black Rolls-Royce came up the driveway, making all the kids gasp.

'A Roller! A real Roller! Look at it!'

'Who is it? Who on earth's got such a swanky car?'

'Oh my, it's fit for a queen!'

'It *is* the Queen,' I said quickly. 'It's my friend the Queen, and she's come to invite me to spend Christmas with her!'

Some of the little ones actually believed me. I started elaborating on the Christmas treats at the palace as I watched the chauffeur get out of the car and open the back door. Then my voice tailed away. I *knew* this silver-haired man in the elegant three-piece suit who stepped out onto the driveway. It was Sir David Royale.

'Never thought the Queen would be wearing a waistcoat and trousers, Elsie Kettle!' said one of the kids, jeering.

'Oh, ha ha,' I said weakly. 'It's not the Queen after all – it's my Sir David!'

'*Your* Sir David? Just shut up telling your stupid stories.'

But within a minute the Matron came into our sitting room. 'Elsie Kettle!' she called. 'You're to come at once. There's a special visitor for you. Run and wash your hands and face and put your coat on, quick sharp!'

All the children gasped and stared. I ran around in a dither, not understanding. I couldn't even zip up my unattractive windcheater because my hands were trembling so much. I darted into the Matron's sitting room.

'Come here, Elsie,' said the Matron. 'Here she is, Sir David.'

'Well well, Elsie Kettle, it's good to see you rushing around! How is your knee?' asked Sir David.

'It's . . . it's very well, thank you,' I said.

'I'm glad that all our patient care has proved so beneficial, my dear. Now, I was wondering if you'd care to come for a little spin in my car with me?'

I nodded dumbly.

'Say yes *please*, Elsie!' said the Matron.

'Yes please,' I whispered.

I didn't know for sure where he was taking me. I could only hope. I got in the back of the Rolls beside him. All the children were staring, their noses squashed flat against the windowpane. I gave them a slow regal wave as if I were the Queen herself.

Then we were off. Sir David sat back, pointing out various landmarks, giving me little lectures on church architecture and war memorials and bomb-sites. I couldn't take any of it in. I kept wanting to interrupt and ask where we were going – but I didn't quite dare, just in case all my hopes were dashed. But then I saw a signpost: GENEVA SANATORIUM.

'Oh!' I gasped.

Sir David smiled at me. 'Yes,' he said, and he patted my hand.

I was out of the Rolls before it was properly parked. I started running – and Sir David hurried with me. He had to steer me through the wards to one right at the end. It wasn't quite as severe as the ward I'd been in before. There were tables and chairs, and most of the patients were sitting up in their dressing gowns.

There was one lady in an armchair, knitting a red jumper with a white polar bear pattern. She had grey hair straggling around her shoulders, but she'd clipped it neatly behind her ears. She was wearing a big tartan dressing gown, but you could tell by her bony wrists and ankles that she was painfully thin. Her face was as pale as paper, and there were sharp creases across her forehead – but to me she looked like the most beautiful woman in the world.

'Nan!' I cried.

She looked up and dropped her knitting. Her mouth worked but no words came out. She blinked as if she couldn't believe her eyes. Then she opened her arms – and I ran into them.

'Nan – oh my nan!' I cried.

'My Elsie!' she said – and we clung to each other as if we could never, ever let go.

AFTERWORD

I did get to live with Nan – but not until the following Easter, when she was completely better and no longer infectious. We couldn't live in our old basement flat because Mum had let it go. We were able to go to the top of the waiting list for a council flat, and we got our own brand-new two-bedroomed flat – very modern, with central heating.

Mum turned up not long after we'd settled in, expressing astonishment that we were both better. She was in a bad way herself. Mr Perkins had left her for a young Canadian lady and she'd had to find her own fare home. She'd had enough of being a secretary and went back into show business. Sometimes she lived with us. More often she was away working.

Nan and I were much happier when it was just the three of us – Nan, me and Princess. Queenie had had a litter of four kittens, one ginger, two ginger and white, and one little snowy-white girl just like her mother. Nurse Gabriel asked if we wanted her – and of course we said yes please.

So we really did live happily ever after – for eight years anyway, until my lovely Nan died. I was devastated, but by then I was old enough to fend for myself. And now I'm even older than my nan was, which feels very weird indeed – but though my own hair is grey and my forehead lined, I'm still me, Elsie, inside. I'm still telling stories too.

Life is very different now. All milk in this country is tuberculin tested and one hundred per cent safe to drink – and hospitals are far more relaxed and child-friendly. I doubt there's another nurse in existence as lovely as my Nurse Gabriel though.

It's nearly sixty long years since the Queen's Coronation, and at the time of writing she's still splendidly reigning. I have my own little grand-daughter now. I wonder if I'll ever get to take her to see a king on his Coronation Day?